FORT PILLOW

FORT PILLOW

Harry Turtledove

 ST. MARTIN'S GRIFFIN ⚑ NEW YORK

www.stmartins.com

Library of Congress Cataloging-in-Publication Data

Turtledove, Harry.
    Fort Pillow / Harry Turtledove.
        p. cm.
    ISBN-13: 978-0-312-35477-0
    ISBN-10: 0-312-35477-0
    1. United States—History—Civil War, 1861–1865—Participation, African
American—Fiction. 2. Tennessee—History—Civil War, 1861–1865—Fiction.
3. Fort Pillow, Battle of, Tenn., 1864—Fiction. 4. African American soldiers—
Fiction. I. Title.

PS3570.U76 F67 2006
813'.54—dc22

                                                                        2006040802

First St. Martin's Griffin Edition: May 2007

10 9 8 7 6 5 4 3 2 1

FORT PILLOW

I

JACKSON, TENNESSEE, WAS A TOWN laid out with big things in mind. The first streets were ninety feet wide. The first courthouse was built of logs, back at the start of the 1820s. Now, more than forty years later, buildings of red and gray brick prevailed. Oaks and elms helped shade those broad streets.

The Madison County seat had not flourished quite so much as its founders hoped. Still, with the Forked Deer River running through the town and two railroads meeting there, Jackson was modestly prosperous, or a bit more than modestly. It was a considerable market for lumber and furs and produce from the farms in the Forked Deer valley.

When civil war tore the United States in two, Jackson went back and forth between Union and Confederacy several times. Confederate General Beauregard made his headquarters there in early 1862. From that summer to the following spring, Jackson lived under the Stars and Stripes as one of U. S. Grant's supply depots. Then Nathan Bedford Forrest's cavalry ran the Yankees out again.

In June 1863, U.S. General Hatch defeated the Confederate garrison and reoccupied the town. Now, in April 1864, Forrest was back, and the Stainless Banner replaced the U.S. flag.

Forrest had his headquarters in the Duke home on Main Street. Two years earlier, Grant had stayed in the same two-story Georgian Colonial house. The Dukes were happier to accommodate the Confederate cavalry commander than they had been to host his opponent in blue.

Although Forrest went to church on Sunday morning, he did not treat the Sabbath as a day of rest. For one thing, he couldn't afford to. For another, his driving energy made him hate idleness at any time. He paced back and forth across the Dukes' parlor like a caged catamount, boots clumping on the rugs and thumping on the oak planks of the floor.

He was a big man, two inches above six feet, towering over the other Confederate officers in the room. He could have beaten any of them in a fight, with any weapons or none. He knew it and they knew it; it gave him part of his power over them. Though his chin beard was graying, his wavy hair had stayed dark. His blue eyes could go from blizzard cold to incandescent in less than a heartbeat.

"I wrote to Bishop Polk last week that I was going to take Fort Pillow," he said. He had a back-country accent, but a voice that could expand at need to fill any room or any battlefield. "I reckon we can go about doing it now. All the pieces are in place."

His aide-de-camp, Captain Charles Anderson, nodded. "Yes, sir," he said. "General Buford's raising Cain up in Kentucky, and we've got enough men looking busy down by Memphis to keep the damnyankees there from moving north along the Mississippi."

"About time we gave that garrison what it deserves," Forrest said. "Past time, by God. Niggers and homemade Yankees . . ." He scowled at the idea.

"Wonder which is worse," Anderson said.

"Beats me." Nathan Bedford Forrest's scowl deepened. That black men should take up arms against whites turned every assumption on which the Confederate States of America were founded upside down and inside out. "You sooner get bit by a cottonmouth or a rattlesnake?"

Dr. J. B. Cowan, the chief surgeon on Forrest's staff, looked up from his cup of sassafras tea. "No," he said. "I'd sooner not."

The concise medical opinion made Forrest and the rest of his staff officers laugh. But mirth did not stay on the commanding general's face for long. Most of the white Union troops in Fort Pillow were Tennesseans themselves, enemy soldiers from a state that belonged in the Confederacy. When they came out of their works, they plundered the people who should have been their countrymen. If half of what Forrest heard was true, they did worse than that to the womenfolk. And so . . .

"We'll move then," Forrest said. "Captain Anderson!"

"Yes, sir?"

"Colonel McCulloch's brigade is at Sharon's Ferry along the Forked Deer, right?" Forrest said. Anderson nodded. Forrest went on, "And General Bell's got his brigade up at Eaton, in Gibson County?" He waited.

Charles Anderson nodded again. "Yes, sir, that's where he was last we heard from him."

Forrest waved dismissively. "Yankees haven't got enough men up there to shift him, so that's where he's at, all right. How many soldiers you reckon McCulloch and Bell put together have?"

Anderson's eyes took on a faraway look. Under his mustache, his lips moved silently. He wore a neat beard much like Bedford Forrest's. "I'd say about fifteen hundred, sir."

" 'Bout what I ciphered out for myself. Wanted to make sure you were with me." Forrest's gaze sharpened. "Now, Captain, how many Yankees d'you suppose Fort Pillow holds?"

"It can't have half that many." This time, Anderson didn't hesitate, though he did add, "They've got a gunboat out in the river to support the place."

"That's bluff country," Forrest said. "Gunboat won't be able to see up high enough to do 'em much good. Send orders to McCulloch and Bell, Captain. Get 'em moving tomorrow. I want them to hit Fort Pillow first thing Tuesday morning. We will take it away from the United States, and we will free this part of Tennessee from Yankee oppression."

"Yes, sir," Anderson said once more. "General Bell in overall command?"

"No, General Chalmers." Forrest made a sour face. He'd tried to have James Chalmers posted somewhere other than under his command, but he'd been overruled both here in the West and by the War Department in Richmond. Chalmers was a good—better than a good—cavalry officer, but not respectful enough of those set above him. In that way, and in some others, he was more than a little like Forrest himself, though he had the education his superior lacked.

"I'll draft the orders, sir, and I'll send them out as soon as you approve them," Captain Anderson said.

"Good. That's good. Tell General Bell especially not to sit around there lollygagging. He's got a long way to travel if he's going to get there by morning after next. He'd better set out just as fast as he can."

Anderson's pen scratched across a sheet of paper. "I'll make it very plain," Forrest's aide-de-camp promised. Forrest nodded. Anderson was a good writer, a confident writer. He made things sound the way they were supposed to. As for Forrest himself, he would sooner pick up a snake than a pen.

Fort Pillow was not a prime post. When it rained, as it was raining this Monday morning, Lieutenant Mack Leaming's barracks leaked. Pots and bowls on the floor caught the drips. The plink and splat of water falling into them was often better at getting men of the Thirteenth Tennessee Cavalry (U.S.) out of bed than reveille would have been.

One of the troopers in the regiment swore as he sat up. "Listen to that for a while and you reckon you've got to piss, even if you just went and did," he grumbled.

"Piss on the Rebs," said the fellow in the next cot.

"Pipe down, both of you," Leaming hissed. He was about twenty-five, with a round face, surprisingly innocent blue eyes, and a scraggly, corn-yellow mustache that curled down around the corners of his mouth. "Some of the boys are still sleeping." Snores proved him right. Quite a few of the "boys" were older than he was.

The bugler's horn sounded a few minutes later. Some of the men slept in their uniforms. The ones who'd stripped to their long johns climbed into Federal blue once more. Some of them had worn gray earlier in the war. Most of those troopers were all the more eager to punish backers of the Confederacy. A few, perhaps, might put on gray again if they saw the chance.

Leaming chuckled softly as he pulled on his trousers. That wouldn't be so easy. The United States wanted men who'd fought for the other side to return to the fold. The Confederates were less forgiving. In places like western Tennessee, the war wasn't country against country. It was neighbor against neighbor, friend against former friend.

Some of the troopers wore government-issue kepis. More used broad-brimmed slouch hats that did a better job of keeping the rain out of their faces.

"Come on, boys," Leaming said. "Let's get out there for roll call. Don't want to keep Major Bradford waiting."

Bill Bradford was a man with pull. The Thirteenth Tennessee Cavalry was his creation. Recruitment and promotion were informal in these parts. Since Bradford came into U.S. service with a lot of men riding behind him, that won him the gold oak leaves on his shoulder straps. And he'd made an able enough commander so far.

Pulling his own slouch hat down low over his eyes, Mack Leaming went outside. Along with the Thirteenth Tennessee Cavalry, four companies of heavy artillery and a section of light artillery were lining up for roll call and inspection. Leaming lips skinned back from his teeth in a mirthless grin. The artillerymen came from colored outfits. The officers and senior sergeants were white men, but the men they led had been slaves till they decided to take up arms against the whites who'd held them in bondage—and who wanted to keep on doing it.

Nigger soldiers, Leaming thought. He didn't like fighting on the same side as black men in arms—he was no nigger lover, even if he fought for the U.S.A. A Negro with a Springfield in his hands went dead against everything the South stood for. Leaming also wondered if the blacks would fight, if they *could* fight.

They looked impressive enough. They were, on average, both older and taller than the men in his own regiment. They drilled smartly, going through their evolutions with smooth precision. But could they *fight?* He'd believe it when he saw it.

Major Booth, who commanded them, seemed to have no doubts. Leaming might have trouble taking colored troops seriously. Nobody in his right mind, though, could lightly dismiss Lionel Booth. He was a veteran of the Regular Army, his face weathered though he was only in his mid-twenties, one cheek scarred by a bullet crease. Though he and his men came up from Memphis only a couple of weeks before, he was senior in grade to Major Bradford and in overall command at Fort Pillow.

Back when the war was new, Confederate General Gideon Pillow ordered the First Chickasaw Bluff of the Mississippi fortified. With customary modesty, he named the position after himself. As the crow flew, Fort Pillow lay not quite forty miles north of Memphis. Following the river's twists and turns, the crow would have flown twice as far, near enough.

General Pillow didn't think small when he built his works. His line ran for a couple of miles from Coal Creek on the north to the Mississippi on the west. The next Confederate officer who had to try to hold the place built a shorter line inside the one Pillow laid out.

That didn't do any good, either. When the Confederates in the West fell back in 1862, Federal troops occupied Fort Pillow. The U.S. Army kept nothing but the tip of the triangle between the Mississippi and Coal Creek. The present earthworks protected only the bluffs at the apex of the triangle and ran for perhaps four hundred feet. The Federals did keep pickets in rifle pits dug along the second, shorter, Confederate line.

These days, six pieces of field artillery aided the defenders: two six-pounders, two twelve-pounders, and two ten-pounder Parrott long guns. They were newly arrived with the colored troops from the Sixth U.S. Heavy Artillery and Second U.S. Light Artillery. Having come under artillery fire, Leaming liked it no better than anyone else in his right mind. He assumed the Confederates felt the same way.

Major Bradford strode up in front of the drawn-up ranks of cavalrymen. Leaming saluted him. "All men present and accounted for, sir," he said. Military formality sounded good. Outside the perimeter defined by the soldiers in the rifle pits, where would the troopers of the Thirteenth Tennessee Cavalry go? If they didn't ride out in force, they were asking to get bushwhacked, to get knocked over the head and tipped into the Mississippi or buried in shallow graves with their throats cut.

"Thank you, Lieutenant." Bradford returned Leaming's salute with a grand flourish. He enjoyed being a major. He didn't much enjoy losing command of the fort to Major Booth. He couldn't do anything about it, though, not unless he wanted to arrange an accident for the younger man. Nodding to Leaming, he said, "Have the men fall out for sick call."

"Fall out for sick call," Leaming echoed.

Four or five men did. One of them shifted uncomfortably from foot to foot. "Sir, permission to visit the latrines?" he said. When Leaming nodded, he scurried away.

Most of the sick men probably had some kind of flux of the bowels. Camp in one place for a while and that would happen, no matter how careful you were. *Bad air or something,* Leaming thought. Doctors couldn't do much about it. An opium plug might slow down the shits for a while.

If you were already plugged up, the surgeon would give you a blue-mass suppository instead. Leaming didn't know what the hell blue mass was. By the way it shifted whatever you had inside you, he suspected it was related to gunpowder.

After roll call, he went up to Bradford and asked, "Any word of trouble from the Rebs?"

"Not here." The other officer shook his head. "I reckon General Hurlbut started seeing shadows under his bed, that's all. Why else would he send us all those damn niggers?" He had even less use for them than Leaming did.

"Worried about Forrest, I expect," Leaming said. "Way he chased Fielding Hurst into Memphis . . ."

Colonel Hurst's Sixth Tennessee Cavalry (U.S.) had had the misfortune of running into a detachment from Forrest's force not long before. Hurst's men were rough and tough and nasty. They needed to be. Like the Thirteenth, they were homemade Yankees, and the hand of every Secesh man in the state was raised against them. However rough, tough, and nasty they were, they couldn't stand up to Forrest's troopers.

Major Bradford chuckled unkindly. "I hear tell Hurst ran away so hard, he galloped right out from under his hat."

What could be more fun than hashing over another outfit's shortcomings? "I hear tell he left his white mistress behind," Leaming said, "and his colored one, too."

Now Bradford laughed a dirty laugh. "He had to have variety— unless he put 'em both in the same bed at the same time." With a sigh, he pulled his mind back to matters military. "But anyway, Forrest isn't anywhere near here. He's off at Jackson, and that's got to be seventy miles away."

"I was talking with one of the officers who came up with the coons," Leaming said. "You know what Forrest had the nerve to do?"

"Son of a bitch has the nerve to do damn near anything. That's what makes him such a nuisance," Major Bradford said. "What is it this time?"

"He sent Memphis a bill for the five thousand and however many dollars Colonel Hurst squeezed out of Jackson while he held it," Leaming said.

Bradford laughed again, this time on a different note. "He better not hold his breath till he gets it, that's all I've got to say. He'll be a mighty blue man in a gray uniform if he does. Besides, that's not all Hurst has squeezed out of the Rebs—not even close."

"Don't I know it!" Mack Leaming spoke more in admiration than anything else. Colonel Fielding Hurst had turned the war into a profitable business for himself. People said he'd taken more than $100,000 from Confederate sympathizers in western Tennessee. Leaming couldn't have said if that was true, but he wouldn't have been surprised. The Thirteenth Tennessee Cavalry had done its share of squeezing, too, but the Sixth was way ahead of it.

"So anyhow," Major Bradford went on, "I don't reckon we've got to do a whole lot of worrying about Bedford Forrest right this minute."

"Sounds good to me, sir," Leaming said.

Corporal Jack Jenkins had always hated Federals. Riding along these miserable roads in the rain did nothing to make him like them any better. Jenkins yawned in the saddle. The order from Jackson had reached Tyree Bell's brigade in Eaton in the middle of the night. Bell got his men in motion by midnight.

"Black as the inside of a hog," somebody near Jenkins grumbled.

"Black as a nigger's heart," somebody else added. The horses' hooves plopped in the mud.

"Plenty of niggers in Fort Pillow," Jenkins said. "Plenty of niggers, and plenty of Tennessee Tories." He had no more love for the men from his state who clove to the U.S.A. than did any other Tennessean who followed the C.S.A.

"Keep 'em moving! Come on, keep 'em moving!" That was Clark Barteau, colonel of the Second Tennessee Cavalry (C.S.). "You want those damn Missourians to get there ahead of us?"

Protected by the darkness, somebody said, "Have a heart, Colonel. They ain't got as far to ride as we do."

Had Barteau been able to see who was complaining, he would have made the trooper sorry for it. As things were, he said, "And you bet your life they didn't set out as fast as we did, either. Sons of bitches are likely asleep in nice, warm beds even now. We've got to work harder, but we'll make all this hard work pay off. Ain't that right?"

Nobody said no, not out loud. Men recognized a loaded question when they heard one. Too much growling and people would get in trouble even if the officers couldn't see who was doing it. They recognized voices—and they knew who was in the habit of saying what he thought.

"When McCulloch's brigade does get moving, I reckon he'll say, 'Hustle it up! You want them bastards from Tennessee and Mississippi to get there first?' " Jenkins said.

He didn't pitch his voice to carry. Several soldiers close by laughed. One of them repeated it for a pal who hadn't heard. The pal passed it on. It made its way down the line of horsemen. Jenkins hadn't particularly meant it for a joke. He knew how officers got men to do what they wanted. You had to coax and cajole. Everybody in a cavalry regiment knew everybody else—people had grown up as friends and neighbors. You couldn't just give an order. Not even the damnyankees could get away with that very often. You had to give a reason, keep people sweet.

Jack Jenkins was not feeling sweet. The horse in front of his kept kicking up mud. He'd got splattered a couple of times, once right in the face. But he had to stay close behind; in this dripping darkness, he could easily lose the road. And if he did, how many men would follow him to nowhere?

Up in a tree, an owl hooted unhappily. It couldn't like the weather any better than he did. With raindrops pattering down, it couldn't hear scurrying mice. And it couldn't see them, either. Nobody could see anything here.

"Come on!" Colonel Barteau called. "Keep moving! Got to keep moving! Y'all want to learn the homemade Yankees a lesson, right?"

"You bet, Colonel!" Was that a trooper who really did feel like punishing the Federal soldiers in Fort Pillow, or was it some lieutenant pretending to be a cheery soldier? Jenkins couldn't tell, which made him suspect the worst.

He was hardened to the saddle, but a ride like this took its toll. When he finally dismounted, he knew he would walk like a spavined chimpanzee for a while. *One more reason to take it out on the coons and the galvanized Yankees in Fort Pillow,* he thought, and rode on.

Maybe Ulysses S. Grant was prouder of the three stars on his shoulder straps than Benjamin Robinson was of the three stripes on his left sleeve, but maybe he wasn't, too. No doubt Grant had risen from humble beginnings. He was a tanner's son. He'd failed at everything he tried till the war began. Only the fighting gave him a chance to rise.

And the same was also true of Sergeant Ben Robinson. Next to him, though, U.S. Grant had started out a nobleman. Ben Robinson was born a slave on an indigo plantation not far outside of Charleston, South Carolina. He'd heard the big guns boom when the Confederates shelled Fort Sumter.

Not long after that, his master ran short of cash and sold him and several other hands to a dealer who resold them at a tidy profit to a cotton planter with a farm outside of Jackson, Mississippi. Not without pride, Ben knew he'd brought the dealer more money than any of the other hands. He was somewhere around thirty, six feet one, and close to two hundred pounds. And he worked hard—or as hard as any slave was likely to work, seeing that he wasn't working for himself.

Once, drunk, his new owner told him, "If all niggers was like you, Ben, we'd have a hell of a time keeping slaves."

The white man didn't remember it the next morning. Ben Robinson never forgot it. He probably would have run off anyway when Federal troops got down to Corinth, Mississippi. He'd long been sure he could run his own life better than any white man could run it for him. But finding out that his master more or less agreed with him sure didn't hurt.

He'd been a stevedore, a roustabout, a strong back for the Yankees, too—till they started signing up colored soldiers. He was one of the first men to volunteer. Even the very limited, very partial freedom he had as a laborer struck him as worth fighting for.

His size and strength got him accepted at once. And, along with the good head on his shoulders, they got him promoted not once but twice. Officers in the Sixth U.S. Heavy Artillery were all white. Most of the sergeants were white, too. For a colored man to get his third stripe was no mean feat.

Ben Robinson had heard that there actually were a handful of Negro officers in the U.S. Army. There was even a major, a man named Martin Delany. But he'd been born in the U.S.A. and educated like a white man. For somebody who'd started out a field hand and who still couldn't write his name, sergeant was a long, long climb.

A soldier in Robinson's company tossed a well-gnawed hambone on the ground. "Is you a pig, Nate?" the sergeant called. "Way you leaves your rubbish all over, I reckon mebbe you is. Take it back to the kitchen an' throw it out there."

Nathan Hunter scowled at him. "Is you happy you gits to play the white man over me?"

A lot of Negro soldiers preferred to take orders from whites, not from their own kind. It was as if they'd been taking orders from white men for so many generations, that seemed natural to them. But if another black man told them what to do, they saw him as a cheap imitation of the real thing.

"Don't want to be no white man." Robinson meant that from the bottom of his soul. All the same, he tapped his chevrons with his right hand. "Don't got to be no white man, neither. All I gots to be is a sergeant, an' I am. This here place bad enough if we do try an' keep it halfway clean. If'n we don't, we might as well be pigs fo' true."

Still scowling, Hunter picked up the bone and carried it away. Ben

Robinson nodded to himself. Military punishments weren't so harsh as the lashes a master or an overseer could deal out—quite a few of the men in the Sixth U.S. Heavy Artillery joined the Army with stripes on their backs. But marching back and forth with a heavy plank on your shoulder or sitting out in the open gagged and with your hands tied behind you and your knees drawn up to your chest, while they weren't painful, were humiliating. For men whose sense of self often was still fragile, stripes could be easier to bear than embarrassment.

Although Robinson had the authority to mete out such punishments himself, he wouldn't have done it. Had he tried, a soldier would have gone over his head to an officer—probably straight to Major Booth. Better to let the men with shoulder straps—and with white skins—take care of anything really serious.

He walked over to the twelve-pounder for which his company was responsible. The smoothbore gun threw an iron ball as big as his fist a mile, or hurled a round of shrapnel just as far. At close range, canister turned the piece into an enormous shotgun that could mow down everything in front of it.

Ben set a proud, affectionate hand on the smooth curve of the barrel, almost as if it were the smoothly curved flank of a woman he loved. He hadn't seen combat yet, but he'd practiced with the gun. He knew what it could do. He frowned. He knew what it could do if it got the chance.

Sergeant Joe Hennissey belonged to Company A. He had no more rank than Robinson, but he had white—very white—skin, red hair, and a beard the exact color of a new penny. He had a better chance of getting something done than Robinson did. The Negro waved to him. "Reckon we got us some trouble here, Sergeant," he said.

"And why might that be?" The Old Sod still filled Hennissey's voice. To most whites, an Irishman was only a small step up from a Negro. To Ben Robinson, looking up at the whole staircase, the distinction between the Irish and other whites was invisible.

"When they made this here fort, they made the goddamn parapet too thick." Robinson kicked at it: eight or ten feet of earthwork.

"Got to be thick enough to be after keeping out the Secesh cannonballs, now," Hennissey said.

"Oh, yes, suh." Ben knew he wasn't supposed to call the other sergeant *sir,* but he did it half the time without even thinking. Calling a white man *sir* was always safe. The redheaded sergeant certainly didn't seem to mind. "But look here, suh. Suppose them Rebels is comin' at us, an' suppose they gets down in the low ground under the bluff. We can't git the guns down low enough—"

"Depress 'em, you mean."

"Depress 'em. Thank you kindly." Robinson was always glad to pick up a technical term. "We can't depress 'em enough to shoot at the Rebs when they is gettin' close to we. Almost like not havin' no guns at all, you know what I's sayin', suh?"

Hennissey scratched his beard. Once he started scratching, he seemed to have trouble stopping—he wasn't scratching for thought any more, but because he itched. Seeing him scratch made Ben want to scratch, too. He was lousy. Most of the men at the fort were.

"We can't be doin' much about where the guns are at," the Irishman said at last. "But I wouldn't worry my head about it too much, Ben me boy. For one thing, we can hit the Secesh bastards while they're still a ways away, so they'll have the Devil's own time coming close at all, at all. Am I right or am I wrong?"

"Reckon you's right, suh," Robinson said.

"Reckon I am, too," Hennissey said smugly. "And even if them sons of bitches do come close, have we got the *New Era* down there on the river, or have we not? Be after tellin' me, if you'd be so kind."

"The gunboat, she there, suh," Ben Robinson agreed.

Hennissey clapped him on the back. "All right, then. You'll fret yourself no more about it, will you now?"

"Reckon I won't," Robinson said.

"Good. That's good, then." Hennissey walked away.

Was it good, then? Still not convinced, Robinson walked over to the edge of the bluff and looked down at the Mississippi. Sure enough, the gunboat floated there. Seen from more than four hundred feet above the river, the *New Era* seemed as small—and as flimsy—as a toy boat floating in a barrel of water. Could its presence make up for the problems with the field guns? Well, he could hope so, anyhow.

Major William Bradford was a lawyer before the war turned western Tennessee upside down and inside out. Since then, he'd stayed busy doing the same thing as a lot of other Tennesseans on both sides: paying back anybody with whom he had a score to settle.

He'd done a good job—better than most. Because of that, he and the troopers of the Thirteenth Tennessee Cavalry (U.S.) he led were marked men whenever they rode out of Fort Pillow. He didn't mind. If anything, it made him proud. They were marked men because they'd left their mark on their enemies. And when those enemies also happened to be enemies of the United States, well, so much the better.

He made himself nod to Lionel Booth when their paths crossed. "Good morning, Major," he said, his voice as smooth as if he were in a courtroom.

"Morning, Major," Booth replied. He spoke with a Missouri twang. He'd been a sergeant major in a Missouri regiment before winning officer's rank. He was shorter and squatter than Bradford—*homelier, too,* thought the Tennessean, who was vain of his looks. But Booth was also senior to him even if younger, and so commanded inside Fort Pillow. Bradford didn't like that, but couldn't do anything overt about it.

"Can your niggers really fight?" he asked Booth.

"I expect they can," the other man said. "And I expect they won't have to. All's quiet around these parts. It'll likely stay that way."

"General Hurlbut doesn't think so, or he wouldn't have sent you up here," Bradford said. Was that bitterness? He knew damn well it was. Fort Pillow had been *his* ever since the Thirteenth Tennessee came down from Paducah in January. Now it wasn't any more. The loss stung. Better not to show it, though. He couldn't get rid of Booth, however much he wished he could.

The senior officer shrugged. "When you build yourself a house, you're smart to dig a storm cellar down underneath. Maybe you won't need it. Chances are you won't, matter of fact. But if you ever do, you'll need it bad. So that's what we are—we're your storm cellar."

Bradford's eyes flicked to the Negroes who'd come north a couple of weeks before. They were going about their business, much as any other soldiers would have. They paraded smartly enough. They probably marched better than the men from his own command, for whom spit and polish was a distinct afterthought. But marching in step didn't make their skins any less dusky or their hair any less frizzy. Bradford had just asked if they could fight. He didn't want to do it again, not in so many words. He tried a different question that amounted to the same thing: "If Bedford Forrest did show up here some kind of way, could we hold him off?"

To a Union man from west Tennessee, that was always *the* question. A preacher face-to-face with the Devil would have had the same worry. How could he help wondering, *Am I strong enough?* Fielding Hurst hadn't been, and Bradford was uneasily aware that the Sixth Tennessee was a bigger, tougher outfit than the one he led.

On the other hand, Forrest's men had caught Fielding Hurst out in the open. The garrison here had Fort Pillow to protect it. And Lionel Booth, maybe because he came from Missouri, didn't hold Forrest in the same fearful regard as local men did. "Major, if he showed up here, we would whip him back to wherever he came from," Booth said, not the tiniest trace of doubt in his voice. "We can hold this fort against anybody in the world—in the world, mind you—for two days."

"I like the sound of that," Bradford said, which would do for an understatement till a bigger one came along.

"No reason you shouldn't. The truth always has a good sound to it." Major Booth tipped his hat and went on his way. He sounded like a preacher who was ready to wrestle with the Devil, all right.

Despite his reassurances, Bradford hoped the Devil stayed far, far away. He was no coward, but he didn't care to borrow trouble, either. And Nathan Bedford Forrest was trouble with a capital T.

Bradford climbed up onto the earthworks enclosing the Federal garrison and peered east. His nerves sent him up there, not his common sense. He knew that. The drizzle—sometimes it was real rain— coming down drastically shortened his range of vision. He could barely make out the two rows of wooden barracks still left from the fort's earlier, larger incarnation, let alone the rifle pits beyond them. He knew those pits were there, and also knew soldiers in blue manned them. But they might have been a mile beyond the moon for all his eyes told him.

What else was out there that his eyes couldn't see? From everything Major Booth said, *he* didn't think any Rebel soldiers were within forty miles of Fort Pillow. Bradford hoped the younger man was right, and had no particular reason to think him wrong. He found himself worrying even so.

Nerves, he thought again, and made himself walk along the parapet for a while before coming down again. A few soldiers, both white and colored, sent him curious looks. He ignored them—he seemed to ignore them, anyhow. Lionel Booth, now . . . He thought Booth really was nerveless. Bradford envied him for that as well as for his seniority. Maybe such calm really did come with combat experience. Bradford hoped so. He'd raised the Thirteenth Tennessee Cavalry only the autumn before. None of the men in it had much.

None of them had much experience in a U.S. uniform, anyhow. More than a few had fought for the Confederacy before switching sides. They'd ridden whichever horse looked like a winner at the moment. Bill Bradford didn't worry about that. They weren't likely to change sides again. Nobody on the other side would trust them now. Whenever they came out of the fort, in fact, they needed to worry about bushwhackers who resented their changing sides once.

A colored sergeant bawled out a private for going around with filthy boots. But for his dialect, he sounded like every other sergeant

Bradford had ever heard. The major wondered how often either Negro had worn shoes before joining the U.S. Army. Not very, not unless he missed his guess. They had them now, though.

And they acted like soldiers now. Would they act like soldiers when bullets flew and cannonballs screamed through the air? Bradford shook his head. He had a hard time believing it.

He shrugged. Before long, Forrest was bound to go back down to Mississippi. Then these coons would go away, too, and whether they could fight or not wouldn't matter a bit.

II

COME ON, RIDE HARD!" COLONEL Robert McCulloch called as the Second Missouri Cavalry (C.S.) squelched west toward Brownsville, Tennessee. "You don't want those bastards from Mississippi to get ahead of you, do you?"

Matt Ward laughed when he heard that. "How many times has Black Bob talked about those Mississippi fellows?" he asked the man riding behind him. "He think maybe we forgot about 'em since ten minutes ago?"

"Beats me," Zachary Bartlett answered. He was doing his best to keep a pipe going in the rain, and not having much luck. Ward had given up trying to smoke till he got somewhere dry. A splat and a hiss declared that the pipe had just taken another hit. "Goddamn thing," Bartlett said without rancor.

"Goddamn rain," Ward said, and his friend nodded. He went on, "How long till we get to this Brownsville place, anyway?"

"Shouldn't be much longer," Bartlett said. He'd said the same thing the last time Ward asked, about an hour earlier. Ward decided that meant he didn't know where the hell Brownsville was, either.

Somewhere between Jackson and Fort Pillow, Ward thought. That took in—what? About seventy miles of ground, anyway. The Second Missouri had been riding west since before daybreak. Ward had done a lot of hard riding in his time. This grinding slog through mud and through streams without bridges was as rough as anything he'd ever tried.

Somebody'd said Bedford Forrest was coming, too, coming after all. He'd started out after the Second Missouri headed for Fort Pillow. Could he catch up? How soon? Was he really coming at all? Or was it just another rumor, one of the nine million that soldiers invented and passed around to give themselves something to do and something to talk about? Ward didn't know. He didn't waste a lot of time worrying about it, either. If Forrest decided to ride west from Jackson, he did, that was all. If he didn't, they could whip the turncoats and coons in Fort Pillow just fine without him. General Chalmers knew what he was doing. And besides . . .

"You own niggers, Zach?" he asked.

"Me?" Bartlett laughed mirthlessly. "Likely tell! My wife's brother bought himself a couple-three, and he's so goddamn proud of it, it's like his shit don't stink. How about you?"

"Nope." Ward shook his head, which made water drip from the brim of his slouch hat. "I got a cousin who does, but he's down in Arkansas somewhere. But I reckon you've been to a slave auction or two, same as I have."

"Well, hell, who ain't been?" Bartlett said. "Good way to kill an afternoon, even if the likes of us ain't got the money to buy. Some of the gals are damn fine lookin', too." His frown looked meaner than it was, for it pulled tight a knife scar at the corner of his mouth. "What you aimin' at, anyways?"

"You've seen all them niggers standing up there on the block," Ward said. "I'm not talking about the wenches, now—I mean the bucks. You reckon somebody you can buy and sell like a sack of flour . . . You reckon somebody like that can *fight*?"

"Not so it matters," his friend answered without hesitation. "I tell you this, though—any nigger who tries pointing a gun at me, that's one dead nigger right there."

"Well, you can sing that in church." Ward was slimmer and darker than Bartlett, and envied the other trooper his scar. He didn't want to get cut or shot himself. He'd seen wounded men, and dead men, too. He knew bullets and knives hurt. But he wanted a mark to show the world—and maybe show himself—he'd been to war.

All over the Confederacy, whites believed Negroes couldn't fight. They believed the Federals were a pack of monsters for putting Negroes in uniform, giving them guns, and letting them fight. And they maintained elaborate organizations designed to crush slave uprisings before they really got started.

Those organizations worked. Rebellions were suppressed so ruthlessly, they didn't happen very often. But having plans to put down revolts said Negroes might fight after all if they ever got the chance.

Matt Ward didn't recognize the contradiction, not with the top part of his mind. Hardly any white Southerners did. But it was there, inescapably there, and it nagged at him the way a tooth will when it hasn't started to ache yet but isn't quite right, either. He sensed it was there, and he wished he didn't.

McCulloch's brigade got into Brownsville a little past noon, riding in from the west. Brigadier General Bell's brigade had just come into town from the northwest. Between them, the two forces stretched Brownsville to overflowing.

Quite a few Negroes were on the muddy streets. There seemed to be more slaves in this part of Tennessee than anywhere else in the state—and there must have been more still before it started slipping back and forth between the C.S.A. and the U.S.A.

"Brunswick stew?" a white woman called, lifting a ladle out of a covered pot.

Ward's stomach was rubbing against his backbone. "Thank you kindly, ma'am." He took the ladle and got his mouth around it like a snake engulfing a gopher. The stew was full of potatoes and mushrooms and some kind of meat. "Mighty fine," he said when he'd swallowed some of it. "What's in there with the vegetables?"

"Squirrel," the woman answered. "Reckon we've got the best Brunswick stew anywhere right here in Brownsville. If it wasn't rainin' like this, I'd give you a biscuit to dip in the gravy."

"I'll take anything I can get." Ward eyed her. She was older than he was—she had to be close to thirty—but she wasn't bad looking. He tried a smile. She smiled back, but not that way. She'd already stuck the ladle into the pot again, and was offering it to somebody behind him. She'd give out Brunswick stew. She didn't seem inclined to give herself away.

With a shrug, Matt Ward rode on. Finding out didn't cost him anything. She might have been interested in a quick poke. Could he have got off his horse, mounted her, and then saddled up again fast enough not to land in trouble? He thought so; he'd gone without for quite a while.

More ladies with pots of stew and rhubarb pie and other good things to eat stood at the edge of the street. Brownsville seemed strongly pro-Confederate. Ward wasn't surprised. Any place where there were lots of blacks and not very many whites, the whites would want to keep them in line, and that meant backing the C.S.A.

He wondered what these nice women thought of the idea of nigger bucks with guns in their hands. Wouldn't they use those guns to outrage Southern womanhood? He'd wanted to outrage Southern womanhood himself only a couple of minutes earlier, but that was different. And he knew exactly how it was different, too: he wasn't a black.

Up ahead, Black Bob McCulloch was shouting, "A guide! We need a guide to Fort Pillow!" His thick, dark beard, with luxuriant mustaches that almost swallowed his mouth, helped give him his nickname.

"I should say you do," a woman told him. "All the swamps and bogs and marshes and I don't know what all between here and the

Mississippi, you'd get lost faster'n greased lightning if you tried to go without one."

"Yes, ma'am." The brigade commander lowered his voice to answer her, then raised it again to a bellow that could carry across a battlefield: "A guide! We need a guide!"

Other officers took up the call, till Brownsville seemed to echo with it. After what the local woman said, Ward hoped they found one. If they bogged down . . . He didn't want to think about what General Forrest would do to them then. He was far more afraid of his own commanding officer than of the damnyankees, and he wasn't ashamed to admit it.

"I can get you there." The answer came almost from Matt Ward's elbow. The man who made it looked as if he'd been through the mill. He wore a collarless shirt with no jacket and a ragged pair of homespun trousers. His eyes were wild in a pale face; his hair stuck out in all directions.

"Who the devil are you?" Ward said.

"My name is Shaw, W. J. Shaw," the wild-eyed man replied. "That Bradford son of a bitch had me shut up in Fort Pillow till yesterday. I managed to sneak off, and I just got here this morning. You bet I can take you back there. Give me a rifle and I'll shoot some of those bastards myself."

He wanted to do it. The eagerness all but blazed off him. It was so hot, Matt Ward was surprised Shaw didn't steam in the rain. The trooper raised his voice: "Colonel! Hey, Colonel! Here's your man, I reckon!"

Black Bob McCulloch had to fight his way back against the tide of cavalrymen moving west. Even when he shouted at the men to get out of his way, they couldn't always. And quite a few of them weren't inclined to, either. Confederate soldiers were always convinced they were just as good and just as smart as the officers who led them.

When McCulloch finally did get to talk with W. J. Shaw, he didn't need long to decide that Shaw was the man they needed. "Give this man some food!" he yelled. "Get him a horse—get him a *good* horse, goddammit! Get him a rifle and some cartridges!"

"Much obliged, sir," Shaw said with his mouth full—one of the ladies on the street was feeding him Brunswick stew. "I'll pay you back for your kindness. And I'll pay that Bradford shitheel back, too, only the other way. Oh, you bet I will."

"Mr. Shaw, we aim to be at Fort Pillow by sunup tomorrow morning," McCulloch said. "You lead us there on time and we'll be in your debt, sir, not the other way around."

"I can do it, but you'll have to ride through the night," Shaw said. "You're damn near forty miles away, you know."

McCulloch nodded. "Oh, yes, Mr. Shaw, I know that very well. But wherever you go, we'll go with you. You don't need to worry about that, not one bit. Some of us rode all through last night. If we have to do it again to clear those niggers and homemade Yankees out of Fort Pillow, we will."

"Colonel, we have a bargain." W.J. Shaw stuck out his hand. Robert McCulloch leaned down in the saddle to clasp it. Shaw went on, "I'd be honored to join this force, not just to guide it."

"And we'd be honored to have you," McCulloch replied. "You do what you say you can do and you won't join as a soldier, either—you'll be an officer straight from the start."

"That's right kind of you," Shaw said. "Right kind." Somebody led up one of the remounts—not a great horse, but not an old screw, either. He swung up into the saddle. Colonel McCulloch nodded. So did Matt Ward. A glance was plenty to show that Shaw knew what to do on horseback.

Black Bob thumped Ward on the shoulder. "Reckon you found us a good one, Matt." Before Ward could answer, the colonel cocked his head to one side. He looked east. "Something going on back there. You make out what?"

Ward looked back the way he'd come, too. Somebody was . . . A broad grin spread across his face. "General Forrest's here, sir!"

Nathan Bedford Forrest stayed happy about sending someone else off to deal with Fort Pillow while he stayed behind in Jackson for about ten minutes. After that, he started to fume. After that, he started another round of restless pacing. And after that . . .

He could feel that he was wearing himself down. "If you want something done right, do it yourself," he muttered, there in the parlor of the house that had held General Grant and now held him.

He'd lived by that notion his whole life long. He'd had to, since his father died young and left him the man of a large family. He'd farmed that way, he'd bought and sold slaves that way—and he'd got rich doing it, too—and he'd used the same rule when he was on the Memphis city council not long before the war.

And he'd used that rule when he fought. He'd enlisted as a private. Now, less than three years later, he was a major general. He had no formal military training. He had next to no formal education of any sort, which was why he so disliked picking up a pen. He couldn't hold a train of thought when he wrote, and he spelled by ear. He knew no other way to do it, but he also knew educated men laughed when someone spelled that way. If he hated anything, it was being laughed at.

But regardless of whether he could spell, he could damn well fight. He'd whipped uncounted officers trained at West Point. They all thought the same way. They all did the same things. They all looked for their foes to do the same things. When somebody did something different, they didn't know how to cope with it.

He had nothing against Jim Chalmers except his—Forrest-like—problem with subordination. The Virginian made as good a division commander as he had. In the end, though, Forrest lost the struggle with himself. *If you want something done right, do it yourself.*

He shouted for Captain Anderson and Dr. Cowan and the rest of his staff officers. "What the devil are we sitting around here for?" he shouted. "We need to get them damnyankees and our runaway niggers out of Fort Pillow."

The surgeon held out his hand to Forrest's chief of staff. "Told you so," he said. Anderson ruefully passed him a brown Confederate banknote.

Forrest turned away so they wouldn't see him smile. So Cowan had expected he wouldn't be able to stay away from a fight, had he? Well, they'd all served with him for a while now, surgeon and chief of staff, paymaster and engineering officer, and the more junior men as well. They had a pretty good notion of how he thought.

He swung back toward them. "What are you waiting for?" he said. "Get your horses saddled up. We've got some powerful riding to do if we're going to catch up with McCulloch's brigade."

Dr. J. B. Cowan gave him a courtly bow. "Sir, most of us have our horses ready. We've been waiting on you."

"Well . . . shit," Forrest said, and the officers laughed. He went on, "While I'm saddling my beast, gather up as much of the Nineteenth Tennessee Cavalry as you can. We'll take some of Colonel Wisdom's regiment along with us so nobody can say we just came along for the fight."

"Even if we did." Dr. Cowan enjoyed poking fun at him, and probably did it more than anyone else had the nerve to.

"Even if we did," Forrest agreed good-naturedly. "Come on. Let's move."

Riding hurt. It had for some time now, and he feared it would till the end of his days. He'd taken several wounds, including one at Shiloh the doctors had thought would kill him and one from the pistol of a junior officer of his. *He'd* thought that one had killed him, and he'd given the lieutenant a knife wound in the belly that brought his end from blood poisoning. Forrest himself, meanwhile, went on.

He went on, and no one but he knew the price he paid. John Bell Hood had lost an arm at Gettysburg and a leg at Chickamauga, and was a slave to laudanum to hold the pain at bay. Forrest, a stranger to whiskey and tobacco, had no more to do with opium in any form. If he hurt, he hurt—and he went on.

On days when he hurt badly, he was apt to be meaner than usual.

If he met the Federals on those days, he took it out on them. He'd lost track of how many U.S. soldiers he'd killed himself; something on the order of a couple of dozen. He didn't think any other general officer on either side could come close to matching his score. If no Yankees were close by when the pain got bad, his own men had to walk soft.

Forrest patted his horse's neck as he rode west. McCulloch's troopers had left the road a chewed-up ribbon of mud. Like any good cavalryman, Forrest took care of his mount before he took care of himself . . . when he wasn't in combat. When he was . . . He wasn't sure whether he'd had more horses shot out from under him than he'd killed damnyankees. It was close, one way or the other.

Bullets that hit the horses were mostly meant for him. He didn't intend to let himself get killed till he whipped the invaders from the north out of the Confederate States. Too bad for the animals, but the country needed him more than it needed them.

"Invaders," he said, and then something more sulfurous still. The garrison in Fort Pillow wasn't even made up of invaders. Yankees at least fought for their own side. You could respect that, even if you thought they'd chosen a bad cause. But the men of the Thirteen Tennessee Cavalry (U.S.) . . .

What could you call them but traitors? They sold out their own land to join the enemy. Some of them had fought for him in earlier campaigns. Maybe they thought they could lord it over their friends and neighbors and kin if they switched sides. Maybe they just thought they'd get easier duty and better rations if they wore blue instead of butternut.

Whatever they thought, he aimed to show them just how big a mistake they were making.

As for the rest of the soldiers in Fort Pillow . . . Forrest muttered again, loud enough to make Captain Anderson send him a curious glance. Angrily, Nathan Bedford Forrest shook his head. Negroes had no business being soldiers, and the damnyankees had no business trying to turn them into soldiers.

Negroes were *property,* like horses and mules and cattle. If any man believed that to the bottom of his soul, Bedford Forrest did. How not, when he'd got rich trading in them? If you put horses and mules and cattle into blue uniforms and gave them rifles, could they fight? Of course not—the idea was ridiculous. Nigger soldiers were just as ridiculous to Forrest.

He hated the Yankees who armed Negroes and tried to train them to fight, not the blacks themselves. He wouldn't have been surprised if some of the bucks in Fort Pillow had been through his slave pens in Memphis one time or another. He had no trouble with blacks—as long as they worked in the fields or in the kitchen or somewhere like that. Deep down in his belly, he was convinced Northerners didn't know anything about Negroes, or they wouldn't try to put weapons in their hands. How could they know, when they didn't live side by side with them the way Southern whites did?

His own slaves had gone to war with him, as teamsters and jacks-of-all-trades. He'd promised to free them when the fighting was over, which no doubt went a long way toward keeping them quiet. In three years of warfare, only a handful had seized any of the countless chances to run off. He took that to mean they were satisfied with their lot.

If it also meant they were scared to death of him, well, that wasn't so bad. And why shouldn't they be? Most of the Federal soldiers who ran up against his dragoons (oh, the Confederates called them cavalry, but they mostly fought on foot; they used horses to get where they were going in a hurry) were scared to death of them, and of him, too.

He got into Brownsville about two in the afternoon. Brigadier General Chalmers greeted him with a half-sour, "Might have known you couldn't stay away."

"Might have known it myself," Forrest allowed. The first word came out *mought*; he was a rich and famous backwoodsman, but a backwoodsman all the same. He said *fit* when he meant *fought,* too, and had several other turns of phrase that marked him for what he was. He lost no sleep over it. To his way of thinking, a man could be a gentleman without sounding as if he had a mouth full of butter. He got straight to business: "You find a guide to take us through the swamps and such?"

"Sure did," Chalmers answered. "Shaw!" he shouted.

When Forrest found out Major Bradford had held W. J. Shaw in Fort Pillow, he sharply questioned the man. The last thing he wanted was a homemade Yankee deliberately turned loose to lead his men astray and bog them down. He didn't need long to decide Shaw was nothing of the sort. What the guide felt toward Bill Bradford was . . . what any good Tennessean should feel for the traitors who wore blue, as far as Forrest was concerned.

"Good enough, Mr. Shaw," he said, setting his left hand—the one he counted of higher worth, for he was left-handed—on the guide's shoulder. "Let's go catch us some Federals."

"I'll get you there, General." Shaw's eyes glowed with pride. So did Nathan Bedford Forrest's—with hunger.

Jack Jenkins yawned as his horse pushed on through the darkness. He'd been in the saddle for twenty-four hours, more or less. He didn't think he'd ever been so weary. He hoped the horse didn't founder. It had carried him for a whole day, and they still had hours to go before they reached Fort Pillow.

Somebody in front of him said, "Reckon we'll surprise the damnyankees when we hit 'em?"

"Jesus Christ, we better," Jenkins said. "Nobody'd reckon we could come so far so fast. Wouldn't believe it myself if I wasn't doin' it."

"Hope that Shaw fella knows where he's goin'," the other trooper said. Jenkins had no idea who he was. He couldn't see the man at all, and made out his horse only as a vague blur. Splashes and drips and hoofbeats did a good job of disguising the other man's voice—and, no doubt, Jenkins's, too.

Not knowing who he was didn't mean disagreeing with him, not when he spoke such plain good sense. "If he doesn't, we're up the creek," Jenkins said. In this part of western Tennessee, that might be literally true.

The Hatchie River bottoms, people called the country between Brownsville and Fort Pillow. Mississippi had some swamps and sloughs and marshes that seemed to go on forever. This country struck Jack Jenkins as being as bad as any farther south, and all the worse at black, black midnight.

"One thing," said the talkative trooper up ahead of Jenkins. "Don't reckon we got to worry about any niggers gettin' ahead of us and warnin' the garrison."

"I should hope not," Jenkins agreed. "Nobody could go faster'n we are. Hell, I don't see how we're goin' as quick as we are." As if to underscore that, a wet branch smacked him in the face.

As he spluttered, the other soldier said, "Not likely, no, but you never can tell what some crazy coon might try an' do. But I don't figure any nigger'd go around after dark in these parts. He'd be sure a hant'd get him."

Another branch tried to yank the hat off Jenkins's head. Only a quick, desperate grab saved it. He jammed it town tighter; with luck, the next branch wouldn't be so lucky. "Weather like this, country like this, goddamn if I don't halfway believe in hants myself," he said.

Plenty of whites raised by Negro mammies and wet nurses soaked up slaves' superstitions almost as readily as pickaninnies did. The only people who'd raised Jack Jenkins and his brothers and sisters were his father and mother and his mother's bachelor brother. They were hardscrabble farmers too poor to do anything but dream of owning slaves of their own.

That didn't mean Jenkins didn't know about hants. He heard about them from his white friends, and from the colored boys who fished in the creeks side by side with him. With kids, the lines of separation between whites and blacks weren't so sharp as they were once people grew up. If a Negro boy was more likely to wear ragged clothes and go without shoes than his white counterpart, the white might be inclined to jealousy, not to thinking he was only a slave and not worth wasting much money on.

So maybe things *did* haunt these woods and swamps. Jenkins couldn't swear they didn't. But he knew Bedford Forrest rode somewhere toward the rear of this column. Jenkins didn't and wouldn't believe any hant ever hatched could shift old Bedford.

Drain Lake River. Spring Lake. Big Slough. The names came out of the night as if hants wheezed them forth. Somebody said the rivers and creeks were full of bigmouthed black bass. Jack Jenkins's mouth filled with spit when he heard that. No time for fishing now, though. No time for anything but riding. Soft, marshy ground close by the countless streams. Woods wherever the land climbed a little higher.

Down by the Hatchie and the smaller streams that flowed into it, cypresses stood tall. Some of them actually grew in the water, their knees sticking up to help support them. Cypresses made Jenkins shiver. In the language of flowers, they stood for mourning and death. Maybe that was as foolish as letting fear of hants keep you inside after dark—but maybe it wasn't, too.

On higher ground, oaks and beeches supplanted the cypresses. Vines hung down from them; Jenkins got more than one wet slap in the chops. Brush and ferns crowded close to the trails. Sometimes it was hard to make out what was trail and what was undergrowth.

Without W. J. Shaw, the Confederate troopers might well have lost themselves in the swamps. Even with him, there were times during that seemingly endless night when Jenkins thought they were lost. In darkness absolute, with no moon or stars overhead, how could you tell where west lay? Shaw seemed able to, or at least was confident he could.

Had such a lean, muscular column—fifteen hundred mounted men—ever penetrated this country by night before? By the way the animals reacted, Jack Jenkins would have bet against it. Wild hogs fled deep into the woods, grunting and squealing. The thought of roast pork made Jenkins's stomach growl. He'd eaten a couple of bites of Brunswick stew and a weevily hardtack biscuit when they rode through Brownsville, but that was quite a while ago now.

Bobcats yowled when they ran away. Raccoons made eerie noises that sounded almost as if they ought to be speech. And once an owl glided by all ghostly not more than two feet in front of Jenkins's startled face. Its wings were silent as a bug inside cotton batting. Had he blinked while it flew past, he never would have known it was there.

What else lived in these woods? Deer and bear, without a doubt. The deer were bound to be long gone, their sharp ears alerting them to danger and their swift legs carrying them away from it. Turkeys probably stayed asleep in spite of the horsemen's racket. *Damnfool birds,* Jenkins thought. If they weren't asleep, they'd be standing under drips with their beaks agape, and some of them would go on drinking till they drowned.

Up above, passenger pigeons would be roosting in the trees. A lot of them would already have flown farther north to breed, but some remained in this part of the world. Jenkins had seen the red-eyed birds flying in the rain before dark. Rain didn't faze them a bit, though sleet might knock them from the sky and fog confused them and made them land wherever they could.

Passenger-pigeon pie made mighty good eating, too. Thanks to the birds, nobody who could afford a shotgun was likely to starve. There were *so* many of them. It was almost as if God put them there as an unending bounty for the whites who spread across His land.

"Stay close to the man in front of you!" an officer shouted. "Don't go wandering off the trail!"

"Yes, Mother," a trooper called. Other riders snickered. Confederate soldiers took their superiors no more seriously than they had to.

Confederate officers knew that as well as their men did. They hated it. This one swore. If the officers had their way, they would turn the Confederate Army into an outfit as full of spit and polish as the U.S. Army . . . wished it were. From what Jack Jenkins had heard, ordinary Federal soldiers gave their superiors a hard time, too. One of their officers was supposed to be known to his troops as Old Bowels.

But the men in gray were looser than the men in blue. People on both sides said so. The damnyankees tried to lord it over everybody, their own soldiers included. Outfits like Forrest's, on the other hand, were even looser than the loose Confederate average. Officers won respect—when they did win respect—because of the men they were, not because they wore bars or stars on their collars.

"No wonder the Yankees want nigger soldiers!" Jenkins exclaimed, all but blinded by the flash of his own insight. If he weren't so tired, it might not have struck him such a blow. As things were, it seemed a truth of Biblical proportions.

"What do you mean?" asked somebody not far away.

"What's a nigger good for? Doin' what he's told, and that's the long and short of it." So said the cavalry corporal, with the assurance of the Pope speaking *ex cathedra*. That he'd had little to do with Negroes bothered him not a bit. He went on, "The Federals, they want everybody to do what they say all the damn time. So niggers with guns are perfect for them."

"Could be," said the other voice in the night. "Just one thing wrong with it, though."

"What's that?" Jenkins demanded, angry that his brilliant perception should be challenged in any way. He was almost too weary to stay in the saddle, but not to ride his hobby-horse.

"You can give a coon a rifle. Hell, you can give a coon a cannon and call the nigger son of a bitch an artilleryman," the other soldier said. "But even if you do, you can't make the black bastard fight."

Jenkins considered that. A yawn almost swallowed his consideration. He welcomed the next wet vine or branch or whatever it was that hit him in the nose; it woke him up a little. "Well, hell," he said, thus revived. "You know that, an' I know that. But what do the damnyankees know, anyways?" He was convinced he'd proved his point. And the other trooper didn't argue any more, so maybe he had.

On they rode, on and on and on. They paused for a few minutes every so often, to let the horses rest a little, drink from streams and puddles, and eat the handfuls of oats their riders doled out to them. The way Jenkins's mount hung its head told him how weary it had to be: as weary as he was, or maybe more, because he didn't have so much on his back.

He patted the horse's neck. "Don't worry about it," he said. "Don't you worry about a thing. We got to be gettin' close to the damn fort . . . don't we?" He wished he hadn't added the last couple of words. They only reminded him he had no idea how far off Fort Pillow was.

With luck, the horse wouldn't know he was bluffing.

It sighed like a tired old man when he swung up into the saddle again. So did he. He felt like a tired old man, though he was only twenty-five. Bedford Forrest drove everybody like hell, himself included. Jenkins had never gone on a ride to compare with this one. He hoped to God he never did again.

On some roads, he might have dozed in the saddle, confident the horse would keep heading the right way even if he didn't pay attention. He nodded off a couple of times, but jerked back to consciousness whenever he did. Too easy to go astray here, to get lost in the swamps. He didn't want to give the officers any excuse to come down on his head.

Every so often, he heard voices stiff with authority screaming at troopers who blundered. No, he didn't want that happening to him. But whenever he yawned, he had to fight to stay awake. And he yawned more and more often now.

Little by little, the rain eased and then stopped. Jenkins needed a while to realize it had. All the leaves and branches were still soaking wet, and drips pattered down on his hat. Some of them slid down the back of his neck, too. He couldn't figure out how they did that. The brim of the hat was supposed to keep it from happening. No matter what it was supposed to do, the back of his neck got wet.

Little by little, also, the shape of the horse in front of him grew more distinct. Little by little, he began to make out the man atop the horse. Up above the clouds that still hid the stars even if they no longer wept, dawn was on the way. It wasn't here yet, but it was coming.

"How much longer?" somebody asked. The words weren't far from a groan. If the answer was anything like *another half day*, despair, if not mutiny, would soak through the ranks.

Alarmed at the thought, Jenkins looked around now that he could see a little farther. Men and horses all had their heads down. No one seemed any peppier than he felt. But no one seemed ready to give up or give out, either. That was good. He didn't want to have to try to turn the troopers around if they decided they'd had enough.

Of course, if they decided they'd had enough, they would have to let Major General Forrest know it. If you were brave enough to do that, weren't you brave enough to face the Federals, too?

"Rein in! Rein in!" The call from up ahead was soft but urgent. "We need the horse holders!" When mounted troops went forward to fight, some of their comrades had to stay behind to hang on to the horses. The usual proportion was about one in four. Forrest used far fewer. He always aimed to get as many of his men into the fight as he could.

"Big Pete, Burrhead, it's your turn," Jenkins called to the men he led. Excitement tingled through him. If they were dismounting, they had to be ready to go into battle, which meant they'd got to Fort Pillow after all, and before the sun came up.

"Big Pete's horse went lame. He's way the hell back there somewhere," a trooper said.

Jenkins swore. He told off another soldier to take Big Pete's place. The soldier swore, too—he wanted to get up there and fight. Few people who didn't want to get up there and fight joined Forrest's cavalry. "Somebody's got to do it, Clem," Jenkins said. "I picked you."

Not far ahead, rifle muskets began to bang.

III

LIEUTENANT MACK LEAMING LAY ON his cot, happily halfway between slumber and wakefulness. Part of him knew reveille would sound soon. The rest was warm and comfortable under a thick wool blanket on an iron-framed bed with a tolerable, or even a little better than tolerable, mattress. A little earlier, he'd been dreaming of a redheaded woman he'd seen in Brownsville. The dream was more exciting than the brief glimpse he'd got of her. He knew he wouldn't get it back—you never did—but he kept trying.

The bugler's horn didn't wake him. The sounds of running feet and shouting men did. "Oh, Jesus Christ!" he said, sitting up in bed and groping for his shoes—like most soldiers, he slept in the rest of his uniform.

His first thought was that some of the men had got into the sutlers' whiskey, of which there was more inside the perimeter of the fort than he would have liked. Dawn was a hell of a time for a drunken riot to start, but you never could tell. That was true of his own troopers. He thought it was bound to be even more true of the colored soldiers just up from Memphis.

Then he heard gunfire, and he flung himself into his shoes and dashed out of the barracks. If his men and the coons were going at each other, then all hell had broken loose. He would have to figure out in a hurry whether to try to put out the fire or to make damn sure the Thirteenth Tennessee Cavalry ended up on top.

But the gunshots weren't coming from inside the earthwork. As soon as he left the barracks, he realized that. The fire was coming from farther away. He looked around, gauging the growing light. It couldn't be later than half past five. A sergeant ran by, as fast as if the seat of his pants were on fire.

"What the hell's going on, Gunter?" Leaming shouted.

"Sir, there's Rebs outside the fort," Sergeant Gunter answered. "They're shooting at our pickets in the rifle pits."

"Rebels?" Leaming shook his head. "There can't be. There aren't any Rebels closer than Jackson."

As if to make a liar out of him, brisk fire came from the south and east. "We sure as hell ain't shooting at each other," Gunter said.

Since Leaming had wondered if the men in the garrison were doing exactly that, he wasn't completely convinced. But the distant catamount screech of the Rebel yell persuaded him that Sergeant Gunter knew what he was talking about.

"What in the name of damnation is going on out there?" Major Bradford asked from behind Leaming. Bradford had taken his own sweet time getting out of bed.

"Sir, the Confederates are attacking the fort," Leaming answered.

"What? Have you gone clean round the bend?" Bradford yelped. "There's no Secesh soldiers within seventy miles of this place."

"I thought the same thing, sir," Leaming said. "But listen."

Major Bradford did. Even in the pale, uncertain light of first dawn, Leaming watched the color drain from his face. *How?* Bradford's lips silently shaped the word. "How could they get here without anybody knowing?" he managed aloud. "Maybe Forrest really did sell his soul to the Devil, the way the niggers say."

"What are we going to do, sir?" Lieutenant Leaming asked.

"I don't know," Bradford said, which struck his adjutant as a fundamentally honest response, but not what he wanted to hear from the regimental commander. Bradford gathered himself, or tried to: "I don't see how we can surrender, though. Lord only knows what Forrest's men would do to us, let alone to the niggers here."

"Didn't Major Booth say we could hold this fort against anybody and anything for a couple of days?" Leaming asked, perhaps incautiously.

"He said it, yes. How old were you, Lieutenant, before you found out what people say isn't necessarily so?" Major Bradford loaded his words with all the scorn his courtroom training could pile onto them. Mack Leaming's cheeks and ears heated. He hoped the light was still too dim to let Bradford notice him flush. He was in luck—the regimental commander had stopped paying attention to him. Bradford was looking toward the tents that housed the newly arrived colored troops and their white superiors. "Where in tarnation *is* Major Booth, anyway?"

Booth chose that moment to pop out of his tent like a jack-in-the-box. The senior officer's tunic had several buttons undone. He wore no hat. His hair was all awry. But his eyes flashed fire even in the gray light before sunrise. "So the Rebs have shown up, have they?" he shouted, a fierce and unmistakable joy in his voice. "Well, good!"

"Good?" Major Bradford might have been looking around for a judge with whom he could lodge an objection.

"Good!" Major Booth shouted again. Mack Leaming inclined toward Bradford's opinion; no visit from Bedford Forrest was good news for anyone who followed the Stars and Stripes. But Booth went on, "We'll give the bastards a bloody nose and a black eye, and we'll send 'em back to Mama with their tail between their legs! Isn't that right, boys?"

The Negro soldiers spilling out of their tents screeched and capered and carried on. But the screeches were defiance hurled at the

Confederates. Many of the capers the black men cut were lewd, but also showed they intended to fight. And the way the colored troops carried on brought smiles to the faces of the Thirteenth Tennessee Cavalry's troopers, many of whom had seemed as uncertain and afraid as Major Bradford and Mack Leaming himself.

"Are we going to fight those Secesh bastards?" Major Booth bellowed.

"Yes, suh!" the colored artillerymen yelled back.

"Are we going to *whip* those Secesh bastards?" Booth bellowed, even louder than before.

"*Yes, suh!*" The Negroes got louder, too. Lieutenant Leaming hadn't imagined they could.

Eyes still blazing, Booth peered this way and that. "Bradford!" he shouted. "Where in God's name are you, Bradford?"

"I'm here, sir," Major Bradford answered. He had to say it again before he could make Major Booth hear him. "What do you require of me?"

"We don't want to let Forrest's men drive our pickets back into the fort right away, do we?" Booth demanded.

Bradford hesitated. Mack Leaming didn't think the Federal garrison wanted to do any such thing. Some of the ground within the large perimeter Gideon Pillow first laid out was higher than the position at the juncture of Coal Creek and the Mississippi the garrison now held. If the Confederates got sharpshooters on that high ground, they could fire *down* on the U.S. soldiers inside the present small earthwork. That wouldn't be good at all.

"Do we?" Major Booth repeated, more sharply than before. He knew the right answer, whether Bill Bradford did or not.

"Uh, no, sir." Major Bradford might not know the answer, but he could take a hint.

"All right, then, goddammit," Booth said. "Get some skirmishers out to help the pickets." He cocked his head to one side, listening to the gunfire out beyond the breastwork. "Don't send a boy to do a man's job, either, Major. The Confederates sound like they're here in numbers."

"Very well, Major," Bradford said, and turned to Mack Leaming. "Order Companies B and C out to the picket line."

"Companies B and C. Yes, sir." Leaming dashed away, shouting, "Company B forward to the picket line! Company C forward to the picket line! We have to hold off the Rebs at long range!"

The men inside Fort Pillow were running around like ants after their hill is kicked. The colored troops' white officers screamed for gun crews to man the half-dozen cannon that had come north from Memphis with them. Negroes not serving the guns took their places along the earthwork with the whites from the Thirteenth Tennessee Cavalry. They started banging away at whatever was out there.

They didn't just shoot at the Confederates, either. To show their scorn for the men who might have owned them in the not-too-distant past, they shouted filthy obscenities out toward the enemy, and backed them up with more lewd gestures.

"Don't you act like those niggers!" Leaming shouted to his white troopers. "Forrest's men are bad enough any which way. You see any sense to ticking 'em off worse?" He spotted one of the officers in Company C. "Logan! Get your men moving faster!"

"Yes, sir!" the young lieutenant answered. "We're doing our best, sir!"

"Never mind your best, dammit," Leaming said. "Just do what you've got to do."

"Yes, sir," Lieutenant Logan said again—what else could he say? Before long, about fifty men carrying rifle muskets and cartridge boxes stumbled out through the mud toward the rifle pits beyond the two rows of disused barracks outside the perimeter.

As Major Booth had before him, Mack Leaming paused to listen to the gunfire out there. Booth had it straight—the Confederates were putting a lot of lead in the air. How many men had Bedford Forrest brought through the swamps east of Fort Pillow, anyhow?

Too many, Leaming thought worriedly. That had hardly gone

through his mind before one of the troopers going out to the picket line caught a bullet in the face and crumpled, his Springfield falling from his fingers. Another soldier also fell, grabbing at his leg. His howl of pain pierced the gravel-on-a-tin-roof rattle of musketry.

How many men have *they got out there?* Leaming wondered, and shivered. One way or another, the garrison would find out.

"Fire!" Captain Carron shouted.

Sergeant Mike Clark pulled the lanyard—the white man was in charge of the gun. A friction primer already stood in the touchhole: a goose quill filled with gunpowder and topped with shredded match. A looped steel pin was fixed in the primer, and the lanyard hooked to the loop. When Clark yanked it out, the match caught and set off the powder below. There was a hiss when the finely ground powder in the friction primer caught, then a roar as the main charge went off. Fire and smoke belched from the twelve-pounder's muzzle. Away flew a shrapnel round, to come down—with luck—on the advancing Confederates' heads.

Sergeant Ben Robinson watched for the burst along with Carron and Clark and with the rest of the colored artillerymen who served the gun. "Long!" the captain said, and then something more pungent. "Robinson! Bring the range down fifty yards!"

"Down fifty yards! Yes, suh!" Robinson said. Fifty yards was two turns of the altitude screw. He had to make sure he turned it the one way and not the other. He didn't want to raise the gun's muzzle instead of lowering it.

Meanwhile, the rest of the crew got the twelve-pounder ready to fire again. One Negro soldier used the worm—a giant two-pronged corkscrew on the end of a pole—to bring smoldering bits of wadding and cartridge bag out of the barrel. Another shoved a dripping sponge down the gun's iron throat to douse any bits of fire that remained. When the sponge was withdrawn, yet another black man shoved in the cartridge full of black powder. While he was loading the next round of shrapnel and the wadding that helped give it a tight seal, Sergeant Clark jabbed a sharp awl through the touchhole and punctured the cartridge bag again and again.

The whole colored gun crew manhandled the piece back into its proper position; even in the mud, recoil had shoved it several feet to the rear. When Captain Carron nodded in satisfaction, Sergeant Clark inserted another friction primer and fixed the lanyard to it.

"Fire!" Carron yelled again. The twelve-pounder roared and jerked backward. Nobody in the gun crew stood behind it when it went off. The heavy carriage could crush a man almost like a man squashing a bug.

Fireworks-smelling smoke made Robinson cough. The shrapnel round burst somewhere between a quarter mile and half a mile away: red fire at the heart of another burst of smoke. A savage glee filled Ben Robinson's soul. That burst and the balls flying from it might maim men who'd bought and sold Negroes with no more thought or care than if they were cattle. What could be sweeter?

"Hey, Charlie!" Ben called to the loader. "Ain't this grand?"

"We finally gits to shoot the buckra, you mean?" Charlie Key said. Robinson nodded. The loader's grin showed a lot of white teeth—one missing in front—in his black face. "The gun go off the first time, I almos' quit this world altogedder."

"Gun go off the first time, I almos' go off myself," Robinson said. Charlie Key laughed. His grin got wider.

"Bring it down again, about a gnat's hair," Captain Carron said.

"A gnat's hair. Yes, suh." Robinson gave the altitude screw half a turn. That was about as small a change as would mean anything at all. Then, grunting with effort, he helped shove the twelve-pounder back up to the parapet.

"Fire!" the white officer yelled. The white sergeant pulled the lanyard. The gun boomed and rolled back. The Negroes who crewed the piece reloaded it and muscled it into position again.

They worked a lot harder than the whites set over them. Ben Robinson had worked harder than the whites above him his whole life long. He knew that wasn't always so. On small farms where the landowner could barely scrape up the cash for a Negro or two, everybody worked like a mule. On plantations like the one where he'd grown up, though, blacks worked hard so whites didn't have to. Whites made no bones about it, either.

Things were different here. Captain Carron and Sergeant Clark knew more about the business of serving a gun than did the men they commanded. And that wasn't the only difference. As Robinson told Charlie Key, he could finally do what he'd wanted to do ever since he was a pickaninny: he could hit back at the whites who'd treated him like a beast of burden almost his whole life long.

The rest of the guns brought into Fort Pillow were banging away, too. Shrapnel rounds and solid shot hissed through the air. "We gots the range you wants, Mistuh Captain, suh?" Robinson asked as the twelve-pounder got ready to fire again.

"What? Oh. Yes." Captain Carron checked himself. "Yes, Sergeant, thank you."

Ben Robinson preened. A lot of whites on both sides of the battle line thought military courtesy a waste of time. Like most colored soldiers, he saw things differently. To him, military courtesy meant treating everybody the way his rank said he should be treated—his rank, not his color. And Robinson had earned enough rank to be treated with respect even by a captain.

Tiny in the distance, a gray-clad soldier threw up his arms and reeled away when the next round of shrapnel from the twelve-pounder burst near him. "You see dat?" Charlie Key whooped. "You *see* dat, Ben? Uh, Sergeant Ben?"

"I seen it," Robinson said. "Dat one dead Secesh!" They both capered and danced in glee. If their company commander and gun chief watched with wry amusement as they carried on . . . If they did, Ben neither noticed nor cared. He wished he could kill all the Confederates from the Mississippi to the Atlantic as easily as he'd slain that one trooper.

With only half a dozen cannon, not all the colored soldiers inside

Fort Pillow had one to serve. Most of them fought as infantry, going through the foot soldier's practiced motions with their Springfields (*Load in nine times! . . . Load!* The drill sergeant had taught them by the numbers, and the training stuck.) and firing at Bedford Forrest's men along with the dismounted troopers from the Thirteenth Tennessee Cavalry.

Bullets came back at them, too. Minié balls—*minnies* to most of the men—whined through the air when they weren't close. When they were, they cracked as viciously as an overseer's whip. Ben found himself ducking whenever he heard one of those cracks. He tried not to, but couldn't help himself.

Shame filled him. The last thing in the world he wanted was to play the coward in front of the whites who'd given him the chance to shoot back at the Confederates. Then he saw that Captain Carron and Sergeant Clark were ducking, too, as were the other Negroes in the gun crew. He realized people couldn't help it when bullets flew by. That made him feel better.

"How's it going here?" Major Booth came up to the gun and peered down the long iron tube at the advancing Confederates. "You fellas giving the Rebs hell?"

"Yes, suh!" Robinson said. His voice was the first and loudest among those of the Negroes serving the gun, but everybody sang out.

"A white crew couldn't do any better, sir," Sergeant Clark said. Hearing that, Ben wanted to burst his buttons with pride. A white sergeant, an experienced artilleryman, said he and his comrades were doing well! If he couldn't feel good about such praise, what could he feel good about?

Major Booth took their good performance for granted, which made Ben Robinson even prouder. "I didn't expect anything different," Booth said. "Not one thing, you hear? Only thing that matters is how well trained a gunner is. The *only* thing—you hear me, Sergeant? The gun doesn't care if the men serving it are black or white or green. It'll shoot the same way for anybody—as long as he knows what he's doing."

"Well, they do, sir," Clark said, and then, "Ain't that right, boys?"

The Negroes raised a cheer. Robinson had been called *boy* before. This didn't feel like that. Clark would—or at least could—have called a group of white soldiers *boys* the same way. He wasn't using it as an insult, or to deny the Negroes' manhood. Just the opposite, in fact.

Major Booth grinned and nodded and slapped Ben on the back. "Well, we've sure as hell trained 'em, all right."

That was true. They'd had to start from the very beginning. Even wearing shoes was something Ben Robinson and a lot of the Negroes had had to get used to. Marching in step seemed pointless, but after a while he realized it did a couple of things. It got him used to automatically obeying the kinds of commands he heard in the Army. And it made him understand he was part of something much bigger than he was. He wasn't taking on Jeff Davis and Robert E. Lee and Bedford Forrest all by his lonesome. He was part of this enormous outfit, and everybody was doing it together. Knowing—understanding in his belly—that he wasn't alone made soldiering a lot easier, even before he started practicing on a field piece.

"We ain't gonna let you down, Major Booth, suh," he said. Most of the rest of the black men serving the gun with him nodded. No matter how scared you were, you didn't want to show it, not in front of the man who'd turned you from a field nigger into a soldier.

"I didn't reckon you would," Booth said. "I wouldn't have let you go into combat if I thought you would." A minnie cracked past overhead. Major Booth ducked, too, just like anybody else. He grinned and chuckled and shrugged. "I don't expect the bullet with my name on it's been made yet. Now you fellows, I know you're going to work hard here, and I know you're going to be brave here. That right?"

"Yes, *suh!*" the gunners shouted as one man,

"Good," Major Booth said. "Now, I've told the sutlers to put out whiskey and dippers along the line. You need a little shot of nerve, you go on and take one. Don't take too much—you've still got to be able to fight the gun. But a little never hurt anybody, white or colored, and that's the God's truth."

After Booth went on his way, Sergeant Clark eyed the gun crew. "Soon as you see me havin' a drink, you can take one yourselves. That sound fair to you?"

The colored artillerymen looked at one another. "Reckon so, Sergeant," Robinson said. The others either spoke words of agreement or nodded. They couldn't very well tell the white man set directly over them no, regardless of what Major Booth said. And Clark's comment *did* strike Ben as fair. He wasn't asking them to do anything he wouldn't do himself.

Brasher than the other Negroes, Charlie Key said, "I gots me a thirst and then some, Sergeant. When you reckon you ply the dipper?" He mimed dipping up whiskey and pouring it down.

Mike Clark looked at him. "Don't aim to use it at all," he answered calmly. As the blacks stared in dismay, Clark went on, "We've got lots of men with Springfields on the line. Some of them get plastered—well, hell, so what? They'll still put a bunch of minnies in the air, and some of 'em'll hit. Half the time, riflemen hardly aim anyhow. But we've only got six guns. We've got to make every shot count, best we can. We better have clear heads for that, don't you think? You with me?"

Ben considered. Yes, they called popskull Dutch courage. But with a big slave trader and his men coming at Fort Pillow, how much extra courage did the Negroes inside need? "Looks to me like you's right," he said to Clark, with regret but without any doubt. "Onliest thing I wish is, I wish we could get them gun muzzles down lower—depress 'em, I mean." He trotted out the word Sergeant Hennissey gave him. "If the Secesh boys slide down under us, we can't touch 'em."

"Damn thick breastwork," Clark muttered. Ben Robinson nodded. He'd said the same thing the day before. The white man went on, "Well, we just got to make sure they don't get that close. Come on, you bucks—quit fooling around here! Let's give 'em another round!"

They served the twelve-pounder with a will.

A minnie cracked past Matt Ward's head, almost close enough to lift the slouch hat right off it. *Almost close enough to drill me between the eyes,* thought the trooper from Missouri. He shoved that down into the nightmare place where such notions naturally dwelt. Losing his hat to a bullet was something he could think about without shivering. But if all the branches and vines in the Hatchie bottoms couldn't steal that hat, he didn't fancy losing it to a damnyankee's Minié ball, either.

Another bullet zipped past, this one not quite so close. Matt didn't think the Federals had a whole lot of men in the rifle pits out beyond their earthwork, but the soldiers they did have were shooting as fast as they could load. A well-trained man with a Springfield could get off two rounds a minute, and the men in those pits knew what they were doing.

A shrapnel round from the fort itself screamed down and burst with a roar off to Ward's right. Along with the rest of Colonel McCulloch's men, he was on the left of the Confederate line, closest to the Mississippi. He and his comrades pushed north toward Fort Pillow. At the other end of the line, Barteau's regiment of Bell's brigade would be advancing west, along Coal Creek.

Ward and his companions nearby were already inside the first line of works around Fort Pillow, the line laid out by the general who'd named the place after himself. That was high ground. From where Ward crouched, he could see into the much smaller perimeter the galvanized Yankees and their colored stooges held. The range was long—it had to be more than a quarter of a mile—but his rifle would reach that far.

A minnie thudded into a stump not far away. "Thank you, Jesus!" yelled a trooper in back of the stump. The garrison inside Fort Pillow hadn't done much of a job of clearing the approaches to their position. The attackers could take cover behind lots of bushes and stumps and fallen trees.

Cautiously, Ward raised his head from behind the stump that sheltered him. He fired at a man in blue in one of the rifle pits. The Enfield carbine he carried bucked against his shoulder. The rifle musket spat fire and a puff of black-powder smoke.

The Yankee in that rifle pit kept moving around, so Ward supposed he'd missed him. "Shit," the trooper from Missouri said, without much rancor. He ducked down and reloaded, biting the paper cartridge and pouring powder and a cloth patch into the Enfield's muzzle, sending the minnie after the powder and wadding and ramming it home, drawing back the hammer to half-cock so he could set a copper percussion cap in place, and then raising the carbine to his shoulder and firing.

This time, the soldier at whom he aimed flinched and crumpled. A Minié ball weighed almost an ounce. When one hit, it hit hard. He bit open another cartridge. After a long fight, soldiers who'd done a lot of shooting had so much black powder on their faces, they looked like refugees from a minstrel show.

Ward wished he had a breech-loading repeating rifle like the ones some Federal cavalrymen were starting to carry. A regiment armed with rifles like that had the firepower of a brigade with ordinary weapons.

"Wish for the moon while you're at it," Ward muttered, tasting sulfur from the powder. Those fancy repeaters needed equally fancy brass cartridges. Even if you captured one, you also had to capture the ammunition to go with it, and keep on capturing more and more. Otherwise the rifle would be useless, except as a club.

Ward wondered why the Confederacy couldn't make rifles like that and the ammunition to go with them. Probably for the same reason it had trouble keeping its men in uniforms and shoes. A lot of the troopers in McCulloch's brigade wore tunics and trousers and shoes damnyankees didn't need anymore. Some of the trousers were still blue. Forrest insisted that shirts, at least, go into the dye kettle right away. If they turned butternut, your buddies were less likely to try to plug you by mistake.

More than a few Confederates carried captured Yankee Springfields, too. Their .58-caliber minnies and the .577 Enfield bullets both worked in both weapons.

If it wasn't for everything the Federals make, we couldn't hardly fight 'em, Ward thought. That was funny if you looked at it the right way. It was worrisome if you looked at it wrong, so Ward did his best to laugh.

He slipped another percussion cap onto the nipple and looked for a new target. There was some damnfool nigger cutting capers on the main earthwork. The black man acted like a drunk. That not only made Ward angry at him, it made the Missourian jealous. He drew a careful bead and pulled the trigger.

He couldn't have missed by much. The Negro's comic tumble behind the breastwork would have brought down the house in a play. But this wasn't a play. It was real. Matt Ward wanted that man dead. Now the coon might pick up a rifle and hurt somebody with it.

Two or three minnies from the fort cracked past the stump behind which Ward hid. They knew he was here, which meant it was time to go somewhere else. He'd fired several shots, and the clouds of smoke belching from his carbine announced his whereabouts to the world.

He scrambled to find fresh cover a little closer to the fort and to the firing pits in front of it. Other troopers were doing the same thing, and cheering one another on as they moved. Only a couple of wounded men staggered back toward the rear. One had a hand that dripped blood. The other . . .

"Son of a bitch!" Ward said softly. He'd seen some nasty wounds, but this was one of the worst. A Minié ball had caught the trooper in the lower jaw and carried away most of it. Blood splashed down the soldier's front. Shattered teeth gleamed inside his mouth. His tongue flopped loose and red, like butcher's meat.

Could you live after a mutilation like that? If you could, would you want to? You'd never be able to show your face—or what was left of it—in broad daylight again. If you had a wife, would she stay with you? If you didn't, how could you hope to get one? Wouldn't you just want to pick up an Enfield or a shotgun and finish what the Yankee bullet had started?

Those were all good questions. Matt Ward did his best not to think about any of them. He tried to move up on the enemy soldiers in the rifle pits.

Major William Bradford had been in some skirmishes before this fight, but never a real battle. This was a different business from everything he'd known up till now. He didn't care for any of the differences.

The Confederates here weren't going to ride off after exchanging a few shots with his men. They meant it. He didn't need to be U. S. Grant to figure that out. They had numbers on their side, too. The volume of gunfire told him that. So did the way they pressed the attack along the whole perimeter, from the Mississippi all the way over to Coal Creek.

Not far from him, a colored soldier from one of the newly arrived artillery units fired his Springfield, calmly reloaded as fast as a white man could have, and fired again. The Negro nodded to him. "Them Secesh keeps comin', suh, we shoots all of 'em," he said.

"Uh, right." Bradford made himself nod. He knew Bedford Forrest's men hated the idea of Negro soldiers. They denied that Negroes *could* be soldiers. If Negroes could fight as well as whites, that knocked the Confederacy's whole *raison d'être* over the head. The Rebs could see as much perfectly well.

But Bill Bradford, though no Confederate, was a Tennessean, and a Tennessean from a county with more slaves than white men. He didn't believe—well, he hadn't believed—Negroes could fight, either. If they made him see they could, he would have to do some fresh thinking, and few men are ever comfortable doing that.

Worst of all, though, was what the battle was showing him about himself. With a major's oak leaves on his shoulder straps, he had rank enough to imagine himself a bold commander like General

Sherman—or even like General Forrest, for whom every U.S. officer had a thorough and wary respect.

Now reality was rudely testing his imagination. What happened when the bullets started flying? He got flustered and fearful, and he knew it. He'd been the next thing to paralyzed till Major Booth told him to send out a couple of companies of skirmishers. Would he have thought of it for himself if Booth hadn't? He hoped so, but he wasn't sure. Dammit, he wasn't sure.

When a minnie struck home, it made a wet, slapping sound that chilled the blood. A white man—a trooper from the Thirteenth Tennessee Cavalry—groaned and clutched at his shoulder. Welling blood made his dark blue tunic even darker. He stumbled away toward the surgeons' tender mercies.

That could have been me, Bradford thought with a shudder. Once lodged in his brain, the idea wouldn't go away. *Know thyself,* some ancient had said. This was knowledge Bill Bradford would rather not have had.

One of the cannon that had come north with the colored artillerymen bellowed. The crew reloaded the gun with the same matter-of-fact competence the Negro fighting as a rifleman displayed. They had a white sergeant and a white captain, but they didn't need anyone to tell them what to do. They knew, and they did it.

No answering Confederate cannonballs came. Forrest's men seemed to have no artillery with them. That was the one bit of good news Bill Bradford saw. Confederate soldiers in gray, in butternut, and even in blue swarmed everywhere out beyond the perimeter. Their fierce yells of fury and defiance put him in mind of the baying of wolves.

Another cannon crashed. Half a dozen guns had seemed plenty to defend Fort Pillow. The earthwork along which they were mounted wasn't very long. But, no matter how many rounds they fired at the Rebs, Forrest's men kept pressing ever closer.

A shell from the gunboat in the Mississippi arched up over the bluff atop which Fort Pillow sat. It burst somewhere to the rear of the attacking rebels. Bradford swore under his breath. The *New Era* had to supplement the firepower in the fort itself.

"Make 'em shorten the range, Theo!" Bradford yelled.

"I'll do it!" His older brother, Captain Theodorick Bradford, passed signals down to the *New Era* with blue wigwag flags. The system had seemed good enough on paper. In the heat of action . . . It was liable to be slower and clumsier than Bradford wished it were.

Major Booth went from one gun along the earthwork to the next, encouraging the crews to keep firing. "Give 'em hell!" Booth yelled. "Those bastards don't know what hell is! Show 'em, damn you!"

And the colored men responded. They laughed and cheered and served their cannon with a will. Not even white men obeyed Bradford so readily. He envied the more experienced officer for his ability to command.

"Major!" he called.

"What is it, Major?" Booth asked, mindful of the civilities even under fire. A bullet snapped past his head. He ducked, then laughed at himself for ducking. "Warm work, isn't it?"

"Er—so it is." Bradford couldn't act so cheerful about it. "They're putting a lot of pressure on the skirmishers, sir. Shall I send out more men, or shall I pull back the ones we've already got out there?"

"Neither," Booth said at once. "If you send out more, we'll lose them. Skirmishers can't stop the Rebs from coming forward. Three times as many men out there couldn't stop them, and the ones we do have are enough to slow the enemy down. If you pull them back into the fort, though, Forrest will push right up to the earthwork. I want to put that off as long as I can."

"Major?" Bradford said, perplexed.

"If we can hold the Rebs out till reinforcements come up the river from Memphis, the fight is as good as won," Booth said. "No way in hell Forrest can overrun us then. His men will skulk off and go back to thieving and murdering and bushwhacking. That's all they're good for, and they can keep doing it from now till doomsday without changing the way the war turns out one damn bit."

"Uh, yes, sir." Bradford wondered if he could have been callous enough to sacrifice the skirmishers in the hope of saving the fort and most of the garrison. He didn't think so, even if he could see it was the right move.

Along with his other talents, Lionel Booth might have been a mind reader. He patted Bradford on the back. "I know they're your men, and I know you're fond of them, Major. But every now and then we need to take some losses for the good of the greater number. Do you see it?"

"I see it. I don't like it." When a minnie cracked past Bradford, he ducked as Booth had. He couldn't laugh about it. It made him feel like a coward, even if it was altogether involuntary.

A wounded man screamed. Bradford set his teeth against the appalling cry. Booth hurried on to hearten the next gun crew.

IV

SURVIVING SKIRMISHERS RAN BACK TOWARD the earthen parapet warding Fort Pillow. Hale soldiers helped their wounded friends. Every so often, a man who'd loaded his Springfield before retreating would fire it at the oncoming Rebs to make them keep their heads down.

Lieutenant Mack Leaming watched a couple of Federals go down, but only a couple. Most of the men who'd set out for the earthwork reached it in safety—or as much safety as U.S. soldiers could find anywhere on this field.

A Minié ball snapped past in front of Leaming's nose, too close for comfort. He flinched. Half a minute later, another near miss made him flinch again. Fifty yards away, troopers from the Thirteenth Tennessee Cavalry shouted that another officer was down. The Confederates seemed to be taking dead aim—though Leaming wished he didn't think of it quite that way—at anyone inside the perimeter who wore shoulder straps and more than his share of brass buttons.

Though clouds still covered the sun most of the time, Leaming didn't think it could be much past eight o'clock. Looking at his pocket watch never even crossed his mind. The Confederates hadn't been attacking for much more than two hours, and they'd already driven the Federals back inside the fortress proper.

That wasn't good, and Leaming knew it. How could the garrison hold out till reinforcements got here from Memphis? Leaming spotted Major Lionel Booth, who was still going from gun to gun encouraging the colored cannoneers. "Major!" he called. "Excuse me, Major . . ."

"Yes, Lieutenant?" Booth sounded as calm as if on parade. Leaming didn't think he really was that calm, but even being able to seem so was a valuable asset to an officer. "What do you need?"

"Sir, how many Rebs do you reckon are out there?" Leaming blurted.

Booth considered. He ducked when a bullet cracked past above his head, but he didn't seem especially flustered. "I'd say fifteen hundred, maybe two thousand," he replied at last. "From the weight of fire, that's about what it feels like to me."

"Is that all, sir?" Leaming said in amazement.

"Isn't that enough? Two and a half, maybe three times what we've got in here," Booth said with a wry chuckle. "More than I figured Bedford Forrest could throw at us, I'll tell you that. But does someone else think there are more?"

"When I asked Major Bradford, sir, he said he thought Forrest had six or seven thousand men," Leaming said.

"Did he now?" Booth started to say something, then visibly changed his mind. What did come out of his mouth after that brief pause was, "Well, Lieutenant, you have to remember this is Major Bradford's first real combat. Your first few times, you're liable to see things that aren't there." He sounded indulgent, like a father talking about a boy who didn't want to go to sleep without a candle by his bed.

Leaming hoped the fortress commandant felt indulgent about him, too. This was also his first real combat, and he was scared. He was scared spitless—the Sahara couldn't have been drier than the inside of his mouth. The first few near misses, he'd almost pissed himself. That would have been a fine thing for an officer to do in front of his men!

"You're getting along just fine, Lieutenant," Booth said, so maybe he could seem paternal toward more people than Major Bradford. "I think there are only a few people who aren't afraid on a battlefield— and they're men who don't care if they live or die. Nothing wrong with being afraid. The trick of it is to go on doing your job whether you're afraid or not. You're not shirking, and that's all anybody can ask of you."

"Thank you, sir." Leaming was no Catholic, but that felt like absolution from a priest.

Major Booth's grin showed crooked teeth. "It's all right. The more Rebs who try to rush this place, the more Rebs we'll shoot, that's all. Let 'em come, by God! How are they going to make it over the parapet? We'll hang on till help from Memphis steams up the river, and then we'll see who runs, and how far."

Shells from the *New Era* climbed high over the bluff, slow enough to be easily visible to the naked eye, then rained down someplace not too far from where Confederate troopers were moving. Seeing those bursts and the clouds of smoke rising from them heartened Leaming. Even so, he said, "I wish we had better signal arrangements with the gunboat. The way things are, she's almost firing blind."

"I won't say you're altogether wrong, but I think we're doing as much as we can," Booth replied. "Signal flags are about as good as we can manage, I'm afraid, even if they aren't perfect—her crew can't see their targets. The ground up here is too high, that's all, and the Rebs are moving faster than we can let the *New Era* know where they're moving to. But some of what the gunboat fires off is bound to come down on their heads."

"Here's hoping, sir," Mack Leaming said. When Booth put things the way he did, the *New Era* didn't seem so very formidable after all. Leaming was glad nobody else inside Fort Pillow had heard the commandant. That left him the only one to have his spirits lowered.

Major Booth seemed unworried about what the gunboat could or couldn't do. He hardly seemed worried about anything. Touching the brim of his black slouch hat, he went back to encouraging the gunners.

Despite their steady fire, and despite the work of the white and colored riflemen behind the earthwork, Forrest's men steadily worked their way forward. They came close enough to let Leaming hear their officers shouting orders, close enough to let him hear their wounded men groan when they were hit.

They came close enough to let him draw his revolver from the holster and fire two or three shots at them: the first shots he'd ever fired with intent to kill. He couldn't see if he hit anybody. That was probably just as well.

And then, instead of sliding forward, the Confederates slid back. They still kept up a steady and galling fire, but they didn't seem to think they could simply storm the parapet any more.

We taught them respect, by God, Leaming thought. Those loping, caterwauling shapes had been everywhere in front of the fort, or so it seemed to him. He found Major Bradford's estimate of their numbers far easier to believe than Major Booth's. Six or seven thousand Rebs? Looking at them out there, he could have believed there were six or seven million of them.

Not far away, two colored soldiers passed a dipper of sutlers' whiskey back and forth. Both of them grinned. One of them raised the dipper in salute to Lieutenant Leaming. "Want a snort, suh?" he called.

"No, thanks," Leaming answered. Dutch courage, nigger courage, what difference did it make? And some of the whites from his own regiment were drinking, too. Put a soldier, white or colored, anywhere near whiskey and he'd find a way to get outside it.

One of the Negroes aimed an obscene gesture at the Confederates out there in the distance. His friend thought that was the funniest thing he'd ever seen, and sent the Rebs something even nastier. Several bullets snarled past them. They went right on laughing.

They weren't afraid, anyhow. And they were fighting the enemy. The colored men at the half-dozen field guns kept firing steadily, while the colored soldiers serving as riflemen loaded and shot shoulder to shoulder with the troopers from the Thirteenth Tennessee Cavalry. Leaming wouldn't have believed it if he weren't seeing it with his own eyes. He had trouble believing it even though he *was* seeing it with his own eyes.

A Negro let out a shrill screech. He staggered away from the parapet, clutching at his left elbow. "Do Jesus! The surgeon gonna cut off my arm!" he wailed. From what Leaming knew of wounds, he was likely to be right. If a bullet shattered bones, you almost had to amputate. Otherwise, the injured man would die of fever. Shy a limb, he might live.

"Po' George," one Negro said.

"Hard luck," another agreed.

They both fired their Springfields less than a minute after George got hurt. The other colored soldiers shot at any Confederates they saw, too. *Niggers really can fight,* Lieutenant Leaming thought in swelling wonder. *Maybe it's not a question of keeping them slaves from here on out. Maybe we were lucky to hold them in slavery as long as we did.*

By now, the white captain and sergeant nominally in charge of Ben Robinson's twelve-pounder had seen that the colored gun crew knew what it was doing. They gave fewer and fewer orders. They gave fewer and fewer suggestions. The black men were doing plenty all by themselves to give the Confederates out beyond the earthwork a hard time.

When Bedford Forrest's troopers pressed close to the parapet, Sergeant Robinson ordered a couple of rounds of canister on his own. He looked back to Captain Carron after he did it, but the officer didn't say a word. He just beamed and nodded, and Ben Robinson went on fighting the gun.

Each round of canister had sheet-metal sides and a thin wooden plug at the top. It held two or three hundred round bullets. In effect, it turned the twelve-pounder into God's shotgun. At short range, it was supremely deadly.

A man caught by the full fury of a blast of canister might be blown to red rags. He might simply cease to be, torn apart so completely that nothing recognizable as a human being was left. Or he might be killed or maimed in any number of more ordinary ways.

The Rebs didn't want to come close to any gun that was firing canister. No matter how much Ben Robinson hated those Secesh sons of bitches, he couldn't blame them for that. He wouldn't have wanted to make the acquaintance of a canister burst himself. Who would?

"Look at 'em run!" Charlie Key yelled. "You ever reckon you see Secesh run?"

Some of the Confederates couldn't run. Some of them would never run again. The rest . . . didn't want that to happen to them.

"Give 'em anudder round, jus' like de last one!" Charlie yelled.

Robinson shook his head. "They outa range now," he said mournfully. "Don't want to waste the canister. We ain't got but a few rounds."

"Too bad," Charlie said. "How come dey don't give us mo'? Powerful good 'munition. Ain't nothin' else make the Rebs scamper like dat." He mimed scampering himself. He was a dangerous mimic.

"Canister shift damn near anything—anything up close," Robinson said. "Out past a couple hundred yards, though, it ain't much. So we got us dese shrapnel rounds an' shot fo' de long-range work."

A twelve-pound iron ball would tear a fearful hole in a tight-packed group of men. Since the Rebs weren't fighting that way, shrapnel bursts did more damage here. Ben Robinson knew he could hurt the white men who'd done so much to make his life a misery. *Sell me away from home, will you?* he thought furiously as he lowered the altitude screw on the gun carriage. *Sell me at all, will you? Treat me like a piece of meat, will you? Treat my sister like a piece of meat, will you?* That was a separate outrage, one that burned all by itself.

Sergeant Clark pulled the lanyard. The shrapnel round roared away. The gun rolled back. As Sergeant Robinson put his shoulder to the carriage to wrestle it forward again, he hoped some of the iron fragments from that round blew a white man's balls off. *Let's see you come round the slave cabins with a bulge in your pants then, God damn your scrawny soul to hell.*

The reloading ritual began once more. It felt almost like a dance. Only the music was missing, and the gun crew didn't really need it. They could go through the steps with no accompaniment but the boom of the Springfields to either side and the whine and crack of enemy minnies darting past.

Like any soldier of any color, Robinson had hated all the hot, sweaty hours he spent on the drill field learning how to handle a cannon. He knew the rest of the colored men in the crew felt the same way. He'd hated white sergeants screaming at him. *Dumb-ass coon! Clumsy fool!* And those were some of the nicer things they said. But they turned raw black recruits into a real gun crew, something that was more than the sum of its parts, and he owed them a reluctant debt of gratitude for that.

He'd also heard that drill sergeants were just as merciless toward whites. That made him feel a little better. Fair was fair.

"Give 'em hell, boys!" Major Booth came up behind the crew. The gunners worked harder than ever under the commandant's eye. That, no doubt, was exactly what he had in mind. When the gun was ready, he tipped his hat to Sergeant Clark and asked, "May I do the honors?"

"Uh, yes, sir." Clark handed him the lanyard. Booth gave it a hearty tug. The gun thundered. Looking pleased with himself, Booth returned the match to the sergeant.

A couple of bullets thumped into the earthwork close by. More cracked past. Enemy fire always picked up when Major Booth was around. "Suh, you wants to be careful," Ben Robinson told him. "They got sharpshooters out there tryin' to pick you off."

Booth laughed lightheartedly. Ben always remembered that—how cheerful the commandant sounded, as if he'd just heard a good joke. "They can try, Sergeant," he said—he was always careful to use colored underofficers' ranks when he spoke to them. "The bastards have been trying for a while, but they haven't got me yet."

"Yes, suh." Ben didn't see how he could say anything else. He couldn't very well tell Major Booth to go somewhere else because when the Rebs were shooting at Booth they were also shooting at *him*. He wanted to, but he couldn't.

And then he heard the unmistakable wet slap of a bullet striking flesh. "My God! I'm hit!" Major Booth exclaimed—a cry more of disbelief than of pain. Booth's hands clutched at his chest. Bright blood welled out between his fingers. "My God!" he said again, more weakly this time. Blood bubbled from his mouth and nose, too. That meant it was a bad wound, about as bad as a wound could be. The thought had hardly crossed Ben's mind before Major Booth's legs gave out and he crumpled to the ground.

"Lawd!" Ben Robinson whispered. Major Booth wasn't just the commandant here. He was the man who'd turned the Negroes he led from field hands into soldiers. If Booth couldn't go on leading, command would fall to Major Bradford. And Booth couldn't—that wound looked sure to kill him, and to kill him fast. As for Major Bradford . . . A lot of the men in the Thirteenth Tennessee Cavalry had no more use for colored soldiers than the Confederates had. They didn't fight for the U.S.A. because they wanted emancipation; they fought for the U.S.A. because they couldn't get along with their neighbors who fought for the C.S.A.

Captain Carron came out of the horrified trance that seemed to grip everyone around the fallen Major Booth. "Take him to a surgeon!" he said. "Maybe the sawbones will be able to do . . . well, something, anyway." His voice trailed off. A surgeon couldn't do much for a chest wound, any more than he could for one in the belly. A man either got better or he died.

Major Lionel Booth was going to die. The way he plucked at Robinson's sleeve when the Negro started to lift him told him as much. Booth tried to say something, but more blood came out instead of words. He fought to breathe—he was drowning in his own blood.

When Robinson and two other soldiers from the gun crew laid him in front of the green-sashed surgeon, the white man said, "Good God, it's the major!"

"Yes, suh," Robinson said. "Help him if you can, suh."

"Help," Major Booth echoed feebly. "Please help. Please . . ." His eyes rolled up in his head.

"He gone?" Charlie Key asked.

The surgeon felt for a pulse at Booth's wrist. "Not yet," he answered. "He's—" He broke off, then said something vile, aimed not at the Negroes but at fate. "*Now* he's gone."

"Lawd!" Robinson said again. "What is we gonna do?"

Major William Bradford felt the weight of the world crashing down on his shoulders. He'd resented Major Booth when the younger officer brought his colored artillerymen up from Memphis. He'd resented him, yes, but he'd come to lean on him, too. Booth knew more about soldiering than he did, and that was all there was to it. Booth didn't get stuffy about passing on what he knew, and Bill Bradford knew he'd learned a lot in the couple of weeks since Booth arrived.

Rather more to the point at the moment, Lionel Booth had kept his head when the Confederates attacked—and when Bradford was on the edge of losing his. Now he was down. Now Fort Pillow was in Bradford's hands again, no matter how much he wished it weren't.

We can hold on. We will hold on, Bradford thought. *And maybe Booth isn't hit as badly as people say.*

No sooner had that hopeful thought crossed his mind than a soldier came pelting toward him from where the surgeon was working. "He's dead!" the man shouted. "He's dead, sir!"

Well, so much for that, Major Bradford thought unhappily. *It's all mine now.* It was his before Booth and his coons got here. He didn't want it back, not like this, but what he wanted didn't seem to matter. He gathered himself, or tried to. "Keep firing!" he shouted to the embattled garrison, and immediately felt a fool. What were they going to do? Stop? Not likely, not with Bedford Forrest's wolves prowling out there. Bradford tried again: "We'll whip 'em yet!"

"You tell 'em, Major!" That was one of his own troopers. They would follow where he led. But what about the niggers? They'd have to, wouldn't they? He was the senior officer left alive, no matter how little he wanted the distinction to land on him at this time in this way.

"Major! Major! Major Bradford, suh!" This time, one of Major Booth's colored soldiers—one of *his* colored soldiers now, for better or worse—dashed toward him from the parapet as if all the furies of hell were at his heels.

"What is it?" Bradford asked. *What is it now?* he almost said, but he swallowed the last word in the nick of time. It would have sounded too much like panic. He felt panic hammering hard inside him, but didn't want to show it. That would only make it spread.

"Suh, the Secesh done shot Lieutenant Hill through the head out by the old barracks," the Negro answered. "He fall down, he twitch a few times, an' he dead now jus' like Major Booth."

"Oh, good God!" Bradford exclaimed. "One thing on top of another!" Hill was—had been—Booth's adjutant, which meant he'd become post adjutant when Booth took command. Now . . . he hadn't outlived his superior by more than a couple of minutes.

"Yes, suh—one thing after another. But I reckon we's hurting the Rebs, too," the Negro said. He still showed fight. That was good.

"We'll just have to carry on the best way we can," Bradford said, and then, "Thank you for letting me know."

"Yes, suh," the colored sergeant answered. He gave Bradford a salute that would have won the heart of any drill sergeant on a practice field. Bradford tried to return it as smartly; he'd already seen the Negroes set more stock in such gestures than did the troopers he led. His salute was spoiled when a minnie cracked past overhead. Both he and the colored man ducked. He would have been humiliated if he did and the artilleryman didn't. As things were, they smiled at each other, both admitting that bullets could scare a man no matter what color he was.

After a bob of the head, the Negro trotted back to his station. "Lieutenant Leaming!" Bradford shouted, and then, when that didn't accomplish anything, "Mack! Where in damnation are you?"

"Right here, sir," Leaming said. "What do you need?"

"A nigger just told me the Rebs have killed Lieutenant Hill out-side the works. That makes you post adjutant again," Major Bradford answered.

"Good Lord!" Leaming said. "I think their sharpshooters really are trying to pick off our officers. We're losing them too fast for any-thing else to make sense. . . . Are you all right, sir?"

"Yes," Bradford lied. He'd always been proud of his major's tunic with its two rows of seven brass buttons each. Now, like Joseph's coat of many colors, his tunic with the many shiny buttons—he made sure they stayed shiny—was liable to land him in danger. He imagined some skinny, mangy Rebel drawing a bead right between the rows, squeezing the trigger, and. . . . He flinched, though no bullet came close.

"What are your orders, sir?" Lieutenant Leaming asked.

"What else can we do but keep on with what we've been doing?" Bradford replied. "Major Booth was sure help would come from Memphis. We just have to hang on till it gets here, that's all."

"Yes, sir." Leaming stepped closer to Bradford so he could lower his voice: "Damned if the coons aren't fighting, sir."

"I wouldn't have believed it, either," Bradford said. "A good thing, though. Without 'em, we couldn't have held this place ten minutes against that swarm of Rebs out there. Thousands of those bastards! Thousands!"

"Sir, Major Booth didn't think there were all that many of them," Leaming said. "He guessed fifteen hundred, maybe two thousand at the outside."

"Nonsense!" Major Bradford said. "Look at them. Just look at them. They've got more soldiers running around than a dog has fleas. And if Major Booth were as smart as he thought he was, he wouldn't have walked into a minnie, now would he?"

"I . . . guess not, sir," his adjutant answered.

"However many Rebs there are doesn't matter anyhow," Bradford said. "Can you imagine what they'd do to us if we surrendered? They hate colored soldiers, and they hate Tennessee Union men. They could have the Army of Northern Virginia out there, and we'd still have to fight. Isn't that right, Lieutenant?"

"Yes, sir, I guess it is, when you put it like that," Leaming answered.

"All right, then. We'll fight on, just the way we would have if Major Booth were still here." Bradford hesitated, then blurted, "I wish he still were." But Fort Pillow was his again, no matter what he wished.

Nathan Bedford Forrest rode toward the sound of the gunfire ahead. It was somewhere near ten in the morning. He'd been in the saddle since setting out from Jackson. He was so tired, he could hardly see straight. His horse had to be every bit as weary. The ideal cavalry trooper was a little bandy-legged fellow who didn't weight more than 140 pounds. Well over six feet tall and somewhere close to 200 pounds, Forrest didn't fit the bill. But he was what he was, and the horse had to put up with it.

He knew exhaustion would fall away from him like a discarded cloak once he got to the battlefield. Most of the time, he was a quiet, soft-spoken man. In a fight, everything changed. His voice rose to a roar that could span the field, no matter how wide. He became a furious and ingeniously profane swearer. Some men turned pale when they fought—they were afraid of what might happen to them. Forrest went hot and ruddy, like iron in a smith's forge. Instead of being hammered, though, he smashed the damnyankees himself.

His nostrils twitched. Yes, that was the brimstone reek of gunpowder in the air. It smelled like Old Scratch coming up from the infernal dominions for a look around. Forrest's lips skinned back from his teeth in a fierce, mirthless grin. He intended to make Fort Pillow into hell on earth, all right.

The ground around the fort was only indifferently cleared. A good many trees still stood, and stumps; fallen trunks lay scattered every which way. Even inside the outermost perimeter, plenty of cover still remained. He watched his men use it to good advantage, scooting forward from one stump to another as if they were in an Indian fight from the days before he was born.

Seeing a trooper not far away, Forrest called, "Where's General Chalmers?"

"Who wants to know?" the man answered, not looking up from the revolver he was reloading.

"Bedford Forrest, that's who." Forrest's voice crackled with danger, the way the air will crackle just before lightning strikes. When the battle fit hit him, he was almost as hard on his own men as he was on the Federals. "Now where is he, you son of a bitch?"

The trooper hadn't been pale. Why should he be, when he was safely out of enemy rifle range? But he went white when he raised his head and saw General Forrest. He almost dropped a percussion cap, and had to fight to say, "He—He—He's over yonder, sir." He pointed west and a little south.

"All right," Forrest said. "I don't see you in the fight once you finish loading that hogleg, though, you'll answer to me, man to man. You hear?"

"Y-Y-Y-Yes, sir," the man answered—not the first time Nathan Bedford Forrest had reduced a man from his own force to frightened stammering. But what he did to the Federals . . .

He found Brigadier General Chalmers about where the trooper said he would. Chalmers was urging his men forward—always a good thing for a general to do, especially when he wasn't far from the firing line himself. Nothing encouraged soldiers like officers who shared their risks.

"How's it look, Jim?" Forrest asked.

James Chalmers whirled. Even in the informal world of the Confederate army, even in the extra-informal world of Forrest's command, an officer who led a brigade didn't expect to be addressed by his Christian name . . . unless a superior did it. "Hello, sir," Chalmers said, saluting. "So you finally made it up here, did you?"

"No, but I reckon I'll get here pretty soon," Forrest answered dryly.

His brigade commander blinked, then decided he was joking and laughed. "Well, I'm glad to hear that, sir. We can use you."

"It looks pretty good, from what I've seen of it," Forrest said.

"I think so." Brigadier General Chalmers nodded. "They sent out skirmishers after we started driving in their pickets, but we shifted them, too. Just about all the Federals are back inside the main position there. They should have hung on to some of the knobs around it. They should have, but they damn well didn't. Now we've got men on 'em, and we can shoot down into their works. This isn't the best place for a fort with a small garrison, no matter what General Pillow thought when he set one here."

"Already knew that myself," Forrest said. "If the Yankees can't figure it out, too damn bad for them. The riffraff they've got in there, they're asking for everything we give 'em."

A bullet cracked past. Chalmers flinched. So did Forrest; he was no more immune to that reflex than most of his soldiers were. It annoyed and angered him, but he couldn't do anything about it. However little he cared to admit it, even to himself, he was made of flesh and blood like any other man.

Straightening, Chalmers said, "You might do well to get down from that horse, sir. It makes you a target for the bastards holed up in there. You wouldn't want some damn nigger to be able to say he shot the great General Forrest, would you?"

"No, but I'm not going to worry about it, either," Forrest answered. "And I want to see this place for my own self from one end to the other, and the horse'll tote me around faster'n I could go on shank's mare." He always carried out his own reconnaissance when he could. More than once, he'd seen things nobody else did. He went on, "You keep crowding our boys forward, you hear, Jim?"

"I'm doing it," Chalmers said shortly.

"I know you are. Keep doing it. Do more of it. Get 'em close to the enemy. Use that high ground. I don't want the Federals moving around a lot in there. They should ought to be scared to death to step away from that parapet."

"I'm doing it," Chalmers repeated. This time, he smiled a little. "I've got sharpshooters picking off the Union officers whenever they see the chance, too."

"There you go," Forrest said. "That's what we need. If those coons and galvanized Yankees haven't got anybody to tell 'em what to do, they won't tend to something that needs tending, and we'll get the bulge on 'em that way."

He started to ride on toward the Mississippi, but a minnie caught his horse in the neck. Blood gushed forth, hideously red and stinking like a smithy. Forrest tried jamming a finger in the wound, a trick that had kept another mount of his alive for some little while. This horse writhed and thrashed and reared, then crashed to the ground, pinning Forrest's leg beneath it.

Pain shot through him. He roared out curses, kicked at the animal with his free leg, and beat it with his fists. It rolled off him and thrashed away its life, kicking slower and more weakly as blood rivered out of it.

General Chalmers ran up to Forrest. "Are you all right, sir?" he asked, alarm making his voice almost as shrill as a woman's. "Can you get up?"

"Don't rightly know." Forrest made himself try it. His breath hissed out between his teeth. Moving hurt like fire. But he *could* move, anyhow. "Don't reckon anything's broken," he said.

His right trouser leg was torn. His flesh was bruised and scraped and battered. The whole leg would be purple and black and swollen tomorrow, if it wasn't already. But it bore his weight even if it screamed. He took a couple of limping steps. Yes, he could manage.

"You were lucky," Chalmers said as he tried to walk off the worst of it.

"Lucky, my ass," Forrest ground out. "If I was lucky, that damned Yankee minnie would've missed my horse. If it did hit the stupid critter, he wouldn't have fallen on me. That there's luck, General. This— you can keep this."

"The fall could have broken your leg—or your neck," Chalmers said. "The minnie could have hit you instead of the horse."

"All that would have been worse," Forrest agreed. "Don't mean what happened was good." He glowered at the beast that had brought him from Jackson. Its writhing was almost over now. Its blood pooled on the muddy ground and started soaking in. A man had an amazing lot of blood in him—you found out how much when he spilled it all at once. A horse had even more. Forrest had had plenty of horses shot out from under him, but he didn't think he'd ever had one hurt him so much when it went down. "Got to get me another animal. Will you tend to that for me?"

"Yes, sir," Chalmers said, and then, stubbornly, "You'd still be safer on foot."

"I'd be slower on foot," Forrest said. "Nothing else matters now. And you don't think dismounted men are getting hit?" A wounded trooper howled and cursed as his friends led him back toward the surgeons. Forrest pointed to him the way a schoolmaster would have pointed to an example on the blackboard. He chuckled when that occurred to him, because his own acquaintance with teachers and blackboards was so brief and sketchy. He could read. He could write, too—after a fashion—however little he cared to do it.

Even if he had no education, he owned other talents in abundance. He had nerve and a fierce and driving energy. He also had an unfailing knack for seeing what needed doing at any given moment. And he could make people listen to him and take him seriously and do what he told them to do. Set against all that, knowing how to spell didn't seem so important. He had men under him who could spell. *He* was the one who set them in motion.

"A horse!" James Chalmers shouted now. "Get General Forrest a horse!"

One of the troopers brought up a large, sturdy-looking beast. A horse needed to be of better-than-average size to bear a man of his weight. "Thank you kindly, Edgar," Forrest said.

"You're welcome, General!" Edgar's face glowed with pride: Bedford Forrest knew him well enough to call him by name! Edgar didn't know Forrest could call most of his men by name. He learned names quickly, and they were the easiest handle you could grab to get somebody to follow you.

Mounting hurt. It would have hurt worse if the blamed horse had fallen on his other leg. Jim Chalmers would have said he was lucky it didn't. Forrest didn't give a damn what Chalmers would have said. Almost getting his leg broken wasn't lucky, not so far as he could see. When he booted the horse into motion, riding hurt, too.

But walking would have hurt worse. And it would have been slower, and speed counted now. Speed always counted to Bedford Forrest. Plenty of people knew how he talked about getting there first with the most. If you got there first, sometimes having the most didn't even matter.

Over the next hour, he painstakingly reconnoitered from the Mississippi to Coal Creek. Like General Chalmers, Captain Anderson begged him to do the job on foot so he would offer the Yankees less of a target.

Voice testy—maybe the pain was talking through him—Forrest answered, "I'm just as apt to be hit one way as another." And he had that sturdy horse shot out from under him (though it was only wounded), but got yet another remount and finished the reconnaissance. When he did, his smile was purely predatory. "We've got 'em," he said.

V

BELOW THE BLUFF ON WHICH the innermost line of Fort Pillow's works sat, a crescent-shaped ravine ran north into Coal Creek. Corporal Jack Jenkins crouched in that ravine, only a few feet away from General Forrest, when Forrest declared that he and his men had the Federals inside the fort.

Jenkins was glad General Forrest thought so. Forrest commonly knew what he was talking about. Jenkins hoped the general did this time. He hoped so, yes, but he was a hell of a long way from convinced.

If Coal Creek Ravine wasn't hell on earth, you could see it from there. Jenkins had ridden through the Hatchie bottoms to get to Fort Pillow. Coal Creek seemed a distillation of everything that was worst about the bottom country. The ground was muddy enough to suck the shoes right off a man's feet. Every sort of clinging vine and thorn bush seemed to grow there, all of them clutching at trouser legs and tunic sleeves when Jack and the other troopers in Colonel Barteau's regiment tried to push on toward the fort.

Poison ivy, poison oak, poison sumac . . . Jenkins tried not to think about any of those. If he broke out in welts later on, then he did, that was all. Now he just wanted to close with the enemy.

One thing worked in his favor, and in favor of the rest of the men in the Second Tennessee Cavalry (C.S.). Because Fort Pillow stood so high above Coal Creek Ravine, and because its earthen rampart was so thick, the soldiers inside the fort had to crawl out on top of the earthwork to shoot down into the ravine. When they did, Confederate sharpshooters farther back and higher up had clean shots at them. After a couple of Federals were wounded, or perhaps killed, the rest seemed less eager to expose themselves.

The cannon inside Fort Pillow would not bear on the ravine at all. Every so often, shrapnel rounds or solid shot would snarl by overhead, but they always came down far to the rear.

That didn't mean the troopers in Coal Creek Ravine went altogether free of bombardment. The Yankee gunboat out in the Mississippi lobbed an occasional shell into the ravine. Jenkins hated the gunboat. It could strike with impunity, for the Confederates weren't able to shoot back at it. But it was firing blind. Just as the bluff and the fort atop it shielded the gunboat from C.S. fire, so they also shielded the Confederates from the sailors who aimed the boat's cannon.

Some of the black men and Tennessee Tories inside Fort Pillow had nerve enough to keep exposing themselves to Confederate fire. One Negro soldier crawled out on top of the earthwork and had his pals within the fort pass him one loaded rifle musket after another, so he sent an almost continual stream of bullets down into the ravine.

Corporal Jenkins took a shot at him. So did a couple of other Confederate troopers not far away. The smoke that burst from their rifles announced where they were. In moments, the Negro sent minnies whistling through the undergrowth close to each of the three men.

As Jenkins reloaded, he said, "To hell with me if that nigger's not too dumb to realize how much trouble he's in."

"I wouldn't be crazy enough to stick myself out there, that's for damn sure," one of the nearby Confederates agreed.

More bullets whipped past the colored man. Had he been white—even if he were only a homemade Yankee—Jenkins would have respected his courage. But the corporal didn't want to admit, even to himself, that a Negro had courage. If a black man could be brave, wasn't he much the same sort of man as a white? And if he was much the same as a white, how could he also naturally be a slave?

Those two things didn't fit together. Jenkins could see that as plainly as Abe Lincoln could. Where it forced the President of the United States to conclude that all men should be free, it forced the Southerner and most of his comrades to deny the possibility that Negroes could show the same sort of courage as white men.

If Jenkins saw a black man exposing himself to enemy fire, then, the blue-uniformed Negro couldn't be brave. He had to be stupid instead.

Another Minié ball clipped leaves and twigs a few feet away from Jenkins. "This here's warmer work than I reckoned it would be," he said.

"We'll get 'em," another trooper said. "Long as they don't get reinforced from down the river, we'll get 'em. And even if they do, we've still got most of the high ground. We'll make 'em sorry they holed up in there."

Squelching through the mire at the bottom of Coal Creek Ravine, Jenkins thought of high ground as little more than a rumor. Something slithered over his boot and vanished in the bushes. Maybe it was just a water snake, not a copperhead or a cottonmouth. He hoped so, because he didn't know how far away it had slithered.

After what seemed like forever and was probably fifteen minutes or so, the Negro soldier let out a holler and scrambled back into the fort. "Somebody nailed the son of a bitch!" Jenkins exclaimed. "About time!"

"You see where he got it?" one of his friends asked gleefully.

"Not me." Jenkins shook his head. "I was ramming a cartridge home." That was true, but he wasn't sorry to have been screened off by the undergrowth. The damn coon had come too close to hitting him a couple of times. "So where?"

"They shot him right in the ass," the other C.S. trooper said.

"Probably give him a brain concussion," Jenkins said. "Remember that Yankee general who said he was going to make his headquarters in the saddle?"

"That was General Pope. He had his headquarters in his hindquarters, just like that nigger," the other man said. "Once he ran up against Bobby Lee, it didn't matter where his headquarters were at anyways."

"You're sure right there," Jenkins said. Every Federal general who'd operated against Robert E. Lee had come to grief. The Confederates' luck wasn't so good out here in the West. But they were still in the fight, and the Union troops holed up in Fort Pillow would pay for forgetting it.

A bullet cracked past Bill Bradford, close enough to make him duck. He imagined he felt the minnie tug at the brim of his slouch hat, but the hat seemed untouched when he took it off and looked at it. He set it back on his head, pulling it down low as if to make himself a smaller target.

Another Confederate fired at him. Again, the bullet made him flex his knees. This time, though, he felt no phantom tugs. He scowled at the cloud of black-powder smoke rising from one of the barracks in front of the fort. The Confederates seemed to infest both rows of wooden buildings.

"Captain Carron!" he called.

"Yes, sir?" the artilleryman answered, standing by his twelve-pounder.

"Will that piece of yours reach those barracks halls? The Rebs have got men in them, and they're close enough to make the fire annoying." That was a polite way to put it. When the Rebs almost parted his hair with a Minié ball, Major Bradford wasn't just annoyed. He was scared green.

Captain Carron shook his head. "Sorry, Major, but I can't do it. The gun won't depress far enough to hit those huts."

"Damnation," Bradford said. "How am I supposed to shift the devils sheltering in them, then?"

"You could burn them out," Carron suggested.

Bradford hadn't thought of that. Now that the artillery officer planted the idea in his mind, though, he found that he liked it. "Lieutenant Leaming!" he said. "Where the—? Oh, there you are."

"Yes, sir. Here I am," his adjutant agreed. "What do you need from me, sir?"

"I want you to gather a—a storming party, I guess you'd call it," Bradford answered. "The Rebs are shooting at us from those barracks." He pointed. "I want the men to take torches along with their Springfields. They are to burn down the buildings and then return to the fort. Is that clear?"

"Yes, sir," Leaming said. "Do you think fifty men will be enough? Shall I send some niggers along with our Tennessee troopers?"

"If fifty can't do the job, no larger number can," Bradford said. "And no, leave the niggers here inside the fort. I don't know how well they'd fight out in the open, and they shouldn't go out where they can be captured, anyway. Forrest's men don't love colored soldiers."

"All right, sir," Leaming replied. "I'll tend to it."

There was some small delay assembling the storming party. There was a larger delay equipping the troopers with torches. But they swarmed out of the fort bravely enough. "Hurrah!" they shouted as they went forward. "Hurrah!" The U.S. war cry wasn't so impressive as the Rebel yell, but they showed good spirit.

The Confederates didn't have many men in those barracks buildings. If they had, they could have slaughtered the onrushing men from the Thirteenth Tennessee Cavalry. They did knock down a couple of soldiers, but only a couple. Then the men in blue reached the first row of barracks.

Major Bradford whooped when smoke began to rise. The rains of the past few days had soaked the wood; he'd feared it wouldn't catch. But two or three of the buildings started burning. His men also fired at the Confederates lurking there. And they'd gone out with fixed bayonets. They could skewer any Reb who got too close.

Most of the time, a bayonet made a good knife and a good candleholder, but not much else. In close combat where a foe might jump out any time, though . . .

The Federal assault naturally drew the enemy's notice. Confederates ran toward the two rows of barracks buildings, too. The Rebs rushing up had no kind of order, but they outnumbered the men from the U.S. storming party.

"Come on!" Bradford shouted to the Tennessee troopers inside Fort Pillow and to the colored artillerymen now fighting as infantry. "Shoot those Rebel bastards! Don't let them gain a lodgement there!" He wondered if the Negroes knew what a lodgement was. It didn't matter. They could see that letting the Confederates shoot at them from cover at close range wasn't a good idea.

As he ordered the black men to shift position behind the earthwork so more of them could fire at the wooden buildings, he paid them the highest compliment any officer from Tennessee could give: he forgot what color they were. He treated them the same way as he treated the troopers from his own regiment. In time of danger, they were all just . . . soldiers.

Maybe some of the Negroes had dipped up a little too much Dutch courage. They capered and gestured to show their scorn for the enemy. Along with obscene taunts, they thumbed their noses and stuck their thumbs in their ears and waggled their fingers. They made ridiculous faces, their expressions all the more absurd because their teeth and tongues and eyeballs showed up so well against their dark hides.

And Major Bradford laughed and slapped his thigh and urged them on. Let the Rebs see his men weren't afraid (even if he was). Let them see Negroes could fight, too. He wouldn't have believed it himself, but he had no more doubts. They could. They really could.

A minnie kicked up dirt between Matt Ward's feet as he ran toward the two rows of wooden huts in front of Fort Pillow. Another snapped past at about breast height. A couple of feet to the right and it would have torn his heart out.

He didn't have time to be afraid—or maybe he was already as afraid as he could be, and one more near miss made no difference. He dashed past somebody who lay on the ground writhing. *Poor bastard,* he thought, and tried not to remember that that could still happen to him. With luck, it was only a flesh wound, and the other man would get better if it didn't fester. Without luck . . . Well, that was one more thing you didn't want to think about.

Then he got in back of the second row of wooden shacks. Bullets stopped flying all around him. His relief lasted perhaps half a minute. After that, he realized the fight went on, and at close quarters. This was different from shooting at the enemy from long range. You had to think about when you pulled the trigger here, because you were hideously vulnerable if you fired and missed and had to reload. Ward wished for a six-shooter instead of his single-shot Enfield.

Wishing didn't make a revolver fall out of the sky. He edged up to the space between two buildings. Ever so cautiously, he stuck out a hand, as if to feel if the enemy was there.

When no one shot at him, he looked into the space. No Yankee rushed toward him or, worse, waited with aimed rifle musket for a target more deadly than a hand. Carrying his own weapon at the ready, he moved up toward the first row of buildings.

Smoke made him cough. The homemade Yankees had already fired some of the barracks. He saw a running shape through the smoke. Friend or foe? The other soldier saw him, too, and started to bring his musket up to his shoulder.

That decided Matt. Anyone who aimed a weapon at him was an enemy, no matter which uniform he had on. Ward shot first. The other soldier screamed and staggered and fell. He fired, too, but wildly, into the air.

He wasn't dead. He feebly tried to crawl back toward Fort Pillow. That told Ward he really was a damnyankee. Rushing forward, the Missourian drove his bayonet home again and again. He'd never used it before, but he'd never been in a mad, cramped fight like this before, either.

He was amazed and more than a little appalled at how many times he had to stab before the other man stopped moving. Sometimes people were harder to kill than anyone who hadn't fought in war could imagine.

Just then, with the Enfield unloaded, Ward felt all too easy to kill. He reloaded as fast as he could, trying his best not to drop the cartridge or fumble with the ramrod or do any of the other stupid things that would waste time. He'd heard of men who, in the heat of battle, rammed home cartridge after cartridge without ever putting a cap on the nipple. With the roar of gunfire all around, they got too excited to notice that their piece wasn't roaring or belching smoke or kicking. Sometimes they *would* cap it with several rounds in the barrel. Then the rifle musket commonly blew up in their face.

Cartridge bitten open and rammed home. Copper cap on the nipple. Enfield half cocked. Ward nodded to himself. He was ready to shoot again. The smoke got thicker. He coughed and rubbed at his streaming eyes. Between the smoke and the black powder he got on his face whenever he reloaded, he hoped his fellow troopers wouldn't shoot him for a nigger.

The row of buildings closest to the fort was on fire. The damned Tennessee Tories had done that much, and Ward didn't see what he and his comrades could do but let those huts burn. The second row remained intact. The barracks there could still give the Confederates good cover . . . if the Federals didn't fire them.

Another indistinct shape came through the smoke. No, this fellow had a torch in his hand, which left no doubt whose side he was on. "Forrest!" Ward shouted, and fired at him.

To his disgust, he missed. Before, he'd sniped at men inside Fort Pillow from several hundred yards, and was pretty sure he'd scored hits. Here he could damn near spit on this bluebelly, but he missed him. It was embarrassing. It happened all the time, but it was still embarrassing.

"Jesus God!" the enemy trooper screeched when the rifle musket roared not thirty feet away and the minnie cracked past him. He

dropped the torch and dashed back toward Fort Pillow in great terrified bounds, his feet hardly seeming to touch the ground. Ward didn't
think a catamount could have caught him, let alone a mere man.

Missing him hadn't been *so* bad, then. He was out of the fight here,
anyway. Matt Ward tried to console himself as he reloaded again. You
could talk yourself into believing almost anything if you tried hard
enough.

More and more men in blue uniforms ran back to the earthwork
on the bluff. Unless the wind suddenly swung, it didn't look as if the
second row of wooden buildings would catch. And if they stayed intact, Ward and the other Confederates who'd saved them would be
able to go on peppering Fort Pillow from the cover they gave. That
was the point of the clash.

For a little while, the smoke and flames rising from the nearer row
of barracks buildings let Lieutenant Mack Leaming believe both
rows were on fire. But the bullets still coming from the wooden
structures soon disabused him of that notion. The men he'd sent
out to burn both rows of buildings at Major Bradford's orders had
torched the first row, but not the second. They wouldn't have the
chance to do it now. They were falling back toward Fort Pillow.
Some of them were running, scrambling up the forward face of the
bluff as far as they could go. Others moved more slowly—those
were men who would pause to shoot at the Rebs when they got the
chance. Still others helped wounded comrades toward what they
hoped would be safety.

A bullet whistled over Leaming's head. He didn't worry about bullets that whistled. They were too far away to be dangerous. Bullets
that cracked by—those were the near misses, the scary rounds. People
said you never heard the one that got you. Leaming didn't know if
that was true, and didn't want to find out, either.

"Lieutenant, why are those men retreating?" Major Bradford demanded.

"Sir, there are probably too many Secesh troopers to hold off," Leaming answered. "If they don't come back, they'll all get killed."

"But they didn't do what I sent them out there to do," Bradford said.

"No, sir," Leaming said. Sometimes—often—the least answer you could give was the best one.

"But they needed to burn those buildings," Bradford said. "We are in danger as long as Forrest's men can fire from them."

"Yes, sir," Lieutenant Leaming said. It wasn't as if Bradford were wrong. They *were* in danger from the Confederates in the barracks buildings. As if to prove as much, a minnie snapped past over the major's head. Bradford automatically ducked. So did Leaming.

"What are we going to do? We can't let them establish themselves there," the commandant said.

We can't stop them from establishing themselves there, Leaming thought. *We tried. It didn't work.* Major Bradford had to know that as well as he did. Since Bradford had to know it, Leaming couldn't think of any answer for him. Then he had a happy thought. "Maybe the *New Era* can shell them out."

"Maybe." Major Bradford brightened. He had great faith in the gunboat in the Mississippi—more faith than its performance so far justified, as far as Leaming was concerned. "Go tell my brother to direct the gunboat's fire against those buildings."

"Yes, sir." Lieutenant Leaming tried to sound cooperative, not resigned. He'd given the major the idea, after all. He trotted over to Captain Theodorick Bradford at the edge of the steep bluff leading down to the river. "Your brother's compliments, sir, and he says for you to tell the *New Era* to pound the stuffing out of the barracks halls and drive the Rebs out of 'em."

"Well, I'll try," Theo Bradford said dubiously. He held up the pair of large wigwag flags and semaphored with great vigor. Leaming peered down, down, down to the *New Era*. From this distance, the gunboat seemed hardly bigger than a toy.

An officer—or maybe a sailor—on her deck signaled back. "What's he say?" Leaming asked.

"Says they'll try—I think." Captain Bradford sounded harried. "I wish to God I had a spyglass so I could make out his flags better. I can't be sure what he's telling me half the time."

"Can he read you?" Leaming asked anxiously.

"I sure hope so," Theodorick Bradford said—not the most encouraging response he could have given.

But the *New Era* had the request. The gunboat did its best to comply. Its guns swung in the direction of the twin rows of barracks halls. Leaming admired that—the sailors far below couldn't see what they were aiming at. One after another, the cannon went off. Fire and smoke belched from their muzzles. He watched the shells rise into the cloudy air, then descend toward their targets. Booms said they'd hit—somewhere.

"Were those on the mark?" Leaming asked.

Captain Bradford shrugged. "Damned if I know. I can see the gunboat, or else I can see what it's shooting at. I can't do both at once." He waved the wigwag flags again. "The more shell the boat puts down, the better the chance that some of them will come down where we want them to."

"I see," Leaming said. He didn't say *what* he saw, which was bound to be just as well. Since he couldn't change anything, complaining wouldn't do him any good. But Major William Bradford plainly thought the *New Era* was a vital part of Fort Pillow's defenses against Forrest's men. And so the gunboat might have been—if only it could hit its targets with something resembling accuracy. As things were . . . Mack Leaming grimaced. As things were, the *New Era* was doing the best it could, and he had to hope that would be enough.

Not long after Nathan Bedford Forrest finished his reconnaissance of the ground in front of Fort Pillow, a soldier in a butternut tunic and blue trousers trotted up to him. He'd issued orders that shirts captured from the Yankees had to go into the dye pots right away so his men wouldn't shoot at one another by mistake. Trousers were supposed to be dyed, too, but that was less urgent.

"What's up, Red?" he asked.

About half a dozen men in his command answered to that nickname. This lanky Mississippian had hair the color of a newly minted copper penny and ears that stuck out a good four inches. He said, "Ammunition wagons just came up, General."

"Did they, by heaven?" Forrest said. "About time!"

"Yes, sir," Red said. He probably didn't worry about the struggle they'd had moving those wagons along the narrow, rutted, muddy roads that went through the Hatchie bottoms, especially the troubles they'd had moving them along in pitch darkness. He did have sense enough to ask, "Any special orders for 'em?"

"Just make goddamn sure you get those cartridges up to the men who need 'em the most," Forrest answered.

Red sketched a salute and went back the way he'd come. Bedford Forrest slowly nodded to himself. Up till now, his men had had only the cartridges they carried with them. They were supposed to bring enough to fight with—a rifle musket and cartridges were all a soldier really needed. But some would have more ammunition, some less, and some none at all. Forrest knew only too well that plenty of soldiers were natural-born knuckleheads.

With the wagons here at last, though, he didn't have to worry about that any more. He wished he would have been able to bring field guns forward, too, but that just wasn't in the cards. One of the Federals' cannon roared. The guns in the fort and the ones on the boat in the river were nuisances, but they weren't anything worse than nuisances. If he could have dropped shells into that cramped space inside the U.S. earthwork, though . . .

He shrugged. Worrying about might-have-beens wasn't his style. Another cannon inside Fort Pillow fired at his men. Those really were niggers manning the guns in there. Easy enough to seem brave when they were shooting from inside an earthwork. They wouldn't act like such big men when they met his troopers face-to-face. His hands folded into fists. He was sure of that. Oh, yes.

For now, though, the coons were having a high old time, skylarking and fooling around and mocking Forrest's men as if the Confederate soldiers would never have the chance to pay them back. They gave the troopers obscene gestures. One Negro even turned around and dropped his pants to show them his bare brown backside.

Forrest hoped that Negro would take a bullet where it did him the most good. No doubt all the Confederates who saw him did their best to give him what he deserved. But he pulled his trousers up again, waggled his bottom at the attackers one last time, and jumped down behind the rampart again.

In spite of himself, Forrest laughed. Say what you would, that Negro had nerve—which only made him need killing more. Ordinary blacks were no great trouble. They did what they were told, the same way ordinary whites did.

An uppity nigger, though . . . An uppity nigger was trouble. He might as well have smallpox or measles or some other deadly, contagious disease. He could infect others with what he carried. And if he did, he made them dangerous to white men, too.

"We got here just in time, sir," Captain Anderson said, coming up beside Forrest. Quiet fury filled the aide-de-camp's voice.

"How's that?" Forrest asked.

"Well, sir, the longer we let these niggers think they're soldiers, the longer they have the chance to believe it, the more trouble they'll be in the long run—not just facing us but spreading their nonsense to other coons," Anderson said. "Better—much better—to nip all that in the bud."

"I was thinking pretty much the same thing," Forrest said.

"If we teach those sons of bitches a good lesson, every smoke who puts on a Federal uniform will remember it from here on out," Anderson said.

"Don't know much about lessons. Don't care much about lessons, neither." Forrest grimaced, remembering his own brief, irregular schooling. "I just want to get in there, clean this place out, and then go give the damnyankees another boot in the behind somewheres else."

"A boot in the behind isn't what that one damnfool nigger deserved." Captain Anderson still seethed. "A minnie up the cornhole—that's more like it."

"He'll get his," Forrest said. "We can find out who he is and damn well make sure he gets his."

"Yes, sir." But Captain Anderson remained discontented. "He's not the only nigger acting that way—he's just the worst."

"I know, I know." A shell from the gunboat in the Mississippi crashed down not far from the row of wooden huts the Confederates had captured. The cannon in the fort wouldn't bear on those barracks buildings, but the gunboat kept pestering them. Another shell burst over there. Somebody screamed—a sliver of iron must have struck home. Forrest pointed that way. "Here's something for you to do, Captain."

"What is it, sir?"

"Find yourself some men who don't look like they're busy doing anything else." Bedford Forrest's mouth quirked in a wry grin—you could always find plenty of men like that on a battlefield. He pointed west, toward the great river. "Take 'em over there. If we have to storm the fort, we'll want to grab the riverbank just as quick as we can. We'll be able to shoot back at that damn gunboat then, and we'll make sure the damnyankees can't land any reinforcements, too."

"I'll do it," Anderson said. "Reinforcements are about the only thing that can save that place, aren't they?"

"Nothing's going to save Fort Pillow," Nathan Bedford Forrest said. "You hear me? Nothing."

"Here they come again!" Captain Carron shouted. Sure enough, a couple of hours after their first headlong assault on Fort Pillow was beaten back, the Confederates made another push. Sergeant Ben Robinson and his crew served their twelve-pounder like steam-driven mechanical men. They sent one round of shrapnel after another at Bedford Forrest's troopers.

But the Rebs were able to get under the range of the gun, the way Robinson had feared they would. Because of the thick earthwork, the crew couldn't depress the cannon enough to bear on them when they drew near. It was up to the soldiers with Springfields then: the colored artillerymen who didn't have a big gun to serve and the dismounted troopers of the Thirteenth Tennessee Cavalry.

They had the same trouble the gunners did, though to a lesser degree. Because of the thick parapet protecting Fort Pillow, they couldn't easily fire down on the enemy soldiers coming up the steep ground toward them. If they tried, they exposed themselves to Secesh sharpshooters. The Rebs were good marksmen; they wounded several Federals who tried to pick off their friends.

All the same, Forrest's men had to run a gauntlet to get too far forward for U.S. gunfire to bear on them. Enough of them got hit to make the rest lose heart. Most of them fell back out of easy range, with only a few hanging on down below where the men in the fort had trouble shooting at them.

Seeing Forrest's fierce fighters move away from Fort Pillow made Charlie Key and Sandy Cole and the rest of the blacks in the gun crew jump in the air and click their heels together. "Look at 'em run!" Charlie shouted. "Just look at 'em run! They ain't so goddamn tough!"

Confederate minnies still cracked past the gunners. "They ain't quit yet, neither," Robinson pointed out. If you forgot that—or maybe even if you didn't—you'd stop a bullet with your face.

Charlie was too excited to care. So was Sandy Cole. "So what if they ain't, Ben—uh, Sergeant Ben?" he said. "So what? You ever reckon you'd live to see the day when we had guns an' the buckra was runnin' from us? Feel so good watchin' 'em go, I reckon I done gone to heaven."

"You keep carryin' on like a damn fool, a minnie send you straight to heaven," Ben said gruffly. He knew what a sergeant was supposed to sound like. He'd had several fine white examples. And his own manner proved him an excellent scholar.

All the same, he knew just what Sandy was driving at. One of the reasons slavery persisted in the South was that whites intimidated blacks. Blacks had always been sure that if they got out of line, if they tried to rise up, whites would fall on them like an avalanche. Whites would be bold, whites would be fierce, whites would be fearless.

Negroes believed it, anyhow. How could they help but believe it when every sign of unrest was ruthlessly put down? Ben Robinson had believed it himself, back before the war started. Whites were so sure of their own superiority, they convinced Negroes of it, too. Didn't most colored men prefer light-skinned women to their duskier cousins? Weren't very black men, men with broad, flat noses and wide lips, reckoned uglier than those formed more in the image of their masters?

But how could you go on thinking somebody was better than you by nature when he ran away for fear that you would blow him a new asshole with your Springfield? Wasn't he a man, just like you? Wasn't he a *frightened* man, just like you?

It sure looked that way to Ben.

Sandy Cole and Charlie Key weren't the only Negroes jeering at the Confederates as they fell back—far from it. The gun crews were fairly restrained; their officers seemed to have them well in hand. But the colored artillerymen serving as foot soldiers alongside the whites of the Thirteenth Tennessee Cavalry were lapping up the sutlers' whiskey as if someone would outlaw it tomorrow. Robinson didn't know if that meant they weren't shooting straight. He didn't need to be Grant or Sherman to see that they weren't thinking straight.

" 'Scuse me, Cap'n, suh," he said.

"Yes, Sergeant Robinson? What is it?" Captain Carron gave his three stripes their due.

"Suh, kin we git the sutlers to put up them whiskey barrels now?"

Robinson asked. "Reckon the men done plenty o' drinkin'. Reckon mebbe some of 'em done too much drinkin'."

"I don't think it's harming them any, Sergeant," the white officer answered. "It keeps their spirits up, you might say." He smiled at his own joke. Ben Robinson didn't. Carron's head swung this way and that as he looked along the line. "The Tennesseans are drinking, too, you know."

"Yes, suh." Robinson's agreement was thick with disapproval. If anything, the troopers made rowdier drunks than the colored ar- tillerymen. One of the white men yelled something at the Confeder- ates that would have made Robinson want to kill him were it aimed his way. "They is actin' like fools their ownselves."

Captain Carron frowned. Ben knew why: he'd called white men fools. Even in the U.S. Army, even when it was an obvious truth, a Ne- gro wasn't supposed to do that. Ben Robinson might not have been a slave any more, but he wasn't exactly a free man, either, not even in the eyes of the power that had put a uniform on his back.

Two colored soldiers, both laughing like idiots, shouted things at the Confederates that made what the Tennessee trooper had said sound like an endearment. That was so funny, they had to hold each other up. Then they shouted something viler yet.

But they might not have said anything at all if the drunken white man didn't give them the idea. Even through the din of cannon fire and musketry, those insults carried. Out there beyond rifle range, some of Bedford Forrest's hard-bitten troopers were shaking their fists at Fort Pillow.

Ben didn't want to make Forrest's men any angrier at him than they already were. Why couldn't anybody else see the plain sense in that?

VI

NOON CAME AND WENT. THE firing from around Fort Pillow and from within the embattled fortress went on and on. Major William Bradford began to have its measure. Indeed, he began to think it mattered less than it did. When Bedford Forrest's men first attacked, Bradford had feared they would storm the earthwork.

They'd tried—they'd tried hard from first light of day till now. They'd tried, and they hadn't had any luck. To Bradford's eye, that meant they couldn't have any luck.

"Keep shooting, men!" he yelled. "Kill 'em all! They'll never break in! Never, you hear me?"

The U.S. soldiers, white and black, cheered raucously. They'd taken fresh courage, too. The colored men, especially, began treating war more as a game than as a serious business. They danced and sang and yelled bits of filth at the Confederates. Men from the Thirteenth Tennessee Cavalry did the same thing.

"Sir, do we really want to tick the Rebs off like this?" Lieutenant Leaming asked.

"What difference does it make?" Bradford said grandly. He felt like dropping his trousers and waving his backside in Forrest's face, the way that one Negro had. He didn't do it, but he felt like it.

But then a minnie snapped past just in front of his nose, so close that he could feel the wind of its passage—or at least so close that he thought he could. He'd seen a couple of men who got hit in the face. He wished he hadn't. Of itself, his hand came up to caress his handsome features. Yes, they were still intact.

Even so, the near miss made him stop thinking about what his soldiers could do to the Confederates and start worrying about what Forrest's men could do to Fort Pillow. He walked over to talk to Theodorick, who was wigwagging signals to the *New Era*. If that also took him away from the Rebels' fire, well, he wasn't altogether brokenhearted.

"Hello, Bill," Theo said. "We're giving 'em hell, aren't we?" As if to prove his point, the gunboat roared out another volley.

Bradford smiled as the shells hissed through the air, and again when they burst among the Rebs. *See how you like it, you bastards,* he thought. But then he brought his mind back to business. "Send a question down to Captain Marshall, if you'd be so kind," he said.

"At your service." His brother looked attentive. "What is it?"

"Ask him if the *New Era* can support us with canister if we have to come down by the riverside."

If the Confederates broke into Fort Pillow, that meant. It sounded much better when he said it the way he did, though. But no matter how he said it, Theodorick understood the true meaning. "Is that likely?" the older officer asked, sudden alarm in his voice and on his face.

"No, no, no," William Bradford said quickly, as much to reassure himself as to ease Theo's mind. "I just want to cover every possible contingency." There was a fine, impressive-sounding word.

"All right, Bill." Theo sounded relieved. He waved his flags to draw the *New Era*'s notice, then started semaphoring again. His younger brother admired his speed and what looked like his precision, though semaphore signals were a closed book to the major.

"Isn't anyone paying attention down there?" he asked.

But then, down on the gunboat in the Mississippi, someone with flags of his own wigwagged from the foredeck. "They have the message," Theo reported.

"Well, what do they say about it?" Bradford demanded.

"Nothing yet," his brother answered. "They have to pass it on to Captain Marshall and wait for his reply."

"All right. I understand." Bill Bradford also had to wait. He liked it no better than any other busy, important man would have—so he thought of himself. After what seemed a very long time but couldn't have been more than a couple of minutes, the sailor with the semaphore flags on the *New Era* started using them.

"At your service in every way, Captain Marshall says," Theodorick told his brother.

"That's good. Thanks a lot, Theo." Bradford took off his hat and waved it in salute to the gunboat, though the sailors far below probably wouldn't notice.

More than a little reluctantly, he made his way back toward the firing. Nothing had hit him yet. Nothing *would* hit him. He kept telling himself so, over and over again. Whenever the law had to say something repeatedly, it was a sign nobody was paying attention to it. As an attorney, Bill Bradford understood that principle. Applying it to his own case didn't occur to him, which might have been just as well.

"Captain Young!" he shouted. "Where are you, Captain?"

"I'm here, sir," John Young answered after Bradford called his name several times. Fort Pillow's provost marshal was a large, solidly built man with a habitual scowl and a black beard so thick it was almost like a pelt. "What do you need?"

Bradford pointed toward the *New Era*. "I want you to get some men to take a store of cartridges down to the riverbank. If we have to fight down there, I don't want it to be just with whatever ammunition we chance to carry with us."

Captain Young's frown deepened. "If we have to fight by the riverbank, that will mean the Rebs have carried the fort," he said. Major

Bradford waited with a scowl of his own. After a pause that stretched, Young added, "Sir."

"Yes, I know it will," Bradford said. "Would you rather *not* nail new shingles on the roof in case of rain?"

Young grunted. "Well, when you put it that way—"

"That is precisely how I put it, Captain." Bradford drew himself up again.

He didn't have to wait so long this time. With a crisp salute, Young said, "Yes, sir. I'll take care of it." He started shouting for soldiers. Before long, he had men lurching and staggering down the side of the bluff, two of them carrying each heavy crate. "All right, sir," he reported when the job was done. "We've got half a dozen cases of minnies down there. If those aren't enough to keep up the fight, God help us all."

"Yes," Major Bradford said. "God help us all."

Bedford Forrest watched the fighting at Fort Pillow from a swell of ground about a quarter of a mile from the Federal earthworks. Sharpshooters from Colonel McCulloch's brigade not far away sniped at the Union men. Unlike the troops farther forward, who simply fired as fast as they could, the sharpshooters took their time and made sure they had good targets before they pulled the trigger.

"There you go!" Forrest shouted encouragement. "Keep banging away at them. They'll fall down."

One of the sharpshooters whooped, so maybe the soldier he'd aimed at *did* fall over. Forrest hoped so. The men in blue inside the fort were putting up a stronger fight than he'd expected. He still thought he could overrun their works—with his men on so many high spots around Fort Pillow, they could fire into the fort with devastating effect, and could keep the enemy from doing as much as he would want to when the final assault came. Still, that final assault was liable to prove more costly than he looked for when he set out from Jackson.

And so . . . A slow smile spread over his face. Even if the colored troops and homemade Yankees inside the fort hadn't fought unusually well, he supposed he would have trotted out one of his favorite ploys. He used it for one simple reason: it worked often enough to make it worthwhile.

"Captain Anderson!" he yelled. "Where in the tarnation is Captain Anderson?" Then he laughed at himself. "To hell with me if I didn't send him down to the riverbank my very own self." He called to one of the soldiers on the little rise with him: "Hey, Zach! Go down to the river and bring Captain Anderson here, will you?"

"Sure will, General." Zach hurried away. Bedford Forrest smiled. Sometimes an order phrased as a request worked better than any other kind. Touchy about their personal pride, a lot of Confederates resented being flat-out told what to do.

Rough, steeply sloping ground and fallen trees made Zach's trip down to the riverbank slower than it might have been. Captain Anderson couldn't come back up much faster, even if he was on horseback. Sketching a salute to Forrest, he said, "What's up, sir?"

Forrest pointed toward the fort. "I'm going to give those people in there a chance to surrender. Sometimes it works, sometimes it doesn't."

"Sure worked in Union City three weeks ago." A smile stole over Anderson's face. "Poor Colonel Hawkins has surrendered to you twice now, even though you were only there once."

"Well, so he has." Forrest grinned, too. His detachment under Colonel Duckworth that intimidated—buffaloed, really—the luckless Isaac Hawkins into yielding Union City was a good deal weaker than the force that surrendered to it. A lot of the Federal officers who went into captivity were furious at their commander—which did them no good at all.

"All right, sir. Let's see if they'll throw in the sponge." Captain Anderson always had paper and pencil handy. "Go ahead."

"Headquarters Forrest's Cavalry. Before Fort Pillow, April twelfth, eighteen sixty-four." Forrest had sent in a lot of surrender demands; he could begin one without even needing to think about it. His aide-de-camp scribbled furiously. Then the general commanding paused. "What's the name of the Yankee son of a bitch in charge there?"

Charles Anderson always had such minutiae at his fingertips; he made a good aide-de-camp. "Booth, sir—Lionel Booth. He's a major."

"Yes, I remembered that. Well, then." He paused again. Captain Anderson poised the pencil. Forrest resumed: "Major Booth, commanding United States forces, Fort Pillow. Major . . ." He weighed phrases in his mind. "The officers and men of Fort Pillow have fought well . . ." As usual, *fought* came out as *fit*. This time, he shook his head. "No, that won't do. It hasn't got the right pitch to it."

"Start again, sir?" Anderson asked; he'd seen Forrest edit despatches on the fly before.

"Reckon I'd better. How's this . . . ?" Forrest said. "The conduct of the officers and men garrisoning Fort Pillow has been . . ." the delay this time was to let Anderson's pencil catch up ". . . such as to entitle them to being treated as prisoners of war." Listening, he nodded. "Yes, that'll do."

"I'm up with you, sir," Captain Anderson said. "What next?"

"I demand the unconditional surrender of this garrison, promising you that you shall be treated as prisoners of war." Forrest knew he'd repeated himself, but let it go. The Federals were bound to be anxious about the point. He went on, "My men have received a fresh supply of ammunition, and from their present position can easily assault and capture the fort."

"Every word of that's true," his aide-de-camp said when he caught up with Forrest's dictation. He grinned again; Forrest and the commanders who served under him had lied like Ananias in several surrender demands, most recently the one that bagged Union City. They didn't always work, either; the fortress up at Paducah, Kentucky, had held out against his forces not long before, even though his men controlled most of the town for half a day. "Now for the warning?" Anderson asked.

"Oh, yes." Even though the Federals inside Fort Pillow couldn't hear him, Bedford Forrest sounded lion-fierce as he continued.

"Should my demand be refused, I cannot be responsible for the fate of your command. Respectfully, N.B. Forrest, Major-General commanding. . . . Read that back to me, Anderson."

"Yes, sir," Anderson said, and then, when it was done, "Does it suit you?"

"Yes, it'll do," Forrest said.

"Shall I deliver it to the enemy myself?" Anderson asked.

"No, I want you back down by the river, fast as you can get there," Forrest replied. "I'll send somebody else." He looked around for another man and spotted one of General Chalmers's staff officers not far away, ready to do anything Chalmers might require of him. *Well, I need him more than Jim does now,* Forrest thought. "Captain Goodman!" he called.

"Yes, sir?" Walter Goodman was not only brave—no one who wasn't brave served under Forrest for long—but had a pretty good head on his shoulders. "What can I do for you, sir?"

"Take a flag of truce and ride up toward the fort," Forrest answered. That drew Chalmers's notice, too; Forrest thought it might. He went on, "Captain Anderson here has written out a call for the Federals to surrender. Will you take it to them?" He held out the paper.

"Of course, sir," Goodman said.

"Good." Forrest nodded to himself; again, he'd phrased the order as a request, but that didn't make it any less an order. "Round up a couple of more officers as you go forward, if you care to—that'll give you a proper-looking truce party."

"I'll take care of it." Captain Goodman read the surrender demand. He looked up with a frown on his face. "Ask you a question, sir?"

"What is it?" Forrest said. "Something not clear?"

"You say the garrison's entitled to be treated as prisoners of war," Goodman replied. "Does that include the niggers, too? The Federals are bound to ask, and they've got a hell of a lot of coons in there."

Forrest grimaced unhappily. What to do about Negroes in blue uniforms had bedeviled the Confederacy since the U.S.A. started arming them. The usual practice, codified by a law out of Richmond, was to return runaway slaves—who formed the bulk of the colored troops—to their owners. Here, though . . . "Yes, dammit, we'll treat the niggers as prisoners of war—*if* they give up now. I want that fort, and I want it before the Yankees can bring reinforcements up the river." He glanced over to General Chalmers. Chalmers didn't look happy about it, either, but he nodded.

Walter Goodman looked sorry he'd asked. "All right, sir," he said, "but a lot of the men won't like it." He wasn't wrong. If anything, ordinary Confederate troopers hated the idea of colored soldiers worse than their officers did.

But challenging, or even seeming to challenge, Nathan Bedford Forrest was the wrong thing to do. Bristling, the general commanding snapped, "If I say we'll take nigger prisoners as long as the Federals give up now, then we damn well will. Have you got that, Captain?"

"Oh, yes, sir," Captain Goodman said hastily.

"All right, then." Forrest's temper cooled as quickly as it rose. "Go on forward and see what this Major Booth has to say for himself."

"If he has any sense, he'll quit now, while he's still able to," Brigadier General Chalmers said. "We *can* storm the place if he's stubborn."

"Looks that way to me, too," Forrest agreed.

Captain Goodman shouted for a white cloth he could make into a flag of truce. When he had one, he started up toward Fort Pillow. Forrest sent Captain Anderson back down to the Mississippi.

"Well," he said, as firing began to fade with men on both sides spying the white flag, "now we see what happens next."

"Look, sir!" an excited trooper from the Thirteenth Tennessee Cavalry called to Mack Leaming. "The Rebs are sending up a truce flag."

"So they are." Lieutenant Leaming didn't sound as happy as the private did. Forrest used flags of truce all the time. He was known to take advantage of them, too, if he saw the chance to do it.

For the moment, though, the rattle of musketry from both sides faded. Major Bradford called out a command to his brother: "For God's sake, Theo, let the *New Era* know we've got a cease-fire!"

"Yes, sir!" Theodorick Bradford waved the wigwag flags as if suddenly stricken with St. Vitus' dance. A few minutes earlier, gunfire would have drowned his voice and his younger brother's. Now they rang clearly, the loudest things on the suddenly quiet field.

"Leaming!" Bill Bradford shouted. "Are you there, Leaming?"

The commandant couldn't have been standing more than twenty feet away from Leaming, but his back was turned so he could call to his signals officer. "I'm here, sir," the adjutant replied.

Bradford turned. "Well, so you are," he said with a sheepish smile. Pointing out toward the approaching Confederate truce party, he went on, "I want you to go find out what the enemy has in mind."

"Yes, sir." Leaming couldn't help blurting, "By myself, sir?"

Major Bradford started to nod, but then checked himself. "Well, maybe not," he allowed. "We don't want Forrest to reckon we can only spare the one man, do we now?"

"That's what I meant, sir," Leaming said gratefully. And it was . . . part of what he meant, anyhow. Going out there alone to face Forrest's fearsome fighters, even under flag of truce, also struck him as too much like sticking his head in the lion's mouth. If he didn't have to admit that out loud, he didn't want to.

"Fair enough," Major Bradford said. "Take Captain Young with you, then. He's a sharp fellow, and solid as a rock. And"—he looked around and nodded toward the first other officer he saw—"take Lieutenant van Horn with you, too, and a few mounted men for swank."

"Yes, sir." Leaming nodded, too. He liked that a lot better. Easier to stay brave when you weren't trying to do it all by yourself. And bringing along Second Lieutenant Dan van Horn was a downright good idea. He came from the Sixth U.S. Heavy Artillery (Colored), and could report directly to his fellow officers—those of them left alive—about what went on.

Van Horn was a young man, younger than Mack Leaming. He still looked excited about the fighting, which was more than Leaming could say. John Young didn't, but he wasn't a man who would rattle easily, either—Bradford was right about that. As for the troopers . . . Leaming picked the first four men he saw and told them to get up on horseback.

Less than five minutes later, he and his companions, carrying their own flag of truce, went down from Fort Pillow toward the Confederates, who waited on the ground that sloped up toward the fort from the end of the battered rows of barracks buildings nearer the Mississippi. All the Rebs were mounted; Leaming, Young, and van Horn moved forward on foot.

"Good morning, gentlemen." Polite as a cat, the C.S. officer holding the white flag saluted his U.S. opposite numbers. "I am Captain Walter Goodman, General Chalmers's adjutant general. Accompanying me are Captain Tom Henderson, commanding our scouts, and Lieutenant Frank Rogers." He didn't bother naming the enlisted men with his party.

"Pleased to make your acquaintance, Captain Goodman." Leaming saluted, too. The formal courtesies of war went on even while men did their best to murder one another. So did life in general: only a few feet away, a robin hopped over the muddy ground, now and then pausing to pull up a worm. Leaming introduced himself, continuing, "I have the honor to be post adjutant. With me are Captain John Young, our provost marshal, and Lieutenant Dan van Horn." Captain Goodman hadn't said what Lieutenant Rogers did; Lieutenant Leaming didn't mention that Lieutenant van Horn led colored troops. He also didn't name the troopers from the Thirteenth Tennessee Cavalry who'd come forward with him.

Goodman held out a folded sheet of paper. "Please take this to your commander, Lieutenant. It is General Forrest's demand for the surrender of the fort."

"I will convey it to him, sir," Leaming said. "May I read it first, so I can clear up with you any questions he is likely to have?"

"By all means." Captain Goodman nodded and gestured. "Be my guest."

Leaming unfolded the paper. From everything he'd heard, Bedford Forrest was not an educated man. By the smooth, flowing script he saw, he doubted the Confederate commander had written this note himself. But it held Forrest's fierce, arrogant tone all the same. "I do have a question," Leaming said when he finished reading it.

"Ask, sir, ask." Walter Goodman was the soul of politeness. He might have been trying to sell Leaming a phaeton or a surrey, not trying to talk him into going into captivity.

He might have been, but he wasn't. "General Forrest says, 'I demand the unconditional surrender of this garrison, promising you that you shall be treated as prisoners of war,'" Leaming read. Captain Goodman nodded again. The Federal officer went on, "You will know we have colored troops inside the fort. Does this promise extend to them as well? They too will be treated as prisoners of war, and will not be killed out of hand or reenslaved?"

"Yes, sir. That is correct. The niggers will be treated as prisoners of war, on the same terms as white men, if you surrender now," Walter Goodman said. "As it happens, I raised this point myself with both General Forrest and General Chalmers, wanting to make sure no unfortunate misunderstandings arose from it. They both stated very clearly that they will accept the colored soldiers under the terms of this demand." Goodman leaned toward Leaming. His politesse did not slip, not quite, but he let the hostility below show through. "Bear in mind also, sir, that if you refuse we shall not answer for the safety of any man within Fort Pillow, black or white. Is that plain?"

"It could scarcely be plainer, Captain." With Captain Young and Lieutenant van Horn beside him, Leaming had to affect a nonchalance he did not feel.

"Very well. Any further questions?" Goodman asked.

"No, sir. I will carry this message to my commanding officer." Leaming had seen that the demand was addressed to Major Booth. Booth would be reading it from the Pearly Gates, from which place his comments were unlikely to return. But the Confederates didn't need to know command had devolved upon a less experienced man. Leaming did not mention Major Bradford's name. He just turned to his companions and said, "Let's go."

"I expect Major Booth's answer in short order," Goodman warned, proving again that he didn't know Booth was dead. "No delay here will be tolerated."

"I will make that very plain, sir," Leaming said. Once more, he said not a word about to whom he would make it plain.

His footfalls and those of the two officers with him and the clop of the horses' hooves and jingle of their harness were the only sounds he heard as he walked back up to Fort Pillow. Guns had been thundering and cannon roaring since first light. The silence now felt almost eerie.

Major Bradford waited just inside the gun port from which the truce party had set out. "What do they want?" he called.

"About what you'd expect, sir." Mack Leaming held out the paper Captain Goodman had handed him. "Here is Forrest's demand."

Bradford rapidly read through it. When he finished, he asked the same question Leaming had: "What about the colored troops?"

"Sir, they are to be included among the prisoners of war," Leaming answered. "I raised the point with Captain Goodman, who delivered the note to me. He said both General Chalmers, whom he serves, and General Forrest agreed they will accept the Negroes' surrender."

"I am not going to decide this all at once," Bradford said. "Have you got paper and a pencil, Lieutenant?"

"Yes, sir." Leaming took the writing tools from his pocket.

"All right, then. Take this down. . . ." Major Bradford hesitated for a moment, perhaps communing with his muse. "To General Forrest, commanding C.S. forces," he said. Mack Leaming wrote it down. Bradford went on. "Sir—I respectfully ask one hour for consultation with my officers and the officers of the gunboat. In the meantime no preparation to be made on either side." He hesitated again, then asked, "Do the Confederates know Major Booth is dead?"

"No, sir," Leaming said. "As you see, their demand is addressed to him. I didn't tell them he'd been hit, and neither did anyone else in the party."

"Likely just as well. They'll think better of Booth than they will of me. He was a real soldier, and I'm just a lawyer, and a Tennessee Tory to boot," Bradford said. Lieutenant Leaming found himself nodding; those were the main reasons he hadn't informed the Confederates of Booth's death. Bill Bradford went on, "As long as they don't know, let's keep them in the dark. Sign it, 'Very respectfully, L. F. Booth, Major Commanding.'"

"Yes, sir." Leaming did as he was asked.

"Good, good. Now—do you have an envelope?" Bradford seemed endlessly worried about tiny procedural details.

"Yes, sir. As a matter of fact, I do." Leaming took one from the left breast pocket of his tunic. He put Bradford's response into it.

"Good. Good. Seal it up. Seal it up tight," Major Bradford said. "And, with a little luck, Bedford Forrest'll give us the hour, and we'll have reinforcements in place by the time it's up, and then we really will be able to tell him to go to the Devil."

"I hope so, sir," Leaming said. Along with the other members of the truce party, he went out of Fort Pillow toward the waiting Captain Goodman once more.

Major William Bradford's dream of reinforcements was Major General Nathan Bedford Forrest's nightmare. Not long after his ultimatum to the men inside Fort Pillow went forward, that nightmare looked like it was coming true. A trooper from down by the Mississippi came up to Forrest, calling, "General! General Forrest, sir! There's smoke on the river, sir! Looks like a steamboat's coming up!"

Bedford Forrest swore horribly. That was the last thing he wanted to hear. "God damn it to hell and gone!" he shouted, and then, hoping against hope, "Are you sure?"

"Sure as I am that I'm Hank Tibbs," the cavalryman answered. "Come see for yourself if you don't believe me."

"I think I'd better," Forrest said grimly, and rode down toward the broad river. He didn't get there as fast as he would have liked; the steeply sloping ground and the number of felled tree trunks made his horse pick its way along. He needed almost fifteen minutes to come to the eastern bank of the Mississippi and peer downstream toward Memphis.

Hank Tibbs didn't have to worry that anyone would fear he wasn't entitled to his own name. Bedford Forrest did some more profane swearing when he spied the steamer coming up from the south. As he'd feared they would be, its decks were blue with the uniforms of U.S. soldiers.

Just to make things worse, a glance north along the Mississippi showed more smoke, as if another steamboat was on the way with aid and comfort for the Federals in Fort Pillow. How was he supposed to take the place if they could pour men into it from the river?

Forrest looked from Fort Pillow out to the gunboat already floating on the Mississippi. The enemy warship was honoring the truce; it hadn't fired a shot since learning the white flag had gone in. But neither the gunboat nor the men in the fort were making any effort to stop the steamer crammed with troops from approaching. In their place, Forrest probably wouldn't have, either. That didn't make him love them any better.

"Captain Anderson!" he shouted.

"Yes, sir?" His aide-de-camp wasn't far away.

"Get as many men down by the riverbank as you can," Forrest said. "Pull some of them down from those buildings we took, and use the little force you already gathered together." He pointed down the river toward the oncoming steamer. "Let those sons of bitches see they'll have a nasty time of it if they try to let their soldiers off."

"I'll tend to it, sir." Anderson saluted and hurried away.

A moment later, Forrest shouted for a runner. When the soldier came up to him, he said, "Get your fanny over to Colonel Barteau in Coal Creek Ravine. Tell him to bring his men out in the open and to take them down by the bank of Coal Creek. I want to make sure the Yankees in that there steamer"—he pointed to the vessel—"can't swing in and land by the creek any more than they can here along the river. Have you got that?"

"Yes, sir," the runner said. When Forrest raised an eyebrow, the man gave back the instructions with tolerable accuracy. Forrest nodded. The runner trotted off toward the far side of the battlefield.

Men in gray and butternut rushed to make themselves visible on the low ground by the base of the bluff. Some of them came up along the riverbank, others down from the buildings they'd gained when the Federals failed to burn them all. Watching, Forrest nodded again, this time to himself. An officer would have to be crazy to try to land in the face of opposition like that.

"General! General! You there, General?" Forrest's head came up like that of a hound taking a scent—he knew Walter Goodman's voice when he heard it.

"I'm here, Goodman!" he called, pitching his voice to carry. He could always make himself heard, even on the maddest, noisiest field. With the guns fallen silent, Yankees out on that steamboat might have heard him. "What do the Federals in the fort say?"

"Here is their answer, sir." Captain Goodman held out a sealed envelope.

"What a pack of foolishness. You could have seen it," Forrest said scornfully. He opened the envelope and took out the note inside. Once he'd read it, he shook his head. "The son of a bitch in there is playing for time, and to hell with me if I aim to let him have any. Can you write down my answer to take back to the U.S. truce party?"

"Yes, sir." Goodman produced pencil and paper. Forrest had thought he would be able to; he served General Chalmers much as Captain Anderson served Forrest himself. "Go ahead, sir."

"To Major L. F. Booth, commanding U.S. forces, Fort Pillow." Forrest paused for a moment, then went on, "Sir—I have the honor to acknowledge the receipt of your note asking for one hour to consider my demand for your surrender. Your request cannot be granted. I will allow you twenty minutes from the receipt of this note for consideration; if at the expiration of that time the fort is not surrendered, I shall assault it. I do not demand the surrender of the gunboat. Very respectfully, N. B. Forrest, Major-General."

"That should do the job, sir," Goodman said. "Let me read it back to you." He did. Forrest nodded. "I'll deliver it, then," Goodman told him, and rode up toward the spot where the truce parties from the two sides were meeting.

Up on the fortified bluff, colored and white soldiers mocked the men emerging from cover to thwart the troop-laden steamship. The men in blue didn't fire on Forrest's troopers, but did their best to provoke them in every other way they could. "We won't give you no quarter if you comes at us!" a drunken Negro bawled.

"After we git you, we git your sisters, too!" another Negro shouted. Forrest could imagine nothing better calculated to inflame his men. The colored soldier probably wasn't joking, either. White troopers from Fort Pillow had ranged through western Tennessee. They'd insulted more than a few women dear to Forrest's soldiers, and outraged more than one. Why wouldn't a black man want to imitate them?

A corporal not far from Forrest growled. "Those sons of bitches'll laugh out of the other side of their faces when we get in amongst 'em." A couple of soldiers shook their fists at the U.S. soldiers inside Fort Pillow, but no one raised a rifle musket to his shoulder and tried to avenge himself upon them. Unlike the Federals, his men showed good discipline—or maybe they were more worried about what he would do to them for going against orders than they were angry at the enemy.

Captain Goodman rode back to him sooner than he'd expected. "What's going on?" Forrest called to him. "Has Booth given you an answer already?"

"No, sir—sorry," Goodman answered. "But some of the Federals in the truce party are saying maybe you aren't really here at all. They're saying it's a bluff like the one Colonel Duckworth used in Union City."

"Oh, they are, are they?" Forrest said. "Will it make 'em happy if I advance and be recognized?"

Goodman's lips quirked upward into something that looked like a smile but was knowing and unamused. "Well, sir, I don't reckon it'll make 'em very *happy,* if you know what I mean, but it'll sure enough take their doubts away."

"Then I'll do it," Forrest said at once. "Lead on, Captain. I think things here are tolerable good—the Yankees won't be able to land, and it looks like they know it."

He followed the junior officer forward, past the barracks buildings and up onto the higher ground that led to the inner position the United States had fortified. The U.S. flag still floated defiantly above Fort Pillow. Forrest felt a peculiar prickling of the skin above his breastbone. If a Federal sharpshooter wanted him dead badly enough to violate the truce, he was within range for a decent shot. But U.S. soldiers had tried to kill him since the war was new. His own horse had come closer to doing it a few hours earlier than most of them had.

Captain Goodman pointed. "There they are, sir."

"I see 'em," Forrest said.

"The big dark one is Captain Young—their provost marshal," Goodman said. "The other officer's Lieutenant van Horn. I don't see Lieutenant Leaming—he's the post adjutant. He must still be inside the fort, talking things over with Major Booth."

"These fellows here can testify for me." Forrest spurred past Goodman and rode up to the Federals. "I am General Forrest," he said. "Will any of you know me by sight?"

"I do, sir." The dark officer sketched a salute. "Captain John Young, Twenty-fourth Missouri Cavalry. Not the way I'd care to meet you, but . . ." He shrugged.

"You do know I am who I say I am?" Forrest persisted.

"Yes, sir." Young did not seem afraid. He probably was—Forrest would have been, in his shoes—but he didn't show it. Most of the time, that was what mattered on the field. Forrest nodded with reluctant respect.

Captain Goodman pointed west toward the Mississippi, where the steamer moving up from the south had come level with Fort Pillow. Her name was painted on her side in huge letters: *Olive Branch*. Bedford Forrest chuckled under his breath.

"Look how many men she's got aboard her, sir," Goodman said. "They can give us a lot of trouble if she lands."

"Don't worry, Captain," Forrest said quietly. "She won't land."

VII

TWENTY MINUTES?" MAJOR BRADFORD STARED in dismay at the note Mack Leaming had just handed him. He saw absently that it was in a hand different from the last one he'd received. "Twenty minutes!" he said again, in even more pained disbelief. " 'If at the expiration of that time the fort is not surrendered, I shall assault it.' My God!"

"What answer shall I take back to the Confederates, sir?" Lieutenant Leaming asked.

"He doesn't even care about the *New Era*," Bradford said. That had nothing to do with his adjutant's question, but he didn't care. He'd counted—he still did count—on the gunboat in the Mississippi to help his men hold their positions against the Confederates. To Bedford Forrest, the gunboat didn't matter at all.

Or Forrest said it didn't matter at all. That wasn't necessarily the same thing. The Confederate cavalry commander was as sneaky a man as God had ever set on the face of the earth. He might be running a bluff, trying to trick the garrison at Fort Pillow into quitting when they didn't have to.

But Bradford was running something of a bluff of his own. He was playing for time, hoping to hold the fort till reinforcements came. And there they were—he could see the *Olive Branch* out there in the river, almost close enough to reach out and touch.

Almost, but not quite. The steamer couldn't approach the bank. The blue-uniformed men she carried couldn't land. The Confederate soldiers moving out to the edge of the Mississippi made sure of that.

Mack Leaming stared bitterly at the troopers in gray and butternut. "They've got no business being there," he said. "It's as though they're taking advantage of the truce."

"Should we protest to General Forrest?" But Bill Bradford knew that would be hopeless as soon as the words passed his lips. The *Olive Branch* was not a participant in the truce. If she were, she wouldn't have been poised to land her troops if opportunity offered. And the Confederates had already seized control of the low ground by the Mississippi—and the ravine in front of the fort on the Coal Creek side, too. Besides, Forrest would just say the Federals could start fighting again if they didn't like what he was up to.

"He wouldn't listen to us," Leaming said, which only confirmed Bradford's fears. His adjutant went on, "Sir, the clock is ticking. You've got to tell the damn Rebs *something*."

"I can't surrender the fort!" Bradford's voice went high and shrill, even though Leaming hadn't come out and suggested that. It was on the major's mind. He didn't see how it could help being on his mind. If he didn't think the garrison could hold the place, didn't he have a duty to the men—and especially to the colored soldiers, who'd fought better than he'd dreamt they could—to yield it and avoid the horrors of a sack?

But he still held hope. Even if the Confederates forced their way inside the earthworks warding Fort Pillow, his men could still drop down to the base of the bluff and keep up the fight there. They had plenty of cartridges waiting for them now, and the *New Era* could sweep the enemy with canister. The gunboat wouldn't be firing blind there. Her men would be able to see exactly what they were aiming at.

"We *can* hold," Bradford said, as if challenging his adjutant to disagree with him.

Lieutenant Leaming didn't—not directly, anyhow. "If we can, sir, you'd better tell Bedford Forrest that we aim to try. And you'd better do it soon, or he'll just up and break off the truce on his own."

No sooner had the words crossed his lips than a couple of shots rang out in the distance. "What's that?" Major Bradford's voice rose in alarm again.

"Sir, the Rebs just fired warning shots at the steamer," answered a soldier by the edge of the bluff who could see down to the Mississippi. A moment later, he added, "She's sheering off. Looks like she's going to head on up the river."

"Damn!" Bradford said feelingly.

"Forrest's men could slaughter the soldiers on her if she tried to land them," Leaming said. "I got a look at her when I was parleying with the Rebs. The way the men are packed on her deck, they can't answer back, or not hardly."

"Damn!" Bradford said again. He knew his adjutant was right; he'd looked at the *Olive Branch* himself. But what a man—even a lawyer—knows to be true and what he wishes were true can often be two very different things. If the steamboat hadn't appeared at all, that would have been bad. To have her appear in what seemed the nick of time, hold out the hope of rescue, and then cruelly yank it away . . . that was ten times, a hundred times, worse. A melodrama with such a scene in it would have been hissed off the stage.

And Lieutenant Leaming wouldn't leave him alone. "Sir, the reply to General Forrest? Whatever you say, you'd better say it fast. The time he gave us has to be almost up."

Bradford didn't like the sound of that. The only ploy he had left was buying a little more time. "Give me a paper and pencil, then," he told Leaming.

"Yes, sir." Leaming handed them to him.

The paper was dirty. There was no envelope. Major Bradford had to make do without them. *Your demand does not produce the desired effect,* he scribbled, and handed the scrap back to Leaming. "There!"

His adjutant read it, frowning because it was none too legible—and maybe for other reasons as well. "What does it mean, sir?"

"Exactly what it says," Bradford snapped. "Now take it out to Bedford Forrest!"

For a wonder, Leaming realized he'd finally pushed too far. With a salute, he said the one thing an adjutant could say that was never wrong: "Yes, sir."

Jack Jenkins stood by the bank of Coal Creek, watching the *Olive Branch* steam up the Mississippi. He breathed a silent sigh of relief. If the Yankees tried landing troops nearby, repelling them would have been rugged work. But they didn't have the nerve. He had no idea where the bluebellies on that steamer were going. They could go wherever it was or straight to hell, and welcome. As long as they didn't stop here, everything was fine.

"Look at those egg-sucking yellow dogs show us their backs," somebody not far away said. "They haven't got the balls to try and stand up against us."

"Damn good thing, too," somebody else said. "Ain't we got enough trouble with the sons of bitches in that there fort already?"

"Well done, men!" Colonel Barteau said. In the watery afternoon sunlight, the three stars on either side of his collar glittered. "Our show of force has successfully deterred the enemy."

"Damn straight," Jenkins said. "We made sure he didn't land here, too."

Clark Barteau smiled. Jenkins assumed that was because he'd agreed with the regimental commander. "Now some of you better hustle back up toward the fort," Barteau said. "If the Federals don't give in, Bedford Forrest'll order the assault, sure as I'm standing here beside you."

"Some of us, sir? Not all of us?" Jenkins asked.

"No, not all of us, Corporal," Colonel Barteau answered. "I'll want some men to stay down here by the water. If we start overrunning the enemy position up on the bluff, what do you reckon the enemy there'll do? What would you do in a fix like that?"

"Try and get down by the river, I expect." Jenkins saw nothing out of the ordinary in a corporal and a colonel discussing tactics. By European standards, both the U.S. Army and the C.S. Army were loose-jointed creatures. The Confederates had less in the way of spit and polish than the Federals did, and Forrest's troopers less than most C.S. outfits. They fought better than most, though, which was all that really mattered. Jenkins added, "That damn gunboat isn't going away, worse luck." He pointed to a crater in the dirt by Coal Creek that marked where a shell from the *New Era* had burst.

"Wish it would," Barteau agreed. "But if it doesn't, I reckon we'll make it sorry. And I think you're right. I think that whole swarm of niggers and Tennessee Tories'll come pelting down to the Mississippi once we get inside their works. And when they do . . ."

"I see, sir!" Jenkins wasn't a man to admire officers just because they were officers. When they showed they were on the ball, that was a different story. "You thought that through real pretty."

"Glad you approve," Barteau said dryly. "If you do see what I mean, perhaps you'll want to stay here." Quite a few troopers were already moving away from Coal Creek along the ravine to get in position to swarm up the bluff against Fort Pillow.

"Reckon I will. It'll be just like coon-hunting back home." Jenkins laughed at his joke, even if he'd made it by accident. "Be *just* like coon-hunting back home."

Colonel Barteau rewarded him with a thin smile. "All right, Jenkins. Maybe you'll have some coons to hunt. You'd best remember one thing, though."

"What's that, sir?"

"These coons can fight back."

"Sir, any coon'll fight back. Bastards are all teeth and claws and mean. A coon dog's a lot bigger'n any coon ever born, but sometimes they'll come out of a hunt lookin' like they been through a meat grinder. Haven't you seen that yourself?"

"More times than I wish I had. I've lost some good dogs that way—who hasn't?—and I've had to doctor plenty more. But I would've had a lot more to worry about if the ordinary kind of coon carried rifle muskets like the ones in there." Barteau pointed up toward Fort Pillow. "I'll leave doctoring bullet wounds to a real sawbones."

Jenkins shivered. *Sawbones* was a name that held too much truth. Too often, amputation gave the only hope of saving a wounded man's life. He clutched his own rifle musket. *It is better to give than to receive,* he thought.

Ben Robinson stared out toward the Confederate officers gathered under the flag of truce. The rest of the colored soldiers in the gun crew were doing the same thing. Some of the Negroes inside Fort Pillow went on jeering at the ragged, skinny white men in butternut outside. Others grew more serious as the gravity of the situation sank in.

Pointing to one officer in particular, Robinson asked, "You reckon that there fella's really and truly Forrest?"

Sandy Cole nodded gloomily. "Reckon he is," he said. "Ain't no use to say Forrest ain't here. I knows him too well fo' that. Any place where there's big trouble, Bedford Forrest, he gonna be there."

"You seen the man yourself? You know his face?" Robinson asked.

"I seen him, all right," Cole answered. "Ain't I a Tennessee nigger? Any Tennessee nigger ever been sold, chances are he been sold through ol' Bedford Forrest's slave lots in Memphis. Yeah, I seen him."

"How'd he treat you when you was there?" Having been sold himself, Robinson had a morbid curiosity about such things. No part of slavery was good, not from the slave's point of view. But being in a dealer's hands, being between masters, was worse than most of the rest. A dealer didn't need to worry about you for the long haul. He just wanted to turn you into cash as fast as he could.

But Sandy Cole said, "Coulda been worse. He give us enough to eat—not fancy, but enough. We had mattresses—didn't got to sleep on the ground. He let us wash—now and again, anyways. Weren't *too* crowded. Yeah, coulda been worse."

"Sounds like it," Robinson agreed. He'd known slave pens where none of what Sandy said held true. But it gibed with other things he'd heard about the C.S. general. Forrest wasn't cruel for the sake of being cruel, the way some dealers were. He was in the business for money, not for sport, and he'd made a pile of it. Even so, the colored sergeant said, "Shame we gots to keep the truce."

"What you mean?" Cole asked.

Robinson pointed out toward Forrest. "There he *is,* damn him. That man deal in slaves. He deal in niggers. You done said so your ownself. Powerful good general, too—likely the bes' general the Rebs got in this part o' the country. An' there he *is.* Don't got to be no great shot to put a minnie through the God-damned son of a bitch. Can't hardly miss, not at this range." He mimed sighting a Springfield at the big man on horseback, mimed pulling the trigger, mimed Bedford Forrest falling over dead.

Sandy Cole laughed, but he sounded a little scandalized, or maybe more than a little. "Can't *do* that, Sergeant, not with the white flags up."

"I know." Robinson sighed. "But dat's how come it's a shame we gots to keep it."

He might as well not have spoken. Cole went on, " 'Sides, s'pose we shoots the general. An' s'pose the Secesh gets inside the fort then. What you reckon they do to us after that? You tell me they don't shoot every one of us, 'less mebbe they hangs some or burns some? *I* ain't brave enough to shoot no Bedford Forrest with the truce flags flyin'."

He had a point. Ben Robinson wished he didn't have to admit, even to himself, how strong a point it was. But he said, "Do Jesus, Sandy, what you reckon the Rebs do to us if they gets in even if we don't shoot Forrest? We ain't sojers to them. We's jus' niggers. Onliest difference 'tween us an' the pigs is, they don't smoke us fo' bacon."

"No, suh." Sandy Cole shook his head. "No, suh. There's another difference—damn big difference, too." He patted the barrel of the gun they served. After more than half an hour of quiet, it was cool enough not to burn his palm. "Difference is, now we kin shoot back."

"Uh-huh." Sergeant Robinson had thought that was a wonderful thing when he first put on the blue uniform. He still did. But it had a drawback he hadn't seen then: "What if we shoots back an' they licks us anyways?"

By the way Cole's face puckered, he might have bitten down on a green persimmon. "Can't let them bastards lick us. Can't do it, Sergeant. They licks us, it's like they really is better'n we is, like they say."

"Long as I kin serve this gun, ain't no white man better'n me," Robinson said. "Mebbe they kin kill me. Do Jesus, I knows they kin kill me. Like I say, they kin lick us. They gots mo' men out there'n we gots in here. But if they kill me, they gots to kill a man who's fightin' back. They ain't gonna kill no nigger, no darkie, no coon. You hear what I'm tellin' you, Sandy?"

"I hears you, Sergeant."

"You believe me?"

"I . . . I'm tryin' to, Sergeant," Sandy Cole said, which struck Robinson as honest enough. The other colored artilleryman eyed him. "You believe your ownself?"

'Course I do. The automatic reply sprang to Ben Robinson's lips. But Cole had given him the truth—or he thought so, anyway. He felt obligated to pay back the same coin: "I's tryin' to, too."

A Federal lieutenant approached the Confederate truce party on foot. Quietly, Captain Goodman said, "That's their post adjutant, sir. His name is Leaming, Mack Leaming. He's been carrying messages back and forth."

"I thank you," Nathan Bedford Forrest said, also quietly. Then he raised his voice so it would carry: "Well, Lieutenant Leaming? What does Major Booth say? He used up all the time I gave him, by God!"

And it didn't do him one damn bit of good, either, Forrest thought. Booth must have been banking on the *Olive Branch.* Too bad for him—that bank had gone bust. The steamboat full of soldiers was leaving Fort Pillow behind. The plumes of smoke on the Mississippi to the north were closer now. Forrest didn't worry about those ships. If this skipper didn't dare to try forcing a landing, theirs wouldn't, either.

Mack Leaming started when Forrest called to him. Forrest wondered what he was so nervous about. Had Major Booth made up his mind to fight? Forrest wouldn't have, not in the Union man's position. But if he had, he had.

"Here is my commandant's reply, sir." Leaming held out a grimy scrap of paper.

Forrest unfolded it. He scowled at the scrawl he had to try to read; it might have been worse than his own hand, something he had trouble believing. " 'Your demand . . . does not produce . . . the desired effect,' " he said slowly. Even after he'd read it, it left him unhappy, or worse than unhappy. "This will not do," he told Leaming. "Send it back, and say to Major Booth that I must have an answer in plain, unmistakable English. Will he fight or will he surrender? Yes or no!"

Lieutenant Leaming turned red. He gave back a salute of drill-field precision, a salute so grand it was almost an insult. "I shall do just as you say, sir," he replied, and did an about-face every bit as fancy. He strode off toward Fort Pillow.

Fussy fellow, isn't he? Forrest thought. He almost laughed at Leaming's retreating back, to see if it could get any stiffer than it was already. He had his doubts. Turning to Captain Goodman, he said, "People go on and on about how I'm an ignorant, uneducated son of a bitch, but by God, Captain, I know how to say what I mean!"

"Yes, sir, you sure do," Goodman said with a small smile. Captain Young and Lieutenant van Horn both stirred, but neither U.S. officer said anything. After a moment, Goodman went on, "Sir, you've done all you need to do right up here—all you need to and more. Might be a good thing if you moved farther away from the fort."

"Ah?" Forrest needed only a heartbeat to understand why. "Reckon so?"

"I do, sir." Goodman pointed up toward the earthwork. "The niggers yonder who're skylarking . . . Well, they're a bunch of damn fools, but they're *only* a bunch of damn fools, if you know what I mean. But the ones looking our way, and the ones pointing our way . . . One of them's liable to pick up a Springfield and point with that instead of his finger. I know they're nothing but niggers, but they don't need to be sharpshooters to hit at this range."

Again, Forrest didn't need long to think about it. He fought ferociously and exposed himself to all sorts of dangers, but that was when his blood was up. It wasn't up now. He could see the good sense in what Captain Goodman said. "All right. I'll do that," he said. "Bring me the Federals' answer as soon as they deliver it." He touched the brim of his hat to Young and van Kirk. "Gentlemen."

"General," both officers said politely. John Young saluted—not to show him up, as Leaming had, but to acknowledge respect even for an enemy.

"You think Major Booth will give up the fort, sir?" Captain Goodman asked as Forrest turned his horse toward the south.

"I am satisfied in my mind that he will," Forrest answered. "In the spot he's in, what else can he do?"

He rode back to the position he'd taken before the Federals demanded proof he was on the field. Among the soldiers and officers gathered there was his bugler, a German named Jacob Gaus. He brandished the bugle the way an ordinary trooper would have brandished a revolver. It was perhaps the most battered musical instrument in the war; along with the dents caused by hard travel were two that came from Minié balls. "Shall I blow the charge, sir?" Gaus asked.

"Not yet," Forrest answered. "I still have hopes that they will see sense and surrender."

"And if they don't?"

"If they don't, Jacob . . . If they don't, they'll wish they had for as long as they live—and most of 'em won't live long."

Mack Leaming was shaking in his boots by the time he got back inside Fort Pillow. He had no doubt that he'd spoken with Nathan Bedford Forrest. He would have believed it even if Captain Young told him the Confederate was an impostor. One look into the big Reb's eyes told him everything he needed to know. Only a killer had eyes like those— hard and cold, always probing for weakness, and always finding it, too.

Major Bradford came up to him. "Well?" Bradford asked. "What does he say?"

"He says he wants your answer in plain English, sir." Leaming took a certain small pleasure in relaying Bedford Forrest's literary crit- icism. He would have enjoyed it more were he less alarmed. "Will you surrender? Yes or no?"

"I can't just come out and *say* that!" Bradford exclaimed.

"Sir, I think you'd better," Lieutenant Leaming replied. "They *will* assault this place as soon as Forrest gives the order."

"So that really is the famous Bedford Forrest, is it?" Bradford tried to keep his tone light, but made heavy going of it. "I saw Young nod, but I can hardly believe it."

"That *is* Nathan Bedford Forrest." Leaming spoke with absolute conviction. "What are we going to do, sir?"

"I won't decide by myself," Major Bradford said. "This is a deci- sion all the officers in the fort need to make."

The ones the Rebs haven't shot, Leaming thought. If only they hadn't shot Major Booth. Bradford no doubt meant well, but he was far out of his depth here. His adjutant knew too well he couldn't do anything about that. Major Bradford was what they had, what the fight left them. Leaming said, "If you're going to hold a council, sir, for heaven's sake do it fast. They are about out of patience with us there on the other side of the breastwork."

Bradford licked his lips. Leaming wouldn't have been surprised if they were dry; his own were. The commandant gathered up half a dozen lieutenants and captains, one of whom had a bloody bandage on his hand but was still at the parapet. "Bedford Forrest demands that we surrender to him at once if we're going to," Bradford said. "I am inclined to fight it out. Does anyone have a contrary view? If you do, speak up now."

"What if they get over our wall here?" asked a lieutenant from the colored heavy artillery; Leaming couldn't call his name to mind.

"We drop down to the bank then," Bradford answered, "and the *New Era* will blast the Rebs from here to Nashville."

"I wish to God the *Olive Branch* could have dropped off her soldiers here," Captain Theodorick Bradford said.

"So do I!" Leaming said. "The Confederates moved up in the ravines to head them off as openly as if they'd captured the fort. We could have given them more trouble if the truce flags weren't flying."

"Forrest wouldn't have listened to us. We already talked about that. And the truce involves his men, the fort, and the *New Era*. The *Olive Branch* was not party to it. Technically, the Rebs were within their rights to refuse her the opportunity to put men ashore," Major Bradford said.

He was a lawyer. There were times when his passion for nitpicking punctilio drove Mack Leaming wild. This was one of them, and worse than most. "Sir, to hell with the Rebels' rights!" Leaming exclaimed. "We're talking about our necks here!"

"We've held Forrest off for this long," Bradford said. "If his men try another push against the fort and fail, I can't imagine how they would be able to nerve themselves for one more after that. I ask again—does anybody feel we should yield?"

No one said a word.

"All right." Bill Bradford was brisk. He nodded to Leaming. "You say Bedford Forrest wants a clear answer, do you?"

"Yes, sir," Leaming answered.

"I shall give him one, then. Let me have paper and pencil, someone." When Bradford had them, he wrote rapidly and handed the paper to Leaming. *General—I will not surrender. Very respectfully, your obedient servant, L. F. Booth, Major Commanding,* Leaming read. "There," Bill Bradford said. "I hope that will be clear enough for General Forrest even without his spectacles, as John Hancock said when he signed the Declaration of Independence." He laughed at his own wit.

Major Leaming laughed, too, more from a sense of duty than for any other reason. "I'll take it out to him, sir," he said. Unlike George III, Forrest had nothing wrong with his eyes. Oh, no.

When Leaming reached the flags of truce, he found the Confederate general no longer waited by them. He handed Bradford's note to Captain Goodman. "Here you are, sir," he said.

"May I ask how your commander replies, sir?" Goodman remained polite.

"We will not surrender," Leaming answered.

Captain Goodman's eyebrows leaped. "Won't you reconsider? We *can* take that place, and it will be terrible if we do. Our men have good reason not to love nigger soldiers and galvanized Yankees. I speak from a concern for the unnecessary effusion of blood, and that effusion will be very great when Fort Pillow falls."

"Major Br—Booth is of the opinion that it will not fall." Leaming corrected himself fast enough to keep the Confederate from noticing his near slip.

"Well, Lieutenant, all I can tell you is that when a Yankee commander believes one thing and General Forrest believes another, General Forrest commonly proves right," Goodman said. "Your superior will not change his mind?"

"He is determined," Leaming replied.

Captain Goodman sighed. "On his head be it. Very well, sir. I shall take his answer to General Forrest, and after that . . . after that, we shall see what we shall see. Good afternoon, gentlemen. A pleasure making your acquaintance." He saluted. So did Captain Henderson and Lieutenant Rodgers.

Leaming returned the courtesy, along with Captain Young and

Lieutenant van Horn. Then they and the common soldiers with them turned around and started back toward Fort Pillow. "Can we really hold this place?" Young asked quietly. "The Confederates' confidence doesn't strike me as their usual bluff and bluster."

"Major Bradford thinks we can. Between the parapet and the *New Era*, he believes we have enough to beat back the Confederates." Leaming paused a moment; leaving it there didn't seem just to the commandant. "He held an officers' council before sending me out with his reply. No one opposed continuing resistance."

"All right." By the frown that further darkened Young's face, it wasn't even close to all right, but he couldn't do anything about it. "We're going to have a hot time of it, a devil of a hot time, but with God's help we'll come through."

He didn't say anything about the gunboat's help. The *New Era* was right down there on the Mississippi. Leaming hoped God was close by, too.

Bedford Forrest watched Captain Goodman ride back toward him. When the junior officer got within hailing distance, Forrest called, "Well, Captain? What will it be?"

Goodman held up a scrap of paper. "You'd better see for yourself, sir."

"That doesn't sound good," Charles Anderson said at Forrest's side.

"No, it doesn't." Forrest nodded. "If the Federals in there think they can hold us out, they've even bigger fools than I credit them for." As Goodman came up, Forrest held out his hand. "Give me the note."

"Yes, sir." Goodman passed it to him.

" 'General—I will not surrender.' " Forrest read it aloud. He slowly nodded a couple of times. Major Booth obliged him on one point: he could not doubt the other man's meaning. "Well, we gave them a chance. If they're such blockheads that they won't take it, it's their hard luck, not ours." Even to himself, he sounded like a judge passing sentence.

"It's their funeral, is what it is," Walter Goodman said. "I tried to tell that to Leaming, but he didn't want to hear it. Reckon he's got his orders, and that's that." He shrugged. "That'll be that, all right."

"I thought they would give up. I really did," Forrest said. "Everybody knows we don't mistreat people who surrender to us. The way our men feel about those damned Federal Tennesseans, and about niggers with guns in their hands . . . Well, Booth'll find out he's made a worse bargain than the one I tried to give him."

Captain Anderson pointed out toward the Mississippi. "What about the gunboat, sir? If the enemy goes down by the river, it's in good position to rake our boys hard."

"We've handled gunboats before. I expect we'll deal with this one the same way," Bedford Forrest answered. "She has to open her gunports to use her cannon. If we've got men blazing away at 'em every time they do open up, she'll lose gunners too quick to stay in the fight for long. Shoot everything blue betwixt wind and water until their flag comes down."

"All right, sir. I'll tend to it," Anderson said. "Colonel Barteau ought to have the same order, in case the gunboat shifts so her guns bear on his men."

"Well, Captain, I can't very well tell you you're wrong, on account of you're right." Forrest called for a runner. He gave the man oral orders to deliver to Barteau over by Coal Creek. When the runner had them straight, he saluted and loped away.

What would the U.S. soldiers be doing, up inside Fort Pillow? Pontius Pilate might have shrugged the shrug Forrest shrugged then. He washed his hands of the Federals. He didn't see what they could do to hold him out except what they were already doing—and that wouldn't be enough.

"General Chalmers!" Forrest said.

Chalmers was talking with Captain Goodman a few feet away. He broke off and nodded to his superior. "Yes, sir? What do you need?"

"Your men ready?"

"Oh, yes, sir. No doubt about it," Chalmers said. "When Gaus blows his bugle, they'll go forward as if it were Gabriel's trumpet."

Jacob Gaus looked at the beat-up instrument he held in his right hand. "God can afford to issue Gabriel something better than this," he said, which set all the officers around him laughing. The bugler added, "Or if He can't, then I am afraid Satan is ahead in the race."

Bedford Forrest was a steadfast believer. That didn't stop him from laughing his head off now; the words, and Gaus's guttural accent, were too funny to resist. Aiming a forefinger at the German, he said, "You are a blasphemous toad, Jacob."

"*Ja,*" Gaus agreed placidly. "But I am *your* blasphemous toad, General."

"That you are—who else would have you?" Forrest needed a moment to bring his mind back to the business at hand. But when he did, he pointed toward the high ground the Confederates had won early in the fight. "You still have plenty of sharpshooters on those little knolls, General?"

"Oh, yes, sir," Chalmers said. "I wouldn't move men off 'em, not when they're up higher than the Federals' position. They can shoot right into the fort, and the troops inside can't do a thing to stop 'em."

"I know. That's why I want 'em there. That's why only a damn fool would reckon he could hang on to Fort Pillow unless he had a big enough garrison for the outer line." Now Forrest pointed ahead, to the ditch in front of the earthwork the U.S. soldiers still held. "And that's why only a damn fool would reckon a no-account trench like that one would keep our boys out of his works, too."

"Easier fighting a damn fool than someone who knows what he's doing," Chalmers observed.

"That's a fact," Forrest said. "All the same, even a galvanized Yankee ought to have eyes to see this. By God, Chalmers, even a nigger ought to have eyes to see this. Your sharpshooters over yonder can fire at *that* stretch of the Federal works so they're shooting along the Yankee's firing line instead of straight at it, and the sharpshooters over *there* can do the same to the other stretch."

"The technical term is *enfilading fire,* sir," Chalmers said.

Was he slyly poking fun at Forrest or really trying to teach him something? Chalmers was not a West Point man, but he'd been to college; he was a lawyer in Mississippi when secession came, and helped lead his state out of the Union. He doubtless looked down his nose at an unschooled nigger-trader like Forrest—he might, but he'd better not show it, not when that unschooled nigger-trader outranked him.

"I don't care much about the technical term, Jim," Forrest said. "I know what I want to do, and I can get it done just fine without fancy talk." He snorted, thinking of the evasive answer the Federals in Fort Pillow tried to palm off on him. Well, they wouldn't get away with it, by God.

"We've all seen that, sir," Chalmers said.

There wasn't—there couldn't possibly be—any mockery in those words. Education or no, fancy talk or no, Bedford Forrest knew without false modesty that he'd done more for the Confederate cause in the West than just about anybody else. When the war was young, he saved a large part of the Confederate garrison in Fort Donelson when his superiors, after breaking out, idiotically marched back in and had to surrender to the Yankees.

He fought hard at Pittsburg Landing, and took a wound that almost killed him; that bullet still lay somewhere near his spine, and still pained him. His first set of cavalry raids up into Tennessee and Kentucky at the end of 1862 did such a good job of wrecking U. S. Grant's supply line that they delayed his attack on Vicksburg by months. He fought at Chickamauga, and still wished Braxton Bragg would have listened to him and pushed the pursuit. That Federal army would be extinct now; the Confederates would hold Chattanooga. Instead . . .

Forrest's hands tightened on the reins. If only they were tightening on Braxton Bragg's scrawny neck. Bragg couldn't win. And when, in spite of himself, he did win at Chickamauga, he frittered away the victory. But he was Jefferson Davis's particular friend, and so his malign influence in the C.S.A. seemed to go on forever.

I should have killed him, Forrest thought. *I should have challenged him. Not even a spineless wretch like that could have wriggled off the hook.* He shook his head. Too late now. Too late for a lot of things in the West.

General Chalmers said something. Lost in his own dark thoughts, Forrest heard his voice without noting the words. "I'm sorry, General," he said, shaking his head again. "That went right on by me."

"I said, will you go forward with the men when they storm the fort?"

"Oh." The question spawned more dark thoughts. Slowly, Forrest answered, "Matter of fact, I wasn't planning to."

"I see." By Chalmers's tone, and by his raised eyebrow, he didn't.

Were Chalmers speaking of some other man, the two-word response might have been an accusation of cowardice. Not with Bedford Forrest. Some gushing Southern newspaper wrote that he'd killed more men in close combat than any general since medieval days. He had no idea if that was so. But he was large and strong and fast, and he usually went straight for the hottest action.

Cautiously, Chalmers said, "Do you mind my asking why, sir?"

"Yes, dammit." Forrest's voice was rough, even harsh. He disliked being put on the spot.

"Very well, sir." By Chalmers's tone, he didn't like it, but he knew he couldn't do anything about it.

Forrest was just as well pleased to keep his mouth shut. If he said he had no stomach for what lay ahead, Chalmers would think him soft. If he said he was afraid he couldn't stop it, Chalmers would think him weak. If he said nothing at all, Chalmers could think whatever he damn well pleased.

He turned to Jacob Gaus. "You ready there?"

"Oh, yes, sir," the bugler answered.

"Anything that wants doing before we sound the assault?" Forrest asked the officers nearby. Neither Chalmers nor Captain Anderson nor Captain Goodman nor any of the others said a word. "Well, then"—Forrest tipped his hat to Gaus—"go ahead, Jacob."

"*Ja.*" Gaus raised the battered bugle to his lips. The fierce horn call belled across the battlefield.

VIII

MAJOR WILLIAM BRADFORD WATCHED LIEUTENANT Leaming and the rest of the truce party walk back from their parley with the Confederates. His brother came up beside him. "Won't be long now."

"No, I don't reckon it will, Theo," Bradford said. The Confederates in the truce party rode off toward the knoll to which Bedford Forrest had repaired not long before. They no longer held up the white flags they'd used to call for the parley.

"Can we hold 'em out?" Theodorick Bradford asked quietly.

"If you didn't think we could, you should have spoken up at the officers' council," Bill Bradford said angrily.

His older brother flushed. "Nobody else did. Damned if I wanted you to reckon I was a quitter."

"I reckoned you were somebody who would tell me what was on his mind. Maybe I was wrong," the garrison commander said.

Captain Theodorick Bradford turned away. "Excuse me, *sir,*" he said, lacing the polite title with disdain. He stormed off without waiting to find out whether his brother excused him or not. Bill Bradford swore under his breath. What could he do about making up with Theo? Nothing, not right now.

About a quarter of a mile away, the Confederates from the truce party were talking with the other Rebs. One of the men on that low rise pointed toward Fort Pillow and then out to a couple of places Secesh soldiers had overrun. Bradford wished he could hear what the enemy soldiers were saying. In war as in cards, one peek at the other fellow's hand was worth all the calculating in the world.

A Confederate soldier raised a bugle. The afternoon sun gleamed off the polished brass as if off gold. For a moment, time seemed to stand still, poised between one thing and another. Then, faint in the distance but very clear, the horn call reached Bill Bradford and the embattled fort.

And it reached the C.S. cavalry troopers all around Fort Pillow. The truce shattered like a crystal goblet dropped on a hardwood floor. A shattered goblet spilled wine. A shattered truce spilled claret of another sort.

A great roar of musketry arose inside the fort and around it. Yelling like fiends, like devils, like men possessed, the Confederates swarmed out of the positions they'd gained earlier in the day and rushed for the bluff. "Shoot 'em!" Major Bradford screamed. "Shoot 'em down like the cur dogs they are!"

All six of the cannon inside the fort bellowed at the same time, sending canister forth against Forrest's fighters. Cursing gun crews wrestled the pieces back into position and reloaded as fast as they could. Not all their curses were aimed at the enemy. "Shit! High!" "High, goddammit!" "Can't we lower them fuckin' muzzles any more?" Bradford heard that again and again. The very way Fort Pillow was made seemed to conspire against the defenders.

But the foul-mouthed colored artillerymen and their equally blasphemous white superiors weren't the only ones battling desperately to keep the Confederates away from the fort. Whites from the Thirteenth Tennessee Cavalry and Negroes from the newly arrived artillery regiments stood side by side behind the earthen parapet, blazing away at the charging, yowling enemy and then ramming fresh minnies into the muzzles of their Springfields. Race, for the moment, was forgotten. Quick firing counted for more.

Bradford ran now here, now there, rushing men from spots that weren't so badly threatened to those in mortal peril. Before long, he hardly knew where to send soldiers and where to hold them back. The whole earthwork seemed in mortal peril.

And, while danger might have made the defenders forget about race, the attackers remembered all too well. Along with the usual Rebel yells and random shouts and oaths, Forrest's men raised another cry: "Black flag! Black flag!"

Ice ran through Bill Bradford when he first made out those words through the din of musketry and cannon fire and other yells and screams. In Bedford Forrest's note demanding surrender, he'd warned that he couldn't answer for consequences if the Federals in Fort Pillow refused. He'd warned, and he hadn't been joking, even if Bradford believed he was. *Black flag!* was the cry for no quarter.

"Hold them out, men!" Bradford yelled. "For your lives, hold them out!"

He drew his army Colt and shot at the Confederates—too many of them were within pistol range. The revolver's cylinder spun. He fired again. He wished his men had even a handful of newfangled Sharps or Henry repeating rifles. They fired so fast, they could easily break a charge like this. You simply couldn't reload Springfields quick enough.

Some of Forrest's troopers fell on the steep slope leading up to the bluff. Wounded enemy soldiers dragged themselves away from the intense gunfire. The dead lay where they fell. *Ravens' meat,* Bradford thought—a bit of perhaps poetry he'd heard somewhere. In this part of the country, turkey buzzards and black buzzards accounted for more unburied corpses than ravens.

The Confederates swarming up the slope clutched their rifle muskets and shotguns and pistols in their fists. Hardly any of them fired.

But not all of Forrest's men were rushing Fort Pillow. Sharpshooters on the knolls a quarter of a mile outside the parapet took a deadly toll on the defenders.

A bullet cracked past Major Bradford's face, so close that it made him jerk back in surprise and alarm. It smacked into the side of the head of a trooper from the Thirteenth Tennessee Cavalry. That sound was too much like the one you made when you chunked a rock at a rotten watermelon. The trooper let out a small, startled sigh—not even a groan—and crumpled as if all his bones turned to water. He died before he hit the ground.

A colored soldier got hit in the side of the neck. Blood sprayed everywhere. The Negro shrieked and dashed wildly through the fort. His wound plainly wasn't mortal, or didn't have to be if someone saw to it, but his pain and fright were liable to kill him if the minnie didn't.

Bradford saw more and more U.S. soldiers hit in the flank. He pointed out toward the clouds of black-powder smoke that marked the Secesh sharpshooters' positions. "Those sons of bitches are murdering us!" he shouted. "Can we stop them?"

"Maybe the cannon can blast them off those knolls," a sergeant said. But he didn't sound hopeful, and Bradford knew why not: the guns inside Fort Pillow hadn't been able to shift the Confederate marksmen since they gained their places. What with all the fallen timber and the stumps on those low rises, the Rebs enjoyed cover almost as good as the earthwork gave the Federals.

"Have to try," Bradford said. But how much good would trying do?

Matt Ward's mouth was dry as the Egyptian desert when the bugle sounded the assault. From the barracks buildings the Confederates had captured, Fort Pillow up on its bluff seemed as towering and indomitable as Goliath the Philistine must have to the children of Israel.

But Goliath fell, brought down by David's sling. Bedford Forrest thought Fort Pillow would fall, too. Instead of a sling, Ward had his

Enfield. And he had friends who would scale the bluff with him or die trying. (He wished he hadn't thought of it that way.)

"Come on! Move out!" Confederate officers and sergeants shouted, all along the line from the Mississippi to Coal Creek. The better, braver ones added, "Follow me!" Where a superior went forward, the men he led couldn't very well hold back.

The cougar yowl of a Rebel yell filled Ward's throat as he rushed toward the bluff and scrambled up it. Where rush stopped and scramble started he wasn't sure, then or afterwards. What seemed like all the Federals in the world were shooting down at him and his comrades. The muzzle flashes that burst from their rifle muskets stabbed out like dragonfire in a book of fairy tales.

He wanted to shoot back. Here and there, some of Forrest's troopers did. Sergeants swore at the men who pulled trigger. Matt understood why, and held his fire. Stopping to reload on this steep slope was asking to get shot. But if a man didn't reload, he had only his bayonet or his clubbed rifle musket with which to face the enemy once he got to the top.

A Minié ball hit the ground a few inches in front of Ward's face with a wet splat. Bits of dirt kicked up into his face. He did stop then, to rub at his eyes with grimy fingers. He might have done more harm than good. He was still blinking frantically and shaking his head when he resumed the upward climb.

Here and there on the muddy slope, Confederates tumbled down or sprawled motionless instead of going forward. Their screams mingled with the battle cries and the gunfire to produce a cacophonous din mercifully unknown outside of war. Ward tried not to hear it, tried not to heed it, but it made him afraid even so.

Screams also rose from the men in blue who fired down at the onstorming Confederates. For a moment, Matt Ward wondered how so many enemy soldiers were getting hurt while his own comrades held their fire. Then he realized the troopers posted on the knolls—he'd been up on one of them himself for a little while, before hurrying forward—were taking a steady toll on the U.S. soldiers at the top of the bluff.

He also realized something else: a galvanized Yankee or even a Negro shrieking for his mother or simply howling out his pain to the uncaring world sounded just the same as a luckless Confederate doing the same thing. Were he a different person, that might have persuaded him of the essential brotherhood of man. Instead, it made him want to hear the foe making those noises instead of his own comrades.

At the top of the bluff, just outside their earthen parapet, the Federals had dug a ditch ten or twelve feet wide and even deeper than that. They likely hadn't dreamt any attackers could come so far, but, like any military engineers who knew their trade, they interposed a final barrier between themselves and the enemy. Or they thought they did.

Some of the Confederates reaching the top of the bluff tried to leap the ditch and scramble up onto the earthwork beyond. Matt Ward didn't see anyone who succeeded; that would have been a formidable jump even for a man not burdened with a rifle musket and enough cartridges to do a deal of fighting.

Most troopers showed better sense than to try to imitate a mountain goat bounding from crag to crag. Instead of jumping over the ditch, they dropped down into it. Ward was one of those. The bottom of the ditch was all mud and puddles; the ooze tried to suck the shoes right off his feet. But he was here, at the top of the bluff. Panting, he paused a moment to catch his breath and try to figure out what to do next.

Were the earthwork that protected the Union troops thinner, they could easily have shot down into the ditch and slaughtered the attackers. Instead, they had to crawl out on top of the bank of dirt to fire into the ditch. When they did, they exposed all of themselves to the distant sharpshooters' deadly fire.

"Now that we're here, that damn earthwork does as much for us as it does for the Federals," said a man near Ward. "We can't get at them, and they can't get at us, neither."

"But we don't need to be *here*," Ward said. The wet squelching as he shifted his feet underlined the point. "We need to be *there*." He pointed to the far side of the parapet. "Long as the bluebellies hold us out, they win."

"Well, it don't look like them sons of bitches is gonna be able to do it much longer," the other trooper said. "Look there."

In the age of chivalry, when knighthood was in flower, besieging an enemy castle was an everyday part of war. Soldiers no more thought of going into battle without scaling ladders than without their pants. Bedford Forrest's troopers knew little of days gone by. They had to improvise if they wanted to get out of the ditch. They had to—and they did.

It all started without orders, which made it seem more marvelous to Ward. Here and there, at the bottom of the muddy ditch, men went down on their hands and knees. Others swarmed up onto them, using them as human scaling ladders to get up to where they could reach the rampart and break into Fort Pillow.

For the first little while, things didn't go smoothly. The would-be ladders didn't perform well. Time after time, they toppled before they got very tall. Then a couple of sergeants who had some idea of what needed doing started yelling their heads off. Most of the time, Matt Ward had no use for sergeants. Just because they had stripes on their sleeves, they thought they were entitled to throw their weight around. Here, though, they turned out to be worth something after all.

With loud, profane encouragement, they got big men on the bottom of what turned out to be human pyramids instead of human scaling ladders. They put smaller men in the next layer up, and smaller men still above *them*. They still had a couple of collapses. . . .

"God damn you, Riley, you stupid, clumsy son of a bitch, why the hell did you have to go and wiggle then?"

"I'm sorry, Sarge. Stinking bug landed right on my eyelid, so help me Jesus. What the devil was I supposed to do?"

"Likely tell," the sergeant said. But he didn't waste any more time scorching the luckless Riley, so if he didn't exactly believe, he didn't exactly disbelieve, either. It wasn't as if he didn't have plenty of other troopers to scream at.

The first Confederate who made it up so he could rush the rampart got shot in the face the instant he showed himself. He tumbled back into the ditch, dead before he splatted into the mud.

"Move!" the closest sergeant bellowed to the men in his pyramid. "That Yankee bastard's gotta reload. If you can get up there before he does—"

More and more men went up. A few of them were hit, and fell in the ditch again. Most, though, gained the narrow strip of ground between the ditch and the earthwork. They crouched there, ducking down behind the piled dirt, waiting for their orders. Matt Ward scrambled up himself. He saw Colonel McCulloch no more than ten feet away, waiting like everybody else.

"Be ready, boys!" McCulloch called. "We're almost there!"

On the other side of the rampart, the Federals had mostly stopped shooting, too. They waited tensely for whatever happened next.

"At my order!" someone shouted—a Confederate, Ward thought, though accent was no help in telling the sides apart with so many Tennesseans on both. The C.S. trooper clutched his rifle musket and braced himself, not that that would do any good if a minnie hit him.

"Is that General Chalmers?" whispered the soldier next to him.

"Beats me," Ward whispered back.

"*Now!*" shouted the officer, whoever he was.

Mack Leaming's saber blade glittered in the sun. He'd never dreamt he might have to fight with his officer's sword. The saber in the scabbard was a mark of his rank, nothing more, and an occasional nuisance that thumped against his leg. But at close quarters a slashing saber was a weapon not to be despised. He wished he had a better notion of how to fight with it, for the coming fight would be at quarters as close as a man could imagine in his direst nightmares.

"Are your pieces loaded?" a Federal officer called to the colored soldiers under his command.

"Yes, suh," they said, and, "Sure is, suh," and, "We ain't afraid of no Rebs."

Leaming wondered why they weren't. He was desperately afraid himself, and trying hard not to show it. Not knowing fear seemed impossible. Carrying on in spite of it . . . A mere mortal might aspire to that.

Somewhere not nearly far enough away, a wounded U.S. soldier howled. While Bedford Forrest's troopers just outside of Fort Pillow mostly held their fire, the sharpshooters on the rises that looked down into the Federal position kept popping away at the soldiers in blue. Every so often, a round struck home.

"This is our big chance, men!" Major Bradford shouted. "If we hold them out now, they're whipped!" Bradford pointed up to the big U.S. flag floating above the fort. Several minnies had punched holes through the Stars and Stripes, but they still proudly waved. "That flag will never come down! Never, do you hear me?"

Together, white cavalry troopers and colored artillerymen raised a cheer. Bradford seemed over the worst of the jitters that afflicted him earlier in the day. Leaming hoped it wasn't too late. He shrugged. Jitters or not, Bradford had done about as well as any man could after Major Booth fell. His adjutant didn't see what he could have done differently if he didn't intend to surrender.

Oh, things might have gone better. If they had, the Federals would have been able to fire all the barracks buildings, not just those in the first row. Then Forrest's men would have had fewer places from which to shoot at the fort from close range. And, more important still, the *Olive Branch* and the other steamboats might have been able to land their soldiers. The Confederates were out there in large numbers. Leaming didn't know whether Booth's 1,500 or Bradford's 7,000 was a better guess, but the garrison was badly outnumbered either way. Reinforcements would have helped the U.S. cause.

If Forrest hadn't sent men to the mouths of the ravines below the fort to scare off the steamships . . . Leaming still thought he shouldn't have got away with doing that under flag of truce, even if it was a truce about which the soldiers aboard the *Olive Branch* knew nothing. No matter what Leaming thought, it was over and done with now.

"Be ready, boys! We're almost there!" a Confederate bawled.

"At my order!" another Rebel shouted. Both voices carried an officer's authority. Perhaps two heartbeats later, the second one cried, *"Now!"*

All along the earthen rampart, Bedford Forrest's troopers popped up, rifle muskets and pistols at the ready. Every Federal soldier with a loaded weapon fired at the same time, at point-blank range. Dead and wounded Rebs spun and tumbled back into the ditch. Screams filled the cool air.

But then the Confederates loosed a volley that dwarfed anything the soldiers in blue could give them. Far more enemy soldiers pressed against the outside of the earthwork than there were Union troops to defend it. Not all of Forrest's men pulled trigger—some held back, so they could shoot when they needed to. But even so, the attackers who fired outnumbered the men inside.

Mack Leaming didn't know how many bullets cracked past him in that hellish instant. He also didn't know how they all managed to miss him. *Thank you, Lord!* ran through his head. Maybe he said it out loud. Maybe he didn't. He never could sort it out afterwards.

He did know that far too many Federals weren't so lucky. All along the earthwork, wounded men reeled back and dead men dropped. The defenders might have taken a sharp right to the chin in a fistfight.

If they went down now, they would never rise again. "Fight!" Leaming shouted. "Fight, God damn you! If we don't fight, we all die!" *Maybe if we do fight, we all die anyway,* some mad and hopeless fragment of his mind jeered.

The Confederates roared and bellowed and screeched their savage battle cry. Leaming had heard people say it was worth a division in battle. Now he understood what they meant—at close range, the

Rebel yell made the hair stand up on the nape of his neck and threatened to turn his blood to water. It made him *want* to run, even if he didn't.

Forrest's men ran—forward. They scrambled up onto the broad rampart and dashed across it, then leaped down into Fort Pillow. Some of them used the bullets they'd held back before. Others stabbed with bayonets or swung their rifle muskets club-fashion.

Whites and Negroes in blue uniforms met them side by side. They didn't need Leaming or any other officer to tell them they had to hold out that swarm of enemy soldiers if they wanted to go on breathing. The colored artillerymen at the center of the U.S. line might not have had much practice with the bayonet, but that didn't keep them from using it when they had to. They fought with the wild courage of men who had nothing to lose. And so they were—the Confederates howled "No quarter!" and "Black flag!" at the top of their lungs.

No doubt the Negroes would have been wiser not to mock Forrest's troopers during the earlier fight, and especially during the truce. Their jeering came back to haunt them now. But, even at close quarters, they showed discipline and courage beyond anything Lieutenant Leaming expected of them. Whites could do no better—the whites from the Thirteenth Tennessee Cavalry fighting alongside them *were* doing no better.

"Hurrah! Hurrah!" Leaming ran at the Confederates, not away from them. Next to the Rebel yell, the Union battle cry seemed flavorless in his mouth, but it was what the Federals had, so he used it.

He slashed at a trooper in muddy butternut. The Confederate brought up his Springfield (or was it an Enfield?) to block the blow. Sparks flew as iron blade struck iron barrel. Another Reb lunged at Leaming with his bayonet. The lieutenant had to leap back in a hurry to keep from getting stuck like a hog. A saber was all very well, but a long bayonet at the end of a long rifle musket had the reach of a spear.

He slashed again, this time at a trooper running by with blood already on his bayonet. The man didn't even seem to see Leaming till the blade bit into his arm. He howled like a wolf and dropped his rifle musket. As blood spurted from the wound, he said, "You son of a bitch! What the hell did you have to go and do that for?"

Instead of answered, Leaming cut at him again. The Confederate scrambled back and tripped over his own feet. Another soldier in butternut (in fact, the man's trousers were blue: surely plunder from a dead Federal) stepped on him. He howled again, and cursed the man on his own side even more foully than he'd sworn at Leaming.

"This way! This way!" an officer in blue shouted, doing his best to rally the Negro troops he led. A moment later, he groaned and crumpled, clutching at a bullet wound in his side.

With him or without him, the colored artillerymen went on fighting. Leaming saw one of them bayonet a Confederate trooper in the belly. The man who fought for Forrest shrieked like a damned soul as he fell. A moment later, a pistol shot at point-blank range blew off half the Negro's face. With a bubbling scream of his own, he went down beside the man he'd speared. Neither of them had a prayer of living.

Forrest's troopers shot down another white U.S. officer, and then another. They seemed to make a special effort to pick off the men with shoulder straps. No doubt they thought the Negroes would fall to pieces without white men to lead them. Before Mack Leaming saw the colored soldiers fight, he would have thought the same thing. Now? Now he had to change his mind.

He wounded another Confederate, and heard another minnie snap past his head, perilously close. Forrest's men brawled ahead. No matter how well the Negroes fought, would it do them any good at all?

When the assault came, the half-dozen gaps cut through the rampart to let the guns of the Sixth U.S. Heavy Artillery (Colored) offered Bedford Forrest's men easy ways into Fort Pillow—or so they thought. Three of them rushed straight for Ben Robinson's twelve-pounder.

He fired the piece himself. Sergeant Clark was down with a leg wound. Unlike some earlier rounds, this one didn't go to waste. Canister blew the Confederates to red rags. One of them managed a wail. The other two . . . simply ceased to be.

Sandy Cole whooped. "Bury them buckra in a jam tin!" he shouted. "Blew 'em right outa their shoes!" Sure enough, several shoes still stood in the gap. One of them had a foot left in it.

"Reload!" Captain Carron shouted. But there was no time. Not all of Forrest's men were rash enough to charge straight into the muzzle of a gun. Many more, great swarms of them, scrambled over the earthwork and into Fort Pillow. Using the worm, swabbing out, shoving in another powder bag and then another round of canister . . . The Rebs would shoot or bayonet them all before they finished the job.

When Robinson grabbed the worm, then, he didn't grab it to pull smoldering bits of wadding from the twelve-pounder's barrel. Instead, he used it like the butt of a spear, or perhaps more like a quarterstaff, driving the twin iron corkscrews at the end into a Secesh soldier's chest. They didn't pierce the Rebel—but, with a startled squawk, his arms flailing, he fell back into the ditch from which he'd climbed.

"That's the way to do it!" Sandy Cole was laying about him with a sponge. It wasn't a weapon that would kill any Rebs, but he had enough reach with it to keep them from bayoneting him where he stood. He knocked a Confederate trooper off his feet, then kicked him in the face as he started to rise. After that, the Confederate stayed down.

Carron's pistol barked—once, twice, three times. In the chaos, Sergeant Robinson had no idea whether the white officer hit anybody. More and more men in butternut dashed up over the rampart and sprang down into Fort Pillow.

Robinson clouted one of them in the head with the worm. It made a much better weapon than the sponge. The C.S. trooper toppled, his face a mask of blood. Robinson snatched up the bucket of water in which the sponge rested when it wasn't swabbing out the twelve-pounder. He threw the water into one startled Confederate's face, then flung the bucket at another.

Yet another Reb fired at him from perhaps six feet away—and missed. The soldier swore and lunged with the bayonet. Ben Robinson beat the blade aside with the worm. "Black flag!" the Confederate shouted. "We're gonna kill us every goddamn nigger we catch!"

"You couldn't catch the clap in a whorehouse," Robinson retorted, cautiously thrusting with the worm.

"Only thing you know about whorehouses is your mama worked in one," the Secesh soldier panted.

"Leastways I know who my mama is. She didn't leave me out fo' the hogs to eat," Robinson said. "Or is you one o' them hogs your ownself?"

The Confederate stared at him with eyes and mouth open as comically wide as a surprised Negro's were said to be. Ben Robinson almost laughed, even though Forrest's cavalryman might kill him yet. The white never dreamt a man he wished he owned might have the nerve to talk back. Well, tough luck for him. Life gave you all kinds of things you never dreamt of. Anybody who'd been bought and sold could testify to that.

And the trooper stayed so surprised, Robinson's next lunge with the worm caught him in the pit of the stomach and folded him up like a lady's fan. Robinson wanted to finish him off. The artillery sergeant wished he had a weapon that could finish off the Reb. He looked around to see if someone had dropped a rifle musket.

Sure enough, several lay on the muddy ground. Robinson snatched one up, only to realize he would die quickly if he stayed where he was to fight with it. Sandy Cole and Charlie Key were still on their feet and fighting, but the rest of the gun crew was either down or fled. Confederates poured past them on either side. Here and there, knots of Union troops still struggled, whites and blacks battling side by side, color forgotten. But Bedford Forrest's men were over the rampart and inside the fort, and God only knew how the Federals were going to throw them out.

Nathan Bedford Forrest raised a polished brass spyglass to his eye to get a closer look at the fight for Fort Pillow. Distance fell away. As with everything else, he paid a price: the image was upside down. He was used to that, and it didn't faze him. The fringes of unnatural red and blue around the edges of things bothered him more.

"Lousy cheap thing," he muttered. He'd had better telescopes, ones where the fringes weren't nearly so bad. But almost three years of constant travel left them water over the dam. He shrugged. This one, borrowed from a Confederate patriot in Jackson, showed . . . enough.

He watched his men go down into the Yankees' foolish, useless ditch and then, only minutes later, scramble out on the far side. He watched his sharpshooters pick off two or three Federals who leaned across the earthwork or crawled out onto it so they could shoot down at the troopers in the ditch. He chuckled a little as he watched; in the spyglass's inverted image, the soldiers on top of the rampart looked as if they were about to fall off the edge of the world.

A moment later, he chuckled again, grimly. The homemade Yankees and runaway slaves inside Fort Pillow weren't really ready to fight, even if they thought they were. They could have made things much nastier for his men if they were bright enough to light the fuses on some shrapnel rounds and toss them over the rampart and down into the crowded ditch. The troopers trapped in there wouldn't have enjoyed that at all.

But neither Major Booth nor any of his officers had the brains to do it. The Federals didn't have long to think of such things, and now, with his own men into place right outside the rampart, it was too late. War didn't give you second chances.

Even across close to a quarter of a mile, the volley the Confederates fired into Fort Pillow sounded like a thunderclap. It must have hit the defenders the same way. Bedford Forrest was sure of that, even if he couldn't see into the fort. That wasn't the sorry spyglass's fault. Several hundred rifle muskets and pistols going off at once didn't just make a thunderclap. They also made the cloud from which it might have sprung. His troopers vanished into that cloud as they swarmed over the rampart and into the fort.

More shots rang out, these spaced far enough apart to be heard individually, not just as part of a greater roar. Through the gunfire, Rebel yells and other cries and the screams of wounded men rang out.

"If we get in, them bluebellies is dead meat," said a soldier near the general, pausing for a moment as he reloaded.

"That's about the size of it, Reuben." Forrest nodded. "And I'll tell you something else, too—we're going to get in."

"Well, hell, yes." Reuben had no doubt in his mind.

Neither did Bedford Forrest, not really. He made hand-washing motions, feeling like Pontius Pilate again. *Well, too bad,* he thought. If the Federals didn't have the brains to quit when he gave them the chance, weren't they asking to get crucified? He nodded again. They were, and his troopers would give them what they asked for.

"Come on, men! We can do it!" Major Bradford shouted. He heard other officers and sergeants in blue yelling the same thing. He really believed it. They'd fought so well for so long. Bad luck Major Booth stopped a bullet, but even so . . .

He never would have dreamt the niggers up from Memphis could fight the way they did. Were they as brave as white men? He still didn't know if he wanted to go that far—he was a Tennessee man himself, after all, even if he did fight for the Union—but they stood by their guns, they fired over the rampart, and they didn't run. What more could you ask?

"We *can* do it!" he yelled again.

Then the Confederates crouched down on the far side of the earthwork rose up like Lazarus and fired a volley that smacked into his men like an uppercut from a prizefighter. As soon as he saw soldiers— black and white—reel away from the rampart, some wounded or slain, others simply terrified, he knew how dreadful the danger was.

"Get back to the earthwork!" he shouted. "We have to keep them out!" He ran forward and shoved at a trooper from the Thirteenth Tennessee Cavalry, a man he knew well. "Get back, Jojo!"

Jojo wasn't inclined to listen. He wasn't inclined to remember military discipline, either. "Get stuffed, Bill," he said, and pushed past his commandant. He hardly seemed to know where he was going— anywhere to get away from the howling, yowling Confederates swarming up and over the rampart.

Bradford could have shot him in the back. A man deserting his post, a man disobeying his superior in combat . . . Nobody would say a word about it, even if anyone from the garrison was lucky enough to be in a position to write reports about what happened here today. Bradford didn't fire. Maybe Jojo would come to his senses in a little while and start fighting again. A dead man wouldn't, not till the Day of Resurrection.

And besides, Major William Bradford knew too painfully well how close to cutting and running he was himself.

Try as he would, he couldn't make himself go right up to the rampart and battle it out with the Confederates hand to hand. He did shoot at one of them who jumped down into Fort Pillow and ran at him with rifle musket clutched by the barrel and swung up over his head. He aimed for the Reb's midsection, but hit him in the left shoulder. His Army Colt pulled up and to the right when he fired.

With a howl of pain, the trooper reeled away. He dropped the rifle musket with which he would have clubbed Bradford to clutch at himself. Bright blood welled out between his fingers. Then a colored soldier hit him in the side of the head with the butt of his Springfield. The blow wasn't sporting, but it was damned effective. The Confederate swayed like a tall tree almost cut through, then fell at full length in the mud. Bradford half expected someone to yell, *Timmmber!*

Another Confederate shot the Negro. He too crumpled, both hands flying to his belly. The best he could hope for was a quick death. Belly wounds almost always killed, if not from the force of the bullet itself then from the fever that followed punctured bowels.

Bradford fired at the soldier in butternut. Even at point-blank range, he missed. A moment later, another black man tackled the trooper. They rolled on the ground, punching and kicking and kneeing and biting in a spasm of hatred and fury.

"Come on! Keep fighting them! As long as they don't get in, we can whip them!" That voice, so like his own, made Bradford's head whip around. His brother Theodorick was still very much in the fight. Theo had a pistol in one hand and one of his blue wigwag flags in the other. He fired at a Reb. The man went down.

"That's the fucker who was signaling the gunboat!" shouted another Confederate—a major. "Nail the lousy son of a bitch!"

Half a dozen of Bedford Forrest's troopers fired at Theodorick Bradford at the same time. At least three bullets struck home—in the chest, in the belly, in the leg.

"Theo!" Bill Bradford cried. He shot at one of the Confederates. The pistol ball caught the Reb just above the bridge of the nose. The man went down without a word, dead before he finished falling.

But Captain Theodorick Bradford was also down, feebly thrashing in the mud. For once careless of his own safety, Bill Bradford knelt beside his brother. "Hurts," Theo choked out. Blood bubbled from his nose and ran from the corner of his mouth. "Hurts bad."

"It'll be all right, Theo," Bradford said, knowing too well it wouldn't.

His brother tried to answer, but only blood poured from his mouth. His eyes rolled up in his head. His chest heaved once, twice, as he fought for air. Then it was still. Bill Bradford smelled a harsh stink. Theo's bowels had let go. It was over.

For those few seconds, no one tried to murder Bradford as he bent over his brother's body. That wouldn't, couldn't, last. No matter what Bradford wanted to do for Theodorick, he had to stay alive or he'd never get the chance. He scrambled to his feet and fired again. The Colt clicked on an empty chamber. He threw it down, snatched up the one Theo had dropped, and fought on.

IX

MATT WARD HADN'T THOUGHT MUCH of the Federals garrisoning Fort Pillow. Half renegade Tennesseans, half coons—what kind of fight could people like that put up? He figured they would throw up their hands and surrender as soon as that first terrific volley tore into them. Of course, from what he heard, Bedford Forrest had thought they would surrender when he sent in the flag of truce.

Forrest proved wrong, and so did Ward. The soldiers in blue fought with as much courage as anyone could want to see. Maybe that was the desperation of cornered rats. Whatever it was, they showed no signs of yielding even if they were badly outnumbered, even if that blast of gunfire killed or wounded quite a few of the men at the rampart.

If they wouldn't give up, they had to go down. A big colored man in a blue uniform swung his clubbed Springfield at Matt Ward's head. Ward ducked just in time. The rifle-musket butt knocked the slouch hat off his head, but didn't knock out his brains. He swore all the same; he liked that hat.

He stabbed at the Negro with his own bayonet. The black man

sprang away. But then he swung again, trying to knock the Enfield out of Ward's hands. Ward wasn't an experienced bayonet fighter. He didn't think any soldiers except former U.S. Army Regulars were expert with the bayonet. But he held on to his weapon, and the black man's swipe left him hideously exposed and unable to get away. Only a sandbag on a practice field could make a more inviting target.

Like anybody who grew up on a farm, Matt Ward had slaughtered and butchered his share of livestock. He knew the soft resistance flesh gave to a knife, knew the feel of a blade grating off a rib and then sliding deeper. But there was all the difference in the world between sticking a hog and sticking a man.

The Negro's eyes opened enormously wide. "Do Jesus!" he screamed. Then he let out a bubbling, wordless shriek of pure agony. He jerked away from the blade and from Ward. An experienced bayonet fighter would have held the lunge and gone on stabbing, twisting the blade to make sure he had a killing stroke. Ward thought the black man would fall over dead. The blood pouring from his side made that seem likely.

Likely or not, it wasn't so. Once free of the bayonet, the Negro went right on fighting—not against Ward, but against a nearby Confederate trooper. That wound had to kill him sooner or later—Ward drove more than a foot of steel into his chest—but it wasn't finishing him fast. As Ward had by the barracks below the bluff, he found out how hard human beings were to kill.

Not far from him, a black soldier threw down his Springfield and fell to his knees in front of a couple of Bedford Forrest's troopers. "Don' shoot me!" he shouted. "Please don' shoot me! I surrender! Ain't gonna fight no mo'!"

"You a runaway, boy?" one of the Confederates asked. Most of the Negroes who fought for the U.S.A. were. By the way this bluebelly talked, he sure didn't come from Massachusetts or New York.

He hesitated a split second, but had to realize lying would do him no good. "Yes, suh," he admitted. "You kin send me back to my massa. I don' care, so he'p me Jesus."

Most of the time, the Yankees complained because the Confederates treated captured colored troops as reclaimed property, not prisoners of war. Forrest had offered to treat the blacks in Fort Pillow as prisoners like any others—he'd offered, and the U.S. commander turned him down. Now the bill for such folly came due.

"I'll send you to your master, all right," the Confederate said. "I'll send you straight to the Devil, because you belong in hell!" He shot the black man in the head from no more than a yard away. Blood and brains and bits of the Negro's skull blew out. The black toppled and lay twitching in the dirt.

"That's telling him, Hank!" said the other C.S. trooper in butternut.

"I should've bayoneted him in the guts, let him die slow," Hank said. "Shooting's too good for a mad dog like that."

"If you can kill 'em fast, you better do it," Ward broke in. "I stuck one, stuck him good, and he's still on his feet, the son of a bitch."

"Niggers is like rattlesnakes—they don't die till sundown." Hank stirred the man he'd just shot with his foot. "Well, this here one's a goner. Bastard's dead as a stump. But Lord only knows when I'll get a chance to reload."

If you didn't carry a repeater or a revolver, that was the rub, especially in a close-quarters fight like this. If you fired too soon, you might come to a point where you desperately needed a bullet but didn't have one. If you waited too long, somebody on the other side was liable to shoot you before you pulled the trigger.

Without a minnie in his own rifle musket, the question was as academic for Ward as it was for Hank. When the Federals mounted a counterattack, he defended himself with bayonet and butt because they were all he had. He might have been one of Julius Caesar's legionaries, except their spears were lighter and longer and less clumsy than his.

But some of his comrades still had loaded weapons. They shot a couple of white officers, after which the Union charge faltered. "Come on!" Ward said. "There ain't enough of 'em to hold us out, no matter how hard they try!"

He waded into the fight. A white Tennessean in a blue uniform tried to bayonet him. He tried to bayonet the homemade Yankee at the same time. His bayonet punched into the enemy trooper's thigh. The Federal's thrust missed him. The Tennessean who fought for the U.S.A. yowled and sat down hard, trying to hold the wound closed with his fingers. Ward never found out what happened to him—whether he bled to death, whether some other Confederate killed him, or whether he ended up getting taken prisoner.

Ward also stopped worrying about what happened to the Tennessee Tory the instant after he bayoneted him. A great cheer rose from the Confederates, a hardly smaller moan of dismay from the Union troops.

The large U.S. flag that had floated over Fort Pillow since dawn's early light was down. If that didn't mean the fort was falling, nothing ever would.

Sergeant Ben Robinson groaned when the Stars and Stripes came down. That was his flag, not any of the ones the Confederates used: not the Stars and Bars, not the Stainless Banner that replaced it because from a distance it looked too much like the flag it sought to supplant, and not the Confederate battle flag with its blue **X** on red. If he belonged to the United States, he had a chance to be a man, an American, a person in his own right. If he belonged to the Confederate States, what was he but a slave, a piece of property, a *thing?* Nothing, nothing at all.

If he wasn't very lucky, he feared he would be a dead man soon. A glance at the sky told him the sun had hardly moved since the Secesh soldiers swarmed over the rampart. He wasn't Joshua, to hold it back in its course. The hand-to-hand fighting inside the earthwork hadn't lasted long—no more than fifteen minutes, twenty at the outside. It only seemed to go on forever.

Well, no matter how it seemed, it wouldn't last much longer. The colored artillerymen and Tennessee troopers inside the fort had done everything flesh and blood could do to hold out Forrest's men, and everything flesh and blood could do wasn't enough. Some people were saying thousands and thousands of Rebs had got into Fort Pillow. Robinson wasn't so sure about that. But he was sure there were more men in butternut and gray than in blue wherever he looked.

"What is we gonna do, Sergeant?" Sandy Cole shouted. He and Robinson and a few other Company D men, Nate Hunter and Charlie Key and Aaron Fentis, formed a little knot of stubborn resistance against the oncoming Confederate tide. Key had served the twelve-pounder; the other two Negroes hadn't. They were riflemen who'd fired over the earthwork at the Confederates. With the gun useless and the earthwork lost, they were all in the same boat. Yes, they were all in that boat, all right, and it was sinking.

"We got to fight," Robinson answered, bending to pick up a fist-sized rock and throw it at the nearest Rebel. "We don't fight, they kill us fo' sure."

None of the other colored soldiers could argue with that. Cries of "No quarter!" and "Black flag!" still rang out. Forrest's troopers were murdering Negroes who tried to lay down their arms and surrender. They were also murdering men from the Thirteenth Tennessee Cavalry who did the same thing. Their blood was up, and they cared about nothing but slaughter.

"Watch yourself, Aaron!" Charlie Key yelled. Aaron Fentis started to turn. He was a squat, broad-shouldered man, strong as an ox but not very fast. He didn't have a chance of knocking away the Confederate bayonet pointed straight at his midriff.

Ben Robinson did. He had a rifle musket of his own now, and swung it at the Reb's piece. The blow caught the weapon squarely and knocked it out of the enemy soldier's hands. Forrest's trooper let out a startled yelp. Aaron Fentis hit the Reb in the head with the butt of his Springfield at the same time as Robinson slammed his rifle-musket butt into the pit of the man's stomach. Down went the Confederate. Somebody stepped on him, shoving his face into the mud. He wouldn't get up soon, if he got up at all.

"We can lick 'em!" Sandy Cole shouted.

The small band of Negroes had licked all the Rebs who came at them. If the other men who garrisoned Fort Pillow could have done the same, the Secesh soldiers would be running away with their tails between their legs. And if pigs had wings . . .

Too many Rebs. That was what it came down to. Now that they were in the fort, the men in blue couldn't drive them out. Robinson knew one reason his little band of soldiers hadn't been badly tested was that they looked and acted tough. Forrest's men were no more eager to risk getting hurt than anybody else with an ounce of brains in his head. They went after people who were hurt or acted afraid. Once all the easy marks were down, they'd deal with the tougher ones.

Somebody close by was screaming for his mother. Ben Robinson couldn't tell if the cry came from a white throat or a black one, from a U.S. soldier or a Confederate. Badly hurt men all sounded pretty much the same. Maybe people should have drawn a lesson from that. In fact, he was sure they should have. He was also sure they didn't. If they did, mad scenes like this wouldn't happen.

"Kill the niggers!" bawled somebody else much too close. Unlike the other, that cry would only come from a Confederate.

"Kill the traitors!" That might have been somebody from the Thirteenth Tennessee Cavalry, but was much more likely also to come from a Reb. Forrest's troopers hated the men who fought under Major Bradford at least as much as they hated blacks. When Ben Robinson came to Fort Pillow, he wouldn't have believed that was possible. After listening to Bradford's troopers talk for a while, he did.

And, after listening to them, he also believed the Confederates had some pretty good reasons to hate them. Some of the things the troopers bragged about doing . . . Of course, they had their reasons for doing those things—they were avenging themselves for other things Forrest's men had done to them and their kind and their friends. How long would that cycle of vengeance go on? How long *could* it go on, before everybody killed off everybody else?

Without Ben's even noticing, Charlie Key managed to reload his

Springfield. When he fired, the muzzle of the piece couldn't have been more than six inches from Robinson's left ear. "Do Jesus!" Robinson yipped, and jumped in the air. "What you shooting at?"

"Damn Secesh bastard." Mournfully, the other colored soldier added, "I done missed the son of a bitch."

"Almos' didn't miss me." Robinson's head still rang. Even after he'd fired the twelve-pounder more times than he could count, that rifle musket made an appalling noise, all the worse because it was so unexpected.

"Shit," Sandy Cole said. "They's in behind us."

Ben Robinson swore, too. The line of soldiers in blue wasn't a line any more. It had broken down into little knots of struggling men, like the one of which he was a part. Each knot fought for itself. Not enough U.S. officers remained on their feet to make the Federals fight as a group any more. And they were going to get defeated in . . . What was the word? In detail, that was it. Robinson felt absurdly pleased with himself for remembering.

But how much good would remembering do him? How much good would anything do him, with the Rebs howling like wolves and his own side falling one man after another? He tried to knock the rifle musket out of another Confederate's hands. He failed—the Reb held on to it. But the man didn't seem quite so eager to gut him like a butchered hog. The way things were going, that was a triumph of sorts.

Major Bradford couldn't even mourn the loss of his brother, not unless he wanted people to be mourning him, too, and in short order. He ran now here, now there, trying to rally the Federal soldiers wherever he could. For a little while, he hoped they could hold Forrest's men out and drive them back.

For a little while, yes—but not for long.

No matter what he'd thought, Bedford Forrest was in deadly earnest when he said his troopers could take Fort Pillow. Between the sharpshooters on the high ground looking down into the fort and the swarm of Rebs coming over the earthen rampart, the garrison had no chance to hold back the tide, any more than King Canute could in days gone by.

When Bradford fired at an oncoming Confederate, he found he'd emptied Theodorick's Colt as well as his own. "Son of a bitch!" he shouted, and then, because that wasn't nearly strong enough, "Shit!"

He threw the revolver in the enemy soldier's face. Whatever the Reb was expecting, that wasn't it. The pistol caught him right in the nose. He shouted, "Shit!" too, much louder than Bradford had. Clutching both hands to the wounded member, he slowly crumpled.

Instead of reclaiming the pistol, Bradford snatched up the Springfield the Confederate had dropped. The Colt was just a lump of iron now. He'd never have the chance to load in bullets and measure out charges of black powder and affix a percussion cap for each cylinder he wanted to fire. With a bayoneted rifle, he carried a spear longer than a man was tall. That was something, anyhow.

Something, yes, but how much? The Federals' defense of Fort Pillow was coming to pieces before his eyes. Things were falling apart. The center could not hold, and the Confederates poured in on both flanks as well. The flag had fallen. In a few minutes, Forrest's men looked likely to kill or capture every Union soldier in the fort.

Biting his lip, Bradford shouted the order he'd hoped he wouldn't have to give: "Down to the river, men! Down to the Mississippi! If the Rebs come after us, the *New Era* will give them canister!"

The gunboat had kept firing all through the fight, even if her shells didn't do so much as Bradford wanted. She hadn't tried lobbing rounds up onto the flat ground atop the bluff, but Bradford could scarcely blame her for that. The shells could, and surely would, fall among his command as well as among the Rebs.

Even breaking contact with Forrest's troopers was hard. The howling men in gray and butternut were mixed in with their foes in blue. Soldiers thrust at one another and swung their Springfields like base ball bats. Whenever somebody managed to load a musket, he fired at the closest soldier in the uniform of the other color. Here and there, men rolled on the ground, kicking and kneeing and choking each other in a struggle old as time.

Little by little, whites and Negroes in blue made for the steep side of the bluff and started scrambling and tumbling down toward the Mississippi far below. If some of the Negroes ran—well, some of the white troopers from the Thirteenth Tennessee Cavalry ran, too. Who wouldn't, with sure death behind and possible salvation ahead?

Bradford wished he could do something about Theo's body. His brother lay where he had fallen. Dead men and writhing wounded lay everywhere inside the earthwork, testimony to how fierce the fighting was. If the Federals still held the fort when the battle was over, Bradford would have to bury poor Theodorick. If they didn't . . .

He shrugged. *If we don't, chances are somebody will have to bury me.*

A heartbeat later, he shrugged again. Even if the Federals held Fort Pillow, he might stop a minnie or get in the way of a Reb's bayonet. He'd worked hard to preserve the Union in western Tennessee and Kentucky. A lot of Forrest's troopers wanted to kill him not just because he was a Yankee officer. A lot of them carried personal grudges. Both as a lawyer and as an officer, he'd harried Rebs and their families as hard as he could. They had it coming, by God! But he couldn't expect Confederate soldiers to love him afterwards. He couldn't, and he didn't.

He carried the Springfield at high port: held diagonally in front of his chest, ready for a lunge or a parry. He wished he'd done more bayonet drill. Because they were cavalrymen, the troopers from the Thirteenth Tennessee had scanted that tiresome exercise, and the officers even more than the men.

The colored artillerymen seemed better at it than their white counterparts. He watched a colored sergeant keep a Reb off him with a few smooth-looking jabs and buttstrokes. The coons had rhythm, no doubt about it. Who would have imagined they could go toe-to-toe with men who might have owned some of them—who might, as a matter of law, still own some of them?

Bradford shook his head. That wasn't so: Lincoln's Emancipation Proclamation superseded what had been the law. When it was first issued, Bradford had no use for the Emancipation Proclamation. It seemed like a sop to Northern abolitionists and nothing more, because it freed slaves only in regions beyond the reach of Union forces. What did that do, except win the President political capital?

But the answer soon became clear. Federal troops might not be able to free Negroes through most of the Confederacy, but a great many slaves were able to free themselves by running off to the closest U.S. garrison. They voted with their feet against the South's peculiar institution.

Southerners still insisted Negroes were slaves by nature, and never could match up against whites on even terms. Maybe they were right. Though a strong Union man, Bill Bradford had always believed that himself. But what the Negroes here at Fort Pillow were doing was making him change his mind.

No, they and their white comrades couldn't keep Bedford Forrest's men out of the fort. But how many more men did Forrest have? And weren't those big black bucks fighting as well as the whites beside whom they stood? Bradford couldn't see that they weren't.

He also couldn't see that he could stay up here on top of the bluff much longer, not if he wanted to go on breathing. Keeping that Springfield between himself and the enemy, he fell back toward the slope that led down to the Mississippi.

Moving a gun was work for a team of mules or horses, not for men. Like the rest of the yelling, cheering Confederates with him, Matt Ward didn't give a damn. They swarmed over the twelve-pounder, literally manhandling it toward the edge of the bluff.

"We hit that son of a bitch of a gunboat a couple times, we'll kill it deader'n a cow that gets in front of a locomotive," somebody said.

More cheers rang out. Not one of the troopers shoving the cannon into place was an artilleryman; Forrest hadn't brought his batteries west against Fort Pillow. Considering the state of the roads the cavalry traveled, that had to be wise. But, like any soldiers, the troopers were convinced they could do anything. They had the gun. They had cannonballs. They had bags of powder. And they had a target. What more did they need?

"Look!" Ward's voice broke with excitement. "There's that stinking scow, just sitting in the water waiting for it. Let's give it to the damnyankees!"

"How?" somebody said. "Damn gun won't point so low."

"We lift the trail up, that'll bring the barrel down," Ward said.

Half a dozen Confederates suited action to work, grabbing the trail and, grunting with effort, lifting it into the air. Then a sergeant said, "That won't work, boys."

"Why not, goddammit?" one of them demanded irately.

"On account of you can't fire steady that way, and on account of the recoil'll run the gun carriage right on over you and squash you like a bunch of bugs," the sergeant answered. "Jesus God, you got to be dumber'n a nigger if you can't see stuff like that."

The trooper remained irate, but he couldn't very well argue because the sergeant was obviously right. "What'll we do, then?" he asked.

"Put stuff under the trail till it stays up and the barrel goes down," Ward said. He wouldn't have insulted the other Confederate the way the sergeant did, but the fellow wasn't what you'd call smart.

Enough "stuff" lay scattered across the grounds of Fort Pillow: boards, barrels, sandbags, what have you. Ward would have used bluebellies' bodies to prop up the trail, but nobody else seemed to want to do that. Even without bodies, they found plenty to depress the gun barrel.

They loaded a sack of powder into the muzzle of the gun. They didn't bother sponging it out first; if any bits of wadding were still smoldering, they might have been very sorry, but luck stayed with them. Somebody shoved a twelve-pound iron ball into the muzzle and rammed it down toward the end of the bore. And someone else, igno-

rant of friction primers, stuck a burning splinter in the touch-hole. . . .
Matt Ward wasn't the only one who jammed his fingers in his ears.

But nothing happened.

"Hang on," the sergeant said. "You got to prick the bag so the powder's loose and the flame can get at it."

Artillerymen, no doubt, had a special iron tool to do just that. Forrest's troopers had to improvise—and they did. Several of them carried horseshoe nails and hoof picks in their pockets. One of those proved long enough and straight enough to do the job. Then Matt Ward put a percussion cap over the vent. "Somebody whack it with a rock!" he said. "If that won't set the blamed thing off, I'm a nigger."

"I'll do it," the sergeant said. "We aimed at that son of a bitch?" He looked down the barrel of the gun, then nodded. "Oh, yeah." He smacked the cap not with a rock but with a hammer he'd picked up God knew where.

Boom! The twelve-pounder's roar was a truly impressive noise. Flame and a great, choking cloud of smoke belched from the muzzle of the gun. Cannon, carriage, and all jerked backward, knocking down the ramshackle support the troopers built under the trail. The sergeant had to spring to one side to keep from getting run over, just as he'd warned the men who wanted to hold the trail up by hand.

They missed the Yankee gunboat. The cannonball kicked up a truly impressive splash about fifty feet behind it and well to its left. There were probably fancy nautical terms to describe that better, but Ward neither knew them nor cared about them. All he knew was, the miserable gunboat still floated.

Several troopers cussed. "We shot the stinking gun once," Ward said. "We can damn well do it again, right?"

"That's the spirit!" the sergeant said. "And even if we did miss, we let those damnyankee bastards down there know this here fort's got it some new owners, right?"

"Right!" the troopers shouted. Maybe they really were heartened. Maybe they just knew better than to argue with anybody who wore three stripes on his sleeve. Under his profane direction, they shoved the twelve-pounder back to the very edge of the bluff. Getting it ready to fire again didn't take so long. Now they had some idea of what they were doing.

They thought so, anyhow. The colored artillerymen whose captured gun they served would have laughed themselves silly. Those colored artillerymen never once entered Ward's mind. Like the rest of the cavalry troopers at the gun, he was intent on the gunboat down in the river.

The sergeant walloped another percussion cap. Again, the cannon bellowed. A gust blew some of the smoke into Ward's face. He coughed and wiped his streaming eyes on his sleeve. More curses erupted from his comrades. This cannonball went into the Mississippi about as far ahead of its intended target as the other one was behind it.

"Well, we scared 'em, by God," Ward said.

"We can still hit that damn thing." The sergeant had no quit in him. "All we've got to do is split the difference between those two. We do that, we put a cannonball right through the blamed boat's brisket."

He seemed to think his makeshift gun crew had the skill to split the difference. Real artillerymen would have, no doubt about it. The Negroes who'd been driven from the gun would have. This swarm of Forrest's troopers? They had enthusiasm and very little else.

They did load the twelve-pounder again. Jostling one another to peer down the barrel, they tried their best to aim the field piece at the gunboat—and to hold it on target with that flimsy pile of stuff raising the trail and depressing the muzzle.

"Here we go! This time for sure!" the sergeant shouted, and brought the hammer down on a third percussion cap.

Fire. Smoke. Thunder. The iron shot splashed into the Mississippi at least as far from its target as either of the earlier two. "Hell's bells!" somebody said in disgust. "We can see the son of a bitch down there. Why in blazes can't we hit it?"

"She," said somebody who fancied himself an expert on things that had to do with ships. "Boats are always *she.*"

"She's a goddamn bitch, is what she is. She don't hold still for nobody," another trooper said.

"Sounds like a woman, all right," Ward said. His own experience in such things was limited—he'd been kissed twice, not counting cousins—but he got a laugh.

"Let's try again, boys." Yes, the sergeant who'd taken charge of the twelve-pounder was as stubborn as they came.

No matter how stubborn he was, three misses made his crew start melting away. "Hell with it," a trooper said as he stooped to pick up his carbine. "I'm gonna go shoot me some niggers and Tennessee Tories. I can damn well hit them bastards."

"That's right." Ward grabbed his Enfield, too. "I know how to aim this critter."

The sergeant squawked, but they all went farther along the edge of the cliff till they looked down on the soldiers in blue scrambling down toward the riverbank. Ward raised the rifle musket and aimed at a white man descending feet first. The homemade Yankee saw him and waved desperately. "Don't shoot!" he cried. "I ain't done nothin' to you!"

Killing a man in the heat of battle was one thing. Killing a man in cold blood, killing a man begging for his life, killing a defenseless man—for the trooper in blue had dropped his piece—proved something else again. With a swallowed obscenity, Matt swung the Enfield away from the other man.

Not all the bluebellies going down the slope and already at the bottom had given up. A soldier down there fired at Ward. He didn't know how to gauge such a steep uphill shot, and the minnie slapped into the mud about ten feet below the Confederate.

If I don't kill 'em, they'll kill me, Ward thought. He aimed at a Negro. This time, nothing stayed his trigger finger. The ball caught the black in the short ribs. Although the runaway slave—for what else could he be?—was halfway down toward the Mississippi, the howl he let out reached Ward up on the bluff. The black rolled and tumbled all the way down to the riverbank.

"Nice shot!" another Confederate trooper said. "He looked just like one o' them clowns in the circus, way he turned somersets there."

"He did, didn't he?" Ward paused in reloading, though not for long—his hands knew what to do even without direction. "Let's see if I can get me another coon like that."

"Well, it ain't like we don't have plenty to pick from," said the other soldier in butternut.

"Yeah." Ward brought the loaded Enfield up to his shoulder and found another target.

A colored soldier rolled past Sergeant Ben Robinson. The man was groaning and trying to clutch at his chest, but his arms and legs kept flying out every which way. "Poor bastard," Sandy Cole said. "He ain't dead yet, he gonna be by the time he fetch up 'longside the river."

"Ain't it the truth?" Robinson said. A Minié ball cracked past his head. A few inches lower and he would have rolled and slid all the way down to the Mississippi, too. The only difference was, nobody would have wondered if he was dead.

Aaron Fentis looked up the slope to the top of the bluff, where Bedford Forrest's troopers were taking potshots at the whites and Negroes below them. "Why the hell those officers of our'n want us to come down here?" he demanded. "Dem Secesh sojers, dey shoot us down like we was so many wild turkeys."

"They say the gunboat keep the Rebs off us," Robinson said.

"Dey say, dey say." Fentis's voice went high and mocking. "I say dey don' know what dey talkin' 'bout. Dey say we hold out Forrest, too. Was dey right? How much good dat damn gunboat do us up till now? Any a-tall? I ain't seen it. You seen it, Sergeant?" Even in disaster, he remembered to stay respectful to Ben Robinson's chevrons.

He should have stayed respectful to the white officers in command at Fort Pillow, too. Robinson should have reproved him for not sounding respectful enough. He knew he should, but couldn't make himself do it. Aaron Fentis might be disrespectful, but that didn't mean he was wrong. The whites in command at Fort Pillow hadn't known what was going on. Well, maybe Major Booth had, but he got killed too soon for it to matter. Since then . . .

Robinson wouldn't have wanted to surrender to the Confederates, even if they did offer to treat Negroes as prisoners of war. But he'd thought, as Major Bradford had thought, that Fort Pillow could hold. That turned out to be mistaken. And now there was no talk of taking anybody prisoner, colored man or white. The Rebs kept yelling, "Black flag!" and firing away for all they were worth.

"Maybe they stop killin' people if we surrender now," Charlie Key said.

"Who kin do it?" Robinson asked bleakly. "Major Booth, he dead. Major Bradford, he want to go on fightin'."

"He git killed, he go on fightin' much longer," Key said. "Then somebody else kin tell the Rebs we is givin' up." He paused, then added, "Do Jesus, I surrender right now if I don't reckon they shoot me dead fo' tryin'."

That was defeatism. Sergeant Robinson knew he shouldn't let anybody get away with it. In happier times, he wouldn't have. But how could you blame a man for defeatism after you were defeated? If scrambling down toward the riverbank with Confederate soldiers shooting at you from above wasn't defeat, Robinson didn't want to find out what was.

If he thought some Reb would let him give up, he supposed he would throw down his Springfield, too. He'd done everything he could reasonably do to defend the fort. But getting anyone in butternut to accept a black man's surrender wouldn't be easy—and might not be possible.

If the Federals couldn't quit, they had to go on fighting. But Robinson couldn't even do that, not now. No Confederate soldiers were within bayonet reach, and he had no cartridges for the rifle musket he'd picked up. He wondered if any of the Union soldiers going down toward the riverbank carried more than a handful of ammunition.

But no sooner had that thought crossed his mind than a white man below him yelled, "You need to shoot back at the stinkin' Rebs, get over here! We got us crates and crates of cartridges."

"Major Bradford, he done thought o' *somethin'*, anyways," Sandy Cole said.

"I reckon," Robinson said. "Reckon that make once, too."

Was he bitter? Just because everything Bradford tried turned out to be wrong? For a moment, he tried to deny it even to himself. He wondered why, when it was so plainly true. Only one thing occurred to him: that as a black man, he had no right to criticize what a white man did.

"Hell I don't," he muttered. What that white man did was altogether too likely to get him killed. Was a damn fool any less a damn fool because he was white? Whites seemed to think so, or at least to believe a damn fool was more a damn fool if he happened to be black.

There were black damn fools. Robinson had known enough of them to have no doubts about that. But there were white damn fools, too. And if one of them wore oak leaves on his shoulders, he could be a damn fool on a scale most Negroes only dreamt of.

Robinson awkwardly made his way down toward the crates of cartridges. If he had to go on fighting, he would make the best fight he could. He was clumsy loading the Springfield, too; most of his training was as an artilleryman, not a foot soldier.

He'd just finished setting a percussion cap on the nipple when a burst of fire came from farther south along the riverbank. Panic swept through him. If the Rebs were shooting at the garrison from there as well as from the top of the bluff, the surviving Federals wouldn't last long. But not many minnies tore into the Negroes and whites in blue uniforms.

Instead, bullets clattered off the gunboat's iron sides. They sounded like hail on a tin roof. For a moment, Robinson wondered what good they would do the Rebs. Ironclads were supposed to be proof against cannonballs, let alone Minié balls.

But then a white soldier standing not far away said, "Fuck me if I'd want to raise the gunports with the Rebs putting that much lead in the air. You do, you'll catch a bullet with your teeth."

"They don't open them ports; they can't shoot!" Robinson exclaimed. "They can't shoot, they don't do us no good."

"You noticed that, did you?" the white trooper said. "Nothin' gets by you, does it, boy?"

Normally, that *boy* would have infuriated Robinson, the more so since he outranked the white. Now he was too appalled to call the other man on it. If Major Bradford was wrong about this . . . *We all die,* the colored sergeant thought numbly.

Up on top of the bluff, a cannon boomed. It hadn't fired for some time, but now the Rebs had got it loaded again. A ball splashed into the water not far from the gunboat. That wasn't great shooting, but it didn't need to be. If the amateur gunners up there—they couldn't be anything else—kept on, sooner or later they might hit. How well armored was the gunboat against fire from above? Ben Robinson had no idea.

Maybe the gunboat's captain didn't, either. And maybe he didn't want to find out. Black smoke poured out of the stack. The gunboat began to move—not toward the riverbank to blast the Confederates and rescue Fort Pillow's embattled garrison, but north, up the Mississippi, away from danger.

"You yellow-bellied son of a bitch bastard!" the white man howled. Robinson nodded helplessly. The gunboat paid no attention to either one of them. Away she steamed, faster and faster.

X

WHEN BILL BRADFORD WATCHED THE *New Era* steam up the Mississippi, he felt like . . . He didn't know what he felt like. Like a man whose intended bride jilted him at the altar? Something like that, maybe. But a jilted bridegroom didn't die at the altar. He just wished he could.

The men defending Fort Pillow, on the other hand . . . Captain James Marshall, the commanding officer aboard the *New Era,* must have decided his gunboat couldn't stand the fire from the riverbank and the cannonballs from the artillery captured up on the bluff. He saw to the safety of his own men. He saw to their safety, yes—but he left the garrison to its fate.

A panicked trooper from the Thirteenth Tennessee Cavalry clutched at Bradford's sleeve and shouted, "What the hell do we do now, sir?" An equally panicked colored artilleryman all but screamed the same question at him.

"Boys, save your lives," Bradford said numbly. "I don't know what else to tell you." He didn't know how to tell them to save their lives. He didn't know how to save his own life, either. The terror that filled the soldiers took root in his own heart, too. What to do? What to do?

From the south came the exultant whoops and jeers of the Confederate cavalrymen who'd forced the *New Era* to flee. "Yellowbellies!" they yelled, and "Cowards!" and "You stinking, gutless sons of bitches!" Hearing the enemy shout exactly what he was thinking was as humiliating an experience as Major Bradford had ever known.

Save your lives. It was easy to say. With Bedford Forrest's troopers already shooting down at the Federals from the top of the bluff, with those Secesh soldiers whooping and jeering by the river, it wouldn't be easy to do. He wondered if the Rebs would accept surrenders now. Part of him wished he'd taken Forrest's offer while he had the chance. Forrest was known for ploys and tricks, but he wasn't fooling this time. Bradford wished he had been.

Yellowbellied coward, Bradford thought furiously. *Stinking son of a bitch.* He stared across the muddy waters of the Mississippi at the receding *New Era*. If he ever met Captain Marshall again, he didn't think God Himself could keep him from punching the gunboat's skipper in the nose. And if Marshall felt inclined to resent that, Bradford was ready to go as much further as the Navy man cared to.

Bradford laughed a bitter laugh. He knew he wasn't a particularly brave man. He did his best to hide that, from others and perhaps most of all from himself, but he knew it. All the same, the prospect of a fight, or even a duel, with James Marshall worried him not a bit. He knew why, too. It was what he would have called a hypothetical question in the courtroom. A lot of things would have to happen for him to face Marshall again. Chief among them was his living through the combat here. And the chances of that didn't look good.

Some of the men still had fight in them. They grabbed cartridges from the crates Bradford had ordered brought here and fired at the closest Confederates. Major Bradford would have expected his white cavalry troopers to show more spirit than the colored artillerymen. The colored soldiers were only niggers in uniform, after all. He would have expected that, but he would have been wrong. Some blacks were terrified and despairing, yes, but so were some whites. The proportions seemed about the same in men of both races.

What that meant . . . was as hypothetical as punching James Marshall in the nose. If Bradford got out of this, he could worry about it later. If he didn't get out of this, he wouldn't worry about anything later.

"Ain't gonna give up to no Secesh sojers," said a colored sergeant ramming a Minié ball down the muzzle of his Springfield. "Even if them fuckers don't shoot me fo' the fun of it, reckon they sell me later. Ain't gonna be no slave again."

Not many of the troopers from Bradford's own regiment showed anything close to that kind of spirit. The white major stared at the black underofficer. Bradford's own opinion of Negroes wasn't that far from Nathan Bedford Forrest's or any other Confederate's. He thought they made good slaves, bad freemen, and worse soldiers. He favored the U.S.A. because he didn't want to see the country broken in two—and because several prominent men in west Tennessee with whom he didn't get along well went all-out for secession. He'd paid them back ten times over. But he was worse then indifferent toward Negro rights; he was downright hostile, and didn't care who knew it.

Or he hadn't cared who knew it. He didn't think he would be smart to go on about niggers and coons where that grimly determined sergeant could hear him. The way the blacks in Fort Pillow fought had surprised him. The way the colored sergeant was ready to go on fighting no matter how bad things looked astonished him.

If we were wrong all along about what Negroes can do, then it doesn't matter if the Confederates win this fight, he thought. *It doesn't even matter if they win this war. Sooner or later, their cause is doomed, and it will fall to pieces. It has to, because it rests on lies.*

On a cosmic level, that might well be so. Back here in the mud by the edge of the Mississippi, who won and who lost mattered very much, because it told who lived and who died. Some of the Federals started south along the riverbank, perhaps hoping to get past the Confederate troopers who'd helped drive off the *New Era.*

A couple of them looked back at him, as if wondering if he would try to stop them. He didn't. For one thing, he wasn't sure they would obey him. Why should they, when his orders had led them to their present sorry state? For another, he wasn't sure they were wrong. What were they supposed to do, wait here for Bedford Forrest's troopers to shoot them to pieces? Certain disaster lay down that road. Maybe, if they pushed hard . . .

And maybe not, too. Every choice Bill Bradford made that day, even keeping his mouth shut, proved wrong. The men in blue fired a few shots—hardly enough to dignify with the name of *volley*—at the Confederates. The roar of musketry that answered sent them reeling back in dismay. Some bled. Some limped. Some didn't even reel, but lay dead or badly wounded by the river.

"They're coming!" a white Federal screamed. "They're on our tails!"

"Dey gwine kill all o' we!" shrieked a Negro beside him. The black's terror and his thick accent made the words almost incomprehensible. But no one could misunderstand the fear that made him push through the crowd of soldiers, that made him throw away his Springfield to run the faster.

And the panic from the men who'd taken that blast of musket fire—and the whoops and Rebel yells from the Confederates who were indeed on their tails—stampeded the rest of the Union troops into motion. What point waiting here for the massacre they all saw ahead? The *New Era* wouldn't rescue them now—they all saw that, too. And so, more a mob, a herd, than anything resembling soldiery, they pelted north, toward where Coal Creek ran into the Mississippi.

One more spooked steer, Bill Bradford ran along with the rest.

A few of the men in Colonel Barteau's regiment along Coal Creek fired at the Federal gunboat as it steamed away from the fight. "No, goddammit! Don't waste your ammunition!" Corporal Jack Jenkins roared, along with other underofficers and officers. "Jesus Christ!" he went on. "You can't hit the son of a bitch at this range, and even if you could, so what? She's iron-plated, for cryin' out loud."

"Have a heart, Corporal," a trooper said. "Damn boat's been shootin' at us all day long. Least we can do is pay her back a little."

"Blow 'em a kiss. Wave bye-bye." Jenkins suited action to word. "Bastard's gone. That's all we've got to worry about. Now reload your damn piece, and don't go shooting at anything till you got somethin' to shoot at."

The private scowled. He muttered. But not only did Jenkins have two stripes on his sleeve, he was also taller and wider through the shoulders and, without a doubt, meaner. If the soldier tried to give trouble, he'd end up getting it instead. He might be a grumbler, but he wasn't a fool. He could see that for himself. And he did need to reload, regardless of whether he needed somebody to tell him to do it. He went right on muttering, but he followed Jenkins's order.

And Jenkins was happy enough to leave it right there. Getting troopers to do what you told them was a never-ending pain in the neck. They always thought they had a better idea, and they were bound and determined to go ahead with it no matter what.

He wondered if he was such a pest before he got promoted. A reminiscent smile stole over his face. He was. Not a chance anyone ever set over him would say anything different. He wondered how sergeants and officers ever put up with him. But the answer to that wasn't hard to find. No matter how big a nuisance he'd been, without even trying he could think of a dozen men who were worse.

"What do we do now?" somebody asked.

"There's damnyankees round the bend of the bluff, down by the Mississippi. You can hear the bastards," somebody else said. "Let's go kill 'em. Them bastards what went up into the fort, they've had all the fun."

Jenkins felt the same way. But a nearby lieutenant shook his head. "We'll just sit tight for a little while, is what we'll do. Aren't a whole hell of a lot of us. We might bite off a bigger chaw than we can get in our cheek."

"Aw, hell sir." Jenkins was still a pain in the neck, whether he realized it or not. "They ain't *real* Yankee soldiers, not hardly. Nothin' but

Tennessee Tories and niggers in blue shirts. One of us has to be worth ... well, a bunch of 'em, anyways."

"I said no." The officer got stuffy, the way officers have since the beginning of time. "If they get through us, it's liable to give them an escape route. Do you want to see that happen?"

"No, sir," Jenkins allowed. He knew how things worked. As long as he kept saying *sir,* he could get away with saying anything else he pleased, near enough. "But they ain't gonna get through us, sir. No way on God's green earth they can do that. You reckon niggers can fight better'n us . . . sir?" If the lieutenant said yes to that, he'd have a fight on his hands even if he did wear two bars on each side of his collar.

But the lieutenant shook his head. "No, no, no—of course not," he said impatiently. "Up till this combat, I wouldn't've reckoned niggers could fight at all: fight like soldiers, I mean." He sounded faintly, or maybe more than faintly, troubled at having to admit even that much, and more troubled as he went on, "They've done better than anybody imagined they could, I'm afraid."

"Well, I'm not afraid, sir. To hell with 'em. To hell with 'em all, and with the homemade Yankees, too," Jenkins said. "Way they were scornin' us and cursin' us during the truce, they must've thought they were somethin' special. They ain't special enough, by Jesus, and they don't fight good enough, neither."

"That's the spirit, Corporal," the lieutenant said. "Don't let anything bother you, do you?"

"Not if I can help it, sir," Jenkins said. "Anything in a blue uniform does bother me, reckon I've got an answer, too." He held up his rifle musket.

The officer smiled. "Good. If it weren't for you and soldiers like you, we'd never get ourselves a free Confederacy."

"Well, hell. We'll manage." Jenkins had as much faith in that as he did in the Resurrection and the Second Coming. "Ain't we whipping the damnyankees out of their shoes here?" He hoped he found a dead Federal with feet his size. His own shoes were falling to pieces.

Around the bend, on the Mississippi River side of the bluff, the gunfire suddenly picked up. So did the shouts and yells. Jenkins had listened with much amusement to the Federals' cries of dismay when their precious gunboat left them in the lurch. After it steamed away, the coons and the homemade Yankees quieted down for a while. Now the fighting picked up again. And by the way the Federals moaned and wailed, things weren't going any too well for them. The Rebel yells that also rang out said those other Confederates on the far side of the enemy were having fun.

And the Federals were heading this way: the shouts were getting louder. For the first time, they also sounded frightened. Gauging things by ear—which was all he could do—Jenkins thought the Federals had put up a pretty fair fight until now. But the men heading this way didn't sound like soldiers under control. They seemed like men who'd had everything they could take, and a little more besides.

Any Union soldier who saw Jack Jenkins's smile would no doubt have called it nasty. No matter how much the bluebellies had taken, they were about to get some more.

"You see, boys?" that know-it-all lieutenant sang out. "We didn't need to go to the fight. It's coming right to us. Y'all ready to give those Federals a little taste of Southern hospitality?"

"We'll give 'em just what they deserve, by God!" Jenkins said, and the lieutenant didn't grumble or fuss one bit. He only nodded. And his smile was every bit as predatory as the corporal's.

"Here they come!" Half a dozen troopers sang out at the same time as the Federals rushed up to Coal Creek and started away from the Mississippi along its southern bank.

They didn't find the safety they hoped for. They were in no kind of order, and didn't seem to be under any officers' control. Jenkins shot the lieutenant a glance of mingled annoyance and respect. Maybe the men who told ordinary soldiers what to do had some uses after all. Maybe.

"Let 'em get close," the lieutenant said now. "Let 'em get close, and then give 'em a good volley at my command. May I face eternal damnation if we don't break those sons of bitches. Hold your fire till I give the order, y'all hear?"

Nobody said no. Even more to the point, nobody started shooting. On came the men in blue. Their "Hurrah!" made a poor excuse for a battle cry, but they used it when they were in good spirits. They weren't cheering now—oh, no. Some of them skidded to a stop when they saw a line of Confederates in front of them. Others kept coming—not so much because they were eager to attack, Jenkins judged, as because they didn't know what else to do.

Only a handful of Federals raised Springfields to their shoulders and fired, trying to clear the way of Bedford Forrest's men. One luckless Confederate howled and crumpled, clutching at a shattered knee.

"At my order . . . ," the lieutenant said, and then, "*Fire!*"

Jenkins's rifle musket bucked against his shoulder. Smoke and flames belched from the muzzle. He took off his hat and fanned the air in front of him, trying to clear it enough to see not just through his own piece's smoke but that from the rest of the rifle muskets as well. The Union charge, such as it was, shattered like crockery on a big rock. Only eight or ten men in blue were down, but even the ones who didn't take a minnie felt the Angel of Death brush them with his dark wings.

"Charge!" the lieutenant shouted. A revolver in one hand and his ceremonial saber in the other, he set his own example.

Against determined foes, it would have been madness. It would have been suicide. But the Federals had no fight left in them. Some turned and pelted back in the direction from which they'd come. Others threw down their guns and tried to surrender.

Sometimes that worked, sometimes it didn't. Jack Jenkins saw some of his comrades send Federals back toward the rear—often with a kick in the rear as they went. Others shot men in blue uniforms at point-blank range or bayoneted them even as they got down on their knees and begged for mercy.

"Don't shoot! Sweet Jesus, please don't shoot!" a Federal sergeant called to Jenkins. He held out empty hands. "See? I ain't got no gun."

He also didn't have an accent like Jenkins's. He was no Tennessean, no homemade Yankee. He really did come from up North; he seemed to pronounce every letter in every word. And that likely meant . . . "You one of those fellows who tell nigger soldiers what to do?" Jenkins barked.

"Yes, that's right," the sergeant answered. "But—"

He got no further. Jenkins pulled the trigger. The minnie caught the Yankee right in the middle of the chest. The man stared in astonished reproach for a moment, as if to say, *What did you have to go and do that for?* He opened his mouth, as if to ask the question. His knees buckled instead. He flopped and thrashed on the ground like a sunfish just pulled from a stream.

"Hold still, God damn you," Jenkins said, and used his bayonet. He stabbed several times, till the U.S. sergeant finally stopped moving. "You turn niggers into soldiers, you deserve worse'n I just gave you."

No sooner were the words out of his mouth than a bullet cracked past his head. For all he knew, a colored soldier fired it. He reloaded his own piece in feverish haste. He felt naked if he couldn't shoot back at the enemy. Some Yankee cavalrymen and even foot soldiers were getting repeating rifles that gave a company almost a regiment's worth of firepower. He thanked heaven nobody in Fort Pillow seemed to have guns like that. The lead they put in the air would have made storming the place gruesomely, maybe impossibly, expensive.

As he stowed his ramrod in its tube under the rifle musket's barrel, he wondered why the Confederacy couldn't make repeating rifles for *its* troopers. U.S. soldiers weren't any braver than their C.S. counterparts; with his own fierce pride, Jenkins refused to believe they were as brave. But the Federals would never lose the war because they ran short on things. Guns, ammunition, uniforms, railroads to take men where they needed to go, gunboats . . . The men in blue seemed to pull such things out of their back pockets, along with more food than they knew what to do with.

As for the Confederates . . . How many of Bedford Forrest's men were wearing captured clothing? Quite a few had blue trousers. A standing order required shirts to be dyed butternut right away, to keep the troopers from shooting at one another by mistake. A lot of Confederates carried captured weapons, too. The South simply couldn't make or bring in enough to meet its need.

Before the war, Southerners sneered at Yankees as nothing more than merchants and factory hands. The charge was true enough. But the South hadn't realized it brought strengths as well as weaknesses. Men fought wars, but they fought them with things. No matter how brave you were, you'd lose if you didn't have food in your belly, if you didn't have bullets in your rifle musket, if you didn't have gunboats to control the rivers. The Federals didn't have to worry about anything like that. The Confederates did, more and more as the fight dragged on.

But not right here, not right now. Forrest's motto was *Get there first with the most men.* He had the most men here, right where he needed them, and the Federals were melting away like snow in the hot sun.

A Negro running in front of Jenkins gave a despairing screech, threw his hands in the air, and wailed, "Do Jesus, don't kill me! I ain't done nothin' to nobody!"

"You one of those niggers yellin' you wouldn't give us quarter?" Jenkins growled.

"Oh, no, suh, not me! I ain't one o' them bad niggers!" The black man shook his head so hard, his cap flew off and fell to the ground beside him. He didn't seem to notice; all his fearful attention was on Jenkins. "I don't want to fight no mo'."

"I bet you don't, boy," Jenkins said. "You a runaway?"

The Negro hesitated. If he said no, the way he talked would betray him—he sounded like someone from the deep South, from South Carolina or Georgia or Alabama or Mississippi. But if he said yes, he was liable to seal his own fate. Jenkins could watch the gears meshing and turning behind his eyes. In the end, all he said was, "Don't kill me, suh. I surrender."

"You had your chance. All of you bastards had your chance. You should've took it when you could." Jenkins squeezed the trigger.

Even he winced at what the Minié ball did. It tore off the bottom half of the black man's face, leaving him gobbling and bleating because he could no longer make sounds resembling human speech. Blood poured down his front. But he would not fall. He would not die. He slumped to his knees and imploringly stretched out his hands to Jenkins. His eyes were enormous in his shattered face.

"Christ!" That was the Confederate lieutenant. He shot the colored soldier in the side of his head with his revolver. The Negro didn't try to stop him—the poor bastard's last gobble before he toppled over might have been meant *Thank you.* The lieutenant shook his head. "I wouldn't let a dog live with a wound like that, Corporal."

"I'm sorry, sir," Jenkins answered; it was horrific enough to sober him, which said a great deal. "I was gonna finish the son of a bitch. I had to reload, that's all." He was doing it as he spoke. He forgot—or maybe he chose not to remember—that he'd bayoneted the white Tennessean after his bullet didn't finish the man right away.

"Well . . . let it go," the lieutenant said. "Stinking bluebellies didn't give up when they had the chance. Now they're going to pay for it."

"Oh, hell, yes." There Jack Jenkins agreed with the officer one hundred percent. He stowed his ramrod and went back to the fight.

The smoke from the *New Era*'s stacks was only a receding stain against the northern skyline. Nathan Bedford Forrest smiled a slow smile, the smile of a big cat that has fed well. The Federals inside Fort Pillow had surely counted on the gunboat's firepower to save their bacon for them. There had to be a great wailing and gnashing of teeth among them now, for they'd leaned on a reed that broke and pierced their hand.

Gunboats were wonderful—where the Mississippi was wide, and

where they could shell soldiers who couldn't answer back with rifle muskets. If a gunboat came close enough to fire canister, though, good shots could put enough minnies through the gunports to remind them that the fight had two sides. Sailors didn't like being forced to remember that.

Now the *New Era* was gone, and Fort Pillow was gone, and nothing remained but the aftermath Forrest foresaw as soon as the U.S. commander refused to lower his flag. *War means fighting, and fighting means killing,* he thought with somber satisfaction. Quite a few generals on both sides shied away from that simple, brutal truth. He didn't. He never had. You did what you needed to do.

And now his men were . . . doing what they needed to do. He was abstractly sorry they were, but knew better than to try to stop them. Nothing so corroded an officer's authority as giving orders no one heeded. If he tried to stop the soldiers from paying back the Federals, they wouldn't listen to him. And so he hung back from the fighting, where usually he led the charge.

Some of the Federals were able to surrender. Grinning troopers herded white soldiers along—and some blacks as well. When the prisoners didn't move fast enough to suit them, a prod with the bayonet worked as well as spurs on a horse.

One of the soldiers in blue, a Negro, waved to Forrest. "I knows you, General," he called. "I knows you, sure as anything."

"Wouldn't be surprised," Forrest answered—the black man looked familiar to him, though he couldn't put a name on the fellow. "You come through my nigger lots down in Memphis?"

"Yes, suh, I done that," the black answered. "I done that a couple times, matter of fact."

Bedford Forrest believed it. A slave who was sold more than once was liable, even likely, to be an uppity nigger, and one who was likely to run off and make trouble. Putting on the U.S. uniform, this one had made as much trouble as he could. Eyes narrowing in concentration, Forrest said, "I still don't recollect your name, but the last time I sold you I got . . . let me see . . . twenty-one hundred dollars for your worthless nigger carcass." He spoke without malice; he might have described a good horse as crowbait the same way.

"That's my price, all right." The Negro's voice held a certain pride, too—it was a good price, a damn good price. Then the man did a double take and stared at Bedford Forrest. "How you remember? How many niggers you done sold since I go through there six, seven years ago?"

"Selling niggers is my business," Forrest said. "I better remember—I'm in trouble if I don't. I wouldn't have got such a good price for you if you didn't have good teeth—I remember that, too. They still sound?"

"Sure enough are, suh." The colored soldier's eyes got wider yet. "Do Jesus! You mus' be some kind o' hoodoo man, you call to mind a thing like that."

"Not me." Bedford Forrest's smile was half reminiscent and, again, half predatory. "Like I say, I've got to remember those things. When I came to Memphis, I didn't have fifty cents in my pockets. When the war started, though, I don't know if I was the richest man there, but hell with me if I can name four who were richer. And I got that way buying and selling niggers. What do you do when you're not trying to murder your masters?"

"I's a carpenter, suh," the black man said. By the way he said it, he was a good carpenter, too, someone who took pains with his work.

That suited Forrest fine. "All right, then," he said. "You'll know when to use oak and when to use pine, when to use nails and when to cut mortises and tenons, what kind of shellac to use, how to match grains—all those kinds of things. That's your business, so sure you know. Well, niggers are my business."

In spite of himself, a certain sour edge touched his voice. No matter how rich he'd grown in Memphis, some people looked down their noses at him because he was a slave trader. That didn't keep them from buying and selling with him. Oh, no. He was useful. But he wasn't welcome in some homes no matter how much money he made.

Hell with 'em, he thought. He'd grown up on a hardscrabble farm, and lost his father while he was still young. He'd had to be the man in his large family himself then, and he'd damn well done it. If the men who owned slaves didn't care for the men who sold them, what did that prove? Only that they were fools. It was like despising the butcher while you ate his beefsteaks.

"Your sojers damn near kill me," the Negro said.

"That's what you get for tryin' to fight white men," Forrest retorted.

"No, suh. I knows about fightin'," the colored artilleryman said. "They killin' lots o' Federals tryin' to give up. Onliest reason I didn't get shot is, trooper who catched me didn't have no bullet in his gun. I was *tryin'* to surrender, honest to God I was."

"Too bad." Bedford Forrest's voice went cold and hard. "I *told* Major Booth I could take that stupid fort. I *told* him he'd pay the price if he didn't give up. He wouldn't listen. Now he is paying the price, and so are you."

"He done paid it, suh. Major Booth, he dead—he got kilt this mornin', 'fo' noon."

"Oh, really?" Forrest heard the surprise that got into his voice in spite of himself. The Negro nodded solemnly. "Then who led the garrison there?" the Confederate commander asked.

"Major Bradford, he been in charge o' things ever since Major Booth die."

"Bradford? That miserable little son of a bitch?" Forrest growled; the head of the Thirteenth Tennessee Cavalry (U.S.) was not one of his favorite people, to put it mildly. The colored soldier nodded again. Forrest aimed a scarred forefinger at him like a pistol barrel. "You say Booth's been dead since before twelve o'clock?"

"Two-three hours 'fo' that, suh. Cross my heart an' hope to die." The Negro matched action to word.

"When we had the truce this afternoon before my men stormed the fort, every single note—every one—the Federals sent out to me had Booth's name on it," Forrest said.

With a shrug, the black man answered, "I don't know nothin' 'bout that, suh. I's jus' powerful glad to be alive."

"And you'll stay alive," Forrest promised. "You told me something I didn't know—something I needed to know, by God. I wish I would've known it sooner, that's all." He stabbed out his index finger again. "What's your name?"

"I's Hiram Lumpkin, suh."

Bedford Forrest laughed. "To hell with me if I know how I ever forgot *that*." He raised his voice to a shout: "Guards! This here nigger, this Hiram Lumpkin"—he spoke the name with enormous relish—"he just did me a favor. Y'all make sure you treat him good. I hear anything happened to him, it'll happen to you, too, only worse. You got that?"

"Yes, sir!" the Confederates chorused. Union troops didn't faze them. Their own fierce leader? That was a different story.

The Negro in blue saluted as if Forrest were one of his own officers. "Thank you kindly, suh. This here nigger, he right grateful."

"Go on, then," Forrest said, and Hiram Lumpkin hurried off into captivity with joyful strides. For his part, Forrest shook his head. "So Booth was dead all along, and Bradford never let on? How about that?" He could see why Bradford kept the senior officer's death a secret. Lionel Booth was a real soldier, and had a pretty good notion of what he was doing. Bradford, on the other hand, was nothing but a lawyer with a loud mouth. Had Forrest known he was in charge at Fort Pillow, he would have pushed the attack harder. Without a doubt, the place would have fallen sooner.

And so Bradford let him think the experienced officer still held command. And it deceived him, too. Bedford Forrest slowly nodded to himself. It cost the Federals in the end. When Forrest demanded a surrender, he was sure Major Booth would have given him one. Booth was no fool. He could see what was what, and he could see the writing on the wall. Bradford pinned his hopes on the *New Era*—and got them pinned back when she sailed away.

Would Bradford try surrendering now? Or would he have the nerve to fight to the death? Forrest had never heard anything suggesting that he was particularly brave. A slow smile spread over his face. He could hardly wait to find out.

Lieutenant Mack Leaming crouched behind a bush halfway down the bluff from Fort Pillow to the Mississippi. He'd watched men in blue run back and forth along the riverbank, pursued first by one band of Confederate soldiers and then by another. They were getting chewed to pieces down there, and more Confederates at the edge of the bluff only made things worse for them.

Part of Leaming wanted to go down by the river with the rest of the Union troops and share their fate. But he could see too clearly what that fate would be. They were getting picked off from three sides at once. The only direction from which nobody was shooting at them was from the Mississippi itself. Some of them threw away their weapons and waded out into the river to try to save themselves from the unending fusillade of lead. It didn't work. Bullets splashed into the water, kicking up little fountains. Although some men waded out up to their necks, that didn't keep them from getting hit.

Trails of blood started appearing in the muddy river. Gators might have followed those trails to see what made them. This far north, though, gators were scarce. It was too early in the year, too cool, for them to be very lively anyhow. The wounded Federals were spared one torment, then. They weren't spared much else.

Up at the top of the bluff, one Confederate trooper nudged the man next to him on the firing line. "Bet you four bits I can hit that nigger in the water there." He pointed.

"Which one?" his pal asked. "I can't see which way your blamed finger's goin'."

"The ugly bald coon, there behind that redhead."

"All right. I see him. You won't hit the son of a bitch." They were both shouting, which let Leaming hear them. Gunfire had likely stunned their ears to anything less than shouts.

"Hell I won't." The first Confederate drew a bead and fired. He whooped. "Did I get him or did I get him? Bastard's headed for hell right now."

"If he is, I better go to heaven, on account of I don't want to spend forever with a stinkin' nigger."

"That's half a dollar you owe me."

"Dumb luck. Dumb fuckin' luck. Bet you can't hit the redheaded Yankee. Double or nothin', all right?"

"Let me reload, by God, and I'll have me a dollar of your money." Methodically, the first trooper started doing just that. He fired again. "There? You see? That damnyankee sank like a rock. I gave him what he had coming, and you can kindly give me a dollar."

"Here, dammit." The other Confederate paid up.

"This here is Secesh paper," the first one grumbled. "It ain't hardly worth what it's printed on. I wanted a real U.S. greenback."

Even the Rebs knew U.S. money was better than their own. The second trooper shook his head. "You didn't say what kind of dollar we were bettin', and you wouldn't give me any better if I won a bet off you. Ought to be grateful you're getting any dollar at all. You sure won't see a different one, and that's the Lord's truth."

"Don't take His name in vain, Cyrus," the first trooper said.

"Bart, you tend to your own little shriveled-up mule turd of a soul, and I'll take care of mine. How does that sound?"

Mack Leaming thought it sounded like good advice. He also thought it was about time to give himself up if he could. Here and there, stubborn U.S. soldiers, white and colored, were still banging away at Bedford Forrest's men. They would undoubtedly wound some, even kill some. They had no chance at all of changing the way the battle was going.

Without even a pistol, he couldn't shoot back no matter how much he wanted to. He'd done what he could with a cavalry saber. He'd done more good for the U.S. cause with only a cavalry saber than he'd imagined he could. Now he had to trust to the mercy of enemies who weren't showing much. He watched a trooper in filthy butternut walk up to a wounded Negro crawling on the ground and blow out the black's brains.

"There you go, Tyler!" another Confederate called as the grubby trooper reloaded.

Up on top of the bluff, where the fighting was about done, things would be calmer. So Leaming reasoned, anyhow. He started crawling up the steep side again. If he could get someone to take his surrender . . .

All I want to do is go on living, he thought. *Is that too much to ask? Please, Jesus, tell me it isn't.*

He got to within perhaps fifteen paces of the top of the bluff before he dared to stand up. When he did, he looked at the saber he still held in his right hand. Then he looked up at the ground for which the Federals had fought, and which they'd lost. Three or four Rebs were watching him intently. They might have been wolves wondering when a sick deer they were chasing would stumble and fall.

Wishing that particular comparison hadn't occurred to him, Lieutenant Leaming tossed aside the saber. He didn't want the Confederates thinking he might make a mad dash up the slope and try to murder them all. He spread his hands and forced a smile he didn't feel across his face.

"I surrender," he called. "You've licked us. We can't fight any more."

Bedford Forrest's troopers glanced at one another. With slow, thoughtful deliberation, one of them raised his rifle musket to his shoulder and peered over the sights down the slope at Leaming. If he pulled the trigger at that range, he could hardly miss. And, Leaming realized with rising horror, he was going to pull the trigger.

Leaming tried to turn away, tried to run. Too late. Too late. The Confederate fired. The minnie caught Leaming in the back, just below his right shoulder blade. His face hit the ground harder than he ever dreamt it could. Blackness covered him.

XI

A FEDERAL—A WHITE MAN—begged for his life on his knees in front of Matt Ward. He had no pride. He had no shame. "Please don't shoot me!" he whined. "I don't want to die!" Tears ran down his terrified face.

"You one o' them bastards who learned niggers how to fight?" Ward demanded. For any Confederate soldier, that was the unpardonable crime.

"No, sir," the bluebelly answered. "Swear to God I ain't! My name's Henry Clay, like the big shot from way back when. I'm Company E, Thirteenth Tennessee Cavalry."

A lot of Forrest's men were Tennesseans. They hated the homemade Yankees in the U.S. Thirteenth Cavalry at least as much as they hated Negro soldiers. Because Ward was from Missouri, he didn't hold so much against the white soldiers in blue. They were just damnyankees to him, not brothers and cousins and friends gone wrong.

He gestured with his bayonet. "All right, Henry Clay. Get up. Turn out your pockets. Whatever you've got in there, it's mine now."

"I don't care," Clay said. "Take it! I got me about ten dollars in greenbacks, and a couple of silver cartwheels, too. And you can have my spare cartridges—don't reckon I'll need 'em no more." He was pathetically eager to give Ward everything he owned. "Got me some hardtack here, and some coffee beans."

"You're a walking sutler," Ward said. He couldn't do anything with the coffee, not till he had a chance to crush or grind the beans. But he broke a chunk off a hardtack cracker, stuffed it in his mouth, and started to chew. The double-baked dough reminded him one of his teeth wasn't as good as it should have been; it twinged when he chewed. His belly growled. His side always seemed to be on short rations, but the Federals had plenty. After he swallowed, he gestured with his Enfield again. "Go on back to the rear. They'll take care of you there."

"Thank you. God bless you," Henry Clay said, more tears drizzling down his cheeks. "You're a Christian gentleman, you are."

"Go on—git. Keep your hands high," Ward said. Clay lurched away, south along the bank of the Mississippi.

Do I feel better because I let him live? Ward wondered. He shrugged. He shook his head. The Federal just didn't seem worth killing. It wasn't the same thing at all. Clay was out of the fight now. That would do.

Another blue-clad soldier tried to give up. Ward might have taken his surrender, too, but a Yankee minnie cracked past his head. His own reaction was automatic. He ducked. Even as he was ducking, he pulled the trigger. The Federal screamed. He thrashed on the ground like a snake with a broken back, clutching his belly and crying for his mother. Ward felt bad about that. He hadn't meant to gutshoot the man. Well, no matter what he'd meant, it was done now.

He reloaded as fast as he could. Some of the colored soldiers and Tennessee Tories were still fighting, as that bullet proved. Fewer and fewer U.S. soldiers kept on shooting, though. A lot of them were down. Others went out into the Mississippi, mostly without their weapons, doing whatever they could to get away from Bedford Forrest's men. And quite a few were trying to give up.

Some, like Henry Clay, succeeded. Others, like the fellow Matt Ward shot without even thinking about it, didn't. The ones who died had only their own officers to blame, as far as Ward was concerned. General Forrest told them he couldn't answer for what his own troops would do if he didn't get a surrender right then. The Confederates' blood was up. Considering the men the soldiers in butternut faced, that was as near inevitable as made no difference. Blacks as soldiers . . . Ward ground his teeth at the very idea—carefully, because the hardtack had shown that that one was tender.

A handful of the bluebellies in the Mississippi were really trying to swim, or at least to float away, letting the current carry them downstream past the C.S. lines. Most just waded out and stayed there. Everybody said ostriches stuck their heads in the sand and left the rest of themselves in plain sight. The Union soldiers were just the opposite. Only their heads stuck out of the water.

Ward aimed at a Negro who had to be unusually tall to have waded as far out into the Mississippi as he had. Before he could fire, somebody else hit the black man. He shrugged. He had plenty of other targets to choose from. He had to swing his rifle musket only a little to the right to bring it to bear on a blond man with a long beard. He fired. The Federal sank into the river.

Bedford Forrest's troopers had already started plundering the enemy. Some of that was rifling pockets, the same kind of thing Ward did to Henry Clay. (The homemade Yankee's name still made him smile.) But much of it was more serious, more essential. Barefoot Confederates stole dead bluebellies' shoes. Troopers in ragged shirts and trousers took what they needed from men who wouldn't be worrying about clothes any more. And fine Springfields lay scattered on the ground like oversized jackstraws. Troopers who'd joined Forrest's force with nothing better than a squirrel gun or a shotgun got weapons as good as any their foes carried.

As good as any their foes here carried, anyhow—Ward silently corrected himself. He longed for a repeating rifle, a Henry or a Spencer. What Confederate cavalry trooper didn't? But the only way to keep a rifle like that in cartridges was to capture them. The Confederate States weren't up to making those fancy brass cases.

Just when Ward thought the fighting was over, it flared up again. A few Federals down here by the riverbank didn't want to give up and didn't think they could get away with surrendering. They seemed bound and determined to take as many Confederates with them as they could.

Ward didn't run toward the new skirmish. Plenty of other troopers were closer to it than he was. He'd already put himself in enough danger for one day. And those coons wouldn't last long any which way.

Sergeant Ben Robinson wondered if he would be the last soldier from Fort Pillow to go down fighting. He could do without the honor; he didn't want to go down at all. Sandy Cole had fallen with a bullet in the right thigh and another in the arm. Charlie Key was shot in the arm, too—if that bone wasn't broken, Robinson had never seen one that was. Aaron Fentis was down with bullet wounds in both legs. He lay groaning somewhere not far away. And somebody'd shot poor Nate Hunter right in the ass.

The little knot of Federals who were still fighting had Bedford Forrest's troopers coming at them from along the Mississippi and from the direction of Coal Creek. More Confederates went on shooting down at them from the bluff. By any reasonable measure, the fight was hopeless.

No matter how hopeless it was, the U.S. soldiers kept on loading and firing, loading and firing. Some were Negroes who'd seen what happened when other colored men tried to surrender. Robinson preferred dying with a gun in his hand to being murdered in cold blood. And some were whites from the Thirteenth Tennessee Cavalry who'd avenged themselves on the Confederates whenever they found the chance and now feared like vengeance would fall on them.

They were a band of brothers now, those last couple of squads' worth of struggling Union soldiers. Race didn't matter any more; neither did rank. Some of them were wounded. Those men loaded Springfields and passed them to others hale enough to use them.

"Here they come!" somebody yelled—the Rebs from the Coal Creek side were dashing forward. The defenders fired a ragged volley of four or five shots to make them keep their distance. The Federals might have wounded one man. Robinson wasn't even sure of that. It didn't matter. The gunshots showed the men in blue hadn't given up. That was enough to stop the Confederate rush.

As if to make up for stopping, one of Forrest's men shouted, "Gonna kill you bastards!"

"Gonna shoot you!" another Secesh soldier added.

"Gonna stick you!" said another.

Another Confederate flavored his words with almost obscene anticipation: "Gonna stick you sons o' bitches *slow* and watch you die an inch at a time." Still others yelled more bloodthirsty endearments.

The white man closest to Ben Robinson grinned crookedly. "Really makes you want to throw down your piece and give up, don't it?"

"Huh!" Robinson said, a syllable half despair, half startled laughter. So many men were down. . . . "Easiest thing to do might be to throw down your piece, all right, an' play possum in wid all the bodies."

"Good luck," the white trooper said. "What do you want to bet the Rebs go around and bayonet everybody on the ground? If you aren't dead beforehand, you will be by the time they get through with you."

"Huh," Ben said again, on a different note: all despair this time. That struck him as much too likely.

Some other white Tennesseans must have thought their chances were better if they laid down their arms. Two white men walked toward the closest Confederates with their hands in the air. Laughing, Bedford Forrest's troopers let them get close—and then shot them. The Federals' screams were as much of betrayal as of agony, though the Rebs put enough minnies into them to finish them in short order.

"You see?" said the trooper by Robinson.

"Reckon I do," the Negro answered.

FORT PILLOW ✦ 183

Less than a minute later, a minnie thudded into the white man's chest. He fired one last shot at the enemy and died in grim, defiant silence. Only a few U.S. Springfields were still firing. The Confederates drew closer and closer.

Robinson was in the middle of reloading when a C.S. trooper shouted, "Drop it, nigger! Drop it right now, or I'll shoot you down like the mad dog you are." The man had friends behind him. All of them were aiming their rifle muskets at the colored sergeant. A wild charge with the bayonet would just get him killed.

All the brave resolve leaked out of him. He let the Springfield fall in the mud. The Confederate hadn't said he'd kill him if he did surrender. Slowly, Robinson raised his hands.

Grinning and laughing, Forrest's trooper shot him.

"Do Jesus!" Robinson screamed, and fell heavily to the ground. Somebody might have dipped his right leg in tar and set it on fire—it hurt that much.

"That'll learn you, you damn coon," said the soldier in butternut. "Just what you deserve. You try takin' up arms against white men, you pay. You'd fuckin' best believe you pay. You hear me?"

Only a groan came from Ben Robinson's lips. The Reb didn't seem to care. He walked on, looking for somebody else to kill. Robinson lay where he'd fallen, writhing and thrashing. He'd never imagined anything could hurt so bad. He clutched his thigh with both hands, as tight as he could. His own hot blood leaked out between his fingers. It leaked, yes, but it didn't flood. Little by little, as his stunned wits began to work again, he realized it wasn't a fatal wound unless it festered.

I'll live, he thought. Right at the moment, everything hurt so much, he wasn't sure he wanted to. A U.S. physician would have dosed him with opium or laudanum, or at least with a big slug of corn squeezings, to ease the pain. He didn't suppose a Secesh doctor would give him the time of day, let alone a painkiller. For one thing, the Rebs didn't have much in the way of medical supplies for their own wounded. For another, he was black. They were more likely to give him a bullet to bite on—or one through the head—than laudanum.

Robinson tried holding still, wondering it that would ease him. It didn't, not even a little. And even if it would have, he couldn't do it. He had to move, and to keep moving. His pain insisted on it. Moving, of course, held dangers of its own. Several Confederate soldiers stalked past him. Any one of them could have decided to finish him off, but none did. Maybe they enjoyed seeing him wriggle and hearing him moan. He wondered about that only later. At the moment, he just thanked heaven.

"Hey, you! Hey, nigger!" The shout came from far away. For a while, Ben Robinson had no idea it was meant for him. Plenty of other colored soldiers were still alive. But then the cry came again: "Hey, nigger! Yeah, you down by the water, the one with the leg!"

He looked toward the top of the bluff. A couple of Forrest's troopers up there were staring down at him. They might have been soaring vultures staring down at a dying donkey. He waved to show he heard them. He didn't want to do that, but he was afraid they would start using him for target practice if he didn't.

One of the Rebs cupped his hands in front of his face. "Come on up here, boy!" he yelled.

"I can't!" Robinson yelled back. "I been shot!"

"You better, Sambo," the Confederate said. "You don't want to get shot some more, you goddamn well better."

They could hit him at that range with no trouble at all. He'd seen them hit men who'd waded out into the river, who were farther away than he was and exposing less of themselves. "I try," he said. Could he crawl? How much would the wound bleed if he let go of it? But that, suddenly, wasn't the biggest worry on his mind. How much would he bleed if they shot him again, and where would they? His belly? His head? He could get better after this wound. Another one might well do him in.

"Come on, nigger! Get movin'." One of the troopers at the top of the bluff started to raise his weapon.

Ben Robinson crawled. He was slow and awkward—even crawling, he couldn't put much weight on the injured leg. Dragging it along the ground hurt like a son of a bitch, too. He bit down on the inside of his lower lip till he tasted blood. Tears streamed down his face. He might have been climbing one of the tall mountains out West, not a riverside bluff.

Getting to the top took more out of him than fighting all day had. Of course, nobody'd put a hole in his leg when he was serving the twelve-pounder and trying to hold the Rebs out of Fort Pillow, first with the worm and then with a Springfield.

The Confederates who'd summoned him scowled fiercely. One was tall and skinny. The other was short and skinny, and so young that pimples still splotched his dirty face. The short one had breath that might have come from an outhouse. When he opened his mouth to speak, Robinson saw that two of his front teeth were black. He came straight to the point: "Give me your money, you damned nigger."

"Money?" Robinson said. "I ain't got no money." That wasn't true, but the words came out of themselves. He hoped the Rebs wouldn't kill him if they found out he was lying.

"Give me your money, or I will blow your brains out," said the soldier with the bad teeth and the horrible breath.

"Hell, Rafe, he's just a nigger. He don't have no brains," the other trooper said. By his loud, braying laugh, he wasn't long on brains himself.

"I ain't got none to give you," Ben Robinson repeated. If he changed his story now, that would make them angry. No, angrier.

"Ought to shoot the son of a bitch anyways," Rafe said. "We shoot all the uppity niggers, the rest'll cipher out they better not mess with us."

"His clothes are pretty good. Let's take what all he's got," said the other soldier, the tall one. He gestured with his rifle musket. "Lay down, you."

Robinson obeyed. In truth, he couldn't have stayed on hands and one knee much longer anyhow. The Rebs pulled off his shoes. They both tried them on, and swore when they found out the heavy leather brogans were too big for Rafe and too small for his pal, whose name turned out to be Willie. The Confederates didn't give them back after that. They tossed them aside so other troopers could try them on if they wanted to.

"Skin out of your pants, boy," Willie said.

"Do Jesus!" Robinson said. "What you want my pants for? They got bullet holes in 'em, an' I been bleedin' all over 'em." They had his money, the money he'd denied owning.

"Skin out of 'em," Willie repeated. "Blood washes out in cold water, and even with holes in 'em they're better'n what we're wearin'."

He wasn't wrong. His own trousers were out at both knees, and inexpertly patched in several other places. Rafe's were worse. One of his trouser legs simply ended halfway between knee and ankle. The other was a tapestry of holes all the way up, including a big one in the seat that displayed his dirty drawers.

Sure the Rebs would kill him if he disobeyed and hoping to live, Ben Robinson undid his belt buckle and slid the pants off. He hissed with pain when he tugged them down over the wound. With the trousers gone, he got his first good look at it. Somebody might have gouged a finger-sized groove in the outside of his thigh. Getting shot was never good, but it could have been a lot worse. *I ought to get over this,* he thought. *It's only a flesh wound.*

He wouldn't get better if they shot him again or if they used their bayonets. And they could. Oh, yes. They could.

Rafe went through his pockets. He came out with a handful of greenbacks and some silver. "Ha!" he said triumphantly. "I knew the nigger son of a bitch was lying!" He kicked Robinson in the ribs.

"Ow!" Robinson howled, and wrapped his arms around himself. He was acting, acting for his life. Rafe could have kicked him harder. If he didn't pretend to be hurt, Forrest's trooper might decide to make sure he was.

"Hey," Willie said. "Half o' that money's mine."

"Hell you say," Rafe told him. "I found it."

"I was the one that said we ought to halloo the coon up here,"

Willie retorted. "Try finding money in the pockets of niggers who ain't here, you're so damn smart."

"Ought to be mine," Rafe whined.

"I ain't askin' for all of it. I ain't greedy like some folks," Willie said. "But you try and steal from me, I'll beat the living shit out of you, and I'm big enough to do it, too."

Rafe reluctantly handed over some greenbacks and coins. With a smug nod of thanks, Willie stuck the money in a pocket of his disreputable pants. The Rebs worried about stealing from each other. Neither one of them cared about stealing from a Negro. Sergeant Robinson didn't point that out. The less attention Forrest's troopers paid to him, the less likely they were to shoot him or stick him or knock him over the head.

Confederate soldiers weren't just robbing blacks. They were stealing from white Federals, too, stripping dead and wounded troopers from the Thirteenth Tennessee Cavalry (U.S.). One wounded white man who made a feeble protest got his teeth knocked out with a rifle butt.

Rafe and Willie dragged Robinson toward several bodies lying close together on the ground. Fear rose up in a choking cloud inside him—were they going to finish him off now? But the minnie or bayonet thrust didn't come. They hurried off to see what other loot they could garner.

Ben Robinson lay where they'd left him. As long as he stayed quiet near dead bodies, maybe Forrest's troopers would think he was dead, too, and leave him alone. Then he noticed he was lying next to Major Booth's corpse. The dead commandant stared at him out of dull eyes. Robinson wanted to reach out and close them; that set, unwavering gaze unmanned him. But he couldn't make himself touch the body. He turned his back on it instead.

Secesh soldiers had already stripped Booth's corpse. He wore only undershirt and drawers. Now that Robinson thought back on it, he'd seen a Reb sporting a tunic with a lot of brass buttons on it.

If that sharpshooter's bullet hadn't found the major . . . Robinson swore softly. Too late to worry about it now. Too late to worry about anything now, except—if God proved kinder than He'd shown himself to be thus far—surviving.

"Surrender? Hell, no, you fucking son of a bitch! You ain't gonna surrender!" a Confederate trooper yelled, and fired at Bill Bradford from no more than fifty feet away. The bullet cracked past the major's head. Bradford turned and ran while the Reb swore. The man who'd led the defense of Fort Pillow didn't know whether he led a charmed life or a cursed one. Every Secesh soldier wanted to shoot him on sight, but so far none of their bullets had bitten.

Not knowing what else to do, he darted into the Mississippi, even though wading out into the river hadn't done his men much good. The water was cold. He waded and floundered and dog-paddled out some fifty yards, then paused, panting and treading water. He could taste the Mississippi mud in his mouth, and prayed it wouldn't be the last thing he ever tasted.

"There he is!" a Reb shouted. "That's Bradford!"

"Blow his head off!" cried another soldier in gray.

An officer pointed out to him. "Come ashore, Bradford, if you know what's good for you!"

"Will you spare me?" Bradford asked. The officer just pointed again, peremptorily. They would surely kill him if he stayed out in the Mississippi. Sobbing from fear and exhaustion, he made his way back toward the riverbank. No sooner had he got to where the water was only waist-deep, though, than the Confederates started shooting at him again. He yelped in fright as bullets flew by and splashed into the water. Again, though, none hit.

The officer who'd ordered him ashore and several others stood around watching the sport. They didn't do a thing to stop it. Sobbing, Bradford dashed up onto the muddy land and started running up the hill. He pulled a soaked handkerchief from his pocket and waved it, again trying to give up. More bullets cracked past him.

At last, he almost ran into a Rebel trooper coming down to the riverside. The Confederate leveled his rifle musket at Bradford's brisket. "Give it up, you Yankee bastard!" he yelled.

"I surrender! Oh, dear, sweet Jesus Christ, I surrender!" Bradford threw his hands in the air as high as they would go. He had never imagined he could be so glad to yield himself.

Then the Reb recognized him. "You!" Now that Forrest's trooper knew the man he'd caught, he looked ready to end Bradford's career on the instant. But he didn't pull the trigger after all. Instead, greed lighting his face, he said, "Turn out your pockets, damn you!"

"I'll do it." Bradford did, without the least hesitation. Being robbed seemed much better than being killed. "Here you go, friend." He handed the Confederate more than fifty dripping dollars. If he held back a double eagle . . . Well, you never could tell when twenty dollars in gold might come in handy.

"I ain't no friend of yours," his captor said, snatching the bills and coins out of his hands. A nasty smile spread across the Reb's face. "No, I ain't no friend of yours, but I like your money just fine."

"Take it, then, and welcome," Bradford said. He could always make more money. He sneezed. The wind on his soaked clothes chilled him to the bone.

Forrest's trooper gestured with the muzzle of his rifle musket. "Up the hill you go, Bradford. I'd shoot you my own self, but I reckon there's others who want you even worse'n I do—starting with the menfolk whose women your damn traitors outraged."

Bradford licked his lips. He tasted more mud; his mustache was wet. But his tongue and the inside of his mouth were dry with fear. "I never gave orders for anything like that," he got out.

"Yeah, likely tell, likely tell," the Confederate jeered. "Now let's hear another story—one I'll maybe believe."

"Before God, it's the truth." Bradford held up his right hand, as if taking an oath. The soldier in butternut laughed. It wasn't a good-natured, mirthful laugh. A cat with a human voice might have laughed like that playing with a cornered mouse. The Reb urged Bradford up the side of the bluff again. Shivering, Bradford went.

It *was* the truth. No one—no one in his right mind, anyway—ordered his men to abuse the women on the other side. But, as Bradford knew and as Pontius Pilate must also have known long ago, there was truth, and then there was truth. West Tennessee was and always had been a Rebel stronghold. Forrest's trooper called the soldiers of the Thirteenth Tennessee Cavalry (U.S.) traitors. To Bradford's way of thinking, the men who were trying to break the Union in half were the real traitors.

If you stayed loyal to the United States, what did you do about treason? What *could* you do about it? You could put it down, that was what. If somebody wanted to see the Stars and Stripes cut down and the Stainless Banner flying in their place, what were you supposed to do? Stand by and watch while he took up arms against your country—against *the* country? Bradford shook his head as he climbed the steep slope. He didn't think so.

And sometimes the game got rough. It got rough on both sides. Plenty of men under his command had had relatives bushwhacked, houses burned, livestock killed or driven off. If they paid the Confederates back in the same coin, who could blame them? Not Bill Bradford, not for a minute. He wanted to make it hard on the Rebs, to remind them they were facing a power strong enough to defend itself, a power strong enough to make anyone who defied it sorry.

Some of the things that happened didn't happen officially. Taking women out behind the barn and doing what you wanted with them—to them—fell in that category. No, nobody would order it. But if you owed vengeance to a particular Reb, if you knew who he was, if you knew where his kin lived, wouldn't you do whatever you could to pay him back? Of course you would.

Some of the soldiers who did things like that bragged about them. Bradford had heard them going on about what they'd done. They fell silent when they noticed him, but often not soon enough. Had he done such things, he would have kept quiet about them till people shoveled dirt over his grave. But he was a lawyer—he knew that talking about something often made it twice as real. Being a lawyer, he also tended to forget that things stayed real even without testimony about them.

As he regained the top of the cliff, he saw a Negro wearing only shirt and drawers lying next to a white man who'd had all his outer clothes stolen. The colored soldier stirred. The white man never would, not till the Judgment Trump blew: Major Bradford recognized Lionel Booth.

Had the Rebs stripped Theodorick the same way? Bradford couldn't stand the idea. He hurried toward the place where Theo had fallen. "Where do you think you're going, you goddamn son of a bitch?" snarled the Confederate who'd captured him.

"To see my brother's body," he answered, not slowing in the slightest. "Wouldn't you do the same for yours?"

The Confederate didn't answer. He also didn't fire. Bradford strode through the chaos of the sack of Fort Pillow. Rebs were busy stripping bodies and plundering sutlers' huts, stealing from the United States all the things their own gimcrack government couldn't give them.

Horrible screams rose from a tent the Federals had been using as a hospital for their wounded. Mixed in with them were shouts of hoarse, drunken laughter. Some of Forrest's troopers must have got into the whiskey Major Booth had ordered put out to fortify the garrison's courage. A couple of soldiers in butternut lurched from the tent. They both carried cavalry sabers dripping blood.

"You scalped that coon just like an Injun would!" one of them told the other. They both thought that was the funniest thing they'd ever heard. They had to hold each other up, or they would have fallen on their faces.

An officious-looking young Confederate second lieutenant rushed over to Bradford. "Where do you think you're going?" he demanded.

Then, recognizing the man to whom he spoke, he did a classic double take. "You!"

"He said the same thing." Bradford jerked a thumb back over his shoulder at the trooper behind him. "I think I'm going to tend to my brother's body, that's what, and see that he gets Christian burial. You are a Christian, I hope?" By the way he said it, he had his doubts.

"I ought to blow your head off right here," the lieutenant said, scowling. If he was a Christian, he didn't believe in turning the other cheek.

"I have surrendered. This gentleman accepted my surrender." Bradford pointed to the trooper again. "If you care to make yourself infamous before God and man, pull the trigger. I shall not run." Soaked and weary though he was, he struck a pose. He'd pleaded for lives before, but never for his own. All the courtroom tricks he'd used for others came back to help him now.

He succeeded in confusing the lieutenant, anyhow. "Don't you go nowhere," the youngster squeaked.

"I am going to find my brother's body," Bradford insisted. "I am going to see him properly buried." *And what I do after that is nobody's business but my own.* When the Confederate lieutenant didn't tell him no, his hopes began to rise.

Mack Leaming lay where he'd fallen. He'd stuffed a pocket handkerchief into the hole below his shoulder blade. The linen square was soggy with blood now, but he did think he was losing less than he had before.

Secesh soldiers and their Federal captives scampered down the side of the bluff and trudged up it. Confederates plundered the dead and robbed the living. They weren't murdering so many as they had in the mad moments after the fort fell, but they hadn't stopped, either. A Negro dashed down to the Mississippi and tried to take refuge in the river. One of Forrest's troopers shot him just as he splashed into the water. His blood mingled with the greater flow of the stream.

Two more Confederates ran over and pulled him out of the water. "Come on, you stinking shitheel!" one of them shouted. "Get up and walk!"

Whatever the Negro said, Leaming couldn't make it out—it was too feeble. "You'd better get up, or you'll never have another chance," the second Reb warned. The Negro managed to reach his hands and knees. Both Confederates laughed. "He crawls like a dog," the second one said.

"He can die like a damned dog." The first Reb put a revolver to the Negro's head and fired once. The colored soldier flopped down, dead. Bedford Forrest's men walked off, laughing still.

A soldier in ragged gray crouched down by Lieutenant Leaming. "Got any greenbacks, Yank?" he asked hoarsely.

Groaning with the effort, Leaming reached into his pocket and pulled out his wallet. "Here," he said, biting his lip against the pain. "Take it. Can I have some water, please?"

He might as well have saved his breath. The Reb was too busy counting his loot to pay any attention to the man the loot came from. "... Sixty ... eighty ... ninety ... ninety-five ... a hundred ... a hundred an' one ... two ... three," the trooper said in an awed voice. "A hundred an' three dollars! Goddamn! I'm rich!" He let out a whoop of joy. Then, like a fox that wanted more than one chicken from the coop, he stared hungrily at Leaming again. "All that money! What *else* you got?"

"Water?" Leaming said again. His throat felt rough as shagreen.

Forrest's trooper didn't care. He frisked the Union officer with ungentle hands, and whooped again when he found Leaming's gold watch. It disappeared into his pocket, along with its heavy golden chain. "Godalmightydamn!" he said, as reverent a blasphemy as Leaming had ever heard. "Wish I had me more days like this here one since I joined up. I am a made man, I am. If you wasn't so ugly, I'd kiss you."

"Give me water," Leaming told him. "I don't need a kiss." Maybe because he was still bleeding, he felt drier every minute. He wondered how long he could last. It seemed to matter only in an abstract way, which probably wasn't a good sign.

He might have been a bank to the Confederate soldier, but he wasn't a human being. The Reb got to his feet. "I find me another Federal even half as loaded as you are, reckon I'm set for life." Away he went, whistling the "Battle Cry of Freedom." Both sides used that tune in this war, though they set different words to it. The U.S. chorus went,

> *The Union forever, Hurrah, boys, Hurrah!*
> *Down with the traitor, up with the star.*
> *While we rally 'round the flag, boys,*
> *Rally once again.*
> *Shouting the battle cry of Freedom.*

By contrast, the Rebs sang,

> *Our Dixie forever, she's never at a loss*
> *Down with the eagle, up with the cross.*
> *We'll rally 'round the bonnie flags,*
> *We'll rally once again,*
> *Shout, shout the battle cry of Freedom.*

To the Confederates in Fort Pillow, freedom seemed to mean freedom to loot. Another Secesh soldier called on Leaming a few minutes after the first one left. "Give me your money, you lousy Tennessee Tory, or you'll be sorry," he said.

"Then I'll have to be sorry," Leaming answered. "Another one of your fellows already took everything I had."

"Now tell me one I'll believe," the Reb said, and searched him with practiced ease that suggested he was either a sheriff or a bandit by trade. Leaming knew which way he would have bet. The Confederate swore when he found Leaming was telling the truth. "Well, I'll get something for myself, anyways," he said, and stripped off Leaming's shoes. They proved too small, which made him swear again.

Then he cheered up a little. "Maybe I can swap 'em with somebody else who's got a bigger pair."

"If you are a Christian man, please let me have some water," Leaming said.

"I am a Christian man, and I hope to go to heaven," the C.S. trooper replied. "But if we met in hell and you were on fire, I'd give you kerosene instead of water. That's what you deserve, you cowardly Yankee piece of shit, for putting guns in niggers' hands and making 'em think they can rise up against their masters. God and Bedford Forrest will punish you for that."

He didn't say whether he trusted more in the Deity or his commanding officer. He did go away, Leaming's shoes in his hand.

The right side of his torso one vast stabbing ache, Leaming lay where he had fallen. He looked up at the sky. The sun was sinking toward the western horizon, but hadn't got there yet. He wondered if he would die before it did. So much had happened so fast. Only a few hours earlier, he was parleying with Nathan Bedford Forrest himself. He'd never imagined it would come to this, to Fort Pillow lost, to finding out what having a bullet hole in him was like.

He grimaced. Some kinds of knowledge were too dearly bought. He'd always been a bright and curious man, but this once he wouldn't have minded ignorance.

A shadow fell across his face. It wasn't a vulture circling close to see if he was dead yet, although the way he felt he wouldn't have been surprised if it were. Not a vulture with feathers, anyhow: another Reb, seeing if he had anything worth stealing.

The Confederate soldier gave him a rueful grin. "Looks like I'm just about too late," he said. "My pals done took all the good stuff off'n you."

"Water?" The more Leaming asked for it, the more he was refused, the more he craved it.

He asked in vain again. The Reb might as well not have heard him. "Reckon I can get more use out of them trousers'n you ever will," he said. "Hike your bottom up so's I can get 'em off you."

"I'm wounded," Leaming got out through clenched teeth.

"I can see that—it's why I don't want your damned tunic," Forrest's trooper said. "Ain't nothin' wrong with your pants, though—hardly any blood on them. So hike up and let me have 'em."

Leaming's wound mattered to him only in so far as it made thievery inconvenient. The Federal officer didn't—couldn't—hike up. His tormentor stole his trousers anyway. Leaming begged for water one more time. He might as well have talked to a deaf man. The Confederate went right on ignoring his pleas. He thought of trying to shame the man, thought of it and decided not to. The trooper who'd stolen his shoes had his own brand of righteousness, however twisted it seemed to Mack Leaming. This fellow might also. And if he did, he might decide to use bullet or bayonet to silence what he didn't want to hear.

And even with the anguish of his wound, Leaming wanted to live. He aimed to die at home, at a ripe age, surrounded by a large and loving family. This muddy bluffside in the flower of his youth? This had nothing to do with what he had in mind. What God had in mind for him . . . he asked himself more and more often as the sun slid toward setting.

XII

WHEN THE FIRING AT FORT Pillow finally slowed, Nathan Bedford Forrest rode forward. His men had had their fun, or enough of it. He knew he couldn't have stopped them even if he wanted to. And he didn't want to. He'd warned the Federals he wouldn't answer for the consequences if they didn't give up. Every time he used that warning up till now, they either surrendered or beat back his men, both of which rendered the threat moot.

But it wasn't moot here. Fort Pillow *did* fall, and so it had to take the consequences. If he tried to hold his men in check after the fall—and if he managed to do it, which wouldn't be easy by a long shot—what sort of threat could he make the next time he wanted to shift some Yankees? He shook his head. None at all.

"Major Booth—no, Major Bradford—you are a damn fool," he muttered.

"What's that, sir?" one of his staff officers asked.

"Nothing. Never mind," Forrest said, annoyed the other man overheard him. He wondered whether Bradford still lived. He was inclined to bet against it, when the Tennessee Tory had so many men who wanted him dead. Bradford's bully boys had harried loyal Confederates in west Tennessee almost as savagely as Colonel Fielding Hurst's outfit. Well, they wouldn't any more—and neither would Hurst for a while.

Forrest's own men cheered him as he neared the position they had stormed. They whooped and grinned and waved their slouch hats. Some of them showed off the shoes and trousers and weapons they'd taken from the Federals. Forrest only grinned when they did. The Confederates had to make war pay for itself when they fought the richer United States.

One trooper waved to Forrest with a fist full of greenbacks. Forrest grinned at him, too, but said, "For God's sake, Lucas, stick that in your pocket! You want somebody to knock you over the head and walk off with it?"

"Anybody tries, I reckon he'll be mighty sorry mighty fast," Lucas answered. With a pistol on one hip and a Bowie knife on the other, he looked ready to raise large amounts of hell.

"Put it away anyhow," Bedford Forrest said. "The less temptation you stir up, the better off everybody is."

Lucas thought about telling him no, then visibly thought better of it. Anyone who told Forrest no was likely to be sorry for it, and in short order, too. If Major Bradford remained alive, he had to wish he'd surrendered. And if he didn't, he would have gone on wishing it till his dying breath.

At the top of the bluff, Forrest dismounted. His horse couldn't cross the trench in front of the U.S. earthworks. But several planks now spanned the ditch. His troopers went back and forth as they pleased.

Under their orders—and under their guns—Federal prisoners were throwing dead U.S. soldiers into the ditch. Bedford Forrest nodded to himself. Why bother digging graves when they already had a big trench handy?

Two Negro prisoners picked up a body. One of them turned to the closest C.S. soldier. "Suh, this here fella, he ain't dead," he said. "I done seen his hand move."

"That's a fac', suh," the other black agreed. "I seen it, too."

"Set him down," the trooper said. The Negroes obeyed. The Confederate soldier stooped for a closer look. His knee joints clicked when he straightened. "Pitch him in," he told the prisoners. "If he ain't dead, he's too far gone for a sawbones to help. He'll be gone by the time they throw dirt on him—and if he ain't, it'll put him out of his misery. Go on—get your lazy black asses moving."

The captives looked at each other. Then, with almost identical sighs, they obeyed. Nathan Bedford Forrest nodded again. What would happen if they refused? Their bodies would lie at the bottom of the ditch—and so would that of the prisoner, who, if he was alive, wouldn't stay that way for long.

More prisoners, these white men, carried the body of a soldier in butternut to lie with his comrades. A junior officer stood over the Confederates' bodies. "What's our part of the butcher's bill?" Forrest called.

"Sir, we've got about twenty dead," the lieutenant replied, stiffening to attention when he realized who'd asked the question. "About sixty wounded, I've heard, but don't hold me to that."

"All right—thanks," Bedford Forrest said. The young officer saluted. Forrest returned it with a gesture more than half a wave. Then he crossed into Fort Pillow. The planks that bridged the ditch groaned under his weight—he was half again as heavy as a lot of the men who served under him. Some Yankee general said small, young, single men made the best cavalry troopers. On the whole, Forrest agreed with him. But he was not small himself, he had a wife, and the pain from his many wounds reminded him he wasn't so young any more, either.

He jumped down from the broad parapet into the fort. Men in blue carried the bodies of their comrades toward the ditch. Forrest's troopers urged them along. If the soldiers in butternut urged blacks more roughly than whites . . . well, too bad. Bedford Forrest shrugged a broad-shouldered shrug. He had no love for Negroes trying to soldier, either.

Other Confederates went on robbing dead and living Federals. Forrest did nothing to stop them. Without Yankee loot, the Confederacy would long since have folded up and died. Having to plunder the enemy to keep fighting him made the war harder, but it went on.

And some of Forrest's troopers went on killing the men they'd overcome. Forrest scowled. "That's enough!" he shouted. "Enough, damn your black hearts! Stop it, or I'll make you sorry!"

Without looking over his shoulder to see who had spoken, a Confederate growled, "Who the hell do you think you are, to try and give an order like that?"

Bedford Forrest trotted up to him and knocked him to the muddy ground, then stood over him with fists clenched. "I'm your general, that's who," he said. "Who the hell d'you think *you* are, to try and disobey me?"

He waited. If the trooper wanted a fight, he could have one. But he quailed instead. Few men did anything but quail in the face of an angry Nathan Bedford Forrest. "I'm sorry, sir," the man mumbled.

"I'll make you sorrier than you ever thought you could be if you go disobeying orders again," Forrest said. "You hear me?" Miserably, the soldier in butternut nodded. Forrest thought about stirring him with his foot, but held back. Treating the trooper like a nigger might make him lash out with no thought for what happened next. Instead, Forrest told him, "Get up and do what you're supposed to do, then."

As the trooper rose, a gunshot rang out not far away. Somebody let out a shriek: a Negro clutching a smashed and bleeding hand. The Confederate soldier who'd shot him cussed a blue streak and started to reload. He'd been aiming for the black man's head, not his hand.

"General Forrest said that's enough," a captain snapped. "You shoot anybody else, or you shoot this miserable son of a bitch again, I'll put you under arrest. Do you want a court-martial?"

"No, sir," the soldier said grudgingly. "But I don't want some dumb fucking nigger trying to kill me, neither." Forrest turned away so the trooper wouldn't see him smile. The captain was right, no doubt about it. Even so, you could always rely on a Southern soldier to speak his mind.

Forrest started to turn back, then stopped short. His pale eyes narrowed. The U.S. officer crouching beside a body had gold oak leaves on his shoulder straps. That made him a major. With Lionel Booth dead, he had to be Bill Bradford. Face grim as death, Forrest stalked toward him.

Major William Bradford had given his parole to a Confederate colonel. The Rebs deigned to take it after they couldn't quite kill him. The officer even gave him something to eat, though Bradford still had his soaked uniform on.

He didn't notice the thump of boots on damp ground till the noise was almost on top of him. He looked up in surprise—and up and up, for he didn't see such a tall man every day, or every week, either. That dark chin beard, that hard mouth, those smoldering eyes . . . With Theo dead, with Fort Pillow fallen, he hadn't thought any worse disaster could befall him. Now, as Nathan Bedford Forrest scowled at him, he wondered how long he could stay even as lucky as he had been.

His knees clicked when he straightened. Even on his feet, he still looked up at Forrest, who was at least six inches taller. "General," Bradford said with such spirit as he could muster, and held out his hand.

The Confederate commander did not take it. Slowly, Bradford let it fall, his face hot with shame and rage. "You damned fool, why didn't you give up when you could?" Forrest demanded.

"Why?" Bradford shrugged. "Because I thought I could hold your men out. And because I feared they would act like beasts if they got in. And I was right, by God!" He pointed toward the heaped and tumbled corpses of Union soldiers, and toward the prisoners carrying bodies to the parapet and flinging them into the ditch.

"That never would have happened if you surrendered," Forrest said.

"So you say now," Major Bradford answered.

For a moment, he wondered if Bedford Forrest would strike him down where he stood. When Forrest grew angry, his whole countenance changed. He went red as hot iron, and seemed to swell so that he looked even larger than he was. "Are you calling me a liar, Major?" he asked softly.

If Bradford answered yes, he was a dead man. He could see that. "I did not trust your earlier assurances, sir," he replied with lawyerly evasion.

"When I say I'll take prisoners, I mean it," Forrest growled, some of that furious color ebbing from his face—some, but not all. "Over at Union City, Colonel Hawkins knew as much. He surrendered to my forces, and he and his men are safe today."

"This makes twice he's surrendered to you," Bradford said scornfully. "He's had practice, you might say."

"Well, you're a damn sight worse off now than if you did show the white flag," Forrest said, and Bradford winced. He could hardly deny that. The Confederate commander went on, "I told you I'd let you surrender, didn't I? Good Lord, I even said I'd let your niggers surrender, and that's something I've never done before and I'm not likely to do again."

"I . . . had trouble crediting it when you did." Bill Bradford picked his words with care, not wanting to inflame Forrest again.

"Too bad for you." Forrest waved back toward the rises outside the Federal perimeter. "As soon as I got men on that high ground, I could cut you to pieces easy as you please. Your soldiers couldn't stick their heads up over the earthwork without giving my sharpshooters perfect targets. Any man with an ounce of sense would have seen as much, and thrown in the sponge." One corner of his mouth twisted into a mocking smile. "Well, I reckon that leaves you out."

"Gloat all you care to," Bradford said wearily. He pointed to Theo's body. "All I aim to do is give my brother Christian burial—

better than chucking him into that mass grave as if he were a butchered beef."

To his amazement, all the high color drained from Bedford Forrest's face. "That's your brother, Major?" Forrest asked, also pointing to the bullet-riddled corpse. Bradford nodded. Forrest startled him again, this time by taking off his hat and holding it over his heart. "Please accept my deepest sympathy," Forrest said. "I lost my own dear brother, Jeffrey, down at Okolona, Mississippi, a couple of months back—you may or may not have heard. But I expect you will believe I have some notion of the misery you feel."

Major Bradford had heard that Jeffrey Forrest was killed in action. It didn't mean much to him at the time: just one more Rebel officer dead, and the wrong Forrest at that. But with Theodorick lying there all bloody, everything changed. Bradford managed a stiff if soggy bow. "I thank you, sir. No one who has not experienced the same thing can hope to understand it."

"That is a fact," Forrest said. "You may give your brother the burial you like." He turned and shouted for one of his aides.

The man came up at a trot—when Forrest said something, people jumped to obey. "What is it, sir?"

"Detail a couple of captured niggers to dig a proper grave for Major Bradford's brother here," Forrest answered. "Even an enemy can bury his dead."

"Yes, sir." No matter what the lieutenant said, he didn't sound happy about it. He looked daggers at Bradford. "Then what do we do with the goddamn son of a bitch?"

"Well, we captured him. He gave his parole." Bedford Forrest didn't sound very happy about it, either. "Now that we've got him, I suppose we have to keep him." No, he didn't seem happy at all.

"I fought hard, gentlemen, but I fought clean," Bradford said.

"Shut up, you lying bastard," snarled the C.S. lieutenant. "What about that poor fellow who didn't like Yankees, and said so, and got his tongue torn out on account of it?"

Major Bradford gulped. "My men never did anything like that."

To his relief, General Forrest nodded. "He's right, Sam. That wasn't his regiment—it was Hurst's. Too damn bad I didn't catch *him* instead of running him into Memphis." But his gaze grew no friendlier as he went on. "What about the women your soldiers molested, Bradford? The women whose menfolks chose the other side?"

"I never gave orders for any such thing, General," Bradford said, as he had before. "As God is my witness, I didn't. They would be an outrage against the laws of war."

But Nathan Bedford Forrest only laughed in his face. "Of course you didn't. However big a jackass you are, you aren't that big." That was a sardonic twist on Bradford's own thoughts. Forrest went on, "But you don't have to give order when you've got your boys all set to do what they crave doing anyways. You just look the other way and turn 'em loose. And your hands stay clean."

You ought to know. Bill Bradford didn't have the nerve to say it out loud, but he would have taken his oath it was true. Did Forrest order his men to slaughter the Federal garrison once they got inside Fort Pillow? Up until this moment, Bradford had thought so. Now he didn't. The Confederate general sounded too much like a man who knew exactly what he was talking about. He'd . . . How did he put it? He'd looked the other way and turned his troopers loose.

And his hands stayed clean, or clean enough, and the Rebs did what they wanted to do anyway. And if the troopers from Bradford's regiment and the colored artillerymen who fought alongside them suffered—Bedford Forrest didn't care.

"See to this fellow," Forrest told the lieutenant, who saluted. Forrest walked off, his longs strides taking him away in a hurry.

The lieutenant scowled at the trooper who'd been watching over Bradford. "What's your name, soldier?" the officer asked.

"Ward, sir. I'm Matt Ward."

"Well, all right, Ward. You heard General Forrest—we've got to keep this bastard alive." With Forrest out of earshot, he sounded downright disgusted. He went on, "We'll let him stick this other son of a bitch in the ground, since he's so damn hot to do it. And then we'll take him along with us. But I'll tell you something else."

"Yes, sir?" Ward sounded as uninterested as a Federal private would have. *You want to run your jaws,* he might have been saying. *Say what you've got to say and leave me alone.*

"If he gets out of line—if he gets even a little bit out of line—you shoot him in the belly," Forrest's staff officer said. "In the belly, you hear? He shouldn't just die. Let him die slow, and hurt while he's doing it. You hear me?"

"Yes, sir," Ward said. "I'll take care of it, sir."

The lieutenant scowled at Bradford. "Do *you* hear me, you goddamned son of a bitch?"

"I hear you, Lieutenant," Bradford answered, as coldly as he dared. "I have given Colonel McCulloch my parole. And do you recollect General Forrest talking about the laws of war? Deliberately abusing a prisoner goes dead against every one of them."

"Bradford, if it wasn't for Colonel McCulloch and General Forrest, we'd roast you and smoke you over a slow fire till we came up with something to really make you suffer," the Confederate officer said. "So thank the high officers and your lucky stars you aren't screaming right this minute."

Major Bradford thanked Nathan Bedford Forrest for losing his brother. He couldn't imagine what he'd do without Theo; they'd been in each other's pockets their whole lives. Yes, the Confederate commander had lost a brother, too, but so what? Jeffrey Forrest really was just a Reb, after all.

And Bradford thanked Bedford Forrest for the loss of Fort Pillow. With the fort, he'd lost any prayer of advancing his own military career, even if he got exchanged. Who would give a fort to a man who'd proved he couldn't hold one? Nobody. And the Thirteenth Tennessee Cavalry (U.S.) was a ruin. All the men at Fort Pillow were either dead or captured. The rest . . . The rest would probably elect a new commanding officer as soon as they found out what had happened here.

Two Negroes came up, shovels on their shoulders like Springfields. Forrest's staff officer scowled at them. "Damn coons got no business wearing uniforms and pretending to be soldiers," he muttered.

"They didn't pretend. They fought." To annoy the Confederate, Bradford concealed his own amazement that the colored artillerymen could do any such thing. One of them looked ready to go on fighting, too, restrained only by the presence of enemy soldiers in overwhelming numbers. The other black was a beaten man, but so were a lot of whites from the Thirteenth Tennessee Cavalry.

"I want to know what you think, I'll ask you," the C.S. lieutenant snapped. He turned to the Negroes. "Dig a hole, and we'll throw the dead Bradford in it. You want to dig a big hole so we can throw both Bradfords in, that's fine by me."

Neither black man rose to the bait. The one who still looked to have fight in him said, "Jus' the two of us diggin', we ain't gonna be done by sundown."

"Then keep digging till you are, damn you," the Confederate said. "You need 'em, we'll have torches up so you can do the job right. General Forrest said we have to do this, so we will." When he spoke of Forrest, he might have been quoting the Gospel.

The Negroes began to dig. Forrest's staff officer watched them for a while. Then, seeming satisfied they wouldn't slack off when his back was turned, he went away to do something else. A few minutes later, he showed up out of the blue to make sure they were still working hard. Bill Bradford nodded to himself. Sure as hell, the lieutenant was used to getting labor out of slaves.

As for Bradford . . . He watched the grave deepen. He watched the sun sink toward the horizon. And, parole or no parole, he watched for his chance.

Corporal Jack Jenkins looked at his rifle musket with a strange mixture of pride and revulsion. He'd never done more killing with the weapon, but it would be a bastard to clean. Not only was the bayonet bloody all the way to the hilt, but the stock was a mess of blood and brains and hair stuck on as if with glue. He'd used it to beat wounded Federals to death so he wouldn't have to waste more ammunition on them.

"Look," he said now. "I've been smashing up niggers and Tennessee Tories." He held up the rifle musket. Some of the strands of hair clinging to the stock were long and blond and straight, others black and tightly curled.

"That's about enough, Corporal," said a captain he barely knew. "You can hear they aren't shooting people up top any more."

"I wasn't shooting 'em down here any more, neither, sir," Jenkins said reasonably. "I was just breaking their goddamn heads." He displayed the rifle musket again to prove his point.

For some reason, the gore-clotted weapon didn't seem to please the officer. He turned away, muttering to himself. After a moment, he made himself turn back. "Just don't kill any more Union troops," he said. "That's an order."

"Not unless they try and give me trouble, sir." Like any soldier who'd served for more than a few days, Jenkins knew how to get what he wanted and seem obedient at the same time.

"Oh, no, you don't." Like any man who'd been an officer for more than a few days, the captain knew when he was hearing disobedience in a compliant mask. "If one of these bastards tries to kill you, you can punch his ticket for him. To *kill* you, you understand?"

"Yes, sir," Jenkins said sulkily.

"All right. Otherwise, you can lift their wallets and clothes, but otherwise leave 'em be," the captain said. "You understand *that?*"

"Yes, sir." Jenkins sounded even more reluctant this time.

He had reason to sound reluctant, too. The Federals alive and unwounded were cringingly anxious to stay that way; what odds that one of them would have the nerve to try to kill anybody? They reminded Jenkins of nothing so much as beaten dogs, rolling over on their backs and baring their throats and whimpering to keep from getting beaten some more.

Even robbing them wasn't much sport now. Almost all of them were barefoot; the ones who still wore shoes didn't wear any that were worth stealing. Jenkins wouldn't have thought Yankees could have shoes as ragged as any that belonged to one of Forrest's troopers, but he would have been wrong.

The same went for their trousers. The whites and Negroes who still wore them were welcome to what they had on.

I can have fun with 'em, Jenkins thought. *That goddamn captain didn't say I couldn't.* He strode up to a white man. "You a homemade Yankee?" he demanded.

Before the Federal trooper answered, his eyes flicked to Jenkins's fearsome rifle musket. If he'd thought about defiance, one look changed his mind. He nodded. "Reckon I am."

"You a dirty, stinking Yankee son of a bitch?" Jenkins demanded. The captive stood mute. Jenkins knocked him down and kicked him in the ribs—probably not hard enough to break any, but you never could tell. Standing over him, breathing hard, Jenkins growled, *"You a dirty, stinking Yankee son of a bitch?"*

"Reckon I am," the prisoner choked out.

"Say it out loud." Jenkins kicked him again, harder this time. "Say it out loud, God damn you, or you'll be sorry. I'll *make* you sorry, you hear?" He kicked the white man hard enough to make pain shoot up his own leg.

"I'm a dirty, stinking Yankee son of a bitch!" the man bawled, plainly as loud as he could. It didn't fully please Jenkins, but it would have to do. He gave the fellow one more boot to remember him by, then moved on to the next closest prisoner, a Negro.

"How about you, Rastus?" he asked, hefting the rifle musket. "You heard that other fella, so what do you reckon you are?"

The black man sang out with no hesitation at all: "I's a dirty, stinkin', Yankee son of a bitch!"

Jenkins knocked him down, too, and kicked him hard enough to make what he'd given the Tennessee Tory seem like a love pat by comparison. "Reckon you can get off easy, do you? Nobody gets off easy today, boy. What you are is, you're a lousy, shit-eating nigger dog. Now let me hear you say *that,* Cuffy, or else the Devil'll roast you even blacker'n you are already."

"I's a lousy, shit-eatin' nigger dog!" the Negro said.

"Louder!" Jenkins kicked him again. This time, the Negro shouted it, tears running down his face. He still wore blue wool trousers. "Turn out your trousers," Jenkins told him.

"I ain't got nothin'—Oof!" The black broke off with a grunt of pain, for Jenkins kicked him yet again.

"Turn 'em out, boy! You reckon you don't got to do what a white man says any more? You better think twice. You used to be a slave?" Jenkins asked. The colored soldier hesitated, no doubt trying to decide whether a lie or the truth would do him more good. "Answer me, you fucking nigger piece of shit!" Jenkins kicked the Negro hard enough to make him groan and clutch at his ribs. No, the captain hadn't said a word about shoeleather. "Answer me!"

"Yes, suh! I was a slave! Do Jesus, don't kick me no mo'!"

"Well, boy, if you was a slave, you know how you're suppose to act 'mongst your betters. I tell you to turn out them pockets one more time, by God, it'll be the last thing you ever hear. You reckon I'm funnin' you? You can find out—you bet you can."

The Negro decided not to take the chance, which proved he wasn't so dumb after all. Out came a grimy handkerchief, some greenbacks . . . and a shiny gold eagle.

"Ain't got nothin', huh?" Jenkins scooped up the money the way a redtail flew off with a chick wandering around the farmyard. The ten-dollar goldpiece went deep into his own pocket. He couldn't remember the last time he'd seen a gold coin. Even silver was in desperately short supply in the cash-strapped South. Federal greenbacks passed for hard money these days, though even they sold at a discount against specie. As for the banknotes Southern banks issued . . . They were like weevily hardtack. You held your nose, you closed your eyes, and you went ahead and used them. "Got any more?" Jenkins barked.

"So help me, that's it," the Negro wheezed, hand pressed against his ribs again.

"Last chance, coon," Jack Jenkins said. "I'm gonna search you. If I find more, you go straight into the goddamn river."

"Ain't got nothin'," the colored artilleryman said. Jenkins patted every pocket he had, felt his chest to see if he was hiding a bag around his neck, even took off his socks and threw them away. He didn't find anything. Either the Negro was telling the truth or he had a devil of a good place to stash stuff.

Corporal Jenkins kicked him once more, almost for good luck. "That's what you get for lyin' to me the first time," he said, and went off to see if he could find another Federal who hadn't been properly frisked. Ten dollars in gold! You could buy a hell of a lot of Confederate paper money for ten dollars in gold. Or you could buy a hell of a lot of things—if anybody in these parts had them to sell.

The sun was going down. Mack Leaming watched it sink with indifference marred by pain and bitterness. *The sun is setting on me,* he thought. If he didn't get someone to help him, if he had to lie on this cold, wet, miserable slope till morning, he feared he wouldn't see the next sunrise.

He'd done everything he knew how to do. Several Confederates went past him, skipping goatlike down the side of the bluff and slogging back up from the riverside. He called out to them—and they paid him no heed.

He even raised his arms in the three motions to shape the Grand Hailing Sign of Distress, but either none of Bedford Forrest's followers was a Freemason or Confederate Masons were a cold-blooded lot indeed, their hearts hardened against their Union brethren. He would rather have believed the former than the latter; Freemasonry was supposed to transcend national allegiances. But regardless of whether the truth lay in ignorance or in malice, it seemed all too likely to kill him.

Leaming must have dozed—or passed out—for a little while.

When he returned to himself again, the sun had dropped closer to the Mississippi and the trees beyond it. He had to look at his arms to see if they still shaped the Grand Hailing Sign. They did, not that it seemed likely to matter.

Someone in boots came down the slope. Leaming didn't bother to turn his head at the sound. But, where so many Confederates passed on the other side like the priest and the Levite in the Book of Luke, this man stopped. Mack Leaming looked up at him. He wore the two bars of a first lieutenant on either side of his collar. Was he, could he be, a Samaritan in this hour of need?

The Confederate officer studied Leaming as he lay there on the ground. After a pause that had to last more than a minute, the Reb coughed a couple of times and asked, "Are you by any chance a . . . traveling man, sir?"

Hope flowered in the wounded Federal. That was a question a Freemason might ask a stranger to see if he too belonged to the order. Careless of the pain, Leaming nodded. When he first tried to speak, only a dusty croak passed his lips. He tried again, gathering his feeble reserves of strength. "I travel . . . from West to East," he got out—the East was the direction from which enlightenment came.

"I thought so," the C.S. lieutenant breathed. "A man does not shape the Grand Hailing Sign by accident. No doubt our forebears chose it for just that reason." He knelt by Leaming. "Well, brother, I will do what I can for you. Where are you hit?"

"Below the shoulder blade," Leaming answered. "I was shot from the top of the bluff, so the minnie went down. . . ." He had to gather himself again before asking, "Could I have some water, please?"

"Of course," the Confederate said, where all his comrades told Leaming no or pretended not to hear him. The man undid the tin canteen at his belt and held it to Leaming's mouth. It was captured U.S. issue, with a pewter spout. Never had Leaming tasted anything more delicious than the warm, rather stale water that ran so sweetly down his throat.

"Thank you," he said when the enemy officer took the canteen away. He could hear how much more like himself he sounded with a wet whistle. "From the bottom of my heart, friend, thank you. You *are* the good Samaritan come again."

"I doubt it. I doubt it very much," the Reb said. "When we attacked this place, I wanted to see every man jack in it lying dead at my feet."

"You've got most of what you wanted," Leaming said. Prisoners were still carrying bodies off the slope and away from the riverside.

"With the force we had and the positions we soon gained, y'all were mad to try to resist us," the C.S. lieutenant told him. Bedford Forrest had said the same thing when Major Bradford refused to surrender. As things turned out, the Confederate general had a better notion of what was what than his Federal opponent.

"We might have held you out in spite of everything if you hadn't moved men forward while the flag of truce was flying," Leaming said.

"We brought them up to warn off the steamer, not to move against the fort," the Confederate lieutenant said sharply. "You could have protested at the time if you thought we were doing anything underhanded, but you never said a word." Leaming bit his lip, for that was true. He wondered if the Reb's anger would drive him away, but it didn't. The Confederate went on, "Let's get you taken care of, if we can."

He straightened up from beside Leaming and shouted. Two colored soldiers hurried over to him. Both were barefoot; one wore only his drawers and undershirt. "What you need, suh?" they asked together. They spoke to the Reb as respectfully as if to a U.S. officer. Maybe they treated him like a master. Maybe they were just afraid he would order them killed if they got out of line even a little—and maybe they were right to be afraid that way.

The lieutenant pointed to Leaming. "Take him up to the top of the bluff. Be as gentle as you can—he's got a nasty wound."

"Yes, suh. We do dat." Again, the Negroes spoke together. One grabbed Mack Leaming's legs, the other the upper part of his body.

He groaned when they lifted him, not because they were harsh but because he couldn't help himself.

Up the steep slope he went. He groaned whenever a Negro's foot came down on the ground. He knew the blacks weren't trying to be cruel—on the contrary, in fact. But the slightest jolt made the long track the Minié ball tore through his body cry out in torment. Tears ran down his cheeks. He bit the inside of his lower lip till he tasted blood.

"Here you is, suh. We lay you down on the ground now," said the black who had him by the shoulders. Leaming yelped like a dog hit by a wagon wheel when they did. After lying still for a moment, he sighed. He still hurt, but with a steady ache, not the sudden, fiery jolts he'd known when they were moving him.

"Do you want some more water?" the Confederate lieutenant asked.

"Oh, please," Leaming said.

"All right. I'm going to lift your head up a little so you can drink easier." Leaming gasped when the Reb did that, but he couldn't deny it helped: not nearly so much water dribbled down the side of his face. And the smoothest whiskey in the world couldn't have done a better job of reviving him than that plain, ordinary water—so he thought, anyhow.

"God bless you," he said, and held out his hand. He was not surprised when the C.S. lieutenant's grip matched his own. They smiled at each other.

A sergeant commandeered the two Negroes who'd carried him up to the top of the bluff. "Come on, damn you!" he yelled. "Don't stand there like lazy niggers, even if you damn well are. Plenty of bodies to dispose of."

Both blacks looked toward the lieutenant. He just shrugged, as if to say he was done with them. Off they went. The sergeant wasn't wrong. Negro and white prisoners were carrying their comrades-in-arms' corpses to the earthwork and throwing them into the ditch in front of it—the ditch that so dismally failed to keep out the Confederaetes.

"There is a man who is not quite dead yet," said someone: a white man, by his voice.

"Put him down." By the authority in the answer, it had to come from a Confederate officer. "If he dies in the night, we can throw him in come morning. And if he's still breathing at sunup . . . Well, we'll worry about it then."

Leaming started to say something to his fellow Freemason, only to discover the man no longer stood by his side. He looked around—where had the lieutenant gone? Leaming couldn't spot him. Was that his voice giving orders over by the sutlers' stalls? Leaming thought so, but couldn't be sure.

He also thought the other man might have done more for him: might, for instance, have hunted up a surgeon to see to his wound. But, although still weak, he no longer feared he would die right away. His wound finally seemed to have stopped bleeding and he felt much better for the water the Rebel lieutenant gave him. He'd been dry as the Utah desert inside.

Not far away, a Negro asked, "Reckon this here's deep enough, suh?"

"Make it deeper, if you please." Mack Leaming blinked in astonishment. That was Major Bradford, sure as hell, and he would have expected Forrest's troopers to kill Bradford out of hand. But the commandant went on, "I want to make sure the scavengers can't get at poor Theo."

"Whatever you say, suh." The black man sounded resigned. Leaming heard first one spade, then another, bite into the ground. Dirt flew out and came down with wet smacking noises.

Bill Bradford still breathing! Leaming shook his head in amazement even though moving hurt. Bradford had done everything he could to make the Rebs in west Tennessee hate him, so why was he still alive after they went on their killing rampage? Try as he would, Leaming couldn't fathom it.

The sun slid below the horizon. Dusk deepened toward darkness.

XIII

MATT WARD LOOKED AT THE hole in the ground in which Major Bradford was burying his brother. By now, it was deeper than the colored gravediggers were tall. It looked blacker than they did, too; in the fading light, it might have gone all the way down to China. Sure as hell, Theodorick Bradford was getting the fanciest send-off of any Federal at Fort Pillow—fancier than the Confederate dead were getting, too.

When Ward glanced at Theo Bradford's body, that thought crossed his mind again. From somewhere, Bill Bradford had come up with a cloth to wrap his brother's corpse. Oh, the shroud was blood-stained here and there from the wounds the older man had taken. But for that, though, he might have died of natural causes.

"Why don't you have some carpenters build him a coffin, too?" Ward asked.

Sarcasm rolled off Bradford like water off a duck's back. "That won't be necessary," the U.S. officer answered. To the colored men roped in to help him, he added, "I reckon you've got it deep enough."

"*I* reckon we done got it deep enough a while ago now," one of the Negroes said. Both of them tossed their shovels out of the grave. One black climbed out at a corner, then reached into the hole to help his comrade out.

"Stick around," Bradford told them. "You'll need to fill it in when I'm done here." They looked at him. They looked at the shovels, and at their hands. They looked at the grave they'd just dug. Neither of them said a word. In their shoes (not that they were wearing shoes), Ward wouldn't have, either. Too easy to knock them over the head and toss them into the ditch outside the earthwork. Whatever happened to them, they wouldn't get a grave like this one. They wouldn't get much of a grave at all.

Major Bradford slid his brother's body into its final resting place as gently as he could. Then he pulled a small Testament from the left breast pocket of his tunic. Almost everyone who carried a little Bible carried it there, in the hope that it would stop an almost-spent Minié ball. Once in a blue moon, it did. Ministers preached sermons about the pocket Testament that saved a life.

Like everything that had to do with Bill Bradford right now, the little book was soaked. He opened it anyway, and frowned. "Too dark to read," he said to Ward. "Would you get me a torch?"

"I ain't your nigger. You can go to the Devil, for all I care," Ward said indignantly. "You want a torch, you can damn well get your own."

"All right, then—I will," Bradford said. He wouldn't have to go far to find one. Plenty of them burned as the Confederates went on plundering Fort Pillow. He came back a few minutes later carrying not only a torch but also a jug. He set that down beside him and offered Ward the torch. "Would you be so kind as to *hold* it for me?"

Grudgingly, Ward nodded. "Reckon I can do that much."

"Thank you kindly." Bradford went through the pocket Testament with care, muttering, "Hope the pages aren't too soggy and stuck together." Then he stopped and nodded. "Here we are." His voice grew solemn: " 'Jesus said unto her, I am the resurrection and the life: he that believeth in me, though he were dead, yet shall he live: And whomsoever liveth and believeth in me shall never die. Believest thou this?' "

"I believe," Matt Ward murmured. The colored soldiers said something, too. The words were probably as familiar to them as they were to him and to Bill Bradford.

Ward thought Bradford would let it go there, but the Federal read some other verses from the Book of John: " 'I am the door: by me, if any man enter in, he shall be saved, and shall go in and out, and find pasture. . . . I am the good shepherd: the good shepherd giveth his life for the sheep. . . . I am the good shepherd, and know my sheep, and am known of mine. As the Father knoweth me, even so I know the Father: and I lay down my life for the sheep. . . . Therefore doth my Father love me, because I lay down my life, that I might take it again. No man taketh it from me, but I lay it down of myself. I have power to lay it down, and I have power to take it again. This commandment have I received of my Father.' "

Major Bradford closed the pocket Testament. He looked at Ward. Feeling something was called for, the Confederate trooper muttered, "Amen." One of the colored soldiers echoed him.

The other one said, "You shoulda been a preacherman, Major. The words, they jus' come right on out."

"I'm putting my brother in the ground," Bill Bradford said. "I don't think I could talk like that for anybody else."

"You want we should cover him over now?" the Negro asked.

"In a minute," Bradford answered. "There's another way to say good-bye to him, too." He picked up the jug. It sloshed. "I managed to get my hands on this before anybody else did. Theo would have liked it this way." He pulled out the cork, raised the jug to his lips, and took a pull. "Ahh!" He handed the jug to Matt Ward. "Here you go."

"I thank you kindly." Ward remembered longing for whiskey early that morning. Had only a day gone by since then? It seemed more like five years. He swigged from the jug. Volcano juice ran down his throat. "Whew!" he said when he could speak again. "That's strong stuff." He started to give the jug back to Bradford.

"Let the niggers have a knock, too," the Federal officer suggested. Ward started to bristle at the idea, but Bradford quickly added, "There's plenty to go round, and they're doing the hard work."

"Well, hell. Why not?" What Ward had just drunk made him magnanimous—or maybe too tipsy to argue. He thrust the jug at the closer Negro. "Here. Go on."

"Much obliged, suh." The black man took the whiskey jug, tilted it back, and then passed it to his comrade. "Mighty nice." The potent stuff didn't faze him at all. Ward wondered if he had a cast-iron gullet.

When Major Bradford got the jug back from the second Negro, he wiped the mouth on his tunic before drinking from it again. Ward would have done the same thing; he didn't want his mouth going where a black's had gone before it. Weren't Federals all hot for nigger equality? He wondered why Bill Bradford, who acted like a Southerner, chose the other side.

Before he could ask, Bradford passed him the jug. Ward didn't mind drinking right after another white man. More tangleleg exploded in his stomach. He looked at the Negroes. "Get to work now."

"Yes, suh," they said together. They weren't rash enough to ask for another pull at the whiskey jug for themselves. They had to know they were lucky to get one. They set to work with the shovels, throwing the dirt they'd dug out back into the grave. It thumped down on Theodorick Bradford's shrouded corpse.

"He was a good man," Bill Bradford said. "He was one of the best." He nodded to Matt Ward. "You have a brother?"

"Not that lived." Ward's head spun when he shook it—that popskull was mean as the Devil. "Had one who died when we were both little. I got me a couple of sisters and a big old raft of cousins." He took another pull at the jug, then offered it back to Bradford.

"Thanks." The Federal officer raised it to his lips. "Cousins are all right, but they're not the same, you know what I mean?" He didn't

seem like such a bad fellow once you talked with him for a while—
and once you'd had enough whiskey to lubricate your brains a little.

"Like I told you, I can't rightly say." Ward eyed Bradford, as well
as he could by the torchlight flickering here and there. Now he asked
his question: "What made you choose the wrong side, anyways?"

"I don't reckon I did," the Tennessee Tory replied, stubborn even
after disastrous defeat. "I believe in building things up, not tearing
them down. The Union's lasted eighty-seven years now. There's
hardly a man alive who wasn't born under the Stars and Stripes. Why
go and tear that to pieces?"

"On account of that damn Lincoln wants to take our niggers away
and tyr-tyr-tyrannize over us." Matt Ward had to try three times before he could get the word out.

"He didn't fire the first shot—you Rebs did that, at Fort Sumter.
And we could have made some kind of arrangement about the niggers. We've had compromises before. We could have found another
one. But Jeff Davis wanted to show what a big man he was, and we've
been shooting at each other ever since."

He trotted the arguments out smooth as you please. Ward remembered hearing he was a lawyer. But he couldn't talk around one thing:
"This here is a Confederate state. If you aren't for the Confederacy,
you're nothing but a dirty old traitor."

"My loyalty is the old one. I'll stick to it." Major Bradford looked
down at his brother's grave. "If you ask me to love the cause that
killed poor Theo, I'm afraid you ask too much."

"Quibble all you care to." Ward hefted his Enfield. "You damn
well lost."

"And isn't that the sad and sorry truth?" Bradford managed a
mournful laugh. He had no weapon, but hefted the whiskey jug instead. "A sorrow I shall try to drown." He drank.

"You already look drowned," Ward told him. "Let me have some
more of that."

"How can I say no? To the victor go the spoils." The Federal officer surrendered the whiskey. Ward raised the jug and took a long pull. Then he took another one.

Next thing he knew, he was sitting on the ground. He didn't know how he'd got there. The whiskey jug sat beside him, though. That was funny. Laughing, he got up and drank some more.

Bill Bradford laughed, too. Ward remembered that.

"Come on!" Nathan Bedford Forrest shouted. "We've got to empty this place out, and we don't have a whole lot of time."

He might have been—he *was*—the best cavalry general in the war. He was proud that his men would throw themselves at the damnyankees sooner than risking his displeasure. But even the mightiest man bumped up against the limits of his power. Forrest's men had fought like fiends. They'd licked the Federals, licked them and plundered them and slaughtered them. Now . . . Now they didn't want to do much more.

Oh, they'd taken the Thirteenth Tennessee Cavalry's horses. You could never have enough remounts. And they would haul off the half-dozen guns they'd captured. Taking the enemy's cannon was proof of your own triumph. But . . .

Bedford Forrest tried again: "We've got all these supplies here. We've got all these cartridges. We need to haul 'em away."

Nobody felt like listening to him. His soldiers had grabbed what they wanted and what they needed as individuals. Right now, he was the only one who seemed worried about grabbing what his ragtag army wanted and needed.

A lot of Confederates had got into the whiskey the Federals put out to nerve their men. Forrest was angry at himself for not laying hold of that as soon as his troops got into Fort Pillow. He should have known better. He *had* known better, but he hung back to let his men have their way with the Negroes and homemade Yankees here. Now he was paying for it.

"Hey, General!" somebody called, his voice full of good cheer and tanglefoot. "Look! We brung you your horse!"

They must have led the animal up the side of the bluff. That surely took a lot of work and trouble. If only they would put so much work and trouble into the things that really needed doing. Bedford Forrest seethed. The worst part was, he had to make them think he was grateful. "Thanks, boys," he said as he climbed into the saddle. Maybe getting up there would do some good. A man on horseback was harder to ignore than a man on foot, even a big, loud man on foot.

Forrest rode over a wounded black man. He thought the fellow was dead, but groans and a feeble effort to get away told him otherwise. The horse snorted and sidestepped; it was no more eager to step on a body, live or otherwise, than any other beast would have been.

Down the slope toward the river, a Confederate who must have been talking to some U.S. prisoners said, "You damned rascals, if you had not fought us so hard but had stopped when we sent in a flag of truce, we would not have done anything to you."

"We didn't reckon we could trust you," came the reply, probably from a Negro's throat.

"How could you have done worse than you did?" the Confederate replied.

"Kill all the niggers," another Confederate said—an officer, by the authority in his voice. A gunshot rang out—a tongue of yellow fire stabbing out down there in the darkness. Somebody screamed.

"No!" another officer shouted. "Forrest says take them and carry them with him to wait on him, and put them in jail and send them to their masters."

He was confused, but he had the general idea. Forrest rode to the edge of the bluff and called, "Yes, I do say that! There's been enough killing, dammit."

A startled silence followed. "Godalmightydamn, that really is Bedford Forrest up there," somebody said.

"Yes, it is. Come on up and help take things out of the fort," Forrest said.

But then someone shouted for him from over near the sutlers' stalls. He started over there. The animal hadn't taken more than three or four strides before more guns barked, down by the Mississippi. A voice floated out of the night: "There's another dead nigger."

Forrest swore softly. He shook his head. The men didn't want to heed him or the officers set directly over them. What could you do? The river had run with blood for two hundred yards when the slaughter was at its height—so someone had told him, anyhow. Maybe that would demonstrate to the Northern people that Negro soldiers could not cope with Southerners.

The horse walked over that colored artilleryman again. His leg was all bloody, and glistened in the flickering torchlight. "What is it?" Forrest called to the lieutenant waving to him from the stalls.

"Sir, I caught this man pilfering goods." The young officer held a pistol on a middle-aged man in civilian clothes.

"Well, what do you need me for?" Forrest said. "Deal with him like he deserves."

"I was not pilfering, by God!" the man said. "I am Hardy Revelle." He struck a pose that suggested Bedford Forrest was supposed to know who he was and what that meant. Forrest stared back stonily. The civilian deflated somewhat. "I am a dry-goods clerk for Harris and Company, whose establishment this is."

"And so?" Forrest growled. "Come to the point and make it snappy, or you'll be sorry."

"After what I've seen today, the murders in cold blood, I am already sorry," Hardy Revelle said. "But I am not pilfering. For one thing, this is my principal's property, so I have more right to it than—" He was likely going to say something like *you thieving Rebs,* but he thought better of it, which was wise. "—than you do," he finished. "For another thing, one of your captains already made me give him a pair of boots. And then after I did, that there captain took me to General McCullough's headquarters—"

"He's Colonel McCulloch." Forrest bore down hard on the last syllable of McCulloch's name.

"Whoever he is, that's where I went." Hardy Revelle didn't care about the correction. He went on, "His surgeon made me show him where the goods were, and a lieutenant with him made off with a bridle and saddle and some bits, and—"

"Wait." Forrest interrupted again, holding up a hand. "What is the name of Colonel McCulloch's surgeon?"

Hardy Revelle frowned. "Durrell? No, that's not right. Durrett." He nodded. "There. Now I have it. And the lieutenant was a big, gawky fellow called Hay."

Bedford Forrest nodded, too, for he was convinced. F. R. Durrett was the Second Missouri Cavalry's regimental surgeon, while J. S. Hay was Colonel McCulloch's ordnance officer. That left only one thing unexplained. "All right, Mr. Revelle—you got these things for the officers, like you say—"

"I sure did." Hardy Revelle might have been the very picture of righteousness.

"Well, fine." Forrest sounded mild—till he suddenly pounced: "So what in blazes are you doing here all by your lonesome? Looks like pilfering to me, by God."

"No, sir. No, sirree. Not me." Now the dry-goods clerk shook his head. "I was just keeping things safe, like."

"Sure you were." Forrest laughed. "Tell me another one."

"What do you want me to do with him, sir?" the Confederate lieutenant asked. "Shall I give him what he deserves, like you said?" He made as if to pull the pistol's trigger. Hardy Revelle quailed.

But Forrest said, "No, let him go for now. These really are his goods to keep an eye on. But if you catch him with his hands full later on, bring him to me again, and we'll see if I change my mind." Of course Revelle was pilfering from his boss's stall. But he did it with enough style to amuse the Confederate general instead of angering him.

"Thank you kindly, sir," Revelle said. "Good to see an honest man can still make his way, it is indeed."

"When you find one, let me know," Forrest told him. Hardy Revelle scratched his head. Forrest laughed some more.

Here came that damned horse again. Ben Robinson couldn't do anything to get out of its way. He had to lie there while Bedford Forrest rode over him for the third—or was it the fourth?—time. Forrest was telling somebody how he got rich trading niggers in Memphis, which wasn't exactly what the wounded black sergeant wanted to hear.

Don't step on me, he thought. *Please don't.* The horse didn't. It had missed him every single time. If it got him, wouldn't that be what they called adding insult to injury? He'd heard the phrase before, but never understood it till now. Getting stepped on by a horse was insulting, sure as hell, and he was already injured.

If he had to get shot to grasp a subtlety of the English language, he would just as soon have stayed ignorant. The wound to his leg hurt worse than anything that had ever happened to him before. It had finally stopped bleeding, or at least slowed down, but he didn't want to do a whole lot of moving around. He was sure that would start it again. Of course, with a gouge bitten out of his thigh he damn well *couldn't* do a whole lot of moving around.

And, at that, he was luckier than most. He could have been screaming for his mother, the way some horribly wounded soldier down by the Mississippi was. Or he could have been dead, the way so much of the Federal garrison was. Every so often, a new body would thud into the ditch beyond the rampart that hadn't helped.

He must have dozed off, because he almost jumped out of his skin when somebody said, "Here's another one of these goddamn nigger sons of bitches."

"Well, you take his feet, and I'll take his head, and we'll fling him in the ditch," another Reb said. "The buzzards and the pigs can squabble over who gets more meat off him, and just what he deserves, too."

"Please don't throw me in dat ditch!" Robinson said. "I ain't dead—I'm only shot."

"Hell," one of the Confederates said, at the same time as the other was going, "Aw, shit." The first one added, "We can kill the bastard pretty damn quick. He ain't dead, but he's sure shot. It ain't like he can fight back."

Ben Robinson got ready to try. How he could fight when he couldn't even walk was beyond him, but he aimed to give it his best shot. Maybe he could pull one of them down, and then. . . . *And then what?* he wondered. *Then they shoot me or stick me, that's what.* But he couldn't just let them murder him.

"General Forrest says we've killed enough of 'em for now," the second Reb said. Ben had never thought he would bless Bedford Forrest's name, but he did then.

The first trooper said something unflattering to his commanding officer. But he said it in a low voice, as if he didn't want Forrest to have any chance of hearing it. Robinson wouldn't have wanted Forrest to hear anything like that, either. The Reb went on, "Well, what the devil shall we do with him, then?"

"There's that hut over yonder, not too far," his friend answered. "We can tote him over there, leave him for the night, and kill him in the mornin'. Nobody'll give a damn about it then, chances are."

"Sounds like a pretty good scheme," the first trooper said, an opinion Robinson didn't share. "Let's do it."

They half carried, half dragged him to the hut. He bit his lip against the pain, but didn't cry out. He was damned if he wanted to show weakness in front of these white men. His wound did start bleeding again; he felt the warm blood trickling down his leg. But there didn't seem to be that much of it. If he could lie still for a bit, he thought it would stop.

When the Rebs got him inside, they dropped him like a sack of potatoes. He did groan then—he couldn't help it. "So long, nigger," one of the troopers said. They vanished into the night.

In spite of the torment from his wound, Ben Robinson started to laugh. Whites reckoned blacks were stupid. As often as not, that meant whites thought they could talk around blacks as freely as if they were by themselves. And thinking they could talk so freely made whites as stupid in truth as they thought blacks were.

We can put him in the hut. We'll come back tomorrow and kill him. Did Forrest's troopers really imagine he'd stick around once he heard that? If they did, they were dumb as rocks. Maybe they figured he was too badly hurt to move. Any which way, they'd be mighty disappointed when morning came and they found their blackbird had flown the coop.

Robinson still couldn't walk. That didn't mean he couldn't move. He wouldn't stick around here for anything, not if he had to crawl on his belly like a reptile to get away. And he damn near did: he hitched himself along on his elbows and one knee. They'd be raw and bloody before he got very far. He didn't care. He'd be a lot bloodier if he didn't get out while the getting was good.

Which way? he wondered once he made it out of the hut. Up on top of the bluff, the Rebs were still doing whatever they wanted. Things seemed quieter down by the Mississippi. And if rescue ever came, it would come by way of the river. Down, then.

Mosquitoes buzzed around him. They came out at dusk. They'd be worse a little further into spring, but they were bad enough now. He didn't care. Confederates with guns were worse than mosquitoes with pointy beaks.

When he went down the side of the bluff, he went slowly—slowly even for a crawling man. He could have rolled down the steep slope in nothing flat, but he didn't know what he'd fetch up against on the way to the bottom. He wasn't in a hurry. Every minute farther away from the hut and those Rebs felt as if it added another year to his life.

Here and there, wounded men groaned in the darkness. Once, Ben heard someone say, "Oh, shut the hell up, you goddamn nigger son of a bitch bastard!" The noise that followed might have been a rock falling on a pumpkin from a tall roof. It might have been, but it wasn't. It came again and again and again. Then the white man grunted—the sort of animal noise he might have made as he spent himself inside a woman—and said, "*He* ain't makin' any more noise."

Another Confederate's voice floated out of the dusk: "You heard what Lieutenant Pennell said about killing people, Jack."

"Yeah, I heard it. So what?" Jack answered. "That's Pennell. You gonna tell me a nigger in a Yankee uniform's a *person?* My ass! A nigger in a Yankee uniform is a snake, is what he is, an' I kill snakes every chance I get."

And snakes'll bite you, too, Ben Robinson thought. He knew damn well he'd killed and wounded his share—more than his share—of Bedford Forrest's troopers, both with the twelve-pounder and in the melee after the Rebs swarmed into Fort Pillow. He knew plenty of other colored soldiers had, too. Yes, they'd lost. But his fellow Negroes hadn't fought any worse than the whites who battled alongside them. The garrison was badly outnumbered, and commanded by a major who wasn't fit to carry General Forrest's boots. Of course they'd lost.

If he lived, if his leg healed up, Ben Robinson was ready to take on the Rebs again. He hated the trooper who'd just beaten a helpless black man to death. He hated him, yes, but he understood him, too. If he got the chance, he'd bite the Confederate States even harder next time.

Ragged wisps of cloud scudded past the moon, now hiding it, now letting it shine down on Fort Pillow. Nearing first quarter, it rode high in the sky, a little west of south. Its pale light would have been better suited to a happier scene, but Bill Bradford couldn't do anything about that.

His head spun. He wasn't so steady on his feet as he wished he were. He'd had to drink a good deal of the vile whiskey he took from the sutler's stall. He'd had to drink a good deal, yes, but he drank a lot less than he pretended to. He might be tiddly, but he wasn't smashed.

The Reb who was supposed to be keeping an eye on him, on the other hand . . . Bradford eyed the young cavalry trooper. The Confederate was still on his feet. All by itself, that said he was a man of impressive capacity. With so much redeye in *him*, Bradford knew he would have curled up asleep somewhere, like a cat in front of a fire.

Asleep the Reb was not. He was singing "O, Susanna"—loudly, and out of tune, in a voice most of an octave deeper than the one he used for ordinary speech. If he'd really had a banjo on his knee, Bradford would have plucked it off and broken it over his head.

Then the trooper stopped. He looked at Bradford. "You're not singing," he said, as if he'd noticed only now. He probably had. He'd been caterwauling away himself for quite a while.

"I just put my brother in the ground," Bradford said. "I don't feel like singing."

"You're a lousy homemade Yankee," the Reb said. "I bet you don't know how to shing—uh, *sing.*"

"I sing in the church choir," Bradford retorted. That was true, even if he hadn't done much of it lately.

"Well, la-de-da," said the Reb—his name was Ward, Bradford remembered. "If you sing there, you can sing here." He wasn't too drunk to remember where his rifle musket lay. "You can sing, or I can blow your fucking head off. Who'd miss you?"

Bill Bradford fought the fear that welled up in him. "Your officers told you to keep me safe."

Ward only laughed. "If I tell 'em you tried to run off, nobody'll give a damn. Hell and breakfast, they'll likely promote me. You stupid son of a bitch, don't you understand that everybody in this whole state wants you dead?"

Everybody in this whole state wants you dead. Bradford knew it was an exaggeration. Tennessee did have its share of Union sympathizers—not enough to keep it from seceding, but enough to make trouble for the Confederate authorities. Even so, the Thirteenth Tennessee Cavalry (U.S.) and other outfits like it were a long way from popular with their neighbors. Ward might be exaggerating, but he wasn't lying.

"I can't sing—it wouldn't be right," Bradford insisted.

"You can if you drink some more." In his own way, the young Reb was a practical man. Now he picked up the whiskey jug and thrust it at Bradford. "Here. Drink, you lousy, stinking bastard."

Bradford drank—some. Then he put his tongue over the opening and pretended to swallow more. That done, he gave the jug back. "Now you."

"What? You reckon I want to drink with a goddamn Tennessee Tory?" Ward scowled at him. Then he seemed to scowl at himself. "But I drank with you already, didn't I? And I sure do want to drink." By the way his Adam's apple worked, he wasn't pretending to pour the rotgut down. "Ahh!" he said, and wiped his mouth on his sleeve. "That's the stuff, all right." Bradford hoped he would forget why they were drinking, but he didn't. On a day full of defeats, here was one more. Ward scowled again. "Sing, God damn you."

And so, standing by his brother's grave, William Bradford sang "O, Susanna" with a drunken Confederate cavalry trooper who would sooner have shot him. Tears streamed down his face. Ward never noticed. *By God, you'll pay for this—you and Bedford Forrest and Jeff Davis, too.*

When the song was finally over, Ward looked at Bradford. "Well, you *can* sing. Who would've thunk it? You may be a lousy, stinking bastard, but you aren't a lousy, stinking, lying bastard, anyways."

"I'm so glad you approve," Bradford murmured. No doubt luckily for him, that went right over the Reb's head. He gestured at the jug. "Have another knock, why don't you?"

"I will if you will," Ward said. "You've got to sing some more, too. You're pretty goddamn good, all right." He picked up the jug and swigged from it, then passed it to Bradford. "Damn thing's almost dry."

And you're still on your feet, goddammit. I thought you'd pass out on me right away. Do you have a hollow leg? Aloud, Bradford said, "I

found that one. I expect I can come up with another one if I need to."
He also drank—again, less than he pretended to. Pretty soon, the Reb
would have to fall asleep . . . wouldn't he?

Not yet. "Sing," he told Bradford, and launched into "Camptown
Ladies." Wincing, nearly sobbing, the Federal officer joined in. The
tune was cheerful, even joyous. His mood was anything but.

Another Confederate soldier wandered over and joined in. Not
too surprisingly, he had a jug of his own. He was a friendly sort, and
willing to share. After a healthy snort, Ward sat down on the ground.
"How come you're shtill shtanding?" he demanded of Bradford, his
voice thick and slurred.

"I've always had a good head on my shoulders." Bill Bradford
wondered why Ward was still breathing, let alone talking and making
some sense. The amount he'd put away . . . He'd pay for it in the
morning. But Bradford wanted him to pay sooner than that.

Ward blinked now, his eyes shining in the moonlight, and shook
his head. "You had a good head on your shoulders, you wouldn't be a
homemade Yankee. You'd be on the right shide inshtead." He
yawned, shook his head again as if annoyed at himself, and then
wagged a finger at Bradford. "Don't you go nowhere," he warned.
But that was the end. He slowly slumped to the ground and slept.

"About *time*," Bill Bradford breathed. Now he had a chance.

"You there! Jenkins!" That sharp, astringent voice could only belong
to Second Lieutenant Newsom Pennell.

"Yes, sir?" Corporal Jenkins fought to sound properly respectful.
It wasn't easy. He didn't like Pennell, and it cut both ways. Jenkins belonged to Company A and Pennell to Company F, but the junior officer went out of his way to find things for him to do, and came down
on him hard when he didn't do them well enough to suit Pennell's
persnickety tastes. That was how it seemed to Jack Jenkins, anyhow.
He never stopped to wonder how it seemed to the lieutenant.

Pennell came up to him, there by the riverbank. The officer was almost too skinny to cast a shadow. He had a narrow, disapproving face, and wore a little hairline mustache that made him look like a French fop. Jenkins was used to beards that were beards and mustaches that were mustaches, not one that looked as if it were drawn on with a burnt match.

"We need a better perimeter around the fort," Pennell declared.

"How come, sir?" Jenkins asked in honest surprise. "We done took the place."

"Yes, yes," Lieutenant Pennell said impatiently. "We took it, and now we have to make sure no one gets out of it."

"I thought we took care of that pretty good," Jenkins said. "We shot most of the bastards in there. The ones that ain't dead ain't goin' anywhere quick." He hefted his rifle musket. Even the moonlight was enough to show the grisly stains on the stock.

But Lieutenant Pennell ignored them, as he ignored Jenkins's comment. "I am going to send you out to the original line of defense around this place, the one that General Pillow laid out," he said, a certain somber glee in his voice. "You and your fellow pickets will stand watch through the night, allowing no one to pass through unless a Confederate soldier or provided with proper authorization. Is that clear?"

"Why'd you pick on me?" Jenkins didn't add, *you son of a bitch,* not where Newsom Pennell could hear it, but he thought it very loudly.

"When I saw you there, I thought how useful an underofficer might be among the pickets," Pennell answered.

When you saw me standing here, you reckoned you'd land me with a crappy duty. That's what it is, Jenkins thought. "Thanks a hell of a lot, sir," he said.

"You're welcome." Pennell either didn't notice the sarcasm— Jenkins's guess—or refused to admit that he did. "Now go take your place. God only knows how many Federals are trying to sneak away even as we speak."

God knows it ain't very many. But, short of bashing in Pennell's brains with the gory rifle musket, Jenkins was stuck, and he knew it. With a martyred sigh, he said, "Yes, sir." He didn't salute as he stomped away from Pennell. If the lieutenant wanted to call him on it, fine. Pennell said not a word.

Even finding Fort Pillow's outer works by moonlight wasn't easy. He might never have done it had he not heard several other disgruntled pickets grousing with one another. They gave the two stripes on his sleeve suspicious looks—they had to wonder if he was coming to make them act like proper soldiers. But when he started discussing Newsom Pennell's unsavory ancestry and inflammable destination, they knew him for a fellow sufferer and relaxed.

One of them had a jug. He was willing to share it. "Leastways you brought a little something out of the fort," another picket said mournfully. "Me, I didn't get no loot a-tall."

"This should've been our chance," another man said. He drew on his pipe. The glowing red coal in the bowl lit up the top of his face from beneath: a strange, almost hellish glow. "Now we're stuck out here, and the others're getting all the goodies."

Jenkins already had some greenbacks and new shoes, and now a knock of whiskey. He didn't know what else he could expect to get, but he joined in the grumbling anyway. When the jug came around again, he took another good swig. Thus fortified, he found a place on the outer line that wasn't too close to anybody else's.

Out in the darkness beyond, a whip-poor-will said its name. Jenkins said Lieutenant Pennell's name, loudly and foully. Nothing was going to happen out here. This was all a waste of time. Here he was, stuck. "I'll pay you back for this, Pennell. See if I don't," he muttered.

XIV

WHEREVER THE REBEL OFFICER WHO was a Freemason had gone, it didn't look as if he was coming back. Mack Leaming lay where the two Negroes who carried him up to the top of the bluff had left him. He was chilly. The gunshot wound pained him and gnawed at his vitality. But he believed he would live. Maybe the water the Reb gave him helped that much. Maybe his bleeding had stopped. Or maybe he was just tougher than he thought after first getting hit.

Every so often, a Confederate would walk by and look him over. Seeing him barefoot and without his trousers, each Reb in turn would realize he'd already been picked clean and go away. A couple of them thought he was dead. They wanted to put him on the pile of bodies not far away.

"I'm still here," Leaming said when one of Forrest's troopers bent to take hold of his ankles.

The man jerked back in surprise—and, if Leaming was any judge, in fear as well. "Goddamn!" he exclaimed. "For a second there, I reckoned you was a dead man talkin' to me."

"Not quite," Leaming answered. "I'm only a wounded prisoner."

He wanted to remind the Reb that Bedford Forrest had taken prisoners; just because he wasn't dead now, that didn't mean the trooper couldn't kill him in a hurry.

"Gave me quite a turn," the enemy soldier said.

"Do you have a canteen? Could I have some water, please?" Leaming asked. Perhaps because of the blood he'd lost, he'd stayed thirsty even after the Confederate Freemason's kindness.

"Sorry. I drank it dry myself during the fight." Unlike a lot of his comrades, this Rebel didn't sound actively hostile.

That encouraged Leaming to say, "Could you get me some water, please? Would you be so good?"

He watched Forrest's trooper think it over. "No, I don't believe I would," the Reb said at last. "You're a homemade Yankee, a Tennessee Tory, a damned renegade. If you was standing here and I was laying there, would you get me water?"

"I hope I would," Leaming said.

But he might as well have kept quiet, for the other man went on, "I don't think so. I expect you'd give me a sermon instead, and tell me how wonderful it was to lick Abe Lincoln's boots and kiss a nigger's ass. I don't care to murder a helpless man, but you get no help from me, neither." He walked off.

If I die because I get no water, won't you have murdered me? Leaming thought. But he did doubt he would die now. He was alive and suffering, and likely to go on suffering for quite a while. The white-hot agony he'd known after he first got shot was duller now, but taking a Minié ball still hurt much worse than anything else that had ever happened to him—and he'd had a toothache that kept him sleepless for two days and nights before a dentist finally did his bloody work.

A couple of white Federals—prisoners, of course—paused to look at him. "Isn't that Lieutenant Leaming?" one of them asked.

"Sure looks like him, poor devil," the other said. "So he got it, too, eh?"

Leaming opened and closed his right hand. "I'm not dead," he said.

Both men from the Thirteenth Tennessee Cavalry (U.S.) started as violently as the Confederate trooper did a few minutes before. "Jesus Christ!" one exploded. His laugh was shaky. "You gave us a hell of a jolt there, Lieutenant."

"That's a fact," the other agreed.

"You're Bill Ryder," Leaming said to him. The Federal nodded. Leaming had to think about the other man's name: "And Elmer Haynes." He got it at last. "What have the Rebs done to you?"

"We been totin' bodies," Haynes answered.

"Hell of a lot of 'em," Ryder added. "They took all the money I had, too. Only good thing about that is, I didn't have much."

"I'm sorry. They robbed me, too." Leaming wished he hadn't had much money. It was gone now, into that thieving Reb's pocket, and his gold watch, too. He asked, "Is there any place where they're taking care of wounded Federals?"

The two troopers looked at each other. Slowly, Haynes said, "They've got some of 'em down in the barracks we tried to burn this morning."

"They've got 'em there, yeah." Bill Ryder seemed content to comment on what Haynes said. "They've got 'em, but I don't know what they're doing for 'em. Don't know that they're doing anything for 'em, tell you the truth."

"Could you men carry me there?" Leaming asked. "Lying on a floor, lying under a roof, has to be better than this."

Ryder and Haynes looked at each other again. They both sighed. They both shrugged. "Reckon we could," Haynes said resignedly. "One more toting job—what the hell?"

"You want the head end or the feet end, Elmer?" Ryder said.

"I had the head last time," Haynes said. "Your turn for that."

"Be careful when you lift me," Mack Leaming said as Ryder stooped by him. "Be—*Aii!*" He bit down hard, but couldn't stifle the yip of anguish as the captured trooper picked him up.

"Where are you men going with that body?" a Confederate officer demanded. "Just throw it in the damn ditch."

"Not a body, sir—he's alive." Haynes spoke as respectfully to the

Reb as he would have to one of his own superiors. Leaming didn't like that, but he was in no position to criticize. Haynes went on, "We were taking him down to the barracks, to put him with the other wounded down there."

He's not so dumb, Leaming thought. By reminding the Confederate that other injured Federals were in the barracks building, Haynes made this transfer seem routine.

Sure enough, the officer nodded. "All right, go ahead. But don't dawdle around. Still plenty of dead ones to get rid of."

"We won't, sir." Bill Ryder sounded respectful, too. Under that respect, though, Leaming heard an old soldier talking. Ryder didn't intend to move one lick faster than he had to.

The Confederate officer turned away. Ryder and Haynes carried Lieutenant Leaming across a plank bridge over the ditch, and then down the front of the bluff. Leaming shook his head in wonder, though the motion made him hurt even more than he already did on account of the jolting journey. Was it only this afternoon that he walked down the same slope to parley with Nathan Bedford Forrest? It was, even if it seemed a million years away.

Just this afternoon, I was spry as a bighorn, he thought. That didn't seem possible, either. He couldn't stand now if his life depended on it. He wondered if he would ever be hale again. He hoped so, but had no notion of how bad his wound was. He couldn't see it. All he could do was suffer, and he was doing plenty of that.

"I do believe I'd sell my soul for a few drops of laudanum," he said.

"We ain't got any, Lieutenant," Elmer Haynes said. Ryder nodded. Haynes added, "Maybe one of the Rebs' surgeons can fix you up."

"Maybe." Leaming didn't believe it. For one thing, the Confederates were always desperately short of everything except guns and ammunition and powder. They never ran low on those, damn them. For another, Forrest's men—with the exception of that one Freemason—seemed unwilling to help Federals in any way. Surgeons were supposed to treat men from both sides, but Leaming wondered whether a physician who served this set of Rebs would meet the obligation.

It turned out not to matter. When the two prisoners set him down on the floor in one of the barracks halls, there was no sign of any surgeon, Union or Confederate. The building was full of wounded men, some badly hurt, others less so.

"Good luck, Lieutenant." For once, Bill Ryder spoke first. He and Haynes vanished into the dusk.

A couple of candles illuminated what looked like an engraving of one of the lower circles of Hell in *The Divine Comedy*. Soldiers writhed and thrashed and groaned. One man had lost an arm; two others were missing legs. They needed laudanum much worse than Mack Leaming did, and they had none. Nobody had anything: no water, no food, no medicine, no surgeons, no attendants. All they had were one another and their shared torment.

Leaming wondered if he would have been better off where he was. It was quieter up on top of the bluff, even if it was colder and wetter. He might have had a better chance of falling asleep.

"Mother!" sobbed one of the men who'd lost a leg. "Mother! Help me, Mother!" No doubt she would have if she could, but she was somewhere far away. And all she could have done might not have been enough for her maimed son.

"Water!" someone else called. No one heeded that prayer, either. If the wounded Federals won longer lives for themselves, they would have to do it each man on his own.

As Ben Robinson lay by the Mississippi, he wondered how big a fool he'd been to come back down to the river. Confederates prowled the riverbank looking for Federals who were still alive. Any live men they found quickly died. Robinson heard only a couple of shots. Those drew irate yells from Secesh officers, who were trying to bring their troops back under control. Most of the prowlers used knife or bayonet or rifle butt, which made less noise.

A couple of Rebs walked past Ben. One of them said, "Will you look at that dead nigger, Eb? Son of a bitch was a sergeant—a nigger sergeant! You ever imagine there was such a thing in all the history of the world before?"

"Reckon not," Eb said solemnly. "Like any nigger can tell somebody else what to do. Well, this bastard got what he deserved."

"You'd best believe it," the other trooper said. "We taught the whole world a lesson here today, we did."

"Bet your ass," Eb said. "The damnyankees reckoned niggers and a bunch of goddamn Tennessee renegades could whip real white men. Honest Abe damn well better do himself some more reckoning, by God. Honest Abe!" He spat in vast contempt.

"They won't never lick us, not if we have to fight 'em the next hundred years," his friend said. "Ain't nobody never gonna tell me no niggers as good as I am. Just on account of Abe Lincoln looks like an ape himself, that's how come he loves them black gorillas so much."

"Expect you're right." Eb spat again. They walked on.

Ben Robinson didn't breathe more than tiny little sips of air till he could hear their footfalls no more. He already knew how Southern whites felt about Negroes. If they didn't feel that way, would they have bought and sold him? And the more whites in the C.S.A. swore at Abraham Lincoln, the more they convinced blacks he was the answer to their prayers. Lincoln wasn't even on the ballot in most Southern states, but if Robinson could have voted . . .

Me? Vote? The more he thought about the idea, the better he liked it. If he was a free man, shouldn't he be able to do everything free men did? He didn't have his letters, but so what? Plenty of white men didn't have their letters, either, but that didn't stop them from voting. And maybe he could learn. Free men could go to school, after all. Teaching them to read and write wasn't a crime, the way it was with slaves in South Carolina.

Then another cloud passed in front of the moon. Darkness poured down on the riverside. New fears filled Ben Robinson—new and at the same time ancient, far more ancient than the simple fear of having Bedford Forrest's troopers smash in his head. Darkness was the time of witches and ghosts and hants, and he lay here helpless, unable to get away.

White men talked about believing in hants and all the other terrible things that prowled the darkness. White men talked about it, but they didn't really do it, not down deep, not where it really mattered. Ben did. He believed in his belly, in his balls. *Something* just out of sight always lay in wait in the dark, ready to reach out and grab, to terrify, to possess, to frighten to death. How many people died all of a sudden, without a mark on them, without a sign of sickness? Too many, far too many. If a conjure woman didn't spell them into the grave, if a hant didn't drag them down into it, why weren't they still alive? Who could answer a question like that? Nobody.

Something buzzed past Ben's ear. Maybe it was only a mosquito. Yes, maybe. But did a mosquito really sound *just* like that? Robinson didn't think so. It might be a hant, waiting for him to fall asleep or just to let his attention lapse.

"Go 'way. Go 'way, bad thing." Those quietly desperate words didn't spring from Ben's throat, but from that of some other Negro not far away. He wasn't the only black man with night terrors, then. Oddly, the other man's fear helped ease his. He realized he wasn't alone. If a hant did try to grab him, somebody might come to his rescue. And, a lower part of his mind added, if he wasn't alone out here, the hant or the ghost or the witch might decide to torment somebody else.

The moon came out from behind a cloud. Pale, cool light spilled across the land. The moon's reflection, shattered and rippled a thousand thousand times by the current, danced on the river. Moonlight was better than darkness . . . wasn't it? Or did it give the things still lurking in black shadow the chance they needed to find a victim?

He didn't know. He was only a man, a frightened, wounded, pain-filled man. Daybreak just past seemed much further away than the moon. The things he'd done since then! The things he'd seen! The things he'd lived through! . . . And the things so many of his comrades hadn't lived through.

Would he live to see the sun rise tomorrow? That seemed even more distant than the dawn that was shattered by Confederate gunfire. If he reached it, he promised he would praise the Lord.

A lot of people must have made a lot of promises while the fighting in Fort Pillow raged. A lot of the people who made those promises were dead now, more than a few of them shot trying to surrender. What did that mean? Were the men who'd made those fancy promises and then died hypocrites and sinners?

Or did God listen to the Confederates instead? No doubt they'd been praying and promising, too. Most of them were alive and well and enjoying the spoils of victory. Did that mean God was on their side? But they were losing the war. If they weren't, the Federals wouldn't hold Memphis. The United States wouldn't have held Fort Pillow.

What did it all mean? The more you looked at it, the less sense it made. Robinson thought of himself as a good Christian man. How could God favor people who wanted to keep him in bondage? But he'd seen enough to know that Forrest's troopers honestly couldn't imagine God favoring someone with black skin at their expense.

As a good Christian man, he shouldn't have feared hants and ghosts and witches. If he followed the Lord, how could they hurt him? He didn't suppose they could have if his soul were stainless. But he knew all the bad things he'd done, and knew how many of them there were. Maybe God would let a hant grab him to pay him back for all his sins. How could you know?

You couldn't. And so he lay shivering, knowing how long this night would be.

Major Bill Bradford looked down at Matt Ward, who lay snoring and curled up like a dog beside his brother's grave. Ward had one protective arm flung over his rifle musket, but Bradford didn't think the cavalry trooper would notice if someone lifted it. He didn't think Ward would notice if a cannon went off beside his head. The Reb had finally drunk himself blind.

"Took you long enough, you son of a bitch," Bradford muttered. He wanted to kick Ward in the face, but didn't have the nerve. The man might wake up in spite of all the rotgut he'd guzzled, or someone might see, or. . . . Bradford had no trouble finding reasons not to dare.

The most important one was, he wanted escape even more than vengeance. No one was paying any attention to him now. If he couldn't seize this moment and disappear, he feared he would never get another chance.

He feared . . . That said it all. The sport the Confederates had with him after Fort Pillow fell, the bullets lashing into the Mississippi all around him . . . He didn't trust any offer of safety from Nathan Bedford Forrest and his officers. It was as simple as that. His parole? Better to get away now and renew the fight another time than to stay a prisoner and suffer an unfortunate accident. He was sure that was how Bedford Forrest would mention it in his reports—if Forrest bothered to mention it at all.

Quick, furtive glances to the right and left convinced Bradford nobody was watching him. Even so, he couldn't just walk away, not in the soaking-wet uniform of a major of the U.S. Cavalry. As casually as he could, as casually as if he had every right in the world to do so, Bradford strolled toward the sutlers' stalls. The Rebs were still ransacking some of them. Others, though, were dark and quiet, which probably meant they'd been picked clean.

Or they'd been picked clean of what the Confederates thought of as plunder, anyhow. Bradford smiled thinly. Right this minute, he was easier to please than Bedford Forrest's troopers.

Looking around again to make sure he went unnoticed, he ducked into one of the dark, deserted stalls. He went behind the counter and felt around there. Nothing. He swore under his breath. Why couldn't this be easy? Why couldn't anything be easy?

Farther back in the stall was the nasty little room where the sutler slept. Bradford wrinkled his nose against the stench when he went in there—didn't the man ever wash? He found what he needed, though: civilian-style trousers and shirt. They too reeked powerfully of their former owner, which might have been why no Confederate lifted them.

Bradford couldn't afford to be fussy. He took off his own soggy pants and the nine-buttoned tunic that made him so proud, then put on the sutler's clothes. They were big and baggy on him; the sutler must have been a larger man. But better too big than too small. If he cinched the belt up tight, the trousers wouldn't fall down, which was all that really mattered.

He started to go, but then abruptly stopped himself. "Good God!" he exclaimed. "I almost forgot about my hat!" It was still wet, too, but that wouldn't show. He pulled off the feather, the gold cord with the acorn finials that marked an officer, and the crossed-swords cavalry badge. That done, he set it back on his head. Now it would pass for an ordinary civilian slouch hat. If he hadn't fixed it, though, it would have betrayed him as soon as the first Reb got a good look at it.

Out of the stall he went, as fast as he could. Fort Pillow always smelled as if several hundred men had been living in it for weeks— and they had. But the air outside seemed sweet as nectar beside what he had been breathing.

A Confederate sergeant walked past him. His heart leaped into his throat. But the Reb strode by without a second glance. Bill Bradford smiled. The Confederates didn't necessarily recognize *him,* then— they recognized a U.S. major. If a frowzy civilian tried to leave Fort Pillow, why should they care? No reason in the world.

Logic might tell him that was so, but how far could he trust logic? If anything went wrong, he was dead.

Yes, and if you hang around here you're dead, too, he reminded himself. Not all Confederates recognized him, but some assuredly did. And he was violating the parole he'd given Colonel McCulloch and General Forrest. If he was going to do that, he couldn't very well do it halfway.

Out of here, then. He hadn't gone more than a dozen paces toward the rampart that had proved so useless before somebody called, "Hey, you! Yes, you in the dirty shirt! Where in blazes you reckon you're going?"

Ice in his belly, Bradford stopped and turned. A young, officious-looking C.S. lieutenant bustled up to him, waiting importantly for his answer. "You people already went and cleaned me out," he said in surly tones, staring down at his shoes so the Reb wouldn't get a good look at his face. "Ain't much point to sticking around, not when I got nothin' left to sell."

"You're a civilian?" the lieutenant asked.

"Don't look like no soldier, do I?" Bradford said. Technically, as the lawyer's side of his mind noted, that wasn't a lie. It also wasn't a direct answer to the question.

That wasn't the reason it didn't satisfy the Rebel officer. "You weren't shooting at us earlier today?" Some of the sutlers had picked up Springfields and joined Fort Pillow's garrison. Much good it did them.

As for Bradford, he shook his head. "Not me," he said. "I'm a what-do-you-call-it—a noncombatant, that's the word." As soon as he spoke, he started to worry. An attorney would know that term, but would a sutler?

"Yeah, sure you are," the Confederate jeered. But then he shook his head. "What else are you going to say? I can't prove you're a liar, so get the hell out of here."

"Thank you kindly, sir," Bradford said. The lieutenant just gestured impatiently. Touching one finger to the brim of his hat in what wasn't quite a salute, Bradford hurried away. He kept looking down at the muddy ground, as if to avoid stepping into a puddle or tripping over a corpse. And he didn't want to do either of those things, but most of all he didn't want to be recognized. If the Rebs should catch him now, in civilian clothes, violating his parole . . . Whatever happened to him after that, they could claim he deserved it.

"Come on, you men! What are you standing around for?" The

loud, angry voice that split the night made Bill Bradford flinch as if the cat o' nine tails had come down on his back. There stood Nathan Bedford Forrest himself, not twenty feet away, still trying to get work out of his men at a time when almost any victorious officer would have let them relax and savor what they'd done. If he turned around and saw Bradford, everything came to pieces.

But he didn't. Someone said, "Sir, we've found some more crates of cartridges over here."

"Have you, by God?" Forrest sounded delighted. "We'll bring 'em away with us. Can't very well fight a war without minnies. Let's see what you got." Despite a limp, his long legs ate up the ground as he strode over to look at his men's latest prize.

And Bill Bradford scurried across the plank bridge the Confederates had thrown across the ditch outside the rampart. How many Federals, white and black, lay in the ditch waiting for somebody to shovel dirt over them? *I spared Theo that fate, anyhow,* Bradford thought. *He won't lie in a mass grave with a nigger on top of him.*

Someone groaned. Bradford's blood ran cold again. He thought the sound came from the ditch below him, though he couldn't be sure. If the Rebs set prisoners to burying those bodies, would they be burying some men alive? He would never know.

His shoes stopped reverberating on the planks. They thumped on the dirt beyond. He blew out a great sigh of relief. Now that he'd made it this far, the Rebs were much less likely to know him even if they saw him. And they were much less likely to see him—torches out here were few and far between.

For the first time since Theodorick fell, he began to hope. He might get away. He might yet live to avenge his brother. As quickly and quietly as he could, he headed away from the bluff and out toward Gideon Pillow's long-abandoned first perimeter.

Corporal Jack Jenkins hated everything and everybody. He'd always hated homemade Yankees and runaway slaves who thought they were soldiers. He'd fed the fires of that hatred today, fed them and slaked them at the same time. He didn't know how many men he'd killed in the fight for Fort Pillow. He did know the number wasn't small.

And he knew one more man he wouldn't mind killing: Lieutenant Newsom Pennell, the miserable, no-good son of a bitch who'd exiled him here. Napoleon on whatever the name of his island was couldn't have been in a more miserable, more godforsaken spot. Did Napoleon have to worry about muddy boots and owls hooting like mournful ghosts in the tall trees? Jenkins didn't think so.

He wanted to wander off and see if that other sentry had some more popskull in his canteen. And he wanted to curl up right where he was and go to sleep. Only one thing held him back: animal fear of Nathan Bedford Forrest. If he broke regulations and something bad happened and Forrest found out about it . . . He shuddered. He didn't want to think about that.

And so he held his ground, certain he was holding it needlessly. Who would come out of the dark from the torchlit bluff by the river? His own forces had a road, or at least a path, they were using, and it took them nowhere near him. That was all right. He didn't much want to see anybody.

As for prisoners, they would have to be lunatics to try to get away. They'd managed to get captured by men who would rather have killed them. Why would they risk that now? If they had any sense, they would be on their knees thanking God for every breath they took.

And then, just when a yawn stretched and wriggled and looked around to see if it was safe to come out, he heard soft, quick footsteps coming his way. His hands tightened on his rifle musket. So somebody was trying to sneak by after all, was he? *I'll fix the bastard,* Jenkins thought.

There he was in the moonlight—some skulking shitheel with his hat pulled down low. "Halt!" Jenkins called. "Who goes there?"

The footsteps stopped. The man looked wildly this way and that, trying to see where the voice was coming from. He couldn't; Jenkins stood in deep shadow. The corporal wondered if he would have some more shooting to do after all. If that fellow started to run, he'd never make another mistake afterwards.

He must have realized the same thing because he stayed where he was. "My name's, uh, Virgil Simms," he said shakily. "I was a sutler at the fort. They said I could go, so I'm getting out of here before they change their mind."

"Who's 'they'?" Jenkins demanded.

"One of your officers—I think he was a lieutenant," the sutler said. "I didn't ask what the devil his name was. I just went."

"Well, Simms, advance and be recognized." The automatic military phrases fell naturally from Jack Jenkins's lips.

He heard Virgil Simms's breath catch. Slowly and reluctantly, the other man came forward. He got within about fifteen feet of Jenkins before he stopped and said, "Where are you? I can't see you."

Jenkins stepped out into the light. The sutler gasped again. Jenkins brandished his rifle musket, enjoying the way the cold, pale moonbeams glittered off the bayonet's polished steel. By the way Virgil Simms gulped, he didn't enjoy it one bit. "You can see me now, by God," Jenkins said. "Come on over here and let me get a look at you."

Even when Simms did, Jenkins couldn't see much. The brim of the sutler's slouch had shadowed his face. His clothes didn't fit him very well, but Jenkins's clothes didn't fit *him* very well, either. His nose wrinkled; Simms was long overdue for a bath.

"Wonder if I ought to take you back to that lieutenant," Jenkins said musingly.

"Whatever you want to do." The sutler didn't sound very happy. Then again, Jenkins wouldn't have been happy hearing that, either. After a moment, Simms went on, "Long way back in the dark. I almost broke my neck a couple times getting this far."

"Yeah." Jenkins had tripped and almost fallen two or three times coming out to take his sentry's post. He didn't really want to go back to Fort Pillow again. He'd just thrown out the words to see if he could rattle Virgil Simms's cage. "Hell with it," he muttered, and then spoke louder: "All right, pass on. Reckon you won't be dumb enough to go on selling shit to the goddamn Federals from here on out."

"Not me." Simms held up his right hand as if taking an oath. "I have plumb learned my lesson."

Jenkins gestured with his rifle musket. "Get the hell out of here, then."

The sutler touched a finger to the brim of his hat. He walked out past the old perimeter to Fort Pillow, and hadn't gone more than a few paces before a cloud passed in front of the moon. Darkness swooped down on the world. By the time the moon came out again, Simms had disappeared into the woods beyond the fort. Jenkins ducked back into his shadow and waited to see if anyone else would come along.

"What time is it getting to be?" Nathan Bedford Forrest asked.

Captain Anderson pulled out his pocket watch. "Sir, it's getting close to eight," he said.

"Thanks. That's about what I reckoned from the moon," Forrest said. "Where in blazes is that damned Major Bradford, then? How long does he need to bury his blasted brother?"

"His brother *was* blasted, by God," Black Bob McCulloch said. Pausing to scratch at his thick, dark beard, the brigade commander went on, "Captain Bradford, whatever the hell his name was—"

"Theodorick," Anderson said helpfully.

"I knew he had some kind of damnfool handle," McCulloch said. "His brother the major had him signaling down to the *New Era*. When we broke into the fort, Theo-whatever took three or four minnies all at once. He died quick, anyway."

"And he's getting buried slow," Forrest growled. "Either Bill Bradford's taking his own sweet time or he's gone and flown the coop on us."

"If he has, we better not catch him again." McCulloch tilted back his head and slashed a thumb across his throat.

"Well, we won't find out standing around gabbing about it. Let's go look." Forrest drummed the fingers of his left hand against his thigh. "I felt sorry for the man, even if he is a Tennessee Tory, on account of I know what he's goin' through. But if he went and took advantage of me after that . . ." Those fingers drummed some more, ominously.

"And of me," Colonel Robert McCulloch added. "I'm the man who's holding his parole. If he ran off . . ." His big hands folded into fists.

"Come on," Forrest said. "His precious Theo was laying over here somewheres."

He didn't need much prowling before he found a freshly dug grave. Next to it, he found a cavalry trooper sound asleep—or rather drunk and passed out, for he stank of whiskey. There was no sign of Major William Bradford. Forrest started to kick the trooper right where it would do the most good. Before he could bring his booted foot forward, Captain Anderson said, "What do you want to bet Bradford fed him all the tanglefoot he could hold, and a little more besides?"

Forrest left the kick undelivered. "I bet you're right, dammit. Hell, of course you are," he said, angry at himself now. "We knew all along he was a sneaky son of a bitch. We should have watched him closer. Easy enough for him to make one private act the fool and then take off." He drank whiskey himself only rarely, for medicinal purposes; he knew what it did to a man who liked it too well.

Colonel McCulloch bent down and shook the trooper. "Come on, Ward! Wake up!" he said.

The cavalryman—Ward—muttered and stirred. Slowly, his eyes came open. "Wahsh up?" he asked blearily.

"That's what we want to find out," Forrest said. "Where the devil's Bradford?"

Ward looked around. His eyes fixed on the grave for a moment, but even in his fuddled state he realized the man in it was the wrong Bradford. Theodorick wasn't missing, nor would he ever be. No matter how plastered Ward was, he took Nathan Bedford Forrest seriously. Anyone who didn't made a dreadful mistake. "Sir, he wahsh—*was*—right here." The young cavalryman looked around in obvious, even if sozzled, confusion. "I don't know where he could've gone, or how he could've gone anywhere. He was drinking as much as me, honest to God he was." He hiccuped.

His words puzzled Forrest, the near-teetotaler. They didn't puzzle Black Bob McCulloch. "Jesus wept!" the colonel burst out. "That's the oldest trick in the world. Make like you're drinking, only don't swallow—more likely, don't even let it get into your mouth at all."

"Oh." Bedford Forrest's voice held a grim rumble.

"Oh!" Ward, by contrast, sounded horrified. "I reckon I messed up."

"I reckon you did," McCulloch agreed. He turned to Forrest. "What shall we do with him, sir? He's one of mine. The blame lands on me."

"Let it go," Forrest answered. "He didn't know Bradford was a snake in the grass, and the reptile"—he pronounced it rep-*tile*—"went and hornswoggled him. Way he'll feel come morning, that'll make sure he remembers he got took."

"Maybe we should have had another Tennessean watching Bradford, not a man from Missouri," Charles Anderson said. "Anybody from this state would have had a better notion of what the man is like."

"We all got fooled," Forrest said. "Every last one of us did, by God. I felt sorry for Bradford on account of I lost my brother, too. Colonel McCulloch trusted him enough to accept his parole. That sneaky goddamn note he sent out this afternoon should have warned the lot of us. 'Your demand does not produce the desired effect.'" He made a horrible face. "Anybody who could write anything like that, he shows you can't trust him from the git-go."

"I fed the man." Colonel McCulloch sounded disgusted with himself. "I offered him a place to sleep in my own tent. I'm lucky he didn't cut my throat in the night, I reckon."

"Wouldn't be surprised." Bedford Forrest nodded. "He might've done it if he didn't get loose this way instead. A reptile, like I say."

Private Ward sat on the ground with his head in his hands. By the way he looked, he already felt bad; he wouldn't need to wait till morning. "I didn't *mean* to let him get away," he said—by the wonder in his voice, he was talking more to himself than to the officers standing over him.

"What you mean is one thing. What happens is something else," Forrest said, not unkindly. "Now we've got to deal with that. Sure as hell, Bradford's got away from Fort Pillow. What'll he do next? Where'll he go?"

"Memphis." Colonel McCulloch and Captain Anderson said the same thing at the same time.

Nathan Bedford Forrest nodded again. Memphis was the great Federal bastion in western Tennessee. The United States had taken the city early in the war, and hung on to it ever since. Any Union sympathizer in these parts would head that way. "What are our chances of catching him?"

"How well does he know the country?" Anderson asked in return.

"Pretty well. He's from these parts," Forrest said unhappily. He tried to look on the bright side of things: "Still and all, ain't but one of him, and there's lots of us. Now that we know he's loose, we've got a chance of running him down."

"He'll be sorry when we do." Black Bob McCulloch didn't say *if.* Bedford Forrest smiled. He liked men like that. Had William Bradford seen that smile, he would have run even faster than he was running. Well, maybe he would see it before too long. No—Forrest took his cue from McCulloch. Bradford *would* see that smile, and soon, and no maybes to it.

XV

AFTER CORPORAL JACK JENKINS LET the sutler pass, he figured his excitement was over for the night. For a couple of hours, he was right. The moon sank toward the Mississippi. Jenkins yawned several times. He didn't lie down. He didn't even squat. He didn't doze—not quite, anyhow. But he'd ridden through the previous night and fought a battle the day before. He wasn't at his brightest and most alert. He didn't think he needed to be.

He yawned again, wider than ever, when the moon set. Darkness came down, a veil of black so thick he could hardly see his hand in front of his face. But he had no trouble picking out the party of horsemen who rode out from Fort Pillow, torches in hand. One of those riders was conspicuously bigger than the rest. If that wasn't Bedford Forrest, Jenkins would have been surprised.

And if that was Forrest . . . then what? *Then something's gone wrong somewhere,* Jenkins thought, never imagining that whatever had gone wrong had anything to do with him.

The riders went along the bank of Coal Creek till they came to the northernmost sentry along Fort Pillow's old outer perimeter. Then they started working their way south, toward Jenkins. As they drew closer, he could hear them talking with the sentries, but couldn't make out what they were saying.

They headed his way. Whatever they were looking for, they hadn't found it yet. He showed he was awake and alert by calling, "Halt! Who goes there?"—as if he wondered.

A dry chuckle came from Forrest. "I'm your commanding general, by God!"

"Advance and be recognized—sir," Jenkins said.

"Here I am." Forrest and his aides slowly rode forward. He held up his torch so that it shone on his face. "Well, soldier? D'you recognize me?"

"Uh, yes, sir," Jenkins answered hastily.

"Who are you? Can't quite make you out in the darkness," Forrest said.

"Jack Jenkins, sir, corporal in the Second Tennessee Cavalry— Colonel Barteau's regiment."

Forrest laughed again. "I know who that regiment belongs to. You'd best believe I do. You were over by Coal Creek before. I've got a question for you, Corporal. Did you let anybody—anybody at all— past you since you came on duty?"

"Yes, sir. One sutler," Jenkins said.

The officers with Bedford Forrest all exclaimed. He held up a hand for quiet. As usual, he got what he wanted. "When was this? What did the fellow look like?"

"Hour and a half ago—maybe two hours," Jenkins said. Forrest's aides exclaimed again, in dismay. A couple of them swore. Jenkins went on, "Couldn't hardly see him—he had his hat pulled down kind of low. He sure smelled bad, though; I'll tell you that."

"I bet he did," Forrest said. "I don't think he was a sutler at all. I reckon you let a polecat get through. Major Bradford broke his parole, and he's nowhere around."

"Bradford!" Jenkins said. "That was Bradford? God damn it to hell! If I knew it was him, I'd've got some more blood on my piece." He held up the rifle musket, which he still hadn't cleaned.

"Don't know for sure yet, but that's the way it looks." Forrest eyed not the ghastly weapon but Jack Jenkins himself. "Why'd you pass him through?"

"He said an officer inside Fort Pillow told him he could go," Jenkins answered uneasily. If his own officers wanted to, they could blame him for letting the Federal get away. And what they'd do to him if they did . . . Trying not to think about that, he went on. "He just seemed like a no-account fellow. And I never reckoned a major could stink like that, neither."

He got a laugh out of Bedford Forrest, but only a sour one. "Oh, you'd be amazed," the general said. He turned to the men who'd ridden out with him. "Any point to beating the bushes for the son of a bitch?"

"Not till morning, sir," one of them answered. "A million places he could hide in the dark. If we didn't trip over him, we'd never know he was there."

"About what I figured myself." Forrest muttered under his breath. "I was hoping you'd tell me I was wrong, dammit."

Jenkins listened to the mounted men with only half an ear. "Bill Bradford?" he muttered. "I had Bill Bradford in front of me, and he slipped through my fingers? Shit!" Bradford wasn't the worst thorn in the side of West Tennessee Confederates; that dishonor went to Colonel Fielding Hurst, who'd been in business longer. But it wasn't for lack of effort on the major's part.

I could've been a hero, Jenkins thought, angry at himself and even angrier at Bradford for fooling him. Killing ordinary Tennessee Tories and smashing in niggers' heads was all very well, but he would have traded the lot of them for Bill Bradford. How many men would have pounded him on the back? How many would have plied him with cigars and whiskey? When word got out, how many pretty women would have smiled at him to show their gratitude, or maybe more than smiled?

"Shit!" he said again.

"We have men down in the south," said one of the officers with Forrest.

"Oh, yes, I know," the general commanding said. "Still and all, I don't much care to have to count on somebody else, not when he shouldn't have got loose in the first place."

"I'm sorry, sir," Jenkins said. "I'm sorrier'n I know how to tell you." He was nothing if not sincere. Had he had the faintest notion who Bradford was, the homemade Yankee's body would lie at his feet. In that case, Bedford Forrest would be congratulating him. The way things were . . .

The way things were, Jenkins didn't want to meet Forrest's eye. Forrest muttered under his breath, then sighed. "Well, Corporal, you're not the only man who messed things up," he said. "Bradford poured spirits into the soldier who was guarding him till the fellow passed out. And he likely did fool an officer or two, else he wouldn't have got out of the fort. He was dressed like a sutler, you say?"

"Yes, sir," Jenkins said. "In ordinary clothes, anyway, not in uniform."

"I bet he wasn't in uniform," Bedford Forrest said. "He took a dip in the Mississippi trying to get away from our boys, and came out soaked to the skin."

"Bastard looked like a drowned rat," one of the other horsemen said.

"He's a rat, all right," Jenkins said.

"He's a rat out of the trap, dammit," Forrest said. "We just have to go on, that's all." He swung his horse back toward Fort Pillow. His companions followed. Watching them go, Jack Jenkins sighed in relief. Forrest hadn't pounded his head against a rock. But if Bill Bradford got away, Jenkins would be pounding his own head for the rest of his life.

Confederate troopers loaded Springfield after Springfield into a couple of wagons. Nathan Bedford Forrest smiled as he watched the work. "This is more like it," he said. "Let's get these taken care of, and then let's get the hell out of here. How many did we capture?"

"About 350, sir," answered Captain Anderson, who as usual had the numbers at his fingertips. He paused significantly. "We brought up 269 of them—that figure is exact, sir—from alongside the Mississippi."

"Well, I can't tell you I'm very surprised," Forrest said. "Half the garrison went down there, did it?"

"More or less, yes, sir." Anderson gave him a quizzical look.

Forrest looked back, bland as butter. He knew what his aide-de-camp was thinking: how could he cipher out a problem like that when he'd had so little book learning? Forrest let Charles Anderson go right on chewing on it. Being such a precise fellow, Anderson would no doubt picture him doing a formal long-division problem inside his head. Forrest could no more do formal long division than he could fly. But that didn't mean he was foolish about numbers. About 600 Federals had held Fort Pillow. Half of six was three; you didn't need to be any kind of scholar to see that. And 269 was close to 300. Nothing complicated about it—unless you tried to make it that way.

He found a different question: "Where are the rest of the Federals' guns?"

"They threw some of them *in* the river, sir," Captain Anderson answered. "A few will have stopped bullets or had their stocks smashed or otherwise become unserviceable. And I suspect a good many of our men have, ah, informally appropriated weapons that took their fancy."

"Well, I suspect you're right about that," Forrest allowed. "Our boys are first-rate foragers—and they need to be, dammit."

"When we have our own country and we chase the damnyankees out of it, we'll be able to make everything we need for ourselves," Anderson said. "We have the wealth, and we have the tools—or we can get what we need from abroad, anyhow. And we have men who can use them as they need to be used."

Bedford Forrest frowned. He was so much a part of the war, and the war so much a part of him, that he hardly thought about what might come afterwards. When he did, he feared the Confederacy could not hope to win. There'd been a last bright spot in the west at the end of the past summer, when Braxton Bragg beat Rosecrans at Chickamauga. If the Confederates could have destroyed Rosecrans's army, if they could have retaken Chattanooga . . .

But they hadn't, and they never would now. The Yankees got their revenge at Missionary Ridge, shattering Bragg's army and—too late—forcing him from his command. When the spring campaigning season started, which it soon would, the Confederates wouldn't be pushing north. The Federals would be driving south instead.

Could Joe Johnston stop them this side of Atlanta? If he couldn't, the war here was lost. He was a good defensive fighter, no man better, but was he good enough? Forrest had his doubts.

And if Johnston lost, if Robert E. Lee lost in Virginia, what was left for the C.S.A.? Forrest saw only one thing: retreating to the mountains and the woods and the swamps and bushwhacking the damnyankees till they got sick of trying to hold down a countryside that hated them and went home. That might take five years. It might take ten. It might take fifty. Forrest faced the idea without enormous enthusiasm, but also without fear. If that was what wanted doing, the South could do it.

The only trouble was, it left little room for Captain Anderson's peaceful Confederacy acquiring the tools it needed to get free of imported goods. Forrest shrugged. That might come one of these days. He didn't think it would come any time soon, no matter what his clever aide-de-camp believed.

He intended to fight as long as the rest of the Confederate States did—and longer, if he had to. If he had no great faith in a Confederate triumph . . . in the end, what difference did that make? He couldn't fight the whole war, only his own little piece of it. Today, he'd done that well.

"Have we taken everything we can from this place?" he asked Anderson.

"I believe we have, sir," the other officer replied.

"Then let's clear out," Forrest said. "Sure as the Devil, we'll have more Yankee gunboats calling on us come morning, and maybe troopships with 'em. We haven't got enough men to hold the outer line of this fort, and the inner line's not worth holding. I can see that, by God, even if Major Bradford couldn't."

"We're ready," Anderson said. "I expect you'll want to leave some pickets behind?"

"I surely will." Forrest nodded. "They'll warn us when the Federals do come around, and they'll help keep the stinking scavengers away."

He and Anderson exchanged glances filled with distaste. Not all men who carried guns in this debatable land fought for the Confederate States or the United States. Quite a few fought for themselves and nobody else. Once the armies moved on, the jackals and hyenas moved in, stealing whatever got left behind and slitting throats when they came upon men they didn't care for.

They were impossible to put down completely. Most of the time, they looked and acted like anybody else: like farmers or tradesmen going about their lawful business. But when the sun went down they picked up shotguns or rifle muskets and rode out to raid. Some inclined to one side, some to the other, some to neither. The Federals in Memphis and Nashville hated them all. Forrest liked them very little better himself.

"Well," he said, "let's go."

Matt Ward poured down one cup of black coffee after another. It made him feel like a wide-awake drunk. He was paying for letting Bill Bradford slip away. He was paying in all kinds of ways. His head pounded; he knew the hangover would get worse later, but it was bad enough now. And he had the joy of realizing Bradford had played him for a fool.

If I could shoot him now . . . But, however tempting that thought was, he shoved it aside. If he fired his Enfield now, he feared his brains would blow out through his ears.

"You awake, Ward?" A second lieutenant from the Second Mis-

souri Cavalry (C.S.) named Tom Bottom sounded as if he would do
something dreadful if he didn't get the answer he wanted.

"Yes, sir." Ward sighed. He knew he'd let himself in for this. That
made him put up with it, but didn't make him enjoy it.

"You'd better be," Bottom growled. "I'll come round again pretty
damn quick to make sure you stay that way."

"Yes, sir," Matt Ward repeated. Bottom was one of the handful of
officers left behind with the pickets now that most of the Confederate
force had pulled out of Fort Pillow. He was acting as if that made him
something altogether grander than a miserable second lieutenant.
Were things otherwise, Ward would have called him on it. With his
headache and with his even more painful knowledge of his own fail-
ure, he kept quiet.

Not everybody who'd stayed behind by the fort was so con-
strained. "Yeah, I'm awake, you whistleass peckerhead," another
trooper rasped. "Are you?"

"What's your name?" Bottom said furiously. "I'll put you on report!"

"My name is Stonewall Jackson, and you can do whatever you
damn well please. But you better not turn your back on your own men
if you try it."

Had Bottom had more nerve, he might have arrested the mocking
soldier. He didn't. He just walked on. Maybe the man's threat un-
nerved him. Everybody heard stories about unpopular officers shot
by the soldiers they commanded. Ward had no idea how many of
them were true—probably not many. If Tom Bottom didn't want to
take a chance on this one, though, who could blame him? Bottom
wasn't a coward—he'd fought well enough in the fall of Fort Pillow—
but he wasn't a fool, either.

As for Ward, he stayed on his feet and kept his rifle musket on
his right shoulder. The lieutenant couldn't complain as long as he
went on doing that. His headache got worse as the night wore
along, and then worse still. He wished for a hair of the dog that bit
him. That might ease the pain. But he didn't ask if any of the other

pickets had a jolt in his canteen. If Lieutenant Bottom caught him doing that, the lieutenant would start roaring at him, and he would deserve it.

And word might get back to Bedford Forrest. Forrest had gone easy on him for letting Major Bradford escape, but if the general commanding got the notion he was a drunk. . . . He didn't know just what would happen then, and he didn't want to find out, either. It wouldn't be pretty. He was only too sure of that.

Here and there, down by the Mississippi, wounded Federals still groaned. Ward couldn't tell whether they were white or colored; all wounded men sounded pretty much the same. Some of them would be dead by the time the sun came up. Others . . . If the Federals sent gunboats up to Fort Pillow soon enough, they might be able to take away the survivors.

"Gunboats," Ward muttered. He shivered, though the night was mild enough. With the blood throbbing inside his sodden brain every time his heart beat, he didn't want to think about cannon going off. If a shell burst close by, he feared his head would fall off regardless of whether any fragments struck him.

The moon sank toward the western horizon. Even its light seemed uncommonly bright, which told him how badly hung over he was. When the sun came up, he wondered if he would bleed to death through his eyes.

"Are you still with us?" Lieutenant Bottom tried to sneak up on him.

Matt Ward thought about coming back with a smart answer, the way Stonewall Jackson had—the way he would have himself had he felt better. But his headache wasn't the only thing that held him back. He had yet to earn the right to do that again, and Lieutenant Bottom *did* have the right—indeed, the duty—to check up on him. Feeling uncommonly small, Ward said, "Yes, sir, I'm still here."

"Good." Bottom nodded and walked on toward the next picket.

Was it? Ward rubbed his throbbing temples, which didn't help much. If he felt this bad now, how much worse would he be come morning? He tried not to think about that. But a long, miserable night loomed ahead.

A horse! a horse! my kingdom for a horse! Bill Bradford remembered some ranting fool of a Shakespearean actor bellowing out the line when a traveling company put on *Richard III* in Memphis. The actor would have done best on a horse that usually pulled brewery wagons, for he was built like a beer barrel himself.

But the cry! The anguished cry! Bradford felt the truth of that, felt it in his very marrow, as he splashed and squelched south through the Hatchie bottoms, heading toward Memphis once again.

He was still wearing his shoes. The mud hadn't pulled them off yet, though it had certainly tried at least half a dozen times. His feet were soaked. In the darkness under the trees, or even out in the open when the moon went behind a cloud, he couldn't see puddles before he stepped in them. Half the time, he couldn't see his hand in front of his face. Pretty soon, the moon would set. He wanted to curl up under the nearest broad-spreading oak and sleep till morning.

He wanted to, but he didn't dare. Bedford Forrest's men would be looking for his trail, sure as hounds went after a raccoon. He'd broken his parole, so he had to make good his escape. The sport they had with him before they finally let him surrender gave a taste of what they'd do if they caught him now.

If he never saw another Confederate soldier, if he never heard the Rebel yell again, that wouldn't break his heart. So he thought for a moment, anyhow. But then he shook his head. Theodorick lay in the cold, wet ground, a shroud the only thing that kept the dirt out of his mouth and nose. The Rebs thought they were getting their revenge for what the Thirteenth Tennessee Cavalry had done to them, did they? Well, he aimed to show them they were nothing but amateurs when it came to revenge.

Maybe—no, probably—General Hurlbut wouldn't give him any sizable command, not after he'd lost Fort Pillow. But if he could have, oh, a company's worth of men who hated the Confederate States and everything they stood for and most especially hated all the people who followed the Stainless Banner just as much as he did . . . If he could have a company of men like that, what a vengeance he would wreak!

"I know where they live," he muttered, and then swore when a hanging vine hit him in the face. And he did. He knew who the leading Confederate sympathizers were, from Paducah, Kentucky, all the way down to Pocahontas, Tennessee. He knew where their brothers lived, and their sons—yes, and their sisters and daughters, too. He hadn't ordered any outrages against their womenfolk. He hadn't, and he wouldn't. But if some happened anyway, he wouldn't shed a tear.

First, though, he had to get to Memphis. *Remember that, Bill,* he told himself sternly. *One thing at a time.* If he made a mistake on the road south, all his hopes for vengeance would go glimmering.

He kept hoping he would run across some homestead out in the middle of nowhere, some place where a farmer scratched out a living with a few crops and whatever he could shoot or trap in the swamps. If the bumpkin had any kind of nag . . .

But he didn't come across any farmhouses, or even trapper's huts. No one seemed to live in these swamps. He knew people did. But one of the reasons they lived in a place like this was that they didn't want anybody from the outside world bothering them. They didn't come out much, and the outside world didn't come in. Bill Bradford suddenly understood why it didn't. It couldn't find anybody here.

Something slithered over one of his shoes. Copperhead? Cottonmouth? Rattler? Only a garter snake? A figment of his overheated imagination? It could have been anything. Whatever it was, it didn't bite. And he didn't yell his head off, though he couldn't say why he didn't. He shuddered and pressed on.

Sooner or later, I have to come out of the bottoms . . . don't I? he thought. When he did, he would surely find a farmhouse. And then, depending on whether the farmer backed the U.S.A. or the C.S.A., he would borrow a horse or talk his way into using one or simply steal one, whichever looked like the best idea.

And then, Memphis. Once he got there, Bedford Forrest's friends would find out they weren't the only ones who could strike by surprise at dawn. "Oh, yes," Major Bradford muttered. "They'll find out, all right."

When the distant thunder of guns woke Mack Leaming, his first reaction was astonishment that he'd been able to sleep at all. He'd thought the pain from his wound would keep him up all night. His second reaction was a groan as that pain, of which he'd been blissfully unaware since whenever he dozed off, flooded back into his consciousness. Did it hurt any less than it had before he fell asleep? Maybe a little, he decided, but maybe not, too. It was still plenty bad.

All around him, other wounded Union soldiers were coming back to themselves with almost identical groans. No one had done anything for any of them all through the night. The only mercy the Rebels showed was not bursting into this miserable hut and murdering them while they slept.

The guns sounded again, closer this time. "What the hell's going on?" somebody said. "Who's shooting at what?"

"Have men marched up from Memphis to chase the Rebs away?" someone else asked.

"Why couldn't they show up yesterday, God damn their rotten souls to hell?" another wounded soldier said.

"It's not men marching—it's a gunboat, dog my cats if it ain't," another man said.

As soon as Leaming heard that, he knew it had to be so. "I love gunboat sailors," he said bitterly. "They sail away when we need 'em the most, but then they come back again after the fighting's done. They're heroes, all right, every damn one of 'em."

That touched off some vigorous and profane swearing from his fellow sufferers. The guns on the river boomed again. Yes, they were definitely closer this time. "You reckon that's the *New Era* comin' back?" somebody asked. "Even though I got me a hole in my leg, there's a few things I'd like to say to the high and mighty skipper who sailed off and left us in the lurch."

More obscenities fouled the early morning air. By all the signs, quite a few men had some things they wanted to tell Captain Marshall if they ever made his acquaintance. Lieutenant Leaming had several thoughts of his own he wanted to share with the *New Era*'s commanding officer.

But another man said, "This here boat sounds like it's coming up from Memphis. The *New Era* steamed north, off toward Cairo"—like anyone from those parts, he pronounced it *Kayro*—"and places like that."

A rifle musket near the Mississippi banged, and then another one. A minute later, the gunboat's cannon responded. "Can't be yesterday's gunboat," a soldier said. "They're shooting at it, and it's got the gumption to shoot back."

Several wounded men swore again. Mack Leaming was not behindhand—far from it. Some of the shells the gunboat fired burst not far from the hut. "I hope they blow the damn Rebs to hell and gone," Leaming said.

As if in response, a Confederate outside yelled, "Come on, boys! Don't just stand there! If we have to pull back, to hell with me if I want the damnyankees to be able to get their hands on one single thing they can use. Burn these buildings, by God! We'll fix this place the way the Lord fixed Sodom and Gomorrah!"

That roused the men inside the hut. "Hold on!" they shouted. "Hold on! There's wounded in here! Let us come out before you fire this place!"

"Devil take your wounded!" the Reb answered. "We have to get rid of this here place right now. Lou! Daniel! Come on! Get moving!"

Somebody with a torch applied it to the corner of the hut. Mack Leaming watched and listened with fearful fascination. He could hear flames crackle, and then he could see them. Terror sent ice along his spine. But ice was not what he *would* feel. Getting shot was bad enough. Getting roasted in the flames had to be ten, a hundred, a thousand times worse.

Men who could limp or crawl made for the doorway as fast as they could go—which mostly wasn't very fast. The more badly wounded men cried out: "Take me with you!" "Don't leave me here to cook!" Leaming added his voice to the chorus. He shouted as loud as he could, and wished he were louder.

"Here you go, sir. I'll give you a hand," a wounded Federal said. He had one hand to give, for his wound was in the left arm. He grabbed Leaming by the collar of his tunic and yanked hard. Leaming groaned—any motion tore at the track the bullet had drilled through him. "Sorry," the other soldier said.

"It's all right," Leaming got out through clenched teeth. It wasn't all right, or anything close to all right. But it was infinitely better than lying there while those vicious orange flames crept closer and closer. Anything, anything at all, was better than that.

The other wounded man dragged him about ten feet out of the barracks hut, then let go of him. "Here you are, sir," he panted.

"God bless you," Leaming said. The right side of his back was in torment, but it would ease. The fire would have given him no relief, no mercy. The man with the injured arm went back into the hut and brought out another wounded soldier who could not move on his own. The hut was burning hard by then, but Leaming didn't think anyone got left behind in it.

Several Confederate soldiers and one officer stood around watching the Federals, but none of them did anything to help. The sun beat down on Leaming's head; it would be a warmer day than the one before. Some of the Confederates had canteens on their belts or slung over their shoulders. He didn't bother asking them for water, though—he knew how poor his chances of getting any were.

A wounded Negro lay not far away. He must have spent the night in the open; as far as Leaming knew, all the men in the hut had been white. One of Forrest's troopers walked over to him and said, "What the hell are you doing here?"

"Suh, I wants to get on the gunboat if she stop," the colored man answered. "Reckon they got a surgeon on bo'd kin cut this minnie out o' me." He pointed to his crudely bandaged calf.

"You want to fight us again, do you?" the Secesh soldier said. "Damn you, I'll teach you!" He brought up his rifle musket and shot the Negro in the chest from a range of no more than a couple of feet. The black man groaned and died inside of a minute or two.

Another black man—he didn't seem badly hurt—stood not far away. Were Mack Leaming in his shoes (not that he was wearing any), he would have got out of there as fast as he could. The Confederates were still shooting wounded Negroes—and the occasional wounded white, too. Maybe this colored artilleryman didn't think they would do anything like that while the gunboat—it was number twenty-eight, the *Silver Cloud*—drew near.

If he didn't, he made a dreadful mistake. The Reb who'd shot the Negro on the ground by Leaming reloaded his rifle musket with a veteran's practiced haste. He hardly even needed to watch what he was doing; his hands knew with no help from his eyes.

Only after the man set a percussion cap on the nipple did the colored soldier seem to awaken to his danger. By then, it was too late for the black to run off. Forrest's trooper would have had no trouble hitting him before he got out of range. Instead of running, he begged for his life: "Please don't shoot me, suh! I ain't done nothin' to you. Honest to God I ain't!"

"You were up in the damn fort, weren't you?" the Confederate replied, taking deliberate aim at the black man's head. "You were shooting one of them goddamn cannon, weren't you?"

"No, suh, not me! Do Jesus, not me!" the Negro said, voice high and shrill, his eyes showing white all around the iris. "I never had nothin' to do with no cannon! Never!"

"You lying sack of shit," the Reb said. "Hell, even if you didn't, you still had a gun in your hands. For all I know, one of my pals is dead on account of you. So you can go to hell along with this other coon here."

He pulled the trigger. The hammer fell—with a loud click and nothing more. The colored artilleryman, who'd seemed on the point of fainting from terror, let out a joyous cry. "You see? You *see?* God don't mean fo' you to take my life. God don't *want* you to take my life!"

"Fuck you, boy," Forrest's trooper said. He thumbed up the hammer and reseated the cap on the nipple. "Didn't have it quite square there." He raised the rifle musket again. "Now I reckon we'll find out what God wants and what He don't."

He fired again. The Minié ball hit the Negro just above the left eye. The man couldn't even scream. The only good thing was, he didn't suffer, not with the back of his head blown out. He hardly even twitched after he fell.

The Confederate spat. "Don't look like God cared much about one worthless nigger after all, does it?"

Leaming had seen too many horrors over the past day. He was numb to them, if not to the pain of his own wound. Fear of retaliation wasn't what kept him from saying anything to Forrest's trooper. What were two more killings among so many? And the officer who stood there and watched his man shoot a pair of wounded, defenseless men? He said not a word, either.

Bedford Forrest hadn't ridden far from Fort Pillow after despoiling the place. The fall he'd taken left him stiff and sore. He camped about five miles from the fort, and passed an uncomfortable, restless night. When he woke before sunup the next morning, he pulled up his shirt and got a good look at himself by the light of a guttering lamp.

"By God!" he muttered. "I'm all over black and blue. Lucky I didn't break anything—mighty lucky."

As long as he was up, he didn't see any reason why his aides shouldn't be up as well. He limped over to Captain Anderson's tent and shook him awake. "What the—?" Anderson said, and then, recognizing Forrest, "Oh. Good morning, sir."

"I've got a job for you, Captain," Forrest said.

"At your service." Yawning, Anderson emerged from the blanket in which he'd wrapped himself like a gray-uniformed butterfly coming out of its cocoon. He started pulling on his boots; like Forrest, he'd slept in the rest of his uniform. "What can I do for you?"

"I want you to ride back to Fort Pillow," Forrest said. "Chances are there'll be Yankee gunboats nosing around. Show a flag of truce and tell 'em they're welcome to take on all the wounded Federals they can hold." He chuckled. "Long as they're doing it, we don't have to."

"I understand, sir." Captain Anderson took a hardtack from his haversack and started gnawing on it. If he went back to the fort, he wouldn't have much chance for any better breakfast. With his mouth full, he asked, "Do you want me to go by my lonesome, or shall I bring a couple of other officers along?"

"Oh, fetch your sideboys, by all means," Forrest said indulgently. "Don't want the Federals to reckon we can't afford to send but the one man. . . . Will you do one more thing for me?"

"Whatever you need, General." Charles Anderson knew the only right answer an aide-de-camp could give to that question.

"General Chalmers is camped a couple-three miles in back of us. Would you be kind enough to stop at his tent and tell him I reckon he did a might fine job yesterday?" Nathan Bedford Forrest sighed. If he was going to bury the hatchet with his division commander, he had to show he appreciated Chalmers's work. He wouldn't lie to do it, but, fortunately, he didn't have to here.

"I'd be happy to, sir," Charles Anderson said. "Isn't Captain Young back at General Chalmers's encampment?"

"Who?" For a moment, the name meant nothing to Forrest, who was thinking of his own officers. Then he remembered the parley of the day before. "Oh, the Federal from Missouri who knew me. Yes, I do believe he is. You want to take him along to Fort Pillow with you?"

"If you don't mind, sir. He seemed to be a pretty sharp fellow, and having somebody like that along may help me dicker with the Yankees in the gunboat."

"It's all right by me, Captain. If he gives his parole not to fight us till he's exchanged, you can let him go, too. I reckon he'll keep his word—not like that Bradford son of a bitch." Forrest's mouth twisted. The way the enemy officer had escaped left him steaming.

"I'll see to it, then." Anderson stuffed the rest of the hardtack into his mouth and left his tent chewing with determination.

Having a little more time on his own hands, Forrest breakfasted on skillygallee: hardtack pounded to crumbs, softened in water, and fried in bacon grease. Washed down with coffee brewed from beans captured at Fort Pillow, it made a tolerable meal. His belly was in no doubt that he'd eaten something, anyhow.

Inside of fifteen minutes, Captain Anderson and three junior officers rode off toward the northwest. Not long after that, Forrest heard the distant thud of a cannon's discharge. He nodded to himself. "Might have known," he said; as usual, the first word came out *mought*. Of course the Federals would be shelling Fort Pillow. It was too late to do them any good, but not too late to salve their pride.

He shrugged. They could have all the pride they wanted. He'd taken the fort. The Thirteenth Tennessee Cavalry (U.S.) wouldn't harry west Tennessee any more. It would be a while before the Sixth Tennessee Cavalry (U.S.) stuck its head out of Memphis, too. As usual, he'd done what needed doing.

XVI

SERGEANT BEN ROBINSON LAY ON the ground watching the
gunboat steam up the Mississippi toward Fort Pillow. Every so
often, the gunboat's cannon would boom, and a shell would
come down somewhere near the Confederates posted in and near the
fort. Some of the Rebs fired back at the ship. It ignored them and kept
on thundering away. Robinson's mouth twisted with a pain that had
nothing to do with his wounded leg. If only the *New Era* showed that
kind of spirit the day before!

Of course, far fewer Confederate soldiers were firing at this ship
than had aimed at the *New Era*. That made a difference. But the *New
Era* really could have done the garrison in Fort Pillow some good.
This gunboat could cannonade from now till doomsday without re-
taking the place. Too late for that now.

Too late for most of the garrison, too. Not sated by the slaughter
the afternoon before, the Confederate pickets were still killing
wounded Federals, mostly Negroes. Whenever Rebs came close,
Robinson played dead and prayed as hard as he could. He didn't
know which worked better, but they hadn't murdered him yet.

The bombardment and the occasional return fire from the riverbank had gone on for a couple of hours when one of the Confederates said, "Here comes an officer with a flag of truce!"

Hearing that, Robinson turned his head. Sure enough, a Confederate officer waving a white flag rode toward the Mississippi at a trot. Ben didn't believe he was one of the Rebs who'd parleyed the day before. With him came three other C.S. officers—and Captain Young, the provost marshal at Fort Pillow.

"Ahoy, the gunboat!" the Confederate shouted, reining in not far from where Ben Robinson lay. The Reb cupped his hands to his mouth to make his voice carry farther. "Ahoy, the *Silver Cloud!*" That was how Robinson learned the ship's name. He'd seen it painted on her, but seeing letters wasn't the same as reading them, as he knew too well. "Will you parley?" the officer yelled.

After a couple of minutes, the answer came back, thin over the water: "What have you got to say, Reb?"

"I am Captain Anderson, General Forrest's assistant adjutant general," the Confederate shouted. "I offer you a truce to take off the wounded. I tried to do the same with the *New Era* yesterday afternoon, but Captain Marshall would not hear me. He sailed away."

One more reason to damn Captain Marshall to the hottest pits in hell, Ben Robinson thought savagely. What was Marshall afraid of? That the Rebs would swarm onto his ship while he was loading casualties? That was a coward's way of thinking, nothing else but.

Again, Captain Anderson had to wait a little while for a response. This time, the men on the *Silver Cloud* said, "I'll come to you in a boat. That way, we don't have to keep screaming our heads off at each other."

Anderson bowed in the saddle. "I am at your service, sir!" he bawled politely.

Four sailors rowed an officer toward the shore. The officer was a young man, and wore two gold stripes near the cuff of each sleeve. "I am Acting Master William Ferguson, Captain," he said. "I'm skipper of the *Silver Cloud.* What do you propose?"

"You came yourself?" Anderson said.

"Here I am," Ferguson replied.

"Well, good for you. As I told you, Captain Marshall showed me only his heels yesterday," the Confederate officer said. "We will give you a truce until, say, five this afternoon. General Forrest desires to place the wounded, white or black, aboard your boat. We have few men still close by, but they will give you what help they may."

Acting Master Ferguson frowned. "White or black, you say? We heard tell you went and killed every nigger you could."

"We killed a lot of 'em," Anderson said matter-of-factly, "but some are left alive. Take a look at this here buck." He pointed to Ben Robinson.

"Oh, yeah?" Ferguson eyed Ben in surprise. The colored artilleryman swore at himself. When he played possum, he fooled the officer on his own side but not the Reb. Much good *that* would have done him. "You really alive?" Ferguson asked.

What would he do if I said, "No, suh, I's dead"? Robinson wondered. But the whimsy died stillborn. This was not the time or place. "Yes, suh, I's here," Robinson answered. "I got shot, but I's here."

"Well, all right," Ferguson said. He turned back to Anderson. "Fair enough, Captain. You can have your truce—on one condition."

"What's that?" the Confederate asked.

"Keep your armed men out of gunshot range of my ship for as long as the truce lasts," Ferguson said. "They were taking potshots at us, and I don't want any damn fool keeping it up while we're in no fit state to defend ourselves."

"Suppose I say that no armed men come within the outermost perimeter of Fort Pillow?" Captain Anderson suggested. "That's about half a mile. There's not a chance in church anyone could hit you from farther off, even if some hothead should try it. And I will issue orders against any such thing."

"Seems acceptable," said Ferguson, nodding. "And you would want this truce to last till five o'clock, you said?"

"Oh, yes, just for the day. That should be plenty."

"I agree." Ferguson walked over to Anderson, who hadn't dismounted, and held out his hand. Anderson clasped it. The two white men got along well enough. Ben Robinson tried to imagine the Reb agreeing to a truce with a colored officer. The picture would not form. "How many wounded are we talking about?" Acting Master Ferguson inquired.

"I don't know, not exactly, but it isn't a small number," Anderson replied. "Perhaps Captain Young here can give you a better notion."

"I'm afraid not," Young answered. "I don't know what happened in the fort after I managed to surrender, and the victors' blood was still running hot at the time." He didn't want to come out and say the Confederates slaughtered the garrison, but he didn't want to lie, either. Ben Robinson granted him reluctant respect.

"I . . . see." Ferguson could add two and two. He went on, "Well, we have a steamer coming right behind us in the hope she would be useful—the *Platte Valley*. I will order her to land alongside us, and we'll do what we can for these poor devils." He looked up and down the riverbank. A lot of bodies had been carried up to the ditch and thrown in, but quite a few still remained. "If you will excuse me, Captain . . ."

Ferguson went back to the boat. The sailors who'd waited in it rowed him out to the *Silver Cloud*. Smoke poured from the gunboat's stacks as she neared the shore. Signal flags and then shouts ordered the *Platte Valley* up alongside her.

Captain Anderson looked at Ben Robinson again. "What did you do to earn those three chevrons, boy?"

"Made myself the best soldier I could, I reckon," Robinson answered. Emboldened by the truce, he answered, "I sure blew some of your sojers to hell and gone while we was fightin'."

"You lost," Anderson said.

"Yes, suh. But we put up the best fight we could with what we had," Robinson said.

The Confederate officer plucked at his beard. "A pity we didn't kill more of you."

"Me, I reckon it's a shame we didn't kill more of y'all." Robinson wouldn't have been so bold if the Reb hadn't tweaked him. He also wouldn't have been so bold if the Federal gunboat weren't lying right offshore. He didn't think the Confederate officer would murder him in cold blood with men from the U.S. Navy watching.

When the Confederate's hand dropped to his revolver, Ben wondered if he'd just made his last mistake. But Captain Anderson let it fall to his side. "Yeah, talk big now, nigger. God help you if we ever catch you again, though."

"I ain't afraid." Ben Robinson intended that for nothing more than a snappy comeback. But he felt the truth and the power in the words and repeated them, throwing them in Anderson's face: "By God, I *ain't* afraid!"

Sailors started taking wounded Federals aboard the *Silver Cloud* and the *Platte Valley*. The men who came for Robinson didn't have a stretcher—nothing but a plank that they carried between them. They set it on the riverbank by the wounded man. "Climb aboard," one of them said. "We'll get you back to the gunboat."

"Thank you kindly," Robinson said as he gingerly flattened himself on the plank. "I is much obliged to you gentlemen."

"Doin' our job," the white man answered, and paused to spit a stream of tobacco juice. Then he said, "You ready, Zeke? We'll lift him on three. One . . . Two . . . Three!"

They lifted together. Both of them grunted. Zeke said, "You sure never missed no meals, did you, pal?"

That reminded Ben how ravenously hungry he was. "I ain't had nothin' a-tall for a whole day," he said. "You got a hardtack you can spare?"

"You want one of those damn things, you must be hungry," Zeke said.

"Wait till we get you in the boat," the other bearer added. "Don't want to have to put you down and then pick you up again."

Robinson couldn't complain about that; it made too much sense.

As soon as they carried him to the rowboat, the sailors each gave him a hardtack. The square crackers tasted like cardboard and weevils, the way they always did. He didn't care. They seemed wonderful.

More wounded Federals filled the rowboat. He was the only Negro in it. Many more whites than colored men seemed to be left alive. The Confederates hadn't murdered so many whites trying to surrender, or after they were already wounded. Oh, they'd killed some, but fewer. The wounded whites were also delighted to gnaw on hardtack.

When the boat was full, sweating sailors rowed the short distance out to the *Silver Cloud*. More men there hauled the soldiers from Fort Pillow up onto the gunboat's deck. The ship's surgeon took a look at Robinson's wound. "Well, you're not too bad," he said, and went on to the white corporal next to him.

Ben wasn't offended. In fact, he found himself nodding. As long as he was on a U.S. Navy vessel, as long as Bedford Forrest's troopers couldn't kill him for the fun of it any more, he wasn't bad at all.

The sun was up, bright and cheerful, promising a day much warmer than the one just past. Bill Bradford wished it would have stopped in the sky before it ever rose. But he was no Joshua, to turn his wish into a command. He would have to make the best of things—if he could.

He still had no horse. He hadn't found a chance to steal one. He hadn't even found a place to buy one, though he would gladly have used the double eagle he'd managed to keep in his pocket. Staying on foot, in a country patrolled by Bedford Forrest's troopers, was asking for trouble.

If I can get past Covington . . . But he'd already had to duck off the road three times to keep mounted Confederates from spotting him. If he was careless even once . . .

And things could go wrong even if he wasn't even slightly careless. Bradford found that out the hard way early in the morning when a shout rang out behind him: "Hey, you! Yeah, you in the scruffy clothes! Hold up, there!"

He whirled. He almost jumped out of the sutler's clothes he'd taken. Four troopers in butternut and gray came trotting toward him. Two carried rifle muskets, or possibly carbines (he wasn't drawing fine distinctions just then), the other two revolvers. He couldn't possibly have seen them, because they'd just ridden out from in back of a stand of oaks he'd passed himself only a couple of minutes before. They must have turned on to the southbound road from a smaller cross-road, because they hadn't been following him before.

What to do? It boiled down to running or bluffing. If he ran, they would ride him down and shoot him. That was only too plain, for he saw no good hiding places he could reach before they caught him. It would have to be bluff, then.

He waved to the Rebs and waited for them to come up. "Mornin'," he said.

His smile didn't seem to warm their hearts. "Who the hell are you, and what are you doing here?" one of them demanded.

"Well, my name's Joe Peterson." Bradford picked something ordinary, but not, he hoped, so ordinary that it roused suspicion. "I'm home on furlough from Braxton Bragg's army. And I was out sparking my girl last night, if you want to know the truth." He smiled again, his expression this time half embarrassed, half ingratiating.

All his acting talents were wasted on the hard-faced Confederate. "On furlough from Bragg's army, are you? Let's see some papers, then."

Bradford went through his pockets. He found no papers of any sort. Even if he had, he couldn't have displayed them—they would have authorized his presence at Fort Pillow. That was the last thing he could afford to do. It was, he judged, much worse than showing that his name wasn't Peterson.

"I seem to have left them in my other pair of pants," he said sheepishly.

"Oh, yeah. I just fuckin' bet you did," the trooper said. He was one of the pair who carried revolvers. He aimed his at Bradford's face. "That other pair of pants—was it gray or blue?"

"I don't know what you mean," Bradford got out through lips numb with fear.

"Hell you don't, you lying son of a bitch," said one of the Confederates with a longarm. He pointed his weapon at Bradford's midsection. "Sure as shit, you done run off from somebody's army. Only question is, you a deserter from our side or the Yankees'?"

"You've got me all wrong," Bradford said. "I—"

"Shut up," the Reb with the pistol said flatly. "We're rounding up deserters. Too damn many fair-weather soldiers reckon they can disappear whenever they find somethin' better to do. That ain't how it works, not when there's a war on. We got three, four other sorry bastards waitin' down in Covington. Take you down there, too, let Colonel Duckworth cipher out what to do with you."

"What to do *to* you," the other rifle-toting soldier added. His voice held a certain grim anticipation Bradford could have done without.

Bradford also could have done without meeting Colonel William Duckworth. The commander of the Seventh Tennessee Cavalry (C.S.) was much too likely to recognize him. *And that won't be good,* Bradford thought desperately. *No, that won't be good at all.*

"You've got me all wrong," he said again.

"If the colonel says so, I'll believe it," said the Reb who did most of the talking. "I wouldn't believe *you* if you told me it was daytime. Roy, why don't you hand me your six-shooter there? That way, this bastard can ride behind you without getting any smart ideas."

"I'll do it," Roy said, "but I'll make damn sure he's not carrying anything, either." He got down from his horse, handed over his revolver, and then walked up to Bradford. "Stick your hands in the air, whoever the hell you are." Numbly, Bradford obeyed. He wasn't armed, so he didn't have anything to worry about on that score. Roy frisked him with a skill that suggested he had practice—and with no respect for his person whatsoever. The Reb nodded. "You'll do. Get up on my horse and slide back of the saddle. You can hang on while I tend to the horse."

"You've got no business doing this to me," Bradford said as he mounted. "I'm on furlough, and I was just going about my business. You've got no right."

"Hell we don't," said the trooper who seemed to be in charge. "Furlough, my ass. You're *somebody's* runaway nigger, sure as I'm a Christian. Don't know whether you ran out on Abe Lincoln or Jeff Davis, but I reckon we'll see." He nodded to Roy, who'd seated him- self in the saddle and taken hold of the reins. "You ready?"

"Ready as I'll ever be," Roy answered. The Confederates booted their horses forward. They went at a walk, so as not to wear down the animal carrying double. *They care more about the horse than they do about me,* Bill Bradford thought bitterly. That wasn't quite true. The Secesh soldiers cared about whether he escaped and whether he could do anything to the man he rode behind. They cared very much about such things. But, without a doubt, they liked the horse better than they liked him.

Because they rode slowly, they took more than an hour to get to Covington. That only gave Major Bradford more time to worry. The seat of Tipton County put him in mind of a lot of other county seats in western Tennessee. The courthouse faced the central square; the cou- ple of blocks around it were given over to businesses. They grew more cotton around Covington than almost anywhere else in Tennessee, and several plantation owners had second houses in town almost as fine as their homes out in the countryside.

The troopers rode down Main Street toward the courthouse. They tied up their horses in front of the brown brick building. Even the columns of the portico were faced with brick. Bradford thought that was excessive, then wondered why he worried about such trifles when his neck was on the line. He supposed it was to keep from worrying about his neck—but he did anyway.

Sentries in front of the door called, "Who y'all got there?"

"That's what we're trying to find out," Roy answered. He gave Bradford an elbow in the ribs. "Get down, you." As Bradford awk- wardly dismounted, Roy went on, "Is the colonel inside?"

"He sure is," the sentry answered. He eyed Bradford with a

frown on his face. "This fellow looks familiar, hell with me if he don't."

"Hell with you anyway, Boone," Roy said. The sentry laughed, which meant they were friends. Roy got down from the horse, reclaimed his revolver, and aimed it at Bradford's chest. "Go on in, you. Colonel Duckworth'll decide what to do with you."

As Bradford walked to the door, he fiddled with his hat, tugging down as low as he could. That might not do him any good, but it couldn't hurt. The troopers herded him along toward the courtroom. A Confederate junior officer stood outside that door like a gatekeeper, which was probably just what he was. "Who's this fellow?" he asked.

"Reckon he's a deserter, Lieutenant Witherspoon. Says he's with Bragg's army and on furlough, but he's got no papers," answered the other soldier with a pistol—Bradford thought his name was Hank, but wasn't sure. "Colonel ought to have a look at him."

Witherspoon rubbed his chin. He was so young, his brown beard was soft and thin. After a few seconds, he nodded. "Well, all right. Bring him in. One way or the other, it won't take long."

"Right," said Hank, or whoever he was. "Come on, you." When Bradford hesitated, another Confederate trooper gave him a shove.

William Duckworth sat behind a table, as if he were a judge. He didn't look like a judge, though. He looked like a Scottish Covenanter, or perhaps more like a slightly deranged Biblical prophet. He was about forty, with dark hair and a dark, scraggly beard that tumbled down his chest to the third pair of buttons on his double-breasted tunic. For reasons known only to himself and possibly to God, he shaved his upper lip. His eyes . . . Bill Bradford would have said they were the coldest and grayest he'd ever seen had he not made the acquaintance of Nathan Bedford Forrest only the day before.

"Well?" Duckworth said, and Bradford had all he could do not to burst into startled laughter, for the Rebel colonel's voice seemed much too high and thin to spring from such a stern, forbidding visage. "Who've you got here?"

"Says his name's Peterson, sir. Says he's on furlough from Bragg's army," Roy answered. "We came across him north of town. Says he was sparking a girl last night, and that's how come he was on the road."

Colonel Duckworth's left eyebrow rose, which only made him look more formidable. "Tell me another one," he said.

Roy nodded. "Yes, sir. That's what we thought. He done run off from somebody's army, sure as hell. Don't know whether it's ours or the damnyankees', but somebody's."

"No doubt." Duckworth studied Bradford with those January eyes. Bradford looked down at his shoes, as he had at Fort Pillow the night before while talking to the lieutenant who let him leave. It didn't work this time. "Shed the lid," Duckworth said sharply. "Let me see who the devil you are."

A sinking feeling in the pit of his stomach, Bradford took off the slouch hat. He looked straight at Colonel Duckworth. If the Confederate officer didn't know him by sight, he still had a chance. But if Duckworth did . . .

And he did, damn him. He did. That eyebrow jumped again, now in surprise, not sarcasm. His eyes widened slightly. He nodded to himself, as if to say that yes, he really was sure. Then he spoke aloud: "You're Major Bradford, aren't you?"

Behind Bradford, Roy and Hank and the other two Rebs all inhaled on the same startled note. The Federal stood there for a few seconds, wondering if he had any chance to brazen it out. He wished he thought he did. Deciding things would go worse for him—if they could go worse for him—if he tried to lie, he gave a weary nod. "Yes, I'm afraid I am."

"I heard Fort Pillow fell," Colonel Duckworth said, and Bradford nodded again. The Reb went on, "So you got out alive, did you? I wouldn't have bet money on that, and there's the Lord's truth."

"We could take care of it for you real quick, Colonel," Roy said. Hank and the other two were quick to add loud, profane agreement.

But Duckworth shook his head. "Can't do it now, not in cold blood—the Federals would raise a stink, and they'd have the right to, dammit. Don't want them murdering our officers if they catch 'em. That's a feud—it isn't war."

"Well, what *shall* we do with him, then?" Hank asked.

The commander of the Seventh Tennessee Cavalry (C.S.) frowned, considering. Elisha might have frowned that way while deciding whether to ask God to have the people who'd mocked his baldness torn to pieces by lions or bears. But Colonel Duckworth, though he had worse than lions and bears at his disposal, seemed milder than the Hebrew prophet of days gone by: "We'll send him on up to Brownsville, that's what. We've got some other prisoners going there tomorrow, anyhow. General Chalmers can figure out what happens to him after that. He'll likely send him on to General Forrest."

"He'll get what he deserves then—hell with me, if he won't." Hank had what was, in Major Bradford's biased opinion, a truly wicked laugh. Of course, Bradford was less than eager to make Bedford Forrest's acquaintance again.

"Where'll we stash him in the meantime?" Roy asked.

That made Duckworth frown again. "Down the hall here, there's some jail cells," he said at last. "We better stick him in one of those. Meaning no disrespect, Major—it's for your own good. There's plenty of men on my side who'd turn handsprings to string you up."

"I'd give my parole," Bradford said. Duckworth didn't know he'd already broken it once. If he could slip away, he might still make it to Memphis.

But the Confederate cavalry officer shook his head. "Afraid I don't trust you that far. You lied about who you were to my men here. You might do some more lying to get away. Or maybe you already did some more, and that's how you got away from Fort Pillow." Despite his wild man's beard, William Duckworth was nobody's fool. He nodded to Bradford's captors. "Take him away. Lieutenant Witherspoon will show you where the cells are."

"Yes, sir," the troopers chorused. Roy—or possibly Hank—stuck his revolver up against Bradford's backbone. "Get moving, you."

Out in the hallway, Witherspoon gaped. "You're Major Bradford?

Well, I'll be a son of a bitch." *I wouldn't be surprised,* Bradford thought, but he held his tongue.

The jail cell was small and dark and dank. The roof must have leaked, because the mattress on the iron cot was damp. Nobody offered to get Bradford another one. He looked out through the barred window and saw . . . the far wall. Experiment proved he couldn't shift the bars. Even if he could have, the window was too small to crawl through. So was the one set high in the wall. He tried pushing at the door—gently, so as not to make any noise. No matter how hard he pushed, the padlock wouldn't give. He'd feared it wouldn't; that lock had looked stout.

Damp or not, he sat down on the cot. Here he was, trapped like a rat. Tomorrow, Brownsville. After that, like it or not, another meeting with Nathan Bedford Forrest.

Mack Leaming watched Federal sailors and Confederate troopers work together to take the U.S. wounded aboard the *Silver Cloud* and the *Platte Valley,* which had pulled up alongside the gunboat. Now the Rebs seemed to be on their best behavior. When he croaked out yet another request for water, one of them gave him some. As it had before, it worked wonders in making him feel better.

Eventually, his turn came. Two sturdy sailors lifted him. When he groaned, one of them said, "Take it easy, Lieutenant. We'll get you onto the steamer in jig time."

"Thanks," he got out. No matter what they told him to do, being moved still hurt like fire. He hoped the wound wouldn't start bleeding again.

The sailor who had hold of his feet said, "Looks like those sorry, raggedy Rebs stole just about everything but your toenails."

"If they could have got those off, they would have taken them, too," Leaming answered. Both sailors laughed, but he wasn't joking.

He groaned again when they set him in the rowboat, and again when other sailors on the *Platte Valley* took hold of him and laid him on the deck. Somebody gave him more water and half a hardtack. Then people seemed to forget about him for a spell.

He dozed a little, only to wake with a start when someone asked, "Where are you hit, Lieutenant?"

"Why do you—?" Leaming stopped. The man crouching by him wore a surgeon's green sash. He had a professional interest in Leaming's wound. "The minnie caught me below the shoulder blade and dug down. It feels as though it stopped in my, ah, rump."

"I see." The surgeon looked up toward Fort Pillow. "Were you by any chance standing on the bluff there, and shot from above?"

"Yes, that's what happened," Leaming said. "Will you cut out the bullet or leave it where it is?"

"If it's where you say, I doubt it's doing you much harm at present," the other man replied. "Digging it out would give you another wound, with all the risk of suppuration and septicemia attendant on such things. So I will let that sleeping dog lie for the time being, I think. Are you in much pain?"

"Some." Leaming didn't want to sound like a weakling. But he didn't want to be a martyr, either, so he added, "Maybe a bit more than some."

"I shouldn't wonder." The surgeon took a small brown glass bottle out of the wooden chest he carried with him. Drawing the cork with his teeth, he handed Leaming the bottle, saying, "Here—take a swig of this."

"What is it?"

"Laudanum, Lieutenant. Best-quality laudanum. I've had excellent results with it in Memphis, and it should help you, too." The surgeon beamed. "Not all drugs in the pharmacopoeia work as advertised—I've seen that too many times to doubt it. But laudanum, by thunder, will shift pain."

Leaming needed no more convincing. He raised the bottle to his lips and drank from it. The taste was strong, and not particularly pleasant: cheap brandy with a heavy infusion of poppy seeds. He had to force himself to swallow. It burned all the way down to his stomach. "It seems—strong." He had to cast about for a polite word.

The physician smiled. "I know it's nasty, but it will turn the trick. This is no humbug. I'll come round again in half an hour. If I have told you a falsehood, call me a liar." He picked up his case and went over to the next wounded man. "Where are you hit?"

Half an hour. Usually, that didn't seem very long. Half an hour walking with a pretty girl went by in the blink of an eye. Half an hour with a gunshot wound . . . was a different story. Leaming couldn't even look at his watch to see how the time passed by. That thieving Confederate had lifted it.

He hardly noticed when his head first began to spin. When he did notice, he blinked in bemusement. He hadn't had much brandy, not very much at all. But it wasn't the brandy that left him floating away from himself: it was the opium dissolved in it. "Well, well," he murmured, and then again: "Well, well." Laudanum really did banish pain, in the most literal sense of the word. The torment didn't disappear, but it went off to a distant province where it didn't seem to matter nearly so much. If that wasn't a miracle, it would do for one till something better came along.

"How are you, Lieutenant?" the surgeon asked. "Sorry to be a bit longer than I said I would—I had to take a poor devil's leg off. God willing, the wound won't go bad now."

"I hope it doesn't. How am I?" Leaming felt . . . untethered, almost as if he were floating above his own body like one of the hydrogen-filled balloons the Federals used in Virginia to peer behind Confederate lines. "I am . . . much improved, thank you." Finding words took a distinct effort.

"I'm glad to hear it." The surgeon smiled. "I'll give you another dose when this one wears off."

"Another dose." Echoing the surgeon was easier. And those two wonderful words held more promise than Mack Leaming had ever imagined.

Matt Ward tripped over a chunk of driftwood on the riverbank. He almost dropped his end of the plank that had a wounded Federal on it. The bluebelly groaned. The Confederate trooper at the other end of the plank said, "Watch what you're doing, dammit! What the hell's wrong with you, anyways?"

"Too much rotgut yesterday," Ward admitted. His stomach was sour, his head pounded, and his eyes felt as sensitive to the light as those of a man long poxed.

"Well, be careful, for God's sake," the other trooper said.

"That's right," the wounded Federal added.

"Shut up, you son of a bitch," Ward said furiously. "I'll take it from him—he's on my side. But I don't have to put up with anything from a goddamn Tennessee Tory, you hear me? I'd sooner tie a rock to your leg and chuck you in the Mississippi than haul you to your damn boat, and that's the Lord's truth."

The wounded man from the Thirteenth Tennessee Cavalry (U.S.) looked to the other Confederate for support. He got none there. "I feel the same way he does," the trooper said. "Just thank your lucky stars I know how to take orders."

"I thank my lucky stars I ain't no nigger," the Federal said. "That's what I thank my stars for. Otherwise, I reckon I'd just be buzzards' meat."

"I thank my lucky stars I ain't no nigger, too," the other Confederate trooper said. "But we weren't fussy yesterday. We got rid of plenty of homemade Yankees, too."

If the wounded enemy soldier had any more clever comments after that, he kept them to himself. That was one of the smarter things he could have done. Nobody was paying a lot of attention to the troopers carrying wounded men. He might have had an accident, and wouldn't that have been too bad?

It certainly would—for him.

A couple of U.S. soldiers brought a wounded Negro to a boat waiting at the river's edge at the same time as Ward and his companion carried up the white man. Like most Confederates, they wanted nothing to do with toting colored soldiers. Blacks were supposed to work for whites, not the other way around.

Both parties of bearers got their men into the boat. "What's it like on your gunboat?" Ward asked one of the sailors.

"Want to see for yourself?" the man answered in a sharp New England accent.

"Can I?" Ward said.

"Why not? There's a truce on," the Yankee said. "You and your friend know how to handle oars?"

"I do," Ward said. The other trooper nodded and started filling his pipe.

"Well, then, why don't you row across? They'll let you up on deck to look around, I figure." The sailor pointed toward the *Silver Cloud*. "Some Rebs on board already."

"We'll do it," Ward said. He'd almost reached the gunboat before he realized he was doing the Federal sailor's work for him. *A good thing he didn't try to get my money, or he'd likely have that, too,* he thought with a wry grin. But pulling a pair of oars seemed to sweat the whiskey out of him better than carrying casualties had.

Sailors on the *Silver Cloud* helped get the wounded men in the boat up onto the deck. They gave Ward and the other Confederate hard looks when they started to come aboard, too. "We don't aim to do any fighting," Matt said. "Fellow back there said we could come and look around." He pointed to the man on the riverbank.

"Cotton always did run his mouth too much," a sailor on the gunboat said, but he stood aside and let the Confederates board. *Cotton?* Ward rubbed at his ear. *Did he say that Yankee's name was Cotton?*

A couple of C.S. officers came out of the chamber where they steered the gunboat—Ward had no better name for it than that—along with a U.S. officer with one gold band at the cuff of each sleeve. Ward couldn't have said what kind of rank that gave him, either. He knew U.S. Army emblems—who didn't?—but not their naval equivalents.

Whoever this fellow was, he and the Confederates were having a high old time. That was literally true, for they were drinking together as if they belonged to the same side. They talked and laughed like old friends. The Confederates told how the *New Era* had sailed away the day before.

"Doesn't surprise me a bit," the Yankee answered. "Captain Marshall always was a little old lady in a blue uniform."

The Confederates thought that was the funniest thing they'd ever heard. One of them almost spilled his drink. "Careful, there," the other one said. "Be a shame to waste it."

"Reckon you're right," the first officer in gray said. Had they really been shooting Federals the day before? All the wounded men in blue on the *Silver Cloud*'s deck said they had.

XVII

CORPORAL JACK JENKINS RODE EAST through the Hatchie bottom country in a perfectly foul temper. The other troopers wouldn't stop ragging on him for letting Bill Bradford slip through his fingers. "Jesus God," one would-be wit said, "if you didn't want him yourself, you should've given him to the rest of us." He might have been talking about somebody who'd thrown away a drumstick instead of putting it back on the platter with the rest of the chicken.

"I wanted him, dammit," Jenkins said. "He fooled me, that's all." *That's all?* he thought bitterly. That was plenty. He'd never live it down. If he got to be an old man with a long white beard, his neighbors would still think of him as the damn fool who let Bill Bradford get away.

"He makes it down to Memphis, he'll stir up all kinds of trouble," another horseman said. "He's a serpent, Bradford is."

"Maybe somebody else'll catch the stinking, rotten son of a bitch," Jenkins said. "It ain't like he paid me to let him get away."

"Ain't enough money in Tennessee for Bradford to pay to get away," the other trooper said. Several men nearby nodded. Jack Jenkins was one of them. He would have paid plenty for the privilege of blowing Bradford's brains out. But he'd had the chance—had it and fumbled it.

He yawned. He could hardly stay on his horse, he was so tired. He'd ridden all day and all night, then fought a battle, then got stuck with that damned sentry duty. So he hadn't had enough sleep to spit at the past couple of days. He wasn't the only man swaying in the saddle, either—far from it.

At least the Confederates weren't going hell for leather now. They'd done what they set out to do. There were no Federals anywhere close by to give them a hard time. They could move at their own pace.

"Wonder where old Bedford'll want us to kick the damnyankees' asses next," somebody said.

"Wherever it is, we'll do it," Jenkins said. He had confidence in Nathan Bedford Forrest, and he had confidence in the men with whom he rode.

Whether they still had confidence in him . . . "Got to make sure they don't trip you when you've got your foot back to kick," one of them said.

"No damn Federal's ever gonna trip me again," Jenkins said furiously. "Ever, you hear?"

The rest of the troopers looked at one another, but none of them said anything. The two stripes on Jenkins's sleeve didn't hold them back; they weren't men who feared sassing underofficers. The growl in his voice, the glint in his eye, the angry flush that reddened his badly shaved cheeks, the hunch of his broad shoulders . . . Any soldier who sassed him now would have to back it up, with fists or maybe with a gun, and some things were more trouble than they were worth.

A great blue heron sprang into the air from the edge of the swamp, a fish in its beak. The bird's wingspan was almost as wide as a man was tall. Jenkins followed it with his eyes. "Wish I could fly like that," he said.

"Who don't?" somebody else said—that seemed safe enough to answer. "I've had dreams where I could flap my arms and go up into the air."

"Me, I've had dreams where I could flap my feet," another trooper put in.

"I believe that, Lou—they're big enough," still another man said. "You find a Federal with shoes that'd cover those gunboats?"

"Sure did—took a pair off a dead nigger," Lou said. "Cryin' shame when a damn nigger's got better shoes than a white man—that's all I've got to tell you."

"It is," his friend agreed. "Well, they're yours now, by Jesus. That lousy black son of a bitch don't need 'em no more."

"What I'd like to do is, I'd like to go up in a balloon one of these days," another Confederate said. "Showmen'll take 'em up at country fairs sometimes. Don't know what they charge for a ride—a quarter-eagle, maybe even a half-eagle. Hell with me if I wouldn't pay five dollars just so as I could say I really flew."

Jack Jenkins thought about doing that. It wouldn't be *bad*—if he had a five-dollar goldpiece, he figured he would plunk it down so he could see what going up in the air was like, too. But it wasn't what he'd had in mind when he spoke; it wasn't what he craved. A showman's balloon was tethered to the ground. Even if the line should break, the balloon was at the mercy of every vagrant breeze.

When he talked about flying, when he thought about flying, he meant flying the way you flew in dreams, flying the way the heron flew. He meant going from here to there because you were here and you wanted to get there. Where here and there were wouldn't matter; you could just hop in the air and go.

Nobody in all the world could do that. Jeff Davis couldn't. Neither could Abe Lincoln. Neither could Queen Victoria, and she had more money than both of them put together. So what did that say about a ragged Confederate cavalry corporal's chances? That they weren't what you'd call good, worse luck.

For that matter, almost anybody in the world could go from here to there on the ground, and where here and there were didn't matter. *Not me, dammit,* Jenkins thought. He was going where he was going because that was where Nathan Bedford Forrest wanted him to go. The privates riding with him were much more likely to pick a fight with him than he was to pick a fight with Bedford Forrest.

Riding to Forrest's will, his backside almost as sore from the saddle as if he were stricken with boils, he came into Brownsville from the west. Had he ridden into it from the east only two days before? That seemed impossible, but it was true. Would he be able to sleep in a bed tonight, or at least under a roof? After all he'd been through, that seemed impossible, too, but at least he could hope.

Pain dulled by laudanum, Mack Leaming lay on the *Platte Valley*'s deck. The world would do whatever it did. For the moment, he couldn't do anything about it. With the brandy and opium coursing through his veins, he couldn't even care about it very much.

Captain Anderson walked along the steamer's deck with the *Platte Valley*'s skipper. The civilian wore a uniform considerably gaudier than a Navy man's would have been. "You will give me receipts for all the men you take aboard, sir?" Forrest's aide said.

"Oh, yes, of course," the skipper answered. "Got to keep the paperwork straight. We'll both wind up in hot water if things don't come out even."

Anderson laughed. "Heaven forbid!" he said. "You Yanks have it worse than we do there, I believe, on account of you're richer than we are—and you have more men to spare for dotting every *i* and crossing every *t*. We've got to make do without so much in the way of spit and polish."

"I'm sure you miss it," said the captain of the *Platte Valley*. He winked at Charles Anderson—Leaming saw in most distinctly.

"Well, now and again I do, to tell you the truth," Anderson replied. "I was a merchant up in Cincinnati before the war, and after that I worked for the Nashville and Chattanooga Railroad. I like having things just so when I can. But when there's no time, and not enough men even if there were time . . . Well, sir, all you can do is your best."

"I suppose that's so." The steamboat skipper pointed up toward the bluff atop which Fort Pillow lay—or had lain. "From what my men say, you Rebs did your best there."

"We shouldn't have had to storm the place, sir," Captain Anderson said. "I gather Major Booth fell early in the fight, and Major Bradford, I'm afraid, didn't have the sense God gave a goose. He thought he could hold us out with Tennessee Tories and niggers, and forced us to prove him wrong."

"Well, you did that, by thunder!" The captain of the *Platte Valley* sounded as respectful—no, as admiring—as if he and the Confederate cavalry officer were on the same side.

Despite the laudanum, dull anger slowly filled Mack Leaming. This plump, easygoing fellow had no business getting so friendly with the enemy. They were doing everything but drinking brandy together. Captain Anderson took out a cigar case and offered the steamboat captain a stogie. That worthy bit off the end, stuck the cigar in his mouth, and scraped a lucifer on the sole of his shoe. Once he had his cheroot going, he gave Anderson a match. They smoked for a while in companionable silence.

What was happening over on the *Silver Cloud*? Was Acting Master Ferguson—a real U.S. Navy officer—as friendly toward the Rebs as this fellow? Was he complimenting them in a professional way for the skill and thoroughness they'd shown in slaughtering the Federals inside Fort Pillow? Leaming didn't—couldn't—know, but he wouldn't have been surprised.

Some Federal and Confederate officers were friends because they'd gone to West Point together or served side by side in the Old Army. Leaming could understand that even if he didn't like it. But it wouldn't be true of someone still wet behind the ears like William

Ferguson. All the same, though, to Leaming's way of thinking Union officers too often bent over backwards to extend all the courtesies to their Confederate counterparts.

That dull anger inside him grew sharper and hotter. He was damned if he would ever give any Confederate more than the minimum due him under the laws of war—if he lived to fight again. Had the Rebels given the men inside Fort Pillow even so much? He didn't think so.

Not far away, a colored artilleryman lay groaning. A bloody bandage only partly covered a huge saber cut on his head, and another wrapped his hand. He was in a bad way; Leaming didn't think he would get better. What would Negroes make of the fight at Fort Pillow? Wouldn't they want to swear bloody vengeance against Forrest's men in particular and Confederate troops in general? Leaming had seldom tried to think like a Negro, but so it seemed to him.

In and around Fort Pillow, the Confederates methodically went on wrecking and burning anything Union forces might possibly use. Forrest's men weren't going to try to hold the place against a U.S. attack. That made more sense than Mack Leaming wished it did. The Federals hadn't been able to keep the Rebs from storming the fortress; the Confederates were unlikely to have any better luck unless they brought in enough troops to man Gideon Pillow's outer perimeter. And what was the point of that?

Smoke from the burning swirled across the *Platte Valley* and the *Silver Cloud*. It made Leaming's eyes sting and burn. It also made him cough, which hurt in spite of the laudanum. He tried to breathe in little shallow sips.

Maybe that helped some. It also made him take longer than he might have otherwise to realize he wasn't just smelling wood smoke. The other odor was scorched meat. His stomach did a slow lurch when he recognized it.

He wasn't the only one. "What are you Rebs doing there?" the *Platte Valley*'s ornately dressed skipper asked Captain Anderson.

"Burning things, sir," Forrest's aide answered matter-of-factly. "Burning things."

"Things—that's fine." The steamboat captain made a horrible face. "Smells like you're burning people, too."

"Not live ones," Anderson said. "I don't know if we got all the bodies out of some of those huts before we fired them. To tell you the truth, I don't much care, either. I am not one of those men who believe the body must be perfect to render Resurrection effectual. My view is that God can provide in such circumstances, and that He will."

Leaming held the same view. That he agreed with the Confederate officer tempted him to change his mind. The skipper of the *Platte Valley* did incline to the literalist view of Resurrection. He and Captain Anderson fired Scriptural texts at each other like Minié balls.

Several real gunshots interrupted them. "What the devil's that?" the steamboat captain exclaimed. "Your men aren't supposed to be carrying arms inside the perimeter."

"I don't know what it is." Anderson sounded strained. If the truce was falling apart, he might not be able to get off the *Platte Valley*.

"They are shooting the darky soldiers!" someone yelled from the shore.

"There is a truce, Captain," the steamboat skipper said. "Your men shouldn't ought to be doing that now."

"I know," Anderson answered, his voice still tight. "If you will let me off this vessel, sir, I will do my best to quell them." He knew his onions. Even if he meant what he said, once he got ashore, he couldn't be made a prisoner.

Don't let him go! Leaming sucked in smoky air to shout it. Before he could, a Confederate officer thundered up on horseback. "Stop that firing!" he roared. "Arrest that man!"

A couple of more shots were fired, but only a couple. "There went some more niggers, God have mercy on their sorry souls," said a wounded U.S. officer standing not far from Leaming. Since he was able to stay on his feet, he could see farther than Leaming could himself.

"This is a bad business," the skipper told Captain Anderson.

"It is indeed," Anderson replied. "I do not know what provoked our soldier to commence firing—"

"Why do you think anything did, except that he was shooting at black men?" the steamboat skipper broke in. "If he was provoked, would your officer have wanted him arrested?"

Bedford Forrest's assistant adjutant general didn't answer, from which Mack Leaming concluded that he had no good answer. Instead, he said, "It's nothing that breaks the truce, anyhow." He seemed relieved, as Leaming would have been in his place.

"No, I suppose not," the captain of the *Platte Valley* replied. "We'll be able to get back to slaughtering each other soon enough, though—have no fear."

"Er—yes," said Charles Anderson. A little later, perhaps feeling he'd worn out what was to Mack Leaming much too warm a welcome, he went back ashore in the rowboat that had brought wounded Federals out to the steamer.

"Ask you something?" Leaming said as the skipper walked past him.

The man stopped in surprise. "Go ahead, friend. Ask me anything you please. I figured you were too far gone to talk."

"I hope not," Leaming said. "Now that you have us aboard, I was wondering where you'll take us."

"I'm bound for Mound City as soon as the truce is up," the skipper answered. "So is the *Silver Cloud*."

"Mound City?" Leaming tried to make his pain-frayed, drug-dulled wits work. He had little luck. "I've heard the name, but for the life of me I can't recall if it's in Tennessee or Kentucky."

"Neither one. Mound City's in Illinois, just up the Ohio from Cairo," the steamship captain said.

"Illinois!" Leaming started to laugh, even though it hurt. He'd been up in Paducah, Kentucky, before the Thirteenth Tennessee Cavalry came to Fort Pillow, but he'd never once crossed the Ohio River to go into Illinois. Kentucky felt like home. Illinois . . . He laughed some more. "Yankeeland at last."

The click of a key in the lock on his cell door woke Bill Bradford from a sound sleep. He was amazed he'd slept at all. Gray predawn light was stealing into the cell through the little barred window in the wall.

With a screech of rusty hinges, the door opened. Three Confederates stood in the hallway. Two of them aimed revolvers at Bradford. "Come on, you," said the third one, who still held the big brass key.

"Let me put my shoes on," Bradford said around a yawn.

"Make it snappy," growled one of the men with a pistol.

"He's a cold-hearted bastard, isn't he?" the other one said. "Damned if I could lay there snoring my fool head off knowing Bedford Forrest was powerful ticked at me."

Bradford looked up from tying his left shoe. "I don't snore," he said with dignity.

The Rebs gave back raucous laughter. "Hell you don't," one of them said. "Either that or somebody went and snuck a sawmill in here when Colonel Duckworth's back was turned." All three of them thought that was the funniest thing they'd ever heard.

"I'm ready now." Bradford got to his feet. "May I have something to eat before you take me to Brownsville?"

"Ought to feed you lead, is what I ought to do," one of the Confederates said, and fear rose in Bradford like a choking cloud.

But another one said, "Duckworth said to give him breakfast."

He got a hardtack and a tin cup of coffee that had to be mostly chicory. It was no worse than what they ate themselves, so he couldn't complain. After that, they herded him along to their encampment outside of Covington. "Got some more prisoners to take up to Brownsville," one of them explained. "Don't reckon they'll try and run off, though, so we didn't have to jug 'em."

"I wasn't going anywhere," Bradford protested.

"Not in a cell, you wasn't," the Reb said. "But you pulled some-thin' funny to get away from Fort Pillow—you must've—so the colo-nel didn't trust you not to do it again."

I would have, in a heartbeat, Bradford thought. Aloud, he said, "That's not fair."

"Too damn bad," the trooper said. "You made your bed. Now you can lay in it."

Lie in it, you ignorant oaf. Bill Bradford knew the difference be-tween transitive and intransitive verbs. The Confederate soldier standing in front of him knew something else: he had a pistol, and Bradford damn well didn't. And when the country was torn in two, when Tennessee was torn in two, who had a gun and who didn't mat-tered a hell of a lot more than the difference between *lie* and *lay.*

The other Federal soldiers—there were four or five of them—looked at Bradford in surprise. He feared he knew what kind of sur-prise it was. *You're still alive?* they had to be thinking.

Yes, dammit, I'm still alive! He wanted to scream it. But that wouldn't do him any good. He made himself seem meek and mild. The less the Rebs worried about him, the better his chances would be. He had got out of Fort Pillow. If he watched for his moment, he would get out of this, too.

But, because he'd got out of Fort Pillow, his captors here weren't inclined to take him on trust. They let the other prisoners mount and ride without restrictions. After he climbed up on his horse, though, they tied his feet together under the animal and they tied his hands to the reins. They tied them tight, and they used plenty of rope.

"This is cruel," he said. "What if I do fall off? The horse will tram-ple me or drag me to death."

"Then don't fall off, you son of a bitch," one of the Confederates said. "Me, I'd pay five dollars in paper or even a dollar in silver to watch that, I would."

"Come on—let's get going," another trooper said. "All this jawin' just wastes our time."

"How come you're so all-fired eager, Dud?" the first Reb asked.

"Anybody'd reckon you got yourself a lady friend up in Brownsville."
He leered.

"Well, what if I do?" Dud said. "It ain't against the law or nothin'.
An' if I get the chance to see her, that'd be right nice."

"See her?" the other soldier said. "Wouldn't you sooner tup her?"
He might have been talking about a ram and a ewe. Most soldiers
came off farms. He was probably more used to talking about animals
than about men and women.

"Never you mind what I'd sooner," Dud said. "Let's ride, that's
all."

They rode. The rest of the U.S. prisoners had it easy. They ban-
tered back and forth with Bedford Forrest's troopers, giving as good
as they got. Nobody seemed to hold anything against them. They
were out of the war now, and they were glad of it. The Rebs seemed
willing to let bygones be bygones.

Not with Bill Bradford. The C.S. troopers snarled at him whenever
he said something. They didn't want to let him down off his horse to
ease himself. "Go ahead and piss your pants," Dud said. "Serve you
right."

"Aw, let him down," another soldier said. "Alf'd be right ticked if
his saddle got piss stains on it. Can't say I'd blame him, neither."

And so, for the saddle's sake if not for his own, Bradford was untied and allowed to go between a tree. He wasn't allowed to go alone,
though. Dud covered him with a revolver as he unbuttoned his fly.
"You try and run and I'll blow it right off you." The Reb sounded as if
he looked forward to it.

After that, relaxing enough to do what he'd come for wasn't easy,
but Bradford managed. He gave Dud no excuse to pull the trigger, no
matter which part of him the Reb aimed at. When he walked back to
the horse, the Rebs tied him on as securely as before.

They rode on through the Hatchie bottom country toward
Brownsville. How *had* Forrest got his men through this ghastly terrain
ahead of the news of their coming? By driving them like cattle before
him, Bradford supposed. If Forrest wasn't a demon in human shape, a

man possessed of superhuman energy and determination, Bradford had never seen anyone who was.

"Boy, this is fun," Dud said as his horse squelched through mud. The other Rebs laughed. So did a couple of the Federal prisoners. Bill Bradford didn't. He just did more marveling. If the roads were bad now, they would have been worse when Forrest and his men came through, because it was raining then. These miserable, narrow tracks had had a day and a half to dry out since the Confederates swarmed west along them.

And how had the Rebs ever found their way through this maze of tracks? Without a guide, chances were they would still be wandering in the swamp. *That man Shaw,* Bradford thought: the Rebel sympathizer who'd escaped from Fort Pillow a day or two before Forrest descended it. Bradford couldn't prove that; he didn't remember seeing Shaw in the fight. But it seemed all too likely.

He wondered if he would meet a gloating Shaw in Brownsville. He wondered if he would meet Bedford Forrest there, too. Forrest wouldn't be gloating. Forrest would be . . . what? An educated man, Bradford didn't need long to come up with the right word. Forrest would be *vindictive,* that was what he would be.

Nathan Bedford Forrest's body felt like one big bruise. He hated staying in the saddle, but he was too stubborn to climb down from his horse. Maybe Captain Anderson could have persuaded him to dismount and rest, but Anderson was still settling affairs back at Fort Pillow. And so Forrest rode on.

He came into Brownsville at the van of his army—and he rode out the other side a few minutes later. "You always were a man in a hurry," J. B. Cowan remarked.

"You ought to know," Forrest told the regimental surgeon. Cowan was his wife's first cousin. The general commanding went on, "Getting there ahead of the other fellow counts for more than almost anything."

"Even if you wear yourself down to a nub doing it?" Cowan asked.

"Even then. Especially then," Forrest replied. "If you do more than the enemy figures you've got a prayer of doing, you hold him in the palm of your hand."

"It's a hard road," the surgeon observed.

"It's the only road I know," Forrest said. "I started with nothing—you know that, dammit—and I made myself a man to be reckoned with. I joined the Army as a private soldier, and I'm a major general now. I'm not so young as I used to be; I haven't got much time to waste. I will take the hardest road I have to, as long as it's the quickest one."

He wondered whether Cowan would go on arguing with him, but the regimental surgeon held his tongue. *He knows better than to try and talk me around,* Forrest thought with an inward smile.

"What will you do when you get to Jackson?" Cowan asked after a while.

"Rest. Let the rest of the men come in—I know they won't all stick up with me." Forrest knew that for a while he would have men scattered all across the seventy miles between Fort Pillow and Jackson, and he couldn't do much about it. Sooner or later, they'd come in. He went on, "Once they're all gathered, I'll cipher out what to do with 'em next—or maybe I'll get orders. Who knows?"

"Will we be able to stay up here in Tennessee any which way?" Cowan inquired. "After what you did at Fort Pillow, the damnyankees will be fit to be tied."

"That was the idea." When Forrest said it, it sounded more like *idear.* "If it gets too hot round those parts, we'll slide on down to Mississippi, that's all. But if they think they can keep me out of Tennessee for good, or even out of Memphis for good, they'd better think again, is all I've got to tell you."

"Out of Memphis? How would you get in there? It's fortified to a fare-thee-well."

"I'll get in." Forrest spoke with supreme confidence. He didn't say how he would get into Memphis, because he had no idea. When the time came, he would come up with something. The West Point men against whom he fought made their plans well in advance. They figured out every little thing before they went and did it . . . and then they thought they would take you by surprise.

Bedford Forrest laughed softly. Once you'd fought one of those fellows, you'd fought all of them. They'd all learned the same way of fighting, and they all had the same bag of tricks. They never figured out that you might know ahead of time what they'd try. The way they were trained, they were *supposed* to think alike.

The Confederacy had a lot of generals and colonels who'd learned at West Point, too. Couldn't they see that the Yankees could read them like a book? Evidently not—and a lot of time both sides seemed ignorant of how predictable they were.

Because Forrest had never learned all the fancy West Point rules and regulations, he was as far beyond the regular officers' ken as a hawk was beyond a snapping turtle's. Things seemed very simple to him. You moved faster than the man you were fighting. You hit him where he wouldn't expect it, where he was weak. You used fear as much as you used bullets. A frightened enemy was an enemy who gave up too soon or who made mistakes that let you lick him. And once you got him scared and jittery, you never let up.

That thought made Forrest mutter into his chin beard. Instead of going all-out after the beaten Yankees at Chickamauga, Braxton Bragg let them retreat into Chattanooga—which meant the only victory that sour-souled son of a bitch ever won turned out not to be worth spit. He had his chance, his single, solitary, glorious chance to bring the war in the West back to life, to make the Confederate presence in Tennessee and Kentucky more than a matter of cavalry raiders. He had it, and he dropped it, and he broke it, and the Confederacy wasn't likely to be able to pick up the pieces ever again.

"I should have killed him," Forrest said. "By Jesus, I should have."

"Who are you talking about, sir?" J. B. Cowan asked. "Major Bradford?"

"What's that?" Bedford Forrest blinked, brought back from what might have been to what was. "No, I wasn't thinking about

Bradford—not that he doesn't rate killing now. I had somebody else in mind."

"Must be Colonel Hurst, then." The regimental surgeon sounded very sure of himself.

"That's right—Fielding Hurst." Forrest let his wife's cousin down easy. Why not? Every Confederate in Tennessee knew Fielding Hurst needed killing. Stories were going round that Forrest had come within inches of challenging Braxton Bragg to a duel, but most people thought they were only stories. Forrest didn't say anything different. What point to it? If the Confederate generals fought among themselves, who gained but the Federals? Still and all, he knew the stories were true—were, if anything, less than the whole truth.

Dr. Cowan grinned, pleased with his own cleverness. Bedford Forrest grinned, amused the other man was so easy to fool. If you let people believe what they wanted to believe anyhow, you could get them to do almost anything.

But then Cowan asked, "What *will* you do with Bradford if our boys catch him?"

The question was unpleasantly sharp. "Don't rightly know," Forrest said, an admission he seldom made. "I hated the son of a bitch before he broke his parole, and he gave me plenty of reasons for it, too. I almost hope we don't catch him. That way, I won't have to make up my mind."

"Almost?" the surgeon said.

Forrest nodded. "Almost."

Word got around. It always did. Jack Jenkins hated that truth, but knew it was one. As he rode east toward Brownsville, he heard the same question over and over again: "How the hell did you let that Bradford son of a bitch get away?"

"It was dark," he said at first. "He said he was a sutler. He was wearing a sutler's clothes, and he stunk like a goddamn polecat. How in God's name was I supposed to know who he was?"

That sounded reasonable—to him, anyway. It didn't satisfy any of the men who flung the question in his face. They didn't really want an answer. They wanted somebody to blame . . . and there he was.

His temper, always short, soon started to fray. Before long, he stopped giving a reasonable answer when people asked him how he let Bradford escape. Instead, he said things like, "It just happened, god-dammit. Bad shit happens all the time. This time it happened to me."

He got no sympathy. He didn't expect any. He wouldn't give anybody else much sympathy for letting Bradford slip through his fingers. The same miserable question came at him even more often.

His answer changed again. He looked around and growled, "Oh, shut up, goddammit!" That did some good. Most of Forrest's troopers were leery of pushing him too far.

"You look like a treed coon," one of them said.

"I feel like a treed coon, too," Jenkins replied—that was one of the few things he'd heard that made sense to him. "Got all these bastards around the tree bayin' their damnfool heads off."

On they rode, into the morning. Every time somebody with a fast horse came up to Jenkins, he heard the hateful question again. And he heard it every time he caught up to somebody with a slow horse. And when they weren't just coming out and asking it of him, they were talking about him and pointing at him. "There's the fellow who . . ."

"Aw, shit," Jenkins mumbled. Yes, he was likely to stay *the fellow who* for the rest of his life. Some mistakes were too damn big to let anybody ever get out from under them. Had he made one of those? He didn't think so, but what he thought didn't matter here. What everybody else thought did. And those nudges and murmurs and pointing fingers went on and on.

"Hey, Corporal, aren't you the one who let Bradford get away?"

"Fuck you up the cornhole!" Jenkins roared. Only after the words were out of his mouth did he realized he'd cussed out a captain. The officer started to say something. Then he got a good look at Jenkins's face. His mouth hung foolishly open for a moment, as if he were a frog catching a fly. He booted his horse up to a trot and rode away.

I bet I had murder in my eye, Jenkins thought, not without pride. *I know goddamn well I had murder in my heart.*

For some little while, nobody bothered him. Oh, people went on pointing and went on talking behind his back, but he knew he couldn't do anything about that. When a newcomer tried to ask him something—and he knew what it would be—somebody softly explained to the man that that wasn't a good idea. *Not if you want to go on breathing, it isn't,* Jenkins thought.

And then every trooper around was cussing a blue streak, and none of it had anything to do with him. He was swearing, too. Whoever was leading them east had led them astray. The path petered out in the middle of a swamp. They were going to have to double back and try again. "God, I didn't need this," somebody groaned, and that summed things up just fine.

"How the hell did we bollix this?" Jenkins demanded. "Lord almighty, it ain't like we're the first bunch to go back to Brownsville. Shouldn't whoever was at the front of this bunch have known where he was going, the rotten skunk?"

Whoever had been at the front of that group of soldiers didn't want to admit it. In his shoes, Jack Jenkins wouldn't have wanted to admit it, either. Something nasty would have happened to him if he did.

Because it had to double back, the group of cavalrymen from Barteau's regiment with whom he was riding didn't get to Brownsville till the late afternoon. By then, the people in the small town had had bands of troopers of varying sizes riding in for hours. Some houses still had the Stainless Banner and the Confederate battle flag and the outdated Stars and Bars flying or hanging on their porches, but no ladies were standing in the street offering the soldiers food, the way they had when the regiment rode west to attack Fort Pillow.

"Rein in, boys!" a first lieutenant called. "We may as well spend the night here. We don't need to ride in the dark today, and we'll make it to Jackson tomorrow any which way."

That was the first piece of good news Jenkins had heard in a long time. Even if he couldn't get a bed for the night—which didn't look likely—he could sleep on a floor or in a shed or somewhere else under a roof. Roughing it was fine when you did it on purpose every once in a while—when you were going hunting, say. When you had to do it day after day after day, it wore thin.

He'd just dismounted when some soldiers came up from the south. "Y'all got lost worse'n we did," he jeered.

"We're not lost," one of them replied. "We're up from Covington with prisoners. We'll take 'em on to Jackson in the morning."

"Prisoners?" Jack Jenkins looked them over. That some wore blue hadn't meant much to him—he'd just thought they hadn't had a chance to dye Yankee plunder. One fellow had on ratty-looking civilian clothes. Jenkins stiffened. He'd seen those shabby clothes before, by moonlight. As casually as he could, he asked, "Need somebody else to help bring 'em in?"

The shabbily dressed prisoner jerked on the horse to which he was tied. He recognized Jenkins's voice. The Confederate captain in charge of the captives nodded. "Sure, Corporal. You can come along."

Jenkins smiled like Christmas.

XVIII

MATT WARD HAD WATCHED THE *Silver Cloud* and the *Platte Valley* steam away late the afternoon before. Chugging north against the current, the gunboat and the steamer she escorted weren't very fast, but they looked as if they would get where they were going.

Here today, Fort Pillow wasn't a fort any more. It was nothing but a bluff next to the Mississippi. Captain Charles Anderson looked around and nodded in satisfaction. "That about does it," he said to Ward and the rest of the Confederates still at the battle site. "I reckon we've done every single thing we set out to do."

Bedford Forrest's aide was bound to be right about that. Forrest's men hadn't just taken the place. They'd run off the Federals' horses and captured all the cannon here. They'd taken more than three hundred rifle muskets; the rest probably lay in the river. They had as much of the rest of the movable property as they could carry away. And now they'd wrecked and burned all the buildings and huts in and around the fort. The Federals wouldn't have anything at all to use if they tried to put men in here again.

Another Federal steamer went by. Maybe it would find Union soldiers who'd got away and were hiding along the river. Ward eyed the smoke pouring from its stack, which mixed with the smoke still in the air from the fires of the day before. "We ought to have boats on the Mississippi ourselves," he said.

Captain Anderson still stood close enough to hear him. "We've got a few," he said. "We can move things across from Louisiana and Arkansas now and again. But we have to sneak, because we can't make ironclads to fight the damnyankees."

"Why not, sir?" Ward said. "*They* can do it."

"They can build them anywhere along the Ohio or the Mississippi and send them downriver," Anderson answered. "We haven't got any foundries on the river to do the job." He made a sour face. "Hell's bells, we haven't got any *towns* on this side of the river. The damnyankees sail up and down, doing as they please. They've cut us in half, may they rot in hell for it."

"That's not good," Ward said.

"No, it isn't," Captain Anderson agreed. "Kirby Smith is doing everything he can over in the Trans-Mississippi, but what he does and what we do don't have a whole lot to do with each other on account of all those Federal gunboats in between."

"What can we do about that, sir?" Matt Ward could look across the Mississippi into Arkansas. If he cared to, he could take a rowboat and get across to the other side—to the Trans-Mississippi, Captain Anderson called it. But if you wanted to move an army's worth of soldiers from one side of the Big Muddy to the other, how would you go about it? You couldn't, not unless you wanted those damn gunboats swarming around you like flies around a fried chicken in summertime.

"What can we do about it?" Anderson echoed. "Keep fighting the Yankees as hard as we can. Keep licking them. Keep making them sweat. Keep making them bleed. Abe Lincoln is up for reelection this fall. If we make the North decide the war is more expensive than it's worth, if we make it decide the war is more goddamn trouble than it's worth, they'll throw that Lincoln son of a bitch out on his ear. Whichever Democrat they put in will make peace and send the bluebellies home. And we'll have our own country then. *That's* what we can do, by God."

"I understand, sir." Ward looked respectfully at the officer, who wasn't that much older than he was. "I really do understand. When I joined up, I did it so I could fight the damnyankees."

"Who doesn't?" Anderson said.

"Yes, sir. But that was all I thought about, you know what I mean? What you said, I didn't think about that even a little bit. How the war and politics fit together, I mean. And they do. They truly do."

"You'd best believe they do," Charles Anderson agreed. "Way things are now, we won't ever drive the United States off our land with guns. Maybe we could have once upon a time, but we lost too many chances. But if we can make those Yankee bastards sick of fighting us, they'll give up and go home. And we win that way, too. So that's what we've got to try and do."

Ward looked at the remains of what had been Fort Pillow. "Well, sir, seems to me we gave them a pretty good tweak right here."

"Seems the same way to me." Captain Anderson eyed him. "When you let Bradford liquor you up so he could get away, I reckoned you were one of those fellows who're good in a brawl but not so good at thinking, if you'll forgive me. But you aren't that way, are you?"

"I hope not, sir. I like to find out how things tick," Ward answered. "Bradford . . . He tricked me, God damn him. I wonder if the son of a bitch got away. Sweet Jesus, I hope not. I'd feel like hell."

"If he did, he'll run into a minnie some other way, that's all." To Matt's relief, Anderson didn't seem to hate him. "For now, we've still got our own war to fight. You ready?"

"Yes, sir!" Matt said.

It's all in your mind, Major William Bradford told himself over. *You're making it up to give yourself something to worry about.* He laughed sourly. As if he didn't have enough already! Here he was, locked up in the Brownsville jail the way he had been the night before in Coving-

ton. Some time tomorrow, he'd head for Jackson and a new con-
frontation with Nathan Bedford Forrest. That wasn't anything to look
forward to with joy and eager anticipation.

But right now it seemed the least of his troubles. He couldn't shake
the feeling that the corporal who'd volunteered to join the guards on
the way to Jackson was the fellow he'd cozened into letting him out
past the original, extended works around Fort Pillow.

Had that fellow out there on sentry had two stripes on his sleeve?
For the life of him—yes, for the life of him—Bradford wasn't sure.
His voice seemed much too familiar, though. And the man had a devil
of a nasty leer, the kind of leer that said he might not have known who
Bill Bradford was before but by Christ now he did, and somebody was
going to pay because he knew.

"Somebody," Bradford muttered. "Me!" What had the Rebs done
to that corporal when they found out he'd let the enemy commander
get away? How much did he have to pay back? And how much did he
hate Bradford for tricking him, for taking away his pride? A lot of
Southern men were touchy as so many greasers about their pride. If
you wounded it, they would pay you back no matter what it cost.

Maybe he's not the one. Bradford tried to make himself believe it.
He stretched out on the lumpy, musty-smelling cot in the little cell and
tried to rest. *It'll be fine tomorrow,* his mind insisted. *You're getting
yourself all worn to a frazzle over nothing.* But even though he closed
his eyes, sleep wouldn't come.

Except it did. When his eyes came open again, the gray light of
dawn seeped into the cell through the little barred window. Outside, a
mockingbird trilled and whistled. Why not? The bird was free.

The jailer gave him bread and butter for breakfast. The butter was
just starting to go off. He could eat it, but it left a sour aftertaste on his
palate that the bad coffee he drank with it couldn't erase. The jailer
watched him eat through the window set into the door. As soon as he
finished, the man unlocked the door to get the cup back. He had a
pistol. Two more men with guns also covered Bradford. "I wasn't going anywhere," Bradford said.

"Not while we can shoot you if you try," one of the guards said.

At noon, Bradford got more bread and butter and coffee. The butter was further gone by then. He ate it anyhow. Time dragged on. The cell got warm and close. Sweat rolled off him. At last, late in the afternoon, the jailer unlocked the door again. "Come on out." That pistol added persuasion to the words.

Out Bradford came. The jailer gestured with the gun. Numbly, Bradford walked outside. The mockingbird he'd heard before—or maybe another one—flew out of a nearby oak, white wing patches flashing every time it flapped. The other Federal prisoners waited out there; they hadn't had to spend the time in jail. The guards who'd brought them up from Covington waited there, too. So did the corporal who'd volunteered to join them.

Was he . . . ? Bradford eyed him with fearful fascination. He couldn't tell. It had been dark, the moon still young and going in and out of the clouds.

"Get up on your horse, Bradford," said one of the Confederate soldiers. "Get up, and I'll lash you aboard." By the way he talked, the Federal officer might have been a sack of dried peas.

"You don't need to tie me—I swear it," Bradford said.

"You swore you wouldn't run off from Fort Pillow, too, you lying son of a bitch." That wasn't the guard who was busy binding Bradford's legs beneath him. It was the newly met corporal. He sounded like a man who knew what he was talking about. Bradford bit his lip. He couldn't even tell the Reb he was wrong. The other trooper tied his hands and tied them to the reins.

"That ought to do it," he said. "Let's ride."

Off they went, not at any particularly fast clip. By now the prisoners, even Major Bradford, were afterthoughts. No need to hurry with them. The battle was won. Sooner or later, they would get to Jackson. When they did, Bedford Forrest would deal with them as he got around to it.

Had Bradford not been a prisoner of war, had he not been tied to the horse he rode, he would have savored the glorious spring day. It was perfect: not too cool, not too hot, with the sun shining cheerily in a sky powder-puffed with scattered white clouds. The grass and growing bushes were green, greener, greenest. So were the leaves on some of the trees. Others, not yet in leaf, remained bare-branched and skeletal.

More mockingbirds sang. Catbirds yowled. A robin hopping around after worms chirped. Somewhere deeper in the woods, a wild turkey gobbled. Once the riders got away from the town stinks of Brownsville, which didn't take long, the very air smelled fresh and clean and pure.

Yes, it would have been a pleasant ride, a more than pleasant ride, if not for the ropes around Bradford's wrists and ankles—and if the corporal who'd added himself to the guard party hadn't kept talking to the other Confederate troopers in a low voice. Every so often, he would point Bill Bradford's way, which did nothing to improve the Federal officer's peace of mind.

"Are you sure?" one of the other soldiers asked, loud enough for Bradford to hear him clearly.

"Sure as my name's Jack Jenkins," the corporal answered. "Sure as that son of a bitch . . ." His voice dropped so Bradford couldn't make out what he said next. Whatever it was, the Federal didn't think he wanted it applied to him.

They'd come perhaps three miles, perhaps five, when one of the troopers said, "We'll stop here for a little bit. Anybody want to ease himself?"

"I do," a Federal said. He swung down from his horse and went off to stand behind a tree. One of the Confederates lit a pipe. The soldier in blue came back buttoning the last button on his fly. He pointed to the pipe. "Can I have a couple of puffs of that?" The Reb passed it to him. He smoked for a little while, then gave it back. "Thank you kindly."

"How about you, Bradford?" the corporal named Jack Jenkins said.

Bradford considered. He didn't particularly need anything, but if he said no the Rebs might use it as an excuse to torment him later by refusing to pause. He nodded. "All right. You'll have to let me loose."

The trooper with the pipe untied him. After Bradford dismounted, he stood by the horse for a moment, opening and closing his hands to work more feeling into them. Then he started for the woods. Jack Jenkins and four other Rebs, one a lieutenant, came with him. "Don't want you wandering off, now, the way you did at Fort Pillow," Jenkins said.

"I wasn't going anywhere," Bradford said, as he had early that morning. His lips were suddenly stiff with fear. That *was* the sentry he'd tricked, and the man knew him for who he was. "Please," he whispered. "I wasn't."

"Well, you damn well won't." The Reb gestured with his rifle musket. "Go on."

Terror making his legs light, his knees almost unstrung, Bradford went. The Rebs urged him deeper into the woods, so that trees hid the path down which they'd been riding. "Let me . . . do what I need to do," he said at last, when they'd gone about fifty yards.

A little to his surprise, they did, spreading out to all sides around the oak he chose so he couldn't get away no matter how much he wanted to—and he did, with all his heart and with all his soul and with all his might. At last, after what seemed a very long time, he finished. He did up his trousers and stepped away from the tree.

"Look!" Jenkins said loudly. "Son of a bitch is getting away!" He swung up his rifle musket. So did the other Confederate soldiers.

"No!" Bradford cried. He fell to his knees. "Treat me as a prisoner of war, please! I fought you as a man, and—"

The guns spoke in a stuttering roar. Hot lead slammed into him from three directions at once. He slumped over. The ground came up and hit him one more blow in the face. He tried to get up, but only his left arm seemed to want to do anything his brain told it to, and it wasn't enough, not by itself.

Corporal Jenkins strolled up and stood over him and slowly and deliberately reloaded. "You shit-eating bastard, you got by me once, but I'm damned if you'll do it twice," he said, and aimed the rifle musket again.

"No," Bradford moaned through blood in his mouth, through nerves telegraphing torment, though darkness swelling before his eyes.

And the rifle musket boomed once more, and the darkness rose up and swallowed everything. Through the rising flood, he heard a laugh and the words, "Shot trying to escape," and then it overflowed, and he never heard or saw anything again.

Illinois. The land of liberty. Abe Lincoln's very own state. A free state. A state where owning a nigger was against the law. Ben Robinson knew there were places like that, but he'd never imagined he would come to one. It was an awful lot like getting to heaven, and nearly made getting shot worthwhile.

Nearly.

He lay on an iron-framed military cot in Ward N of the Mound City general hospital. A big sign said it was Ward N. People talked about it a dozen times a day. Now he knew what an N looked like. Benjamin Robinson. He had four of them in his name. It wasn't much of a start for learning his letters, but a start it was.

Colored soldiers from Fort Pillow, a couple of dozen of them, crowded the ward. Charlie Key was here, and Sandy Cole, and Aaron Fentis, too. They'd all survived their wounds, same as Ben had. Dr. Stewart Gordon, the white surgeon who ran the ward, said they were all likely to get better. He seemed to know what he was talking about, and to know what he was doing, too. Only one man had died since the *Silver Cloud* and the *Platte Valley* brought them up here, and poor Bob Hall had been in a bad way: a Reb had hacked up his head and his hand with a saber while he lay sick down at Fort Pillow. Another soldier, Tom Adison, had lost an eye and a chunk of his nose to a Minié ball. He wasn't in good shape; Dr. Gordon looked worried every time he examined him. The rest were going to make it.

Every time Dr. Gordon changed his dressing, Ben stared at his own wound. Every time, he liked what he saw. Oh, yes, he would have liked not getting shot in the first place ever so much better. But the edges of the gouge in his thigh were healing together. The wound wasn't festering. It didn't have pus dripping from it. It didn't stink. It was—he was—getting better.

One morning—Ben thought it was ten days after the fight at Fort Pillow, but he might have been off one either way—the surgeon came into Ward N earlier than usual. "I want you to listen to me, boys," he said. "Something's up."

He was younger than a lot of the colored soldiers he was talking to. But he'd treated every last one of them, and was plainly doing the best he could with them. Ben traded glances with Sandy Cole and Charlie Key, but he was inclined to give the surgeon the benefit of the doubt.

"Something's up," Gordon repeated. "We're going to have men from the Joint Committee on the Conduct of the War visit you today: Senator Wade and Congressman Gooch."

Even a colored artilleryman who'd been a soldier for only a little while knew about the Joint Committee on the Conduct of the War. When something went wrong with the Union war effort, the members of the committee swooped down like eagles—some said like vultures—to pin the blame on whoever deserved it (or whoever they thought deserved it). They could blight an officer's career. They could, and they had, and by all accounts they liked doing it.

"Do Jesus! Us niggers gonna be in trouble for losing the fight?" Robinson asked in more than a little alarm.

But the surgeon shook his head. "No, no, no. So help me, no. As far as they're concerned, you're heroes for fighting as well as you did. No, what they're after is making Bedford Forrest out to be a monster on account of the massacre. They aim to use it to fire up people in the North to fight the Rebs harder."

"I got you," Ben said, but he couldn't help adding, "If you was ever a slave, you already got all the reason you need to fight them Confederate bastards hard as you can."

"There are no slaves up here," Dr. Gordon reminded him. "A lot of people up here have never set eyes on a colored man, let alone owned one. The men from the committee want to remind them what the war is all about. There's an election coming up, you know. If Honest Abe doesn't go back to the White House, the Democrats will give the damn Rebs whatever they want."

"Do Jesus!" Ben said again. He'd imagined the Federals beaten. He knew the Confederates fought hard. But he'd never dreamt the United States might just give up the fight.

He felt better when he saw the members of the Joint Committee on the Conduct of the War. Congressman Daniel Gooch was about forty, with a round face, reddish hair and beard, and worried eyes behind small, oval spectacle lenses. Senator Benjamin Wade was at least twenty years older, and quite a bit tougher. He combed his graying, thinning hair straight back. His eyes were narrow and shrewd, his mouth a disapproving slash across his clean-shaven face. He effortlessly dominated the proceedings.

"We are going to get to the bottom of the bad faith and treachery that seem to have become the settled policy of Forrest and his command," Wade declared in a rasping voice that brooked no argument. "We must convince the authorities of our government of this fact. Even the most skeptical must believe that it is the intention of the Rebel authorities not to recognize the officers and men of our colored regiments as entitled to the treatment accorded by all civilized nations to prisoners of war. And at Fort Pillow the brutality and cruelty of the Rebels were most fearfully exhibited."

A secretary took down his words as he spoke them. *This man means it,* Robinson realized. He'd always known the Rebs were in grim earnest. He'd sometimes doubted his own side was. Here, though, here stood a man with as much iron in his spine as even Nathan Bedford Forrest had.

Congressman Gooch started questioning the colored man closest to him, Elias Falls of Company A. Falls spoke of what he'd seen and heard during the fight. He said Bedford Forrest had ordered the firing stopped, and that a Secesh officer had threatened to arrest a soldier for shooting a Negro. The secretary wrote down his words just like Senator Wade's.

When Falls finished testifying—he didn't take long—Ben Wade spoke again: "That will be about enough of that. We are here to show the people of the United States what monsters the Rebels are. We are going to do that. If you men want to testify to anything else, do it before the Confederate Congress. Do you understand me?" After that, no one talked much about officers trying to stop the shooting.

Congressman Gooch asked most of the questions. Senator Wade chimed in now and again. They worked their way through the ward, coming closer and closer to the cot where Ben Robinson lay. At last, the secretary told him, "Raise your right hand." When he did, the white man said, "Do you solemnly swear to tell the truth, the whole truth, and nothing but the truth, so help you God?"

"Yes, suh," Robinson answered, impressed by the gravity of the phrases.

"I have sworn in the witness, sir," the secretary said formally to Daniel Gooch. "You may proceed."

"Thank you." Gooch's voice was a light tenor. His New England accent gave Ben a little trouble, but he managed. "Were you at Fort Pillow in the fight there?" Gooch asked.

"Yes, suh," Ben said. The secretary scribbled, taking down his words for all time.

The Congressman took him through what had happened and how he got shot. Gooch asked if he had seen the Confederates burn any soldiers. He said no, because he hadn't. Gooch's mouth tightened a little, but he went on to ask about burials, and whether Ben had seen anyone buried alive. Robinson mentioned the one Negro who was still working his hand when he went into the ground.

"Were any Rebel officers around when the Rebels were killing our men?" Gooch asked.

"Yes, suh—lots of them," Robinson answered.

"Did they try to keep their men from killing our men?"

"I never heard them say so." Ben explained how Bedford Forrest had ridden his horse over him three or four times.

Daniel Gooch let him finish, then asked, "Where were you from?"

"I come from South Carolina," Robinson replied.

"Have you been a slave?"

"Yes, suh."

"Thank you, uh, Sergeant." Gooch went on to the colored man in the next bed, a private from Company B named Dan Tyler. He asked him the same sorts of questions he'd asked Ben. He and Senator Wade continued through the ward till they'd heard the stories of most of the Negroes there. Even badly wounded Tom Adison got to speak his piece.

"Thank you, men," Ben Wade said when they finished. "Thank you for your bravery down South, and thank you for what you told us here today. We aim to make it so that everyone in the whole country will remember Fort Pillow for as long as this nation lives. It deserves remembering, and that's a fact. Men will go into battle crying, 'Remember Fort Pillow!' And we will pay the Rebels back in their own coin. Never doubt it, men, for we will!"

He lumbered out of the room, Congressman Gooch and the secretary hurrying along in his wake. "We was part of history," Ben Robinson said in wonder as the door closed behind them. "We reckoned we was just soldierin', but we was part of history. I be damned. Me—a part o' history." Up till now, history, like freedom, had been something for whites only. In an odd way, a completely unexpected way, he felt more of a man than he ever had before.

Mack Leaming wasn't happy, and the pain from his wound wasn't the only thing to make him unhappy. Like everyone else who'd lived to come north from Fort Pillow, he knew the officials from the Joint Committee on the Conduct of the War were on their way west to find out what went wrong.

He knew when they reached Mound City, and he knew when they

questioned the Negroes who'd survived Bedford Forrest's murderous attack. Senator Wade and Congressman Gooch got to the coons before they asked the white survivors a single question. And if that wasn't wrong, Lieutenant Leaming had never run into anything that was.

Not until the following day did Wade and Gooch and their obsequious secretary come to Ward B, where Leaming lay recuperating. The surgeon, a tall, thin, doleful-looking man named Charles Vail, came early in the morning to change his dressings. Vail also stopped by the bed of Captain John Potter, who lay not far away. He looked at Potter—who'd led Company B of the Thirteenth Tennessee Cavalry—and shook his head.

"No change?" Leaming asked.

"I'm afraid not," Dr. Vail answered. "With a head wound like that, he's in God's hands, not mine. And God hasn't doled out many miracles lately. Potter's almost hopeless. I wish I could tell you different, but . . ." He spread his hands.

While Leaming was digesting that, the secretary who'd accompanied Messrs. Wade and Gooch to Mound City came into the ward. He spoke with Vail; the surgeon led him over to Leaming's bed. "Good morning, Lieutenant," the secretary murmured. His voice and clothes were prissily precise. *A cornholer?* Leaming wondered. *Wouldn't be surprised.*

But that was neither here nor there. "Good morning," Leaming said.

"I hope you continue to improve," the secretary told him.

"He's making good progress," Dr. Vail put in. "His prognosis is favorable, unlike poor Captain Potter's."

"I am glad to hear it." The secretary gave his attention back to Leaming. "The gentlemen from the Joint Committee are most desirous—*most* desirous, sir—of presenting the massacre at Fort Pillow to the people of the United States in terms as emphatic, and as condemnatory of Bedford Forrest and his brigands, as possible. Any assistance you can offer towards that end will be greatly appreciated. Do I make myself plain?"

"I think you do, sir," Leaming answered. Wade and Gooch wanted him to slang the Rebs, and they wouldn't mind if he stretched things a little to do it. Neither would he. After everything that had happened at Fort Pillow, he wanted to pay them back any way he could.

The effete secretary withdrew, to return a few minutes later with the Senator and the Congressman. He administered the oath to Leaming, then took out his notebook and pen while Daniel Gooch started the questioning. With the secretary's encouragement, Leaming wasn't above stretching things when he talked about the truce. He complained that the Rebs who'd come down to the riverside to meet the *Olive Branch* took advantage of the white flag to improve their position. Because the steamer was not a party to the cease-fire, that wasn't exactly so, but it felt as if it ought to be. Congressman Gooch nodded gravely. The secretary's pen slid across the paper.

Leaming told how he'd been shot and robbed and succored only by his fellow Freemason. When he described how he'd been carried aboard the *Platte Valley,* Senator Wade took over for Gooch. He wanted to know who'd been drinking with the Rebs. Leaming hesitated about putting U.S. officers in hot water, and truthfully said he hadn't seen anyone doing so. Wade did not look happy. Leaming got the idea he seldom looked happy, but he looked even less so now.

"Do you know what became of Major Bradford?" Wade asked.

"He escaped unhurt, as far as the battle was concerned," Leaming answered. "I was told the next morning on the boat that he had been paroled. I did not see him after that night."

A little later, Congressman Gooch asked, "What do you estimate Forrest's force to have been?"

"From all I could see and learn, I should suppose he had from seven thousand to ten thousand men," Leaming answered. Major Booth hadn't thought so, but Major Booth was dead . . . and the larger number better suited the Union cause. A few questions later, Leaming got the chance to trot out one more rumor: "I have been told that Major Bradford was afterwards taken out by the Rebels and shot. That seems to be the general impression, and I presume it was so."

"Thank you, Lieutenant," Gooch and Wade said together. "No further questions," Wade added.

After the secretary closed his notebook and put away his pen, Daniel Gooch nodded to Leaming. "Thank you, Lieutenant," he said. "That was very effective testimony."

"I was doing my best to help, Your Excellency," Leaming replied.

"Well, your best is damned good, son," Ben Wade rumbled. "We'll hold Bedford Forrest's toes to the fire with what you had to say—just see if we don't." His face darkened with anger. "And we'll put a stop to the despicable practice some of our officers have of treating white men on the other side better than they treat colored soldiers in their own uniform. Despicable, I say, and we will stamp it out."

"Er—yes, sir." Till he'd seen the Negro artillerymen at Fort Pillow fight, Mack Leaming would have been that kind of Federal officer himself. Fighting for the Union and fighting for the Negro had seemed two very different things to him. They still did, as a matter of fact—but he had more sense than to admit it to the implacable Senator from Ohio.

"If I may be permitted to say so, Lieutenant, your testimony was exactly along the lines envisioned by the committee when it voted to send Senator Wade and Congressman Gooch west to investigate this tragic incident," the secretary observed.

You told them what they wanted to hear. Leaming heard the words behind the words. "Good," he said. The secretary had told him what the distinguished gentlemen wanted, and he was glad to oblige. This was a war of soldiers and cannons and gunboats, yes. But it was also a war of politics. He could see November ahead, just as Wade and Gooch could. If Lincoln failed then, if the Democrats prevailed then, all the Union's sacrifices would be for nothing.

He and his comrades had lost the battle at Fort Pillow. They might yet win the struggle to define what happened there, and winning that struggle would go some little way toward winning the war as a whole. Leaming shifted carefully on the cot. His wound still pained him. Wounded or not, though, he might still pain Nathan Bedford Forrest.

"Shot trying to get away, was he?" Bedford Forrest said, stalking through the parlor of the Duke house in Jackson as he had while ordering the attack on Fort Pillow.

"Yes, sir," Captain Anderson said stolidly. "So the men who were bringing Major Bradford and the other prisoners here report."

"Well, Lord knows he's no loss. He's a gain, by God." But Forrest studied his assistant adjutant general. "So they say, eh? But you don't believe 'em, do you?" Anderson shook his head. "How come you don't?" Forrest asked.

"Well, sir, for one thing, among the men who were supposed to be bringing him in was Corporal Jack Jenkins," Anderson answered.

"Corporal . . . ? Oh!" A fortnight after the fight at Fort Pillow, Forrest needed a moment to place the name, but only a moment. "The fellow he gave the slip to getting out of the fort!"

"The very same," Anderson said.

"You reckon Jenkins got his own back, then?"

"Sir, I can't prove a thing. All the men tell the same story," Anderson replied. "And it certainly is something Bradford *might* have done, when you consider that he did break his parole in leaving Fort Pillow."

"Uh-*huh*." Forrest wondered what to do—but, again, not for long. "Well, Charlie, I don't suppose I need to ask any more questions. Bradford got what was coming to him, and by my lights he earned it. If anybody ever kicks up a stink about it—and who would kick up a stink about a skunk like that?—'shot trying to escape' ought to quiet things down, eh?"

"Yes, sir. I suppose so." Captain Anderson didn't sound overjoyed at his decision, but he didn't sound as if he wanted to make a fuss, either. That suited Bedford Forrest fine. Major Bradford hadn't been worth a fuss while he was alive, and sure as hell he wasn't worth one dead.

"Anything else I need to know?" Forrest asked.

"News from Memphis is that a couple of Federal Congressmen are nosing around, trying to figure out where the blame goes for losing Fort Pillow," Anderson said.

"Are they, by God?" Forrest said. His aide nodded. Forrest threw back his head and laughed. "I'm glad to hear it, the Devil fry me black as a nigger if I'm not. I was starting to believe our side was the only one with fools in Congress."

"They're shouting and wailing about how we massacred all the poor darkies—and the homemade Yankees, too," Anderson said.

"They can shout and wail as much as they please. Bradford had the chance to surrender, and he damn well didn't take it. I told him I wouldn't answer for my men if he didn't, so he only got what was coming to him," Forrest growled. "Besides, we *did* take prisoners. We gave some of 'em back to the Federals by the river—"

"I did that myself," Anderson said.

"Of course you did," Bedford Forrest said. "And we've got more prisoners going on down to Mississippi with the men. And there are niggers in both batches. Am I right or wrong?"

"You don't need to ask me, sir," Captain Anderson said loyally. "I know damn well you're right."

Nathan Bedford Forrest dropped it there. He'd won at Fort Pillow, which was all that really mattered. But he also knew—however little he cared to admit it—his men had got out of hand when they took the fort. Going up against Negroes with guns and Tennessee Tories, it wasn't surprising. He'd expected it after Bradford refused his surrender demand; he might even have had trouble enforcing a peaceful surrender had the Federal commander yielded. His soldiers hated the men they were fighting: it was as simple as that.

"They say all the Yankees' nigger troops are taking an oath to avenge Fort Pillow," Anderson added.

"They can say any stupid thing they want, and the niggers can swear any stupid oath they want," Forrest said scornfully. "It won't amount to a hill of beans next time they bump up against our boys. With an oath or without one, nigger troops can't stand up against white men."

"I should hope not, sir!" Anderson said.

"Don't worry about it, Charlie, because they damn well can't. Just remember the bloodstains in the Mississippi." Forrest remembered them himself, with somber satisfaction. He didn't care to remember how long the garrison in Fort Pillow had fought, how defiant the enemy had been, or how outnumbered they were. Since he'd won, he didn't need to remember any of those things. *Get there first with the most men.* He'd done that. Whenever and wherever he had to do it again, he expected he could.

He had less faith in the Confederacy's other generals, with the partial exception of Robert E. Lee. Joe Johnston was bound to be an improvement on Braxton Bragg. Forrest couldn't think of anything breathing that wouldn't be, including the mangiest Army mule. But could Johnston stand against the Federals when they finally started south from Chattanooga? Could anyone? Nathan Bedford Forrest didn't know.

In one way, it wasn't his worry. He'd done what he aimed to do, and he saw no reason he couldn't go on doing it for a long time. But if the great Confederate armies fell, what difference did it make? Could he go on bushwhacking even after they fell?

If I have to, I will, he thought grimly. *If it means holding the niggers down, I will.* He wasn't afraid; what concerned him were ways and means.

He shrugged broad shoulders. Thinking about bushwhacking and defeats to other generals was also borrowing trouble. The day-to-day routine of war was enough to worry about and then some. Soon he and his staff would follow the rest of his men down to Mississippi. "We'll lick 'em yet, Charlie," he said.

"Of course we will, sir," Anderson answered. Bedford Forrest hoped he meant it.

HISTORICAL NOTE

Sergeant Benjamin Robinson, Lieutenant Mack Leaming, Major William Bradford, and, of course, Major General Nathan Bedford Forrest are historical figures. Private Matt Ward and Corporal Jack Jenkins are fictitious. The Thirteenth Tennessee Cavalry (U.S.) was also known as Bradford's Battalion and as the Fourteenth Tennessee Cavalry (U.S.) (there was another Thirteenth Tennessee Cavalry [U.S.] that served mostly in the eastern part of the state); because contemporary sources discussing the events of April 12, 1864, call it the Thirteenth, I have used that name here. Coal Creek is now more often known as Cold Creek. Again, as the first name seems in more common use at the time of the fight at Fort Pillow, I chose it here.

Piecing together exactly what happened at Fort Pillow on that eventful day is anything but easy. There are four principal primary sources: the contemporary reports from both sides in *The Official Records of the War of the Rebellion*; the testimony collected by Messrs. Wade and Gooch of the U.S. Congressional Joint Committee on the Conduct of the War immediately after the engagement and published as *The Fort Pillow Massacre*; the Confederate rejoinder in Jordan and Pryor's 1868 book, *The Campaigns of General Nathan Bedford Forrest and of Forrest's Cavalry* (in essence, Forrest's own military memoir); and Wyeth's 1899 biography, *The Life of General Nathan Bedford Forrest,* which is written from a Southern point of view and is generally sympathetic to Forrest and his men.

The problem is that reconciling events in the contemporary documents—particularly in *The Fort Pillow Massacre*—and those of the two accounts inclining more toward Bedford Forrest's viewpoint—is often next to impossible. Knowing whom to believe—or whether to believe anyone—gets tricky. The accounts of Forrest's backers are unabashedly racist. In them, that Negro troops are none too brave and that blacks are mentally inferior to whites are givens. They seem to imply that the insults the colored artillerymen hurled at Forrest's troopers from the earthworks of Fort Pillow justified a massacre in and of themselves.

This should leave *The Fort Pillow Massacre* as a more reliable source . . . except that it is a propaganda piece in its own right, designed to paint the Confederates in general and Bedford Forrest in particular in colors as dark as possible. Forrest's force of about 1,500 men was inflated to from 7,000 to 10,000. The account emphasizes the slaughter of soldiers white and (particularly) black after the surrender of Fort Pillow—but there was no surrender, not in any formal sense. Bradford, acting in the dead Major Booth's name, refused to give one, and the fort was taken by storm.

Trying to find out what happened to Major Bradford after the fighting ended is another case in point. Pro-Confederate sources say that he was well treated, was given dinner by Colonel McCulloch, and gave his parole not to escape so he could bury his brother, Theodorick, who was killed when Fort Pillow was stormed. Bradford broke his parole, was recaptured in civilian clothes, and was shot while being taken from Brownsville to Jackson, where Forrest was. Jordan and Pryor say (p. 455, note), "On the way, he again attempted to escape, soon after which one of the men shot him . . . mainly due to private vengeance for well-authorized outrages committed by Bradford and his band upon the defenseless families of the men of Forrest's cavalry.

[While at Fort Pillow] [h]e was treated with the utmost consideration and civility." Wyeth, writing a generation later (p. 588, note), says, "There is nothing in the records to show that the men who murdered Major Bradford were ever brought to trial for this unwarrantable act": he does recognize that it should not have been done. My account of Bradford's last moments is based on the testimony of trader W. R. McLagan, as reported in *The Official Records of the War of the Rebellion,* which shows that he was shot in cold blood rather than after an escape attempt.

Meanwhile, though, what motivated Bradford to break his parole? An affidavit from two U.S. lieutenants (*Fort Pillow Massacre,* p. 105) states, "Major William F. Bradford, commanding our forces, was fired upon after he had surrendered the garrison. [He never did so.] The rebels told him he could not surrender. He ran into the river and swam out some 50 yards, they all the time firing at him, but failing to hit him. He was hailed by an officer and told to return to the shore. He did so. But as he neared the shore the riflemen discharged their pieces at him again. Again they missed. He ran up the hillside among the enemy with a white handkerchief in his hand in token of his surrender, but still they continued to fire upon him. . . . [W]hen they found they could not hit him, they allowed him to give himself up as a prisoner and paroled him to the limits of the camp." Pro-Confederate sources say . . . nothing of any of this. If a tenth of it is true, Bradford had good reason to mistrust the Rebels' "consideration and civility."

The same affidavit, composed only six days after the combat at Fort Pillow, also asserts, "They [the Confederates] immediately killed all the officers who were over the negro troops, excepting one who has since died from his wounds. They took out from Fort Pillow about one hundred and some odd prisoners (white,) and forty negroes. They hung and shot the negroes as they passed along toward Brownsville until they were rid of them all. Out of the six hundred troops (convalescents included) which were at the fort they have only about one hundred prisoners (all whites,) and we have about fifty wounded who are paroled."

These claims are, in detail, demonstrably false. Forrest's official report and Jordan and Pryor list by name 226 U.S. prisoners. These include three officers set above the colored artillerymen and close to 60 enlisted men, almost all of them black, from those units: these in addition to the wounded taken up to Cairo and Mound City. Nor were Negroes hung and shot on the way to Brownsville.

Nevertheless, the Union officers' affidavit touches on something vitally important in the Civil War as a whole and in the fight at Fort Pillow: the matter of race. Anyone who doubts that slavery played the most important role in causing the war need look no further than South Carolina's Ordinance of Secession and the Confederate Constitution, which did its best to make the peculiar institution legally impregnable for all time to come.

At Fort Pillow, both white and black Union troops suffered heavy casualties at Confederate hands once Forrest's men broke in. Proportionately, though, blacks had about twice as many killed as whites. This cannot be and surely is not coincidence. To quote from the lieutenants' affidavit once more, "Major Anderson, Forrest's assistant adjutant general, stated that they did not consider colored men as soldiers, but as property, and as such, being used by our people, they had destroyed them."

But this "property" had just spent several hours firing cannon at the Confederates and shooting rifle muskets at them. Are we to believe that Forrest's troopers disposed of them the way they might have, for instance, burned down a barn that sheltered (white) Federal soldiers? It seems unlikely, to say the least.

As Bruce Catton and others have noted, hand in hand with the belief that Negroes could not fight went another, almost directly opposite, belief: that they would fight like demons if they were ever roused. Forrest's men seem to have been reacting to this fear, and to have been trying to make sure blacks stayed intimidated by the whites who had ruled and owned them for so long. They were as outraged and alarmed by Negroes in arms as matadors would have been by bulls that could use swords of their own.

This effort at intimidation failed. "Remember Fort Pillow!" became a rallying cry for colored soldiers in blue for the last year of the war. In the Civil War, untrained black troops generally performed about as well as untrained white troops, this despite their own superiors' frequent lack of confidence in their abilities and the Confederates' strong motivation to oppose them as fiercely as possible. That such questions do not arise today is in no small measure due to the sacrifices these men, so many of them born into servitude, made.

Pro-Confederate sources deny that any massacre took place, or blame the killings that did take place on the fury and excitement accompanying the storming of the fort. The second of these may well have some validity; the first does not. It is plain that killings continued well after Fort Pillow fell. That similar things happened in other things is true, but does not erase the unprovoked slaughter of men trying to yield.

It should also be noted that while the colored artillerymen in Fort Pillow suffered more than their white counterparts, the troopers of the Thirteenth Tennessee Cavalry (U.S.) did not have an easy time of it. In Tennessee, as in Kentucky and Missouri, the Civil War was not country against country or state against state but neighbor against neighbor. Because the war was so personal, it was uncommonly ferocious. People knew who was on which side—knew and made foes pay.

Jordan and Pryor (pp. 422–23) write: "Many of Bradford's men were known to be deserters from the Confederate army, and the rest were men of the country who entertained a malignant hatred toward Confederate soldiers, their families and friends. . . . Bradford and his subalterns had traversed the surrounding country with detachments, robbing the people . . . besides venting upon the wives and daughters of Southern soldiers the most opprobrious and obscene epithets, with more than one extreme outrage upon the persons of these victims of their hate and lust."

Col. Fielding Hurst, commanding the Sixth Tennessee Cavalry (U.S.), also operated in the same area. He levied contributions on towns in western Tennessee to keep them from supporting the Confederates; in 1865, *U.S.* Brigadier General Edward Hatch noted that "Hurst has already taken about $100,000 out of West Tennessee in blackmail when colonel of the Sixth Cavalry (Union)." This supports Forrest's assertion of March 22, 1864, that "on or about the 12th day of February, 1864, under threats of burning the town," Hurst extorted $5,139.25 from the citizens of Jackson, Tennessee. Forrest also accused Hurst's men (as noted in Wyeth, pp. 339–40) of torturing, mutilating, and murdering captured Confederates. Whether this is true cannot be certainly known 140 years after the fact, but it was a hard war in those parts.

When the Confederates had more soldiers in the neighborhood than the Federals, did they fight a kinder, gentler war? To put it as mildly as possible, that is hard to believe. They had exactly the same sort of scores to settle as their U.S. counterparts, and just as much zeal to settle them. And, at Fort Pillow, two groups of men they hated more than anyone else on earth were delivered into their hands. Bedford Forrest had warned Major Bradford he could not answer for his men if they got into Fort Pillow, and they proceeded to prove he knew what he was talking about.

Of course, Forrest issued the same warning whenever he assaulted a U.S. garrison. The most compelling piece of evidence that he meant it this time was his decision to hang back from the fighting. In almost every engagement where men he commanded went into action, he fought at the fore. True, this time he was dazed and bruised after his horse fell on him when shot, but that seems too small a reason for a man who ignored gunshot wounds to stay out of the fray. More likely he understood what would happen if his men got into the fort, understood they *would* get in, and stayed away while the savagery was at its worst to keep from having to try to play King Canute against the blood-dimmed tide.

We remember Fort Pillow today because it is a microcosm of what the Civil War was all about. It showed that blacks *could* fight, could be men like any others, and it showed how determined white Southerners were not to give them the chance. It also showed that an inexperienced major was no match for the best cavalry commander on either side, even with earthworks and a gunboat to help him.

Forrest won the battle. The Union won the war. In many ways, the South won the peace for the next hundred years. Only in the past couple of generations have we begun to confront the issue of how to make the black man truly equal to the white. We still have a long way to go. Looking back at what happened at Fort Pillow, though, tells us how far we've come.